THE SHANGANI PATROL

Can even the bravest survive?

It is 1889 and the great powers of Europe are scrambling for territory in Africa. The last prize is the kingdom of Matabele and Mashonaland, and the South African millionaire Cecil John Rhodes wants the land at any price. Recently returned from Khartoum, former captain and army scout Simon Fonthill needs a new mission. On meeting Rhodes, he agrees to lead an expedition trek to King Lobengula's *kraal* to seek his agreement to land settlement, but the king's court is a cauldron of intrigue and Fonthill and his comrade '352' Jenkins must fight in one of the most famous last stands in Britain's colonial history.

THE SHANGANI PATROL

THE SHANGANI PATROL

by

John Wilcox

Magna Large Print Books
Long Preston, North Yorkshire,
BD23 4ND, England.

British Library Cataloguing in Publication Data.

Wilcox, John
 The Shangani patrol.

  A catalogue record of this book is
  available from the British Library

  ISBN 978-0-7505-3380-5

First published in Great Britain in 2010 by
Headline Publishing Group

Cover illustration by arrangement with
Headline Publishing Group

The right of John Wilcox to be identified as the author of this work has
been asserted by him in accordance with the Copyright, Designs and
Patents Act, 1988

Published in Large Print 2011 by arrangement with
Headline Publishing Group Ltd.

Magna Large Print is an imprint of Library Magna Books Ltd.

Printed and bound in Great Britain by
T.J. (International) Ltd., Cornwall, PL28 8RW

In memory of my friend Liam Hunter

Acknowledgements

I owe a debt to my editor at Headline, Sherise Hobbs, for her infinite attention to detail and, in particular, her intuitive sense of pace, of knowing where passages need more action and less of my regrettable tendency to let my characters talk too much. I must also thank my copyeditor, Jane Selley, for her care in tidying up my prose. I wouldn't be a writer without my agent, Jane Conway-Gordon, and I appreciate her constant support. As I do that of my wife, Betty, my devoted research assistant, proofreader and first critic of all my work.

These four have been a constant in most of my writings so far, but in the case of this particular book, my biggest vote of thanks must go to Dave Sutcliffe, an ex-Rhodesian now living in Newcastle, KwaZulu Natal, South Africa. For various reasons, I was unable to get into Zimbabwe to carry out basic research, and Dave, ex-surveyor, naturalist, guide and historian in his own right, did not hesitate to fill the gap by supplying detailed maps and local knowledge. Any mistakes that may have crept into the narrative concerning historical events and flora and fauna, however, are mine, not his.

As always, the London Library proved invaluable in supplying books about the period. However, I could find few definitive accounts of Rhodes's invasion of Matabeleland and Mashonaland either in the UK or during an all too brief visit to South Africa. Nevertheless, contemporary copies of *The Times*, kept in a pristine state at the London Library, proved useful, as did the following books:

A Flag for the Matabele by Peter Gibbs, Frederick Muller Ltd., London, 1955

To the Victoria Falls via Matabeleland, the diary of Major Henry Stabb, 1875, edited by Edward C. Tablet, C. Struik (Pty) Ltd, Cape Town, 1967

Rhodes by J.G. Lockhart and the Hon. C.M. Woodhouse, Hodder and Stoughton, London, 1963

Cecil Rhodes by John Flint, Hutchinson, London, 1976

And that great old stand-by, *The Colonial Wars Source Book* by Philip J. Haythornthwaite, Arms and Armour Press, London, 1995

Alas, many of these books will be out of print, but the London Library and the British Library should be able to help.

Chapter 1

Just inside the southern border
of Matabeleland, late 1889

They stood in silence in a rough half-circle on the beaten earth in the centre of the kraal, all eyes on the tall, thin figure of the black man with a long stick on the edge of the circle. It was not yet quite light and the stars were still pricking the indigo blue of the darkness above them. Simon Fonthill, ex-soldier, army scout and leader of the group, shivered – and not just because it was bitterly cold in these few minutes before dawn.

'Lion,' said Mzingeli, their guide. 'We go to kill him but he very dangerous animal. He also very shy...'

'Ah well,' murmured 352 Jenkins, 'then p'raps it would be rude to bother 'im, eh?' Jenkins, Fonthill's long-standing comrade, was the inevitable jester of the group. But this time no one smiled.

'...and he run from us in daylight. But at night he can see in dark and we cannot. So he attack us then without fear. That is why we go now, in light, just as sun comes up.' The tall man looked at them in turn. 'We hear him and his ladies roaring in bush last night and we know he make kill. So we follow his spoor now until we find where he lie down to sleep his meal away, and then you, Nkosi,' he nodded to Fonthill, 'or you,

Nkosi,' he inclined his head towards Jenkins, a touch less deferentially, 'will kill him.'

No one spoke. Mzingeli was their servant, but he spoke with an air of quiet authority that shrugged off questions of rank, class or race, and it would have seemed an act of lese-majesty to have interrupted him at this point. His name meant the Hunter, and he looked the part. Some six feet tall, he was slim and probably older than his athletic frame suggested, for the tightly curled hair that lay close to his scalp was now quite grey and his eyes seemed to reflect the sadness of great years. His nose was long, with flared nostrils, and his lips were thin. He wore the dress of the Afrikaner – dirty corduroy trousers and a loose flannel shirt – but his feet were bare, showing white patches between his toes as though from the touch of a paintbrush, and totemic beads hung around his neck. An old Snider rifle was slung across his shoulder, but now he was drawing in the dust with the end of his stick.

'This is animal,' he said, and suddenly the silhouette of a male lion appeared at their feet. He stabbed at a point just above the left front leg of the animal. 'Here you shoot. Here is heart and lungs.' His stick moved again quickly, and the impressive outline of a charging lion, head on, materialised. 'Lion can jump twenty feet,' he went on, 'so you do not want to see him like this. Only way to kill him like this is here.' He jabbed the stick between the eyes of the animal. 'No good down here,' he gestured at the chest beneath and behind the mane, 'because chest has about nine inches deep of muscle, and although your bullet

14

may kill charging Zulu,' a smile appeared, showing perfect white teeth, 'it no go through lion chest.'

Fonthill shot a quick glance at Alice, his wife. She was listening with rapt attention, a tiny pink sliver of tongue showing between her lips. But he noticed that despite the cold, small beads of perspiration had appeared on her forehead. Like him, she was apprehensive but exhilarated. Why the hell had she insisted on coming? She would have been safe enough staying here in the kraal. Then he gave a slight shrug of the shoulders. He knew well enough now that Alice Fonthill could never be dissuaded from a course of action on which her mind was set. But Mzingeli was continuing.

'We hunt lion and two lionesses. We find the kill then we track spoor. We do not make noise. Walk in straight line. I lead, then come Nkosi Fonthill, then,' he nodded at Alice, 'Nkosana, then Nkosi Jenkins, then my boys.' The two black bearers stood leaning on their spears, not understanding a word. 'When we find lions, I do not point with hand or move quickly. I point gently with head and eyes. Watch me. Then, Nkosi, you walk very quiet ahead and kill animal.'

Simon nodded. 'Yes ... hum ... yes. Yes, of course.'

'Very quietly,' added Jenkins.

'Mzingeli,' Alice interjected.

'Nkosana?'

'You said that there is one male lion and two lionesses who have been attacking the cattle compound.'

'Yes, Nkosana.'

'Are there no cubs? Do they not form a pride?'

15

Mzingeli nodded at the relevance of the question. 'It is usual, yes. But this is just one man and two ladies. Male must have fought with previous lion and killed him, or perhaps other lion was old and died. New one now comes in and kills all cubs and starts again with these lionesses, so no family yet.'

Alice wrinkled her nose. 'How disgusting. Does this mean...' and her voice faltered for a second, 'that we must kill all three?'

The black man shook his head. 'No, unless they all attack us. We kill only lion. His ladies then go away and find another mate. I don't think they come back here.' Mzingeli looked around enquiringly, as though waiting for further questions. Then his eyes widened and he added slowly, 'This dangerous. Everybody go very, very careful.'

As though on cue, the tips of the mopane trees fringing the compound became suddenly alight as they caught the first rays of the rising sun. The little party turned to leave and began making for the opening at the edge of the thorn hedge that encircled the village. There, as if from nowhere, the village *inDuna*, or headman, materialised, spoke briefly to Mzingeli and then smiled and nodded to Fonthill.

'He thank you for what we do,' said the tracker.

Simon returned the smile and gave an acknowledging nod. But he felt not at all confident about their mission, and despite Mzingeli's competence, nor did he feel assured that they could bring it to a successful conclusion. When they had recruited Mzingeli in the Transvaal – on the warm recommendation of an old army acquaintance in the

16

Cape – they had had no intention of hunting lion or other big game, or even of crossing the lazy Limpopo into the wilderness that was Matabeleland. They had merely wished to travel in a leisurely manner through the rolling grasslands of the veldt, shooting a few guineafowl and buck, camping under the stars and breathing the fresh, clear air of the country. A holiday, but also a way of forgetting the sadness they had left behind them at home in Norfolk. A brief change of direction for the three of them: Simon, Alice and, of course, Jenkins, Fonthill's former batman, now lifelong friend, and survivor, with Simon, of a dozen or more dangerous encounters on campaign with the British Army. This was to have been a few weeks of indulgence, far from danger, and with a first-rate tracker to guide them through the country and help them find game when they needed it.

It had been Mzingeli who had suggested that, as they were so near to the Matabele border with the Transvaal, they should cross the river and spend a couple of nights at his home village, thus allowing him to see again his elderly father, who was the *inDuna* there. There would be no need to seek permission from the all-powerful Matabele king, Lobengula, to enter his country. They would slip in and move out again without detection. The tracker had explained that he himself was a member of the Malakala tribe, a minority clan who lived on either side of the Limpopo. A non-militant, reclusive people, they had been completely subjugated by the Matabele, who used them as a source of plunder and slaves. His fellow tribesmen, he said, would see that the

17

party were completely hidden from the king's men during their short stay.

Fonthill gave a wry smile as he trod carefully behind the tall figure of Mzingeli. He was still unsure whether the tracker had known, as he neared his old home with his employers, that his village's slender stock of cattle – those few still left to them by the Matabele – was being ravaged by the lions, or whether it was a mere coincidence that they should arrive when the white man's legendary firepower and hunting skills were so sorely needed. Either way, Simon had felt quite unable to resist the request that they should rid the village of this terrible scourge. He smiled again. He felt a little like the young hero of a medieval tale, called upon to slaughter the terrible dragon that was terrorising the hamlet and taking away the young maidens. Except that he knew nothing about dragon-slaying and even less about lion-killing. Thank God for Mzingeli – except that, of course, they wouldn't be in this mess in the first place if it hadn't been for the crafty old tracker. He shrugged. Ah, well. He and Jenkins had been in more dangerous situations than this and survived. If only Alice hadn't insisted on coming too!

He turned and tried to smile reassuringly at his wife. They were walking in single file, as Mzingeli had instructed, except that for some reason, the two bearers, Ntini and Sando, carrying their spears and light shoulder packs, had overtaken Jenkins, leaving the latter at the back. Fonthill caught the Welshman's eye.

'I'd be grateful,' said Jenkins, in a hoarse whisper that seemed to boom back at them from the trees, 'if I could be relieved of this postin' at the back, see, before we come up with these bleedin' lions ... oh, beggin' your pardon, Miss Alice.'

Alice sighed, stopped and turned. 'Three five two, if you're going to apologise every time you swear, it is going to make for a very long day. Let me remind you that I am a brigadier's daughter, I have served as a war correspondent on almost as many campaigns as you and Simon, and I have heard language that might make even your hair curl. So do feel free to swear as much as you bloody well like.'

Jenkins bit into his huge black moustache. 'Yes, miss. Sorry, miss. It's just that I'd rather be up front to face the bugg ... beggars when they come than at the back 'ere, with me arse sort of exposed, look you.'

Mzingeli held up his hand. 'No talk now.' He spoke curtly in his own language to the two bearers, who sheepishly moved behind Jenkins. Then they all moved on.

Within what seemed like only moments, they had been swallowed up by the bush. Mzingeli had called this terrain mopane woodland, named after the mopane itself, a deciduous tree with butterfly-shaped leaves that cattle loved to chew, and he had told them that it stretched in a broad belt for miles along the low veldt north of the Limpopo. Yet it bore little resemblance to any woodland that Fonthill remembered from England. The mopane jostled for space with the much larger baobab tree and the smaller thorn trees and bushes. Visibility was only about one hundred yards, and the terrain could not have been more different from the rolling grassland that they had left behind them in the Transvaal.

The night had brought them little sleep, for the bush had been alive with noise: the squeal of hyenas, the barking of baboons, the grunting of dozens of other, unknown animals, and above all, the roar of lions – that primeval sound that made them pull their blankets under their chins and ensure that their rifles were within reach. Lions feared no one; even elephants were likely to form a defensive circle when the king of beasts was on the hunt. Now, however, as they walked, the woodland had turned into a sleepy, seemingly quiet environment. But it was not a tranquil place. They trod carefully yet they continually disturbed guineafowl, which suddenly flew up ahead of them, squawking, flapping and sending their hearts into their mouths. Simon became aware of a distinctive smell of ... what? Ah yes – cinnamon. He realised that it emanated from the miniature kopjes of dried clay constructed by ants that now began to appear among the trees. The rainy season had long since passed, and underneath their boots the soil was dry and powdery. Strange new country. Good country for lions. He licked his dry lips and gripped his rifle tightly.

None of them carried weapons ideal for big-game hunting. They had set out originally armed mainly with light rifles, like the small-calibre Westley Richards that Alice now cradled. Ideal for bringing down antelope and buck but capable only of wounding a charging lion. Mzingeli's Snider was an old rifle that had been replaced as British Army issue long before the Zulu War ten years ago, and although the man had already proved himself to be a good shot with it, it too seemed inadequate for today's purpose. The bearers had their assegais, razor sharp but best used for skinning and cutting up a carcass rather than killing. That left the Martini-Henry rifles carried by Fonthill and Jenkins. These had been used by the pair at the end of the abortive Sudan campaign four years ago, and thrown into the back of their wagon almost as an afterthought when they had set out from the Cape, merely a precaution in case danger should ensue from hostile natives. They packed a heavy .45 cartridge that, as Mzingeli had reminded them, could be effective against a charging Zulu. But a lion...? Fonthill looked down and checked that he had inserted a round 'up the snout'.

Simon himself, at thirty-four, was no longer the apprehensive young subaltern who had first landed in South Africa exactly ten years ago. The decade spent as a highly irregular army scout in Zululand, Afghanistan, the Transvaal (twice) and Egypt had lined his face a little and brought a light dusting of grey to his temples. Some five feet nine inches tall, his figure had filled out a little but his waist was slim enough, his shoulders broad and he carried himself lightly. He certainly looked the part of a hunter, in his light khaki shirt and trousers. The brown eyes, narrowed now under his wide-brimmed Boer hat as they peered into the bush, still, however, carried a trace of uncertainty, although the Pathan musket that had broken his nose had left it hooked and given his face a predatory air.

He turned his head to look at his wife stepping behind him. Exactly the same age as Simon, Alice Fonthill had matured into a fine-looking woman: erect, slim, with long fair hair tied into a serviceable bun behind the brim of her bush hat, her grey eyes steady and meeting those of her husband with a ready smile, although they too displayed a hint of something – sadness? – that gave her face a haunting, perhaps melancholy element. Alice's chin was perhaps a little too strong and square to bestow conventional beauty, but she carried herself with an air of charismatic attractiveness that had served her well in the masculine world of journalism, especially during her time covering the campaigns of Queen Victoria's army over the last ten years.

Behind them both, Jenkins carried his rifle at the slope over his shoulder, as befitted an ex-soldier of Her Majesty's 24th Regiment of Foot. It was at the regiment's hospital on the Welsh borders that he had met Fonthill, becoming the young subaltern's servant-batman, mentor and friend. Always known as 352 – the last three figures of his army number, and used to distinguish him from the many other Jenkinses in this most Welsh of regiments – he was some four years older than Simon, although no flecks of grey had yet dared to fight their way through the thicket of black hair that stood out vertically on his head, or into the great moustache that swept across his face. Seemingly as broad as he was tall (he stood at about five feet four inches), Jenkins exuded strength. He was as muscled and broad-chested as a pit bull terrier – Welsh, of course.

Now the three walked in self-absorbed silence, slowing a little in pace with Mzingeli, who had changed direction to the right and begun pushing through the thorns into a little clearing. As he did so, two hyenas squealed and ran away in their hangdog way and, in an indignant beating of wings, a brace of vultures rose into the air. Underneath them, the bones of an impala were picked almost clean.

Mzingeli held up his hand to keep them away from the carcass. Then he bent his knees and began examining the sandy floor near the bones, squatting and peering carefully at the earth, occasionally poking at it with one long black finger.

He stood and beckoned Simon. 'The three killed here,' he said. 'Maybe three hours ago.'

'Are they nearby still?'

'No. They go to find somewhere in shade to sleep. Look.' He pointed to the ground. 'Big lion – probably more than four hundred thirty pounds. See here, where he lies down. Big mane.' Fonthill bent to examine the scuffed sand but could see nothing distinctive.

'Were the two lionesses with him?' he asked.

'Oh, yes. They kill impala. Old lion just come up and do eating when hunting is done. Good life for him.'

Ntini called from the edge of the clearing. Mzingeli nodded. 'Good, we have spoor. We follow.' He addressed them all now in a soft voice. 'I do not know how far away they are. I think not far, maybe half a mile. So we go very quietly. Very dangerous now.'

'Oh blimey,' murmured Jenkins. 'Let me come

up front with you, bach sir.'

Fonthill shook his head. He was under no illusion that Jenkins was concerned about his own safety. The Welshman had the heart of a lion himself, and Simon knew of only three things that daunted him: water (he couldn't swim), heights and crocodiles. No, he would wish to be near Fonthill to protect him. A crack shot, he knew that Simon was still only a moderate marksman and that the opportunity of firing off a second round after a missed first shot was unlikely to present itself. By the time the second cartridge could be inserted into the breech of the single-shot Martini-Henry, the lion would have sprung. He wished to take up his post, familiar to him over the years, at Fonthill's shoulder.

Simon smiled. 'No thanks, old chap. Stay just there. Behind Alice.'

In single file again, they moved off. This time the two bearers, who previously had been conversing in very low voices so that Mzingeli could not hear up ahead, were silent, the whites of their eyes showing prominently and their assegais held firmly across their bodies. They had dropped back a little from the quartet ahead. They were undoubtedly apprehensive. Perhaps their fear had communicated itself to the others, for everyone was now stepping with great care and peering cautiously into the foliage that pressed in on them on either side – everyone, that is, but Mzingeli, whose eyes remained fixed on the sandy track ahead of him.

Eventually, after half an hour, he raised his right hand slightly in a signal to halt. The bush had thinned noticeably, and ahead of them the track had widened until it admitted a rocky outcrop. The tracker, his eyes still fixed to the front, motioned over his shoulder for Fonthill to join him.

He nodded to the ground ahead and then whispered, 'See mark in front of lion's paw, like brush mark.' Simon squinted but could see nothing of the kind. 'Lion tired,' continued Mzingeli. 'He drag front of his paw as he lift it up.' The tracker gently nodded his head. 'I think they found place to rest and digest meal, up there, behind rocks.'

'What about our scent?' asked Fonthill.

'We are upwind. They do not smell us.'

Fonthill felt a hand on his shoulder. Alice whispered in his ear, 'They're up there, aren't they? Up in those rocks?'

'Yes. Mzingeli believes so.'

'Don't go in alone. Take 352 with you.'

Simon fought back a flash of irritation. 'No. He must stay here with you. I can kill this damned lion. In any case, Mzingeli will probably come with me—'

He was interrupted by the tracker, who turned, his finger to his lips. 'We go together round to right,' he whispered. 'Stay very close. Be ready to shoot quickly if lion sees us. Very quiet now.'

Gesturing to Jenkins to stay close to Alice, Fonthill gave a twisted smile to his wife – somehow the muscles on his face seemed to be set rictus-like, not allowing him to give her the reassuring beam he intended – and followed Mzingeli at a crouch, his rifle clutched across his breast. The two men stole away to the right of the rocks, the tracker gently pulling away branches and holding them until Simon could take them in turn and pass through. They climbed a little through the bush and moved in a semicircle until they began to edge around the end of the highest rock, some ten feet away from it. Mzingeli was ahead, his bare feet making no sound as he placed each one carefully in front of the other on the now stony ground. Then he froze and, his eyes staring ahead of him, motioned for Simon to come alongside.

Ahead of them was the lion, stretched resplendent in the shade of the overhanging rock. His great head lay away from them, the tangled mass of the dark brown mane contrasting with the tawny colour of the body, and he seemed huge in that confined space, the end of his tail almost, it seemed, within reach. His head rested on one side; the one eye that could be seen was closed, and his chest rose and fell in gentle rhythm. There seemed to be a look of beatific satisfaction on the giant beast's face in repose. It had been a good meal and he was sleeping it off. Of the lionesses there was no sign.

A smile creased Mzingeli's face. He gestured with both hands to Simon as if tracing a circle, and mouthed, 'Big.' Then he moved slightly to his right and nodded his head forward. The signal was clear: kill. Kill now.

Fonthill licked his dry lips and inched forward, raising his rifle to the shoulder. Where was the target spot? Ah yes, just above and behind the front leg. Not easy to define from the rear, with the mane spreading so far down the body. He squinted through the foresight. Damn! It was set

26

at one hundred yards. At point-blank range he would overshoot by miles. Feeling Mzingeli's disapproval radiating towards him, he lowered the rifle and, with infinite care, pushed down the sight, then raised the rifle once more and focused on the sleeping animal. His finger tightened on the trigger ... *squeeze, don't pull* ... and there it stayed, until the end of the long barrel began to sway a little with the weight of it.

The lion was sleeping, *sleeping.* Fonthill had killed many men in the heat of battle or in one-to-one combat over the preceding years, but he had never killed anything that was not erect and facing him. This magnificent beast lay a few yards from him in perfect somnolence, completely unaware of the danger. It seemed somehow unfair, completely unfair, to kill him like this. It was not a killing, more an execution. He could not do it. Give the animal a fighting chance, at least.

So Fonthill shouted, 'Get up, you lazy bastard.'

Immediately the sleeping thing became alive, very much alive. The lion was on its feet within a second, turning its great head towards the danger, its mouth open showing yellow incisor fangs and emitting a roar that boomed back from the rocks around. At that moment, Fonthill fired.

The bullet tore through the muscles just behind the animal's head, cutting a furrow through the mane and causing blood to spurt. Then, with one bound, the beast had gone, leaving behind the echo of the shot and a bloodstain on the rocky ground. From the other side of the rock came two responding roars and a scuffle as the lionesses, unseen, followed him.

Fonthill and Mzingeli were left staring at each other. Neither spoke for a second or two, then Simon cleared his throat. 'Sorry. I just couldn't kill him while he was asleep. It seemed so ... so ... unfair somehow. I am sorry, Mzingeli.'

Slowly, a smile spread across the tracker's face. 'I think I understand, Nkosi.' Then the smile disappeared. 'But now we have big problem. We cannot leave wounded animal. We must follow into bush and finish him. If he stay alive with wound, he cannot chase properly to hunt and he turn to eating men. Becomes man-killer. We must track him now into bush. Very dangerous.'

'What happened?' Alice and Jenkins had suddenly materialised, Alice's eyes wide. Behind them – at some distance – appeared Ntini and Sando. 'Oh, thank goodness you are all right.' Alice clutched Simon's arm. 'What happened?'

'Well, I ... er ... missed. That's it really. No, it isn't.' Fonthill's face was crestfallen. 'The fact is, I just couldn't kill the bloody thing at point-blank range when it was sleeping.'

Mzingeli's face was once again illuminated by his great grin. He interjected, 'Nkosi shouted, "Wake up, lion" to make it fair. It is the English way, I think. I don't see this before.'

'Well,' Jenkins's expression was lugubrious, 'it's not the bloody Welsh way, I can tell you, Jelly. I would 'ave shot 'im up the arse if necessary, see.'

Fonthill cleared his throat again. 'Yes, well. I couldn't do it and that's that. Then I missed, although I wounded the beast. Now I must follow him and finish him off. It should be quite easy. I will have a blood spoor that will lead me to him, and this time I promise I won't miss. You must all stay here because the lionesses are still about, but I would like Mzingeli to come with me, please.'

'Don't talk nonsense, Simon.' Alice's voice was quite determined. 'We will all come with you. This time it will be more dangerous because the animals will be alerted – and they will probably be in the bush, and not,' her voice took on a gentler tone and her eyes were soft, 'lying on a nice clean rock waiting for you to shoot. Don't worry, my love, the odds will be much more equal this time.'

'Oh bloody 'ell,' said Jenkins.

Mzingeli gestured to the two bearers and spoke to them in their own tongue. Then he turned to the others. 'I think we take cup of tea and something to eat before we follow. There will be time.'

They set off again within the half-hour, moving more quickly this time. The trail was easy to follow and it led in a straight line, deeper into the bush. Then, after a while, the drops of blood became more irregular until finally they disappeared and Mzingeli was forced to deploy his arcane tracking skills again. Not that this was too difficult, because the three animals seemed now to be moving abreast through the bush, flattening the long grasses that had become a feature of the terrain.

As they progressed, a new and deeper air of tension began to pervade the little group. The bush seemed very, very quiet now, as though all of its occupants were standing off, silently waiting for the denouement that was surely to come. Somewhere a jackal barked, and high above an eagle wheeled, but otherwise the eerie stillness seemed to grow as they trudged along, watching carefully to ensure that they did not tread on a puff adder that might lurk in the sandy hollows that were becoming more prevalent and whose bite could be fatal. On either side of them the grasses seemed to have become longer and more impenetrable.

They reached a little clearing and Mzingeli held up his hand. He nodded at the ground. 'He stop bleeding,' he said. 'Not hit bad, then, and maybe close. He very dangerous now. I think he very angry.' As he spoke, the others were aware of a strange, musky smell.

'Yes,' said Jenkins, 'well I would be if I'd 'ad a bullet through me–'

He was silenced by the most frightening sound Simon, Alice or Jenkins had heard since they had first landed in South Africa. From somewhere nearby, out in the bush but beyond their vision, came a low, rumbling growl. Its source was hard to place, but it was immediately followed by another from a different direction and then a third, again with a different origin. The sound was other-worldly – malicious and menacing, as though Satan himself was watching them from the surrounding bush and giving a warning of intent. The three Europeans all immediately felt a prickling at the nape of their necks.

'The buggers 'ave surrounded us,' breathed Jenkins.

Fonthill pulled Alice to his side and looked at Mzingeli. The tracker's eyes were wide and he was turning slowly, examining each section of the undergrowth in turn, his rifle at the ready. The six had instinctively moved together now, so that they stood in a tight circle, almost back to back, except for Sando, who for some reason had stayed slightly apart, his eyes fixed on some long grass underneath a thorn tree.

In a flash of tawny flesh, the lioness broke out of the grass, ran towards the bearer and then sprang on him. Sando just had time to sink on to his haunches and dig the butt of his long spear in to the earth, its blade pointing at an angle of about forty-five degrees straight at the lioness. It seemed that the animal hit Sando and the blade of the assegai at exactly the same time. The spear head penetrated its throat, snapping the shaft, but the lioness seemed to engulf the bearer, knocking him backwards, its jaws seeking his throat, despite the tip of the blade protruding from the back of its neck.

With speed matching that of the lioness, Ntini plunged his own assegai into the side of the beast, at the top of and just behind its foreleg. He withdrew it quickly and then thrust it into the stomach, this time twisting it as he pulled it out with that familiar sucking sound, *iklwa*, that Fonthill had first heard on the battlefield of Isandlwana a decade before. The lioness became suddenly still. From underneath its body, a bloodstained Sando began the struggle to free himself.

The others, however, had no time to help him, because the little clearing now erupted into a maelstrom of action. From the right, the lion broke cover with ferocious speed and sprang at Fonthill, as though recognising him as his earlier tormentor. Instinctively Simon leapt aside, firing as he did so. At such short range, the force of the bullet had the effect of making the beast twist in mid-air, although it had only entered that mass of muscle under the chin, not quite penetrating it. As the lion hit the ground, however, Alice's much lighter cartridge took him at the side of the head. The second shot had the effect of stunning the beast for a moment, and fumbling a second round into the breech of his Martini-Henry, Fonthill had time to leap forward and deliver the *coup de grâce* at point-blank range into the lion's heart. The beast's head sank forward with a sigh and he lay still.

From the left, the second lioness had timed its attack to coincide exactly with that of its mate and it bounded towards Jenkins. The latter's shot took her just above the right eye and that of Mzingeli directly in the open, snarling muzzle. She lay as still as the others.

'Well,' gasped Jenkins, 'we weren't very quiet but we seem to 'ave done the job, isn't it?' In moments of great anxiety, Jenkins's Welshness always seemed to increase.

Simon gathered Alice into his arms. 'Well done, my love,' he murmured into her ear. 'Good shooting. I doubt if I could have finished him myself. Are you all right?'

'Quite all right, thank you. Well done yourself.' But her voice carried a tremble. She gently disentangled herself. 'What about Sando?'

Mzingeli and Ntini, with gun and spear, were labouring to lever the dead lioness off the struggling bearer, who eventually emerged covered in blood, although whether his own or that of the lioness it was difficult to tell. Closer inspection, however, disclosed an ugly strip of flesh hanging from his shoulder, like an unbuttoned epaulette, although his teeth were flashing in a broad grin. He was clearly going to live to fight another lion on another day.

Mzingeli looked up and grinned. 'Very good shooting,' he said to Fonthill. 'Better this time. Not easy to move *and* fire. Nkosana very good too.'

'Thank you,' said Alice, then she frowned. 'But I am sorry we had to kill the females, too. Why did *they* attack us, Mzingeli?'

The black man shrugged. 'I think they knew we going to kill lion. They frightened too, you know.'

'Ah well.' Alice looked down at Sando and then bent and examined his shoulder.

'Mmm. Not good. This will need stitching. Where's my medical bag?'

Jenkins picked up the pack that Ntini had dropped and presented it to Alice. He looked at the wound and wrinkled his nose. 'Blimey, miss. There's not much you can do with that, is there?'

'Oh yes.' Alice rummaged through the pack and extracted a small but quite heavy leather bag. 'I took an instructional course in basic medicine at the London Missionary Society before we left,' she said. 'Just as well, I would say, the way this so-called holiday is going. Here, hold this.' She held out a small bottle. Jenkins wiped his hands on his trousers and took it, then received a small package wrapped in oiled waterproof paper.

Alice kneeled down beside the stricken bearer, whose face was now creased in pain. His eyes widened in anxiety when she produced another bottle from her bag, and then a small, tube-like instrument with a thin needle point at its end. She called to Mzingeli.

'Please come and interpret for me. Please explain to Sando that this is not witchcraft but white man's medicine to make him better. Tell him that I will use this needle.' She turned to Simon and Jenkins, now watching with as much anxiety as Sando, and held up the hypodermic syringe. 'It's still quite new, I think; it's called the Pravaz syringe back home.' She showed it to Mzingeli. 'I will use this to put some fluid into his veins that will stop the pain. Then I will very carefully clean the wound and sew the skin and flesh back on to the shoulder. He will feel no pain while I do this, although later on it will hurt a little. He must not touch it afterwards.'

Mzingeli nodded and translated. Sando, the whites of his eyes showing and his mouth open, said nothing, but watched Alice with awe as she went about her work: first pouring a little water on to her hands, washing them with a tiny bar of soap from her box and drying them, then slipping the needle end into the little bottle, pulling the morphine into the syringe and, with great care, injecting the fluid into the arm. The bearer winced but seemed as fascinated by the procedure as the four others, who were all looking on, quite engrossed. Alice poured a little liquid from the bottle on to a swab from the package that Jenkins held and then gently dabbed it on the open wound to disinfect it. This also had the effect of stopping the bleeding. Wiping the wound dry, she selected a needle from her box and then threaded it with a fine gut.

'Simon,' she called, 'wash your hands and put a little of this disinfectant on them. Then pull back the flesh that is hanging down and hold it in place while I sew. Three five two – if you're going to be sick, I would rather you did it away from my patient, thank you.'

'Thank you, miss. Oh bloody... 'Ere, Jelly, 'old this bottle, quick.'

The operation continued until the flesh had been sewn into place, with Sando's head nodding now, his eyes half closed, as the morphine took effect. 'There,' said Alice, making a tight little overstitch to complete the sewing. 'Just as well that I was always a good seamstress.' She looked up at Fonthill. 'Don't you think, darling?'

Simon shook his head and blew out his cheeks. 'Not to put too fine a point on it, my love, I think you are bloody marvellous. Killing a lion one minute, then performing surgery on your knees the next. You continue to amaze me. I may have to marry you again if you go on like this.'

'Very good, very good, Nkosana,' added Mzingeli, his face beaming. Then he prodded Sando awake and spoke to him sharply.

'No,' said Alice. 'Let him be for a while. He will need to recover from the shock.'

Fonthill stood upright and nodded to the carcasses of the dead beasts. 'What should we do with these?' he asked the tracker. 'Just leave them for the scavengers to clear up?'

Mzingeli looked shocked. 'Oh no, Nkosi. They very valuable. Meat no good for eating, but skins good, particularly lion's tail. Fetch much money in Transvaal and Cape. Ntini and me do it now. Then we carry back to kraal.'

'Very well. I'll get Jenkins to make us some tea ... when the poor lamb has recovered, that is.'

A fire was soon lit and a shame-faced Jenkins set their little black kettle on it, and as Alice carefully repacked her bag, Mzingeli and Ntini began to the skin the carcasses, using very sharp hunter's knives. Within minutes, the skins were stretched over bushes to dry and everyone settled down to drink strong black tea – even a woozy Sando, who kept looking at his shoulder in puzzlement.

It was, then, a peaceful scene that was interrupted by Jenkins, who looked up from his mug and murmured softly, 'Oh, shit!'

Out of the bush had materialised some ten or twelve natives. They were tall men, superbly built, with very black skins that seemed to shine over rippling muscles in the sunlight. They wore girdles of monkey's tails and headdresses of black ostrich feathers, extending over their necks and shoulders and reminding Simon of the fur tippets worn by fashionable ladies in London. Each warrior – for they seemed to be in war dress – carried a long shield of hide, like that used by the Zulus of the south, and a short stabbing assegai, except that, unlike the Zulus of the south, the blades of their spears were not silver but quite black. They moved around the edge of the clearing so that the little group was surrounded, and then stood, watching them silently.

Fonthill shot a quick glance at Mzingeli. It was the first time he had seen fear on the face of the tall man.

'Matabele,' said the tracker. 'Black blades. Bad men. Very bad.'

Chapter 2

Fonthill slowly stood. 'What do they want, do you think?' he asked Mzingeli.

'I ask. But they don't like Malakala people. Take us for slaves.' He licked his lips and spoke to one of the Matabele, who had advanced a little ahead of the rest. He wore a waxed circlet of fibre woven into his hair, like the Zulu elders, and had the air of an *inDuna*.

The man looked at Mzingeli scornfully and then, ignoring him, advanced towards Fonthill and stood for a moment, slowly turning his head to look at Alice and Jenkins before moving his gaze back to Simon. He gestured to the carcasses of the dead animals and then spoke angrily.

'He say why do we kill King Lobengula's lions and why do we come into Matabeleland without king's permission?'

Out of the corner of his eye, Fonthill saw one of the Matabele pick up Alice's rifle and then her pack. A second native moved towards Jenkins's Martini-Henry. Simon took a deep breath, then slowly bent down and picked up his own rifle, which lay at his feet.

'Pick up your rifle, 352,' he said softly. Then he sighted the long barrel over the shoulder of the

37

Matabele chieftain and fired it into the skull of the lion, causing it to jerk. The noise of the report caused all of the natives to jump and sent echoes bouncing back from the surrounding bush. Fonthill nonchalantly reloaded his rifle, cocked the mechanism and slowly raised the muzzle until it was pointing directly into the eyes of the man facing him.

'Tell him,' he called to Mzingeli, 'to order that man to replace Alice's rifle and pack on the ground, otherwise I will blow his head off.'

'No, Nkosi.'

'Yes. Tell him.'

The tracker cleared his throat and spoke slowly. The Matabele's eyes widened for a moment, and Simon thought he detected fear in them as he regarded the muzzle of the gun, aimed so menacingly close to him. But he remained still and stood silent. At last he turned his head and nodded towards his follower. Sulkily the man dropped the rifle and the pack and Alice stepped forward to regain them.

It was a victory of a sort. Simon smiled and lowered the rifle, and nodded cordially to the *inDuna*. 'Now,' he said to Mzingeli, 'please explain the circumstances – how we were asked by your village to shoot the lions, which were attacking their herd.'

For the first time, the *inDuna* deigned to notice the tracker and stood frowning as the story was told. When he responded, it was with perhaps just a little less antagonism than before.

'He say,' said Mzingdi, 'that we should not have entered country without king's agreement.'

'Very well. Please explain that we were on our way to – what's the place that is supposed to be the guardian entrance to Matabeleland?'

'Makobistown.'

'Yes, that's it. I had forgotten. Please explain that we crossed at the Tati border and were on our way to Makobistown to gain permission when emissaries from your father's kraal asked us to remove the danger of the lions. We have skinned the beasts and were about to travel to Bulawayo to present the skins and the lion's tail to his majesty, as a gift from us.'

For a brief moment a smile flickered across Mzingeli's face before, sombrely, he translated.

The lie – probably supported by Fonthill's intransigence – was obviously convincing, for the *inDuna*'s attitude changed. He turned to Mzingeli, nodded and waved his assegai. Immediately his companions, their faces still imperturbable, squatted on the ground, their spears at their sides.

'Phew,' murmured Jenkins. 'Shall I make us all a nice cup of tea, then, bach sir?'

'Good idea. Mzingeli, ask the chief if he would like English tea.'

The tracker did so, and a brief, guttural interchange took place.

'He say no. Rather have brandy.'

'Very well. Three five two, see if you can find a drop of brandy. Not the good French, mind you. That Boer Cape stuff that you like so much.'

The Welshman made a face. 'What a terrible waste.' He shuffled across to Sando's pack and withdrew a bottle and an extra tin cup. Simon, Jenkins and Mzingeli threw away the tea dregs at the bottom of their own cups and joined the Matabele. Fonthill clinked cups with the *inDuna* and raised his mug in an unmistakable gesture. 'To King Lobengula,' he toasted. The others followed suit and the Matabele, grinning, nodded his head and joined them. Then he spoke again to Mzingeli, who now seemed to have earned his approval.

'This not good,' explained the tracker. 'He say they take us to Bulawayo to king's kraal. He say Lobengula like English. He say we should start now.'

'Oh blast! Will it be dangerous, do you think?'

'Cannot say, Nkosi. King cruel man. When some man accused of stealing his cattle, he kill him, of course. But very cruelly. He strip off skin from forehead and pull it over eyes that saw cattle. He cut off nose that smelled them. He cut off ears that hear them. He put out eyes that seen them. Then he throw man to crocodiles. Very cruel.'

'How disgusting.' Alice had joined them, after seeing to her patient, who was now fully conscious.

'Yes, Nkosana. But is true he seem to like English. Some traders stay in Bulawayo and one missionary. Other men come from other countries to try and get treaty to dig for gold and other things in ground, but king very careful. I hear perhaps he sign treaty with Nkosi Rhodes from Cape. But I am not sure.'

'Cecil John Rhodes. Ah.' Fonthill nodded his head. 'He's a shrewd devil, that one. I met him once, years ago. I wonder...'

His musings were ended by the *inDuna*

climbing to his feet. The Matabele spoke briefly to Mzingeli then to his men, who all stood.

'I'm sorry, Alice,' said Simon, 'but it seems we are all off to Bulawayo to pay homage to the king, whether we like it or not.'

She frowned, then her face relaxed into a smile. 'Ah well,' she said. 'At least it should be interesting. Just don't get caught stealing his cattle, that's all I can say.'

Three long, thick branches were cut from the bush by the Matabele and the skins carefully draped over them. The ends of the poles were lifted on to the shoulders of six of the warriors and then they were off. As they left the clearing, the hyenas were already gathering around the carcasses of the lions.

They moved at what seemed at first to be a slow pace, set by the *inDuna*, but his loping stride was deceptive and the three British soon began to feel the heat, as they left the bush and began to traverse stony, sandy terrain. Around them, but unseen, baboons began to bark and troops of more courageous chattering monkeys formed company with them as they marched. Alice became concerned that the unremitting pace might displace some of Sando's stitches, and she insisted that the party halt, while she made a makeshift sling for the man's arm.

This attracted the *inDuna*'s attention, and he gazed in astonishment at the neat array of stitches that patterned the ugly wound in the bearer's shoulder. He demanded to know who had made this decoration, and his jaw dropped as Mzingeli explained what Alice had done. He became noticeably deferential to her afterwards.

'He think you powerful lady witch doctor,' Mzingeli told her.

'So she is,' grunted Simon. 'So she is. I should know.'

Alice aimed a playful blow at him. But her eyes were dark. 'I only wish I was,' she said.

Gradually they passed out of the mopane woodland and moved into more open country, still dotted with bush but also studded with rocky kopjes that rose from well-grassed veldt. These were interspersed with low rocks, smooth and sun-burnished, that swelled up from the grassland like whales stranded on a seashore. It was obviously better country for cattle, and they passed many small kraals before stopping at one to spend the night. That evening, as they sat around an open fire eating black bread and the meat of a young duiker buck, the Matabele party, including the *inDuna*, kept well away from the British and their bearers. Fonthill, however, noticed that the Matabele were casting envious eyes on the rifles and the packs.

'Ah,' said Mzingeli, 'Matabele are thieves. Everyone knows this. We must be careful with our things.'

'Tell me about them. What sort of race are they?'

The tracker curled his lip. 'They are the conquerors of this region. Everyone afraid of them – like Zulus in south. The men think war and hunting only things for men to do. Leave every-thing else to their women. They take everything they see because they think it is their right.'

'I see. Where did they originate?'

'They really Zulus. They come from Zululand long time ago – maybe fifty years, maybe more – in the time of the great Zulu king Shaka. They had their own chief, Mosilikatze. He have trouble with Shaka and lead his clan north. They fight Boers in Transvaal and move north again. Come here and settle. Kill men of many tribes, including my own, and also big tribe in north, the Mashonas. Make these people their subjects and slaves. They good hunters and warriors. Everyone afraid of them.'

The flames from the fire flickered across the tracker's face. Usually passive, his features were now set grimly and his eyes were cold. 'They kill my two brothers. So I leave village as young man and cross Limpopo and go south. Work for Dutchmen on farms in Transvaal and become good tracker and hunter.'

Mzingeli fell silent, and the two men stared into the fire for a moment. Fonthill looked across the flames and saw that both Alice and Jenkins were asleep under their blankets, their heads resting on their folded outer garments, their rifles tucked under the edges of their coverings. Most of the natives of the kraal had crawled into their beehive-shaped huts, and the Matabeles from Bulawayo were stretched out on their sleeping mats.

Fonthill reached into the pack at his feet. 'A little brandy, Mzingeli?' he enquired. 'I think we deserve one, after all the fuss of the day. We call it a nightcap back home.'

The pain left the tracker's face and he gave one of his rare smiles. 'A nightcap? Ah, good word.

Let us put on a nightcap then, Nkosi.'

Simon extracted the bottle and two tin cups and poured a little of the amber liquid into each. Suddenly he became aware that they were not alone.

'If there might be a drop to spare, bach sir,' said Jenkins, close to his right ear, 'then I could just be persuaded, see.'

Fonthill sighed, took out another cup, and poured a dram. 'Very well,' he said, 'but I refuse to drink with a man who is in his underpants. For goodness' sake, Jenkins, go and put your trousers on.'

Jenkins slipped away and Simon turned back to Mzingeli. 'Have the Matabele been at war lately?'

'In some ways they always at war, because they kill anyone who argues or stand up with them. But they careful with white men, because Lobengula hears about power of white men in south. He know they beat Zulus.' The tracker took a sip from his cup, grimaced and wiped his lips with his hand. 'This is problem for him. He has about twenty thousand warriors, maybe more, who have not washed their spears for long time – some of them never. They want ... what you call it ... honour from war and also things they take from it.'

'Plunder.'

'Yes. King must hold them back all the time. Like holding lid on boiling cooking pot.'

A trousered Jenkins had now rejoined them. 'Will they attack the Dutchmen in the Transvaal, then, Jelly?' he enquired.

'They would like to. If Matabele have guns, perhaps. But they have only a few. And Boers

44

have many.'

Fonthill took a sip of brandy, coughed a little and asked, 'What about the king?'

Mzingeli's smile reappeared. 'He has sixty-three wives. Likes beer, brandy and champagne...'

'Champagne?'

'Yes. Traders bring it in for him. He drinks much. He just want to be left to his wives, his cattle and his white man's drink. He don't want war. Although...'

'Yes?'

'He like to kill. Bulawayo mean Place of Man Who Was Killed. My father tell me – he the one that tell me all this – my father say that Lobengula six months ago or so send *impi*, war party, to punish two villages where men defy him. They kill all the men, and the children and girls taken as slaves. Then the wives and older women made to carry all good things ... what you say, plunder ... back to king's kraal. Then they pushed into circle with spears and women all killed by two young warriors, who so wash their spears.'

'Miserable bastards,' murmured Jenkins.

Fonthill frowned. Then he drained his cup and stood. 'It seems we shall have to handle King Lobengula with care. Bed now, I think. Good night.'

Mzingeli put a restraining hand on his arm. 'Nkosi, it was very good shooting today. Very fine. No one afraid. And you did clever talking with Matabele. Very good.'

'Well, thank you, Mzingeli. I am just sorry that I was stupid the first time. Thank you.'

The little party made equally good time the

45

next day, and after midday they began to climb, so much so that the three British began to gasp a little, reminding Fonthill that this country was some four thousand feet above sea level. They emerged on to a plateau, in good open country, well watered, with a smudge of high hills on the horizon to the north-east. The pace eased a little now and the party settled into a rhythm that lasted for another two and a half days. By the time Bulawayo came in sight, Simon estimated that they had travelled some eighty miles or so from the border.

Lobengula's capital was not as big as Fonthill had expected; not as large, for instance, as he remembered Ulundi, the capital of Zululand, but big enough, perhaps half a mile in diameter. The kraal was enclosed by a great thorn fence that undulated up and down the plateau and within which hundreds of wickerwork beehive huts had been erected for Lobengula's subjects. Grazing cattle – long-horned oxen, many of them distinctively black in colour, domestic cows and steers of a provenance unknown to Fonthill – were dotted on the plateau, almost as far as the eye could see. Smoke from many cooking fires arose and a distinctive smell came drifting across to them: a mixture of cooking fat, cattle manure and human excrement.

Fonthill wrinkled his nose and exchanged glances with Alice. A thought struck him. 'Do you think these fellows will say that they killed the lions themselves and will get the credit for bringing them back to the king?' he asked Mzingeli.

The tall man nodded his head slowly. 'It could

be. They like that.'

'Right. Please tell them that we would like to take our skins to the king straight away.'

The *inDuna* nodded his head curtly in response. Soon they were surrounded by dozens of dogs that yapped all around them and snapped at their heels, together with troops of naked children, who looked at the white people with wide-eyed curiosity and teeth that flashed in the sun. The children were joined by two tall Matabele carrying assegais, who, on being addressed by the *inDuna*, turned and immediately ran back to the kraal as fast as their long legs could carry them.

'They go to warn the king that we are coming,' confided Mzingeli. 'They also go to prepare the praise-singers.'

'The what?'

'When king meet new people, they have to wait outside his house while they are told, in song, of how wonderful king is. It is custom. It can take half an hour.'

'Oh, bloody 'ell,' wailed Jenkins. 'I could do with a drink, see, not the chapel choir.'

They entered through a gap in the thorn hedge, where a huge pile of oxen horns had been stacked to one side. 'This to show everyone how rich king is,' whispered Mzingeli. 'All cattle are owned by him. He has about three hundred and likes to count them into cattle kraal every night and see them out to graze every morning.'

Flies were now hovering around them, feasting on the perspiration that dripped down their cheeks and the backs of their shirts. The flies intensified as they neared the king's cattle compound, now empty, and set beside a smaller enclosure within which grazed goats and some horses. Both were adjacent to the king's kraal, a separately ringed fence of thorns enclosing huts for his wives and important members of his household. The king's own dwelling stood out by its singularity in this uncivilised setting. It was a not unpleasant-looking low thatched house, one storey high, with a veranda running the length of its front, European style.

Mzingeli caught Simon's eye. 'Built for him by European trader. Man called Grant. He dead now.'

To one side of the main house and near the goats' kraal stood a round hut built of sun-hardened mud and topped with a conical thatch. It shared with the goats the intermittent shade bestowed by a tall indaba tree, whose roots twisted and curled above ground like giant pythons frozen in time. Before the hut the ground had been beaten flat by thousands of feet, so that it seemed to glisten in the sun.

'That where king has court,' explained Mzingeli. 'Gives wisdom.'

They were halted by the *inDuna* and the skins were lowered to the ground. Immediately two Matabele appeared, caparisoned in monkey skins and ostrich feathers, their faces and bodies streaked with red ochre and carrying what appeared to be fly whisks. They immediately began to chant, swaying in unison and beating time with their whisks. At once a crowd began to gather and started to repeat the words of the singers in a hypnotic ululation, stamping their feet

48

to the rhythm.

'The praise singers,' confided Mzingeli.

'What are they saying?' asked Alice.

The tracker listened for a moment, his head on one side. 'Silly words,' he said. 'They say that Lobengula is King of Kings, Lord of White Men, Slayer of Men, Devourer of Whole Earth and so on ... silly words.' His lip curled in contempt. Then, as if suddenly remembering something important, he gestured to Simon, Alice and Jenkins to come close and, raising his voice to be heard above the chanting, said, 'I forget. When you meet the king you must not address him standing. You must sit. He must always be above you. The Matabele always move before him in bent position, with hands resting on knees.'

'To hell with that,' said Fonthill. 'We would not do that for our Queen, so I don't see why we should do it for some other monarch. I suggest we just bow our heads when he approaches.'

The chanting continued for at least half an hour, while the British three stood in the hot sun, shifting their weight from one foot to the other and wiping away the perspiration that dripped down from under their hats and beneath their shirts. Eventually the singing stopped and was replaced by a roar of acclamation as a tall figure emerged from the door of the house and slowly crossed the veranda threshold. Immediately, all the Matabele sat. It was the cue for the visitors to bow their heads, although Mzingeli and his boys squatted also.

From under his eyelashes, Fonthill observed the king closely. He was about six feet tall and of massive proportions. At first glance he seemed to be almost completely naked, his skin very black. Then it could be seen that his huge stomach hung down above a narrow strip of hide that encircled what once had been his waist and from which a profusion of monkey tails dangled. His posture was erect and magisterial and his features were regular and quite handsome, with the flat nose and thick lips of the Zulu, and the Zulu elder's narrow band of fibre oiled and bound into his tightly curled hair. His eyes seemed cold until they fell upon the lion skins; then they lit up and he smiled, gesturing towards the trio with the long assegai he carried and speaking in a low, guttural voice.

Fonthill leaned down to Mzingeli. 'Can you translate for us?'

'He is asking the *inDuna* where they come from. And,' he waited a moment, 'man is telling truth.'

The king frowned for a moment, then his face split into a smile and he nodded cordially to the trio. He beckoned behind him, and a large wooden chair was brought and set under the broken shade of the indaba tree, and then a collection of goat skins were scattered before him. Lobengula lowered himself into the chair and beckoned with his assegai for the three to sit before him on the skins. Simon grabbed Mzingeli by the shirtsleeve and dragged him down beside him.

The king was speaking. 'He say that you very welcome to his home and he thank you for gifts,' interpreted Mzingeli. 'He say that lion is not hunted here for sport because animal can contain spirit of past Matabele chiefs and bad to kill him. But if lion is attacking cattle then he must be a bad chief. King thanks you for protecting cattle of his people.'

'Well that's very nice of 'im, I'm sure,' whispered Jenkins. ''P'raps 'e's goin' to offer us a drop of somethin' to drink now, d'you think?'

As if the king had heard, he turned his head and shouted an order over his shoulder towards the interior of his house. Immediately – someone must have prepared them already – gourds of beer were brought out and presented to the three Britains. Fonthill took a grateful gulp. It was similar to the Kaffir beer he had drunk in the Transvaal: made from corn, the grain from which had been left to vegetate, dried in the sun, pounded into meal and gently boiled. Cool now, and with a slightly acidic taste, it was delicious. Noticing that nothing had been brought for Mzingeli and his boys, he handed his half-full gourd to the tracker. Alice did the same with hers to Sando and, with rather less grace, Jenkins followed suit with Ntini.

'Tell the king,' said Fonthill, 'that we are grateful for his welcome. We are sorry not to have sent ahead to ask for permission to cross into his land, but we were diverted by the people of the village near the Limpopo.'

The king waved his assegai in airy acknowledgement of the apology and spoke again. 'Why did you not come here on horse or wagons, as all white people do?'

'Because,' replied Simon, 'we left our horses and wagon at the village and set out to kill the lions on foot. We expected to return to the village but we were brought to you immediately.'

On translation, a frown immediately descended on the royal features, and then they twisted into an expression of fury. Within seconds the benevolent, welcoming monarch had changed into a despotic tyrant, hurling abuse at the *inDuna*, who bowed his head and knelt in submission, his forehead touching the ground.

'He say that the man has caused king to lose honour with white visitors by bringing you here without horses, wagon and clothes,' translated Mzingeli quietly. 'I think they take him away to kill him now.'

'Oh no. Tell him that we were so anxious to meet the king, about whom we had heard so much, that we were happy to leave our things behind. The *inDuna* must not be blamed.'

Hearing this, Lobengula's face lightened and he waved his assegai to the *inDuna* in what appeared to a gesture of forgiveness. The man sat up slowly and shot a quick glance of thanks at Fonthill. But the king was speaking again.

'He want to know if you have met Queen Victoria.'

Simon smiled. 'Tell him yes. I met her at her palace in Windsor. So too did Mr Jenkins here.' Fonthill was not lying. Both he and Jenkins had attended investiture ceremonies at Windsor Castle when they had received the order of Companion of the Bath and the Distinguished Conduct Medal, respectively, for their services on General Wolseley's abortive expedition to relieve General Gordon at Khartoum. The king gave an expansive smile.

'He say he has written to Queen Victoria and

she has written to him.'

'Ah. How ... er ... very interesting.'

Lobengula now broke off to give a string of orders to his attendants and then turned back to his visitors.

'King say that he will send people to my father's village to bring horses and wagon here. He also give hut for you to live in and send food. He want you to stay a while as his guest. He say he have other white people here but they have not met Queen Victoria. He say that he don't think big man in south, Nkosi Rhodes, has met queen either. But you have. He like to talk to you later.'

'Oh blimey,' muttered Jenkins. 'I don't like the sound of that.'

'Neither do I,' whispered Alice. 'I wonder what's wrong with his foot?' For the first time, Fonthill noticed that the king's right foot seemed swollen around the big toe, and remembered that he had limped as he had come towards them. 'I would say he's got gout,' Alice continued. 'Too much champagne and brandy, I would think.'

Lobengula rose slowly to his feet to indicate that the audience was at an end, and Simon and the others rose too. Fonthill bowed his head in acknowledgement.

'The king is very kind,' he said as Mzingeli interpreted, 'and my wife, servants and I would be honoured to stay for a short time as his guests. But we must return to the south soon, for we have urgent business in Cape Town. In the meantime, however, we are at the service of your majesty to give you whatever assistance we can.'

With that, the king gave a cheery smile, barked

further commands to his attendants and then limped back into his house. The *inDuna* leaped to his feet and beckoned the visitors to follow him. They all walked out of the king's enclosure towards where a party of Matabele women were hurrying in and out of a large beehive hut set apart from the rest, crawling agilely on their hands and knees through the narrow opening carrying blankets, drinking vessels and other domestic utensils.

At the entrance, Fonthill paused and, with one restraining hand on the *inDuna*'s shoulder, addressed Mzingeli. 'Tell him,' he said, 'that I would like proper accommodation also to be given to you and your boys.'

The tracker shook his head. 'Thank you, but is not right here, Nkosi. We just slaves here.'

'No you are not. The British abolished slavery in 1807 and I don't recognise it anywhere. Go on, tell him. The man owes me a favour, dammit.'

Hesitantly Mzingeli translated. Simon's request was treated with a frown but the Matabele shrugged his shoulders and then nodded his head in acquiescence.

Once inside the hut, Alice spread a sleeping mat, laid a blanket upon it and sat down. 'Well, my darling,' she said with a warm smile to Simon, 'do you know, I didn't realise that you were so well acquainted with our gracious Queen. As a result, it seems you have just been appointed Grand Vizier Extraordinary to his fat majesty here, and we are doomed, it seems, to stay here while you advise him for years and years and bloody years. Eh?'

Fonthill returned her smile sheepishly. 'Well, I

only answered a question.' He looked around. 'It's not exactly the Ritz, I agree, but it will serve until our transport arrives. Then we shall be off, I promise.'

That evening, a young goat was delivered to Mzingeli from the king with instructions to slay it and cook it for his master. It came with a calabash of beer, a sack full of corn and a basket containing the delicious local umkuna plums. Later, they gathered outside the hut, squatting by firelight under the stars in the cool of the evening, tearing chunks of the goat meat apart with their hands and washing it down with the beer.

'Well,' said Jenkins, inevitably, 'I'm startin' to take to this postin' now, bach sir. The old king is lookin' after us right well, I'd say.'

Their meal was interrupted towards its end by the arrival of a visitor. A portly, bearded white man, dressed in conventional slouch hat, loose cotton shirt and corduroy trousers, he stood deferentially for a moment at the edge of the light cast by the fire before stepping forward to introduce himself.

'James Fairbairn,' he said. 'I trade here. Thought I would walk over and introduce myself and welcome you to this Paris of Africa. I've heard that you came here in a bit of a rush, so I've brought you a few things you might need, toothbrushes, soap and the like. All from the store. You can pay me later,' he added hurriedly.

'My word, you are welcome,' said Alice. The introductions were made and Fairbairn joined them at the fireside and helped them to munch the plums and drink the beer. He was, he said, one of a small group of traders who had made their homes in Bulawayo some years ago and eked out a not particularly profitable living. They existed under the eye of the king but they were more or less left alone, as long as they gave Lobengula presents from time to time, 'as a kind of fee for being allowed to stay,' he explained. But it wasn't a bad life. 'At least we are all our own men.'

There was, he added, a local British missionary who spoke the Matabele language fluently and who had become intimate with the king, drafting the occasional letter for him to the authorities in the Cape Colony and even, once, to Queen Victoria. The man ran a school for the children but so far had made no conversions to Christianity.

'Why are you here?' Fairbairn asked.

Simon explained the circumstances.

The trader seemed relieved. 'We are getting a lot of white visitors here now,' he said. 'Usually they cause trouble.'

'Why?'

'Well.' Fairbairn scratched his beard. 'I don't know too much about politics back home, or in Europe for that matter. And I am no mining engineer. But I do know this much – the scramble for Africa by the white man is still going on and old Lobengula's kingdom is one of the juiciest bits that is still available, so to speak. Available, that is, if you can get the old rogue to put his cross on a piece of paper and then move in and develop it.'

'Cecil John Rhodes?'

'Yes, but not just him. Look.' Fairbairn pulled a stick from the edge of the fire, snapped off its charred end and used it to sketch a rough map of southern Africa in the dust at their feet. 'Here is Matabeleland, including Mashonaland to the north, which the king controls anyway. The British are well entrenched down at the bottom in South Africa, here. The Portuguese have vast territories in Mozambique in the east and Angola in the west, right next door, so to speak. Belgium has the Congo in the centre of Africa to the northwest here. We've got the Germans, under ... what's his name?'

'Bismarck?' prompted Alice, her chin in her hand.

'That's the chap. Yes, the Germans here, in Damaraland, to the south-west, just itching to get more land. Then, very importantly, old Kruger with his Boers in the Transvaal here, just south of the border with Matabeleland, all cock-a-hoop after rubbing our noses in the dirt at Majuba. He wants a route to the sea for his state and reckons he can best do it through Lobengula's nation. On top of all that there's the French at the top of Africa and in the Sahara who would love to put our noses out of joint by taking the king's land. Everybody thinks that there is gold here. There's a bit of mining at Tati just over the border to the south, as you know, but no traces have really been found anywhere else around here, as far as I'm aware, although the king has not really let anyone mine in his land yet. So everyone seems to be beating a path to the old devil's door.'

Fonthill smiled. 'For someone who doesn't know much about it, that's what I would call a pretty fair summing-up of the situation, Mr Fairbairn, and matches what I heard in the Cape.'

The trader looked a touch embarrassed and scratched his head. 'Well, it's important to us all, I suppose.'

'But you said that all these visitors cause trouble.'

'Yes. Everybody makes all kinds of promises to Lobengula – promises that they don't keep. He's no fool, you know. He knows the white man pretty well now. It is true that he is well disposed towards the English – mainly I think because we knocked over the Zulus a few years ago, and also because the stories of the wealth created by the British in the diamond and gold fields down south are rife here. So he thinks we are strong. But he says that all white men are liars.' Fairbairn grinned. 'And so we are, I reckon.'

Jenkins had been listening with care. Now he lifted his head. 'Tell me, Mr Fairbairn, why do people want this land anyway? It don't look much good to me, see. Lot of woodland and these big high rocks stickin' up all over the place.'

'I suppose it's the promise of gold and other minerals, as I've said, although there's good farming land around here and in Mashonaland. But Matabeleland is also the route to the north, to the big lakes up there. You've got to go through here to get there, to get to whatever they've got to offer.' He scratched his head again. 'Seems to me that the powers in Europe have gone a bit mad about all this. I can see it leading to a scrap in the end.'

The little gathering fell silent for a moment as the flickering flames lit their faces spasmodically. Somewhere far away a hyena barked and caused Fairbairn to look up. 'Bad sign, that,' he said.

'The little devils are getting more adventurous. Coming close to our huts and stealing the rubbish.'

'What about the British in all this, Mr Fairbairn?' Fonthill asked. 'Mzingeli here tells me that he believes that Rhodes from the Cape has entered into some sort of deal with Lobengula.'

Fairbairn's teeth flashed in the firelight. 'Yes, he has. In fact his people have just left, after being here for months. He got the king to put his cross on the paper what seems like ages ago, giving Rhodes the right to prospect for minerals, mainly gold, of course. In return Lobengula has been promised all sorts of things: guns, ammunition, money and so on. But nothing has materialised. That's why he says all white men are liars. At the moment, I don't think that treaty is worth the paper it is written on. The king won't really understand what he's signed anyway. But the others are still sniffing around here, to get him to let them have rights, too.'

'Who are they?'

'Well, the Dutchmen from the Transvaal are always pulling at his sleeve, but he hates the Boers so he won't do anything with them. No...' The trader's voice faded away for a moment. 'The worst are the Portuguese.'

'Why?'

'They think this territory is theirs anyway, because they've been next door in Mozambique for bloody centuries. But they've never really had the guts just to come in and invade and settle the land, which is what is called for. The main problem is that they are insistent. They've got a man

59

here now. His name is Manuel Antonio de Sousa – very fancy bloke to match his fancy name. But everybody calls him Gouela. He's a slave master in his own right and a cruel bastard – ah, excuse me, ma'am.'

Alice, whose eyes had never left Fairbairn's face, nodded her acceptance.

'He has abused all the tribes in his territory to the east. He rapes and flogs, but he's got a silver tongue from what I hear and he is here to rubbish the British to the king and to get him to sign a treaty with the Portuguese. He's got silly airs and graces but the king gets taken in by all this stuff. So Rhodes ought to watch out.'

Fonthill slowly nodded his head. 'Fascinating,' he said. 'Now, Mr Fairbairn, we have just a little drop of Boer brandy left. Will you take a dram?'

Fairbairn stood. 'No, thank you kindly. I must be getting back.' He looked down at the bundle at his feet. 'I will leave all this stuff with you. Take what you want and bring the rest back to the store and ... er ... you can pay me there. It's about three hundred yards that way, outside the outer fence. Now, I'll say good night to you all.'

After his departure, Alice drew her knees up under her chin and stared into the embers of the fire reflectively. 'I have to say, Simon,' she said, 'that I don't like the sound of all this. You must be careful not to trade on your incredibly close relationship with our Queen,' she looked up and grinned, 'because you would just be the latest in a long line of interlopers here who couldn't deliver. You mustn't be a scapegoat for Cecil John Rhodes.'

'And, look you, I don't like what I 'ear about this Portuguese chap,' said Jenkins. 'Manuel Saucepot or whatever 'is name is. I fancy 'e could be trouble.'

Fonthill rose to his feet. 'Well, I'll try and stay out of this mess if I can. But I can't see us getting out of here before our transport arrives. We are in the hands of the king, for better or worse. So let's go to bed.'

Chapter 3

The next morning Fonthill, stripped to the waist, was washing outside the hut in a bowl of cold water when he saw a strange apparition approaching. A white man, resplendent in a yellow uniform, complete with gold buttons and red braid at the shoulders and a sword at his waist, was being slowly borne towards him on a palanquin, or litter, carried by two Kaffirs. At the door of the hut, the litter was carefully lowered to the ground and the man put out his jackbooted legs, stood stiffly and inclined his head.

He said something quickly in a language foreign to Fonthill and waited for a reply. 'I am sorry,' said Simon, hurriedly towelling himself. 'You must forgive me, but I don't speak that language.'

'Of course not.' The man's English was highly accented but it was clear that he was being contemptuous. 'Why is it that you English do not speak any language other than your own?' It was not a question, more a condemnation. Fonthill studied him carefully. He was of medium height – a little shorter than Simon – strongly built and with a face that reflected a life spent in the tropics: pockmarked and yellow-tinged. Beneath the peaked cap that matched the uniform hung hair in waved ringlets. He must be, of course, the Portuguese spoken of last night by Fairbairn.

'I am afraid that with most of us that is true,' Fonthill replied, pulling over his head the coarse shirt that Mr Fairbairn had supplied. *'Though not all of us. Mais si vous parlez Francais, peut-être je peux vous aidez,'* he added, 'or *vielleicht wäre die Deutsche Sprache lieber?* However, I do apologise, for I do not speak any of the lesser languages, such as Portuguese.'

A distant chuckle came from within the hut. The Portuguese's eyes hardened. 'English will do,' he said. 'I speak it fluently.' He jerked his head forward. 'Manuel Antonio de Sousa, agent for the King of Portugal in Matabeleland and Mashonaland, at your service.'

Fonthill took a pace forward and extended his hand. 'Simon Fonthill. How do you do.' He shook the man's hand, an action that resembled handling a damp, warm fish, then gestured. 'I am sorry I cannot ask you inside, but my wife is completing her toilet. We had rather a long day travelling yesterday.' He indicated a log nearby. 'Won't you sit down?'

'No. Your wife is with you?' De Sousa seemed surprised.

'Yes. We were on holiday, travelling in the Transvaal, when we crossed into Matabeleland to help one of the Malakala villages, whose herd was being attacked by lions. We met up with a party of the king's men and were brought here.'

'Ah, that explains the skins. Or does it?' The sneer had returned. 'You don't expect me to believe that, do you? You are, of course, working for Rhodes.'

Fonthill felt his temper rising but took a deep breath. 'No, I am not. I have no interest in Mr Rhodes's activities. As I explained, I am on holiday. Now, Mr de Sousa, what can I do for you?'

For a moment, de Sousa's black eyes gleamed in anger. Then he laughed. 'Listen, my friend,' he said. 'When you return to your master, tell him that King Lobengula has no further interest in the false promises of the British. This is Portuguese territory and Lobengula is a Portuguese subject, and he has agreed to allow my people – *not the British* – to develop this country. Rhodes – and you – would be well advised to stay out of my way.'

Jenkins chose that moment to crawl out of the hut. He looked at the Portuguese's litter, with its two bearers standing idly by, and spoke with exaggerated concern. 'Oh, somebody ill, then? Goodness me. It must be the heat, I suppose.' Then, pretending to see de Sousa for the first time, 'Ah, good morning. Would you like to come inside out of the heat and lie down, perhaps?'

De Sousa looked at the Welshman in astonishment. Then his lip curled. 'This is your wife?' he asked with a sarcasm to match that of Jenkins.

'No,' replied Fonthill evenly, 'this is the only accommodation we have at the moment, until our wagon arrives from the border, so we are forced to share. Now,' his voice took on a harder tone, 'I do not like being threatened, Mr de Sousa, and I can only repeat once again that I have nothing to do with Mr Rhodes. As for staying out of your way, I shall go where I like in this territory, subject to the approval of the king. I know as well as you do, sir, that Matabeleland is not under the suzerainty of Portugal and remains an independent country. If this was not so, you would not be here. Your behaviour, sir, is not that of a gentleman and I would be grateful if you would leave.'

The two men remained glaring at each other for a moment, and then the Portuguese walked slowly to his litter, lay down upon it and, with a flick of his wrist, bade his bearers carry him away.

Fonthill and Jenkins watched him go with smiles on their lips. 'What a pompous bit of offal,' said the Welshman. ''E looks an' sounds like a tin soldier, don't 'e?'

'I'm not so sure about that.' Alice had crawled out of the hut and joined them. She put a hand on her husband's arm. 'You were right to tick him off, my love, but I have a feeling that you have just made a rather dangerous enemy.'

Simon puffed out his cheeks. 'I didn't have much choice, actually. He was bloody rude from the start so I had to put him down. Obviously the man is a bounder. You'll remember what Fairbairn said about him last night. And of course he was bluffing about Matabeleland being Portuguese territory...'

'Yes, my dear, but I believe that they have always claimed it as being ... what is the phrase? "In their African sphere of influence." Maybe this is recognised in Whitehall. Don't forget that Portugal is supposed to be our oldest ally. So perhaps they have some sort of case. All I am saying is that you should stay away from him.'

'Yes, well, if you say so, Alice. But I shan't lose any sleep in worrying about him.'

They were interrupted by the *inDuna*, who approached them accompanied by Mzingeli. The tracker looked concerned. 'King want to see you now,' he said.

Fonthill wrinkled his nose. 'Very well. Let me just make myself presentable for his majesty. You had better come with me, Mzingeli, to interpret, please.'

This time Fonthill and Mzingeli were ushered straight into the king's house. They found him half sitting, half lying on a chaise longue, but dressed very differently now. Despite the warmth in the dark interior, he wore a pair of cord trousers, rather the worse for wear, a dirty flannel shirt, a tweed coat and a billycock hat in which was stuck a feather. One foot was encased in a lace-up boot; the other wore an old carpet slipper with its end cut away to reveal a swollen, obviously inflamed big toe.

The total effect was incongruous and Simon bit back a smile. Instead he bowed his head in greeting as Lobengula waved him to sit on a pile of skins before him. Mzingeli squatted at his side and the king gestured to him to interpret.

'He ask,' began the tracker, 'how was Queen Victoria when last you see her?'

'Er ... very well, thank you, sir. Ah, she is still sad, of course, because her husband died – even though this was about twenty years ago.'

'She got no other husbands left?'

'No. It is our custom only to have one spouse at a time. And she has never married again.'

'That very silly. But your business. Give her my salute when next you see her.'

'I will indeed, sir.'

The king shifted his afflicted foot slightly and grimaced in pain, but he continued, through Mzingeli: 'You know Rhodes?'

'Only slightly. I have met him once, but that was eight years ago.'

'He never come to see me. Only send his people. If he so interested in my land, why he no come and talk to me himself?'

'I don't know, sir. However, I do know that he is very busy with affairs of state in the Cape Colony. I understand that he may soon be elected prime minister there.'

'Humph. That not king.'

'No, sir. But it means he is the leader of this very big land.'

'Not as big as my land.'

'With respect, sir, it is about twice as large.' Fonthill was not sure about this, but he rather doubted if the king would be able to check the fact.

A silence fell on the gathering, only broken when a huge black woman entered, bearing a gourd of beer for Simon. She wore native dress, which meant very few garments. The king nodded towards her. 'This my sister, Nini. She not married.'

Unsure about the significance of this last piece of information, Fonthill struggled to his feet and

66

bowed. Mzingeli, aware of the proprieties, inclined his head from the sitting position. But Nini strode forward, seized Simon's hand and shook it vigorously, an act that made her huge bare breasts sway alarmingly. 'How is you?' she asked, disdaining to use Mzingeli's interpretive skills.

'I is ... I am very well, ma'am. I am delighted to meet you.'

'You have wife?'

'Yes, she is with me.' A look of what might have been disappointment came across Nini's otherwise happy features. 'You know Queen Victoria?'

Fonthill shifted uneasily from one foot to the other. This was all getting rather out of hand. 'Only very slightly, ma'am.'

It was clear that the king's sister's knowledge of English was being exhausted, for she now nodded to Mzingeli to translate. 'She know that Queen has sons. She would like to marry one. You help her?'

Simon gulped, quickly dismissing from his mind the irreverent vision of the portly Prince of Wales and the eighteen-stone Princess Nini attempting to copulate. 'I fear that would not be possible, ma'am. The Queen's sons are married already, and our religion and constitution allow only one husband at a time.'

The princess nodded, seemingly not disconcerted by the news. She pointed to the gourd. 'Good beer. I make. Goodbyeing.' Then, with a cheerful grin, she left.

Fonthill squatted again and, although not exactly yearning to drink beer at half past eight in the morning, took a sip from the gourd. Nini was right. It *was* excellent. Perhaps she could have made a match of it with that famous *bon vivant* Prince Edward after all... But the king was speaking again.

'I trust you. Anyone who is friend of great English Queen must be honourable man. Everyone I talk to from other countries want me to give them my land. They say to dig in it but I think they put their own people on it. I know that world is changing and not like that of my father. Perhaps I must give in to these strong countries, like yours.'

The king was now looking hard at his guest and his face wore an expression of ... what? Pleading? Desperation? Simon experienced a sudden sympathy for this man, who just wished to be left alone to live as his forebears had, but who clearly saw that he must somehow move with the times. A man who realised that he must change but not knowing which way to turn. A man under great pressure.

He cleared his throat to reply, but the king was continuing. 'I say to Rhodes he can come here and dig. In return, he promise me,' and he slapped one finger after another on to his palm, 'one hundred pounds your money on first day of every lunar month, a thousand rifles with hundred thousand bullets, and steamboat for me on Zambezi. What happen? Nothing. Now, Portuguese, Germans and other English tell me I have done wrong and should sign with them. My *inDunas* say I must not sign my country away. What do I do? You honest man. You know great Queen. Tell me, what do I do?'

Fonthill frowned. What the hell to say? He took another, reflective drink from the gourd. Then, 'I am English, of course, and your majesty will think that because of that I will favour the English in my reply. But I will attempt to be objective.' He waited for Mzingeli to translate, for it was important that the tracker found the right words. Then he continued.

'You know that the British Empire is the largest in the world. It has territories that are...' his brain attempted to find a comparison that would be roughly accurate and also meaningful, 'a hundred, hundred, hundred times bigger than Matabeleland and Mashonaland combined. It has ships that control the wide oceans and armies that exist in fifty countries or more. I myself have fought in these armies in five countries in the last five years and seen their power. If your majesty feels he must side with one of these great nations, then I have to say that he should choose the strongest, which is Britain.

'As for the offers you are receiving from other English companies, I understand that you have already signed a treaty with Rhodes. I do not know this man well, but he is very rich and powerful – he owns many, many more oxen even than your majesty. He is a man of distinction in the Cape, and because of his prominent position, he would not – he could not – avoid keeping his word to you. So I recommend that you should put your trust in him.

'However...' Fonthill paused to allow Mzingeli to keep pace, but also to gather his thoughts. He found himself empathising with the king's appeal. Could he help? 'As you know, I wish to return to the Cape as soon as possible. I promise you that I will see Rhodes and explain to him your concern. I will say to him that whatever problems he has in keeping his word to you, they must be overcome, otherwise he will lose his contract with you. I hope that may help your majesty. I fear I can do no more.'

The king listened carefully, and when Mzingeli had finished, he sat for a while looking at Fonthill. Then: 'Wise words. Yes, I keep with Rhodes, but only as contract said: he can dig, but not to settle people here. Yes, please. You talk to him in Cape. I am glad you help me.'

Fonthill bowed his head in acquiescence, and as silence descended again, he took another sip from the gourd. Then, however, a further thought occurred to him.

'Your majesty has a Portuguese agent visiting you?'

'Yes. He important man.'

Simon coughed and wondered how to go on. 'I am afraid, sir, that he does not appear to me to be a gentleman. I understand that he treats the tribes that come under his command to the east very badly. Making slaves of them—'

The king interrupted Mzingeli quickly at this point: 'That is good. Some people no good for anything but slaves. I have slaves.'

Damn! Fonthill had to recover. 'Yes, sir. But you treat your slaves well. I understand that he does not. He rapes and whips them. That is not the action of a white gentleman.'

'Ah yes. It is right, you are different. But he is

friends with King of Portugal. He is agent.'

'I believe that he merely has duties involving the native tribes to the west of Mozambique. But also he has threatened me this morning' – Simon felt at this point that he was behaving rather like the school sneak, betraying another boy to the headmaster, but he ploughed on anyway – 'saying that I must not interfere with your plans to give digging rights to other countries. I think you should know, sir, that I do not think he is to be trusted.'

Another silence descended, and it was clear that Lobengula was not comfortable with the accusation. Fonthill, however, refused to retract it. De Sousa had thrown down the challenge, and this opportunity for creating bad odour between him and the king was too good to be missed.

Eventually Lobengula spoke. 'King hear your words. He think about it.'

Silence once more. It seemed as though the king had something else to say but was almost embarrassed to say it, or could not find the words to do so. He stirred on his couch, and once again a grimace flashed across his face.

'Your majesty is in pain?'

This seemed to open a door of opportunity for the big man. 'Yes. My foot gives me much hurt. It is curse put on me by my enemies.' His face took on a diffident expression, as though about to seek a favour but not knowing how to ask it of this strange, highly placed white man, who had brought him gifts but had so far asked nothing of him. Then he seemed to pluck up courage.

'Your lady has power of witchcraft, my people

71

tell me.'

'Oh no.' Fonthill smiled. 'She is no witch doctor.'

'Ah, but she heal shoulder of the Malakala man. Put back flesh torn by lion. No one get better after lion bite or claw. They die. This man good now, I hear. Could she come and take curse off my foot?'

Consternation settled on Fonthill. First he was a close friend of Queen Victoria, the most famous and powerful monarch in the world. Now he was married to a witch doctor! He thought quickly. Alice had only rudimentary medical knowledge, given to her over four days by doctors at the Missionary Society who knew the territory and its dangers. But there was no way she could cure gout. Or was there...? Perhaps she could alleviate the pain a little. To do so would put them in good standing with the king. If she failed, however, this could diminish them both in Lobengula's eyes. Anyway, he could hardly refuse the man's request.

'Your majesty will know,' he began, 'that we do not believe in curses. The problem with your foot will be a medical one...' He sought for simple words that would explain it. 'It will be the result perhaps of something you have eaten or drunk too much of. Or maybe a thorn that has settled deeply in the foot.'

The king scowled. The scowl was reflected in Mzingeli's translation. 'He say he know all about thorns. No thorn in his foot.'

Simon bowed his head. 'Very well, sir. My wife is not a witch doctor, but nor is she any other sort of doctor. She does, however, have some basic skills in healing that might help you and perhaps relieve your pain. I will ask her.'

The big smile returned to Lobengula's face. 'Good. Ask her come soon. Now, I give more food to you tonight. Is there more you want?'

Smiling, Fonthill shook his head. 'Only our horses and wagon from the border, sir. We are anxious to travel south.'

'My men go get them today. Is good you go soon – to see Rhodes.' Then he added quickly, 'After your lady help me.'

Fonthill rose, pulling Mzingeli with him, and they both bowed and shuffled out of the room. As they trudged back to the hut, Simon confided, 'I shall be glad to get out of here, Mzingeli. I seem to be getting deeper and deeper into I don't quite know what. But I don't like it.'

The tracker nodded. 'King is cunning. You must be careful.'

Alice herself was just returning to the hut as Fonthill approached. 'I've been to Fairbairn's store to pay him,' she said. 'I've left Jenkins up there, trying to haggle with him about the price of a bottle of whisky. The man was not exactly giving anything away last night, but I don't begrudge him what he charges. He lives behind the shop, so to speak, and I can't help feeling that he doesn't have much of a life. But it's his choice. Now, what did his majesty want?'

They both sat on a log and Simon recounted his conversation with Lobengula, beginning with the king's request for help with Rhodes.

Alice pulled a face. 'I have never met the great Cecil John,' she said, 'but he sounds a bit of a slippery customer to me. I would not like you to become too involved with him.'

'Oh, as millionaires go, I don't think he's too bad. Of one thing I am sure – he's a genuine patriot. When I met him in Kimberley seven or eight years ago, he gave me his vision of a British route to the north, with much of his map painted red. Then, he was just the company secretary of a mining outfit. I have read since that he has made two fortunes: the first in diamonds, of course, and the second from gold in the Transvaal. It's my bet that he is not really interested in Matabeleland or Mashonaland for the mineral rights. He would rather settle the land with Britishers if he could and then try and build a road, or even a railway, to the north. The king is a shrewd old cove and I believe that he suspects this is what Rhodes is up to and he is worried about it.'

Alice sniffed. 'Well on that matter, I would be on Lobengula's side. I know he is a cruel old despot, but he has done nothing to harm the British or any other Europeans, for that matter. Why can't we leave him gradually to slip into the nineteenth century in his own way and his own time? We've got the biggest blasted empire the world has ever seen. Why do we need to add a few more African acres to it?'

'I don't quite agree, my love.' Simon smiled. They had been over this ground before. Alice's radical views were familiar to him. She yearned for the return to power of William Ewart Gladstone as prime minister of Great Britain, and for a resumption of a Liberal government's anti-imperialist policies. As a war correspondent for the *Morning Post*, she had even managed to infiltrate her views

74

into her reports for that most Tory of newspapers.

He looked around him and gestured towards the rolling grassland behind the barrier of thorns. 'I've seen enough to know that this is good land,' he said, his eyes crinkled. 'And I gather it is even better further north in Mashonaland. As it is, it is not developed at all, and the Matabele seem to know nothing about agriculture. They will never make the most of this fertile ground. I am talking about cultivating it, not digging for gold, silver, copper or whatever might be beneath these grasslands. I wouldn't mind at all farming here.' He grinned at her. 'Bit less boring than Norfolk, anyway.'

But Alice was not smiling, and remembering the king's other request, Simon was glad of the chance to change the subject and put Lobengula's plea to her.

'What?' His wife's face was a study in consternation. 'Good lord. I am not a doctor, Simon. You know that.'

'Yes, Alice. I did try and explain, but it seems you have acquired a reputation as a magnificent witch doctor after stitching up Sando's shoulder. Perhaps there is something you could do to ease Lobengula's pain?'

'I don't know. Perhaps there is something in the self-help medical book the missionaries gave me. I will go and get my bag.' She stood to move into the low opening of the hut, but Simon held her back.

'I'll go. I need to oil the rifles, anyway.'

He crawled through the opening and stood for a moment in the dim interior, trying to accustom

75

his eyes to the poor light, before bending down to look under Alice's bed for her bag. Suddenly a movement caught his eye. On the low wooden-framed bed by the door – *his* bed – something was moving, undulating under the blanket that had been lightly thrown there. Then, slowly, a cold-eyed flat head emerged to regard him, followed by the coils of a body.

It was a puff adder.

Fonthill felt his mouth go dry. He made to move back towards the hut opening, but the snake followed him with his head and then slipped from under the blanket on to the ground. It was cutting him off from the exit. Where the hell were the rifles? His eye caught them: the two Martini-Henrys and Alice's gun, neatly stacked against the wall – just by the entrance. The snake, of course, was between him and the guns.

He looked hard at the reptile, which had now formed itself into a tight coil, with its head held high and back, in an 'S' shape. Simon licked his lips and tried to remember what Mzingeli had told them. The puff adder was, he recalled, the most dangerous snake in Africa. Its bite could penetrate leather and its poison was extremely toxic. It could kill a man and frequently did so in this part of Africa.

The thing was now uncoiling and moving towards him slowly, hissing, its mouth wide open and revealing its fangs. Even in the semi-darkness he could see the dark bands around its eyes. Uncoiled, it revealed itself to be about three and a half feet in length. Fonthill felt the hairs begin to stand up on the back of his neck.

He took a deep breath and shouted, 'Alice. Do not crawl into the hut. There is a snake in here. It is between me and the rifles and the door. Get 352 or Mzingeli quickly – and a gun. Quickly now.'

There was no reply. He called again. Silence once more. He looked round for some sort of weapon. His hunting knife was hung up above his bed and unreachable, but even if he could have got to it, it would have been useless against the adder, which could strike so quickly. The thing was slowly slithering towards him now. Fonthill felt completely vulnerable in his lightweight cord trousers and slip-on shoes. He had even left his socks off today, of all days. What could he use to distract the snake?

He felt behind him with one hand, encountering Alice's bed. The blanket! Slowly he pulled at it until he felt it come loose and slide on to the floor. Could he hear voices now, from outside? He called out: 'Don't come in,' and pulled the blanket towards him until he had a large portion wrapped around his wrist. He took a gentle step forward towards the snake. Immediately, it coiled its head back again. With a jerk of his wrist, he flicked the blanket at the adder, so that it almost touched the square head, now held nearly upright. The snake hissed and struck at the blanket with what seemed like the speed of light. The two, slightly back-curved fangs snapped together on the frayed edge of the cloth and immediately became entangled in the coarse wool fibres.

Fonthill tugged the blanket back, but it remained caught in the snake's fangs, pulling the thing towards him. He sprang to the side, caught his leg on the foot of Alice's bed and fell to the ground. He threw the rest of the blanket at the snake and, rolling over, saw it thrashing its head under the folds of the cloth as it tried to free itself.

This was his chance. He hurled himself towards the doorway and landed on his stomach at the foot of his bed. Scrambling to his knees, he pulled his own blanket from the bed and held it as a feeble barrier between him and the snake, like some grounded matador, in the hope that he could slip through the doorway behind its cover. The snake, freed now, had followed him and struck at the blanket, tearing it from his grasp as though it was a mere sheet of paper and tossing it aside. This time, its fangs had not become entangled.

With only inches between them, the serpent and its victim stared at each other, eye to eye. Simon saw the adder open its jaws and pull back its head to strike. He held up a hand and closed his eyes.

The shot that echoed within the confined space of the hut sounded like a howitzer cannon being fired. Fonthill felt something fall across his knee and he recoiled. When he opened his eyes, he saw the body of the headless serpent twitching on the ground by his kneecap. Turning his head, he saw Jenkins lying on his stomach, halfway through the doorway of the hut, Mzingeli's Snider rifle at his shoulder. His head lay to one side and he was being sick.

Simon could hear Alice shouting from outside, 'Let me in, let me in.' He summoned up a feeble croak. 'It's all right. Jenkins has got him. We are both all right.'

At this the Welshman raised his head, vomit on his chin. 'He didn't bite you then, bach sir?' he whispered. 'The 'orrible thing didn't get you?'

Fonthill stood slowly, shaking off the body of the snake with a shudder. Of its head there was no sign, except for a red smudge of some undefined matter on the wall of the hut. Jenkins's shot had shattered it completely. He walked over to his comrade and knelt by his side, only to see the Welshman disappear slowly backwards on his stomach through the opening, as if by magic. Having pulled him clear, Alice appeared, her face ashen.

She crawled into the hut and put her arms around her husband. 'Thank the Lord you are all right.'

'Mind where you put your feet, my darling,' Simon whispered into her hair. 'I'm afraid poor old 352 has been a bit poorly. I'd forgotten how frightened he was of snakes.'

Outside, Mzingeli, Sando, Ntini and a still trembling Jenkins awaited them. Simon pulled the Welshman to his feet and regarded him severely. 'You've made a terrible mess of our living accommodation,' he said and punched him on the shoulder. 'God bless you, old chap.' He took his hand and pumped it. 'I am just so grateful that my best friend just happens to be the finest shot in the world.'

'Not with that bloody old thing he ain't, look you.' Jenkins wiped his chin and gestured towards Mzingeli's rifle. 'If the range had been a foot or so longer I would have missed. It fires up, y'see, but anyway, I was trembling so much.' He turned to

Alice and wiped away the perspiration from his face with a very dirty handkerchief. 'Sorry about the mess, miss. Can't stand snakes, see.'

She kissed him. 'I don't know how many times I have had to thank you for saving my husband's life, 352,' she said. 'But this surely must have been the closest thing. My word, it must.' She turned towards Fonthill. 'I heard you shout, Simon, and immediately ran for Mzingeli, who of course had the only other gun. Then I saw dear old 352 coming down the hill.'

Mzingeli coughed and nodded towards Jenkins. 'I want to go in because is my gun – only one outside hut – but he say no. He best shot. I think he right.'

Fonthill shook his head again. 'Right. Let's clear up inside and get rid of what's left of the brute. Three five two, get yourself a whisky. You are relieved of duty for at least ten minutes. Then we must all talk.'

Later, the six of them squatted on the beaten earth outside the hut. 'Now,' began Fonthill, 'I want to ask you something, Mzingeli. Could that snake have crawled in through the doorway of the hut on its own?'

The tracker shook his head. 'No. Snake don't like people, although it will attack when people come close.' He gestured with his arm. 'Too many people here. Snake never live in village. Out in woods and stony holes. Not here.'

'That's what I thought.'

'What?' asked Alice. 'You don't think it was planted, Simon, do you?'

'I don't know.' He struggled to his feet. 'Excuse

me for a moment.' He was back within a minute. 'As I thought, someone has cut a hole in the wickerwork at the back of the hut and closed the gap with a large stone. The snake was obviously slipped though the hole. The noise outside the entrance would probably have stopped it from escaping that way. By the time I got inside, it was a rather angry snake, I would say.' He turned to Mzingeli. 'Did you or either of the boys see anybody approaching, perhaps, say, carrying a sack?'

The question was translated but received no affirmative reply.

Fonthill frowned. It had to be de Sousa. The bastard! He looked ruefully at Alice. 'You were right. I *must* have upset him. Must be very sensitive people, these Portuguese. What a nasty piece of work!'

'What are you goin' to do about 'im, then, bach sir?' enquired Jenkins in a low voice. 'Let me nip over with me knife to where 'e lies on 'is fancy bed, like.'

Fonthill shook his head. 'No. The king obviously respects the man for some reason. I certainly don't want to have blood on my hands while I am in his kraal – and neither did de Sousa, for that matter. That's why he used the snake. A very African way to kill a European, don't you think? He wouldn't have been suspected.'

He mused for a moment. 'I think I will let the matter rest.'

Jenkins's black eyebrows almost met his moustache. 'You don't mean lettin' 'im get away with it? 'E will just try again, won't 'e – an' keep tryin' till he gets you.'

81

'He might, but that's a risk we just have to take.' He looked at them all in turn, resting his eyes last on his wife. 'We must all be on our guard.' He rose to his feet. 'Anyway, we shall be getting out of here soon, when our transport arrives. I would give it only a few days now. It's not far from the frontier.'

'Yes,' said Alice glumly. 'And I have become the Royal Physician. I must get my bag and bone up on gout, or whatever it is that's wrong with the old boy.' Her face fell further. 'What if it's syphilis, or something like that? I shall be a bit stumped then. What the hell would Florence Nightingale have done?' She rose to get her bag, then, at the hut opening, paused for just a moment.

'Let me go first,' said Fonthill hurriedly. 'I'm sure there is not another one in there. But if there is, don't worry. I can fight snakes single-handedly now. Just give me a blanket. Oh ... and perhaps Jenkins with a rifle.'

With a grin, he crawled in and Alice followed him.

Chapter 4

Three days later, they were on their way to the border, relieved to be rid of the hothouse atmosphere, the ever-present scent of danger, that characterised Lobengula's kraal. The king's men had arrived with their wagon and horses remarkably quickly and the monarch himself waved them off, shouting, 'You come back,' as they rode away. The sun sent shafts of welcoming light across the plain and it was pleasant as, blessedly on horseback again, they followed the faint trail across the veldt. Mzingeli loped on ahead, his Snider over his shoulder, with Sando at his heels and Ntini handling their team of oxen from his seat on the wagon at the rear.

Alice, riding a little behind Simon, allowed her mind to dwell on the last three days. She had visited the king twice, on successive days, and she grinned as she recalled the details. She had been apprehensive about her ability to make a correct diagnosis, but she need not have worried. There was no thorn or broken bone under that cutaway slipper that protected the swelling – and how had that cosy item of Victorian domestic footwear come to be worn by an African chieftain? – but a significant clue was provided by the pile of empty champagne and brandy bottles that glittered in the corner of the hut. Gout, it had to be! Her little handbook on African diseases made no mention of this malady, but her father had suffered a little from it. Too much meat, port and red wine was the cause, the local general practitioner had lectured. A balanced diet was the cure.

She had alleviated the pain on both visits by administering a little morphine into the naked bottom of the monarch as he lay on his couch. Lobengula had taken it well and had called in his *inDunas*, wives and children to witness his bravery. They had all applauded when he waved airily to them as the needle entered the great rump.

But he had taken less well Alice's injunctions to

give up the white man's drink, reduce the amount of beef he ingested and eat more berries and other fruits. She knew that it would take more than the homilies of a white woman to change these indulgences, so she had visited Fairbairn to ask him to refuse to sell the bottles to Lobengula. The trader had smiled, waved his pipe and delivered his own lecture on the inadvisability of him telling the King of the Matabele how to live. 'He's God around here,' he had explained. 'If he wants champagne and brandy, then by golly I've got to sell it to him.'

So Alice had shrugged and taken her bag away. On the morning of their departure, however, the king had summoned her and given her a bottle of splendid French cognac, vintage 1880. Whatever his vices, the man had good taste – and a sense of humour. 'For your man,' he had boomed, pressing the bottle into her hand. 'Be careful he don't get goot.' She had decided that she liked the old ruffian. And oh how the little children had gasped, laughed and applauded as he presented his buttocks to the needle.

As she summoned up their laughing faces, Alice's eyes filled with tears. Sniffing, she blew her nose, gulped and then gently urged her horse forward until she rode side by side with her husband.

'Our son would have been four just the other day,' she said.

Simon nodded his head, looking straight ahead but gripping her hand tightly. 'I know,' he said. 'The day we shot the lions.'

They rode hand in hand for a few minutes, lost in their own thoughts. Intuitively Jenkins had let his own mount fall back a little as soon as he saw their hands meet. His godson, their son – George Jenkins Mustapha Fonthill – had lived only a few minutes after his birth at their farm in Norfolk, back in 1885. The pregnancy had been difficult and Jenkins had always had his doubts about the survival of the babe. Perhaps its unconventional conception in the sands of the Sudanese desert, amidst the trauma after their escape from the Mahdi's camp, might have had something to do with it. He sighed. It was rarely spoken of now and it was clear that their attempts to have another child since had failed. He knew that the two people he loved most in the world carried with them this constant sadness, and he in turn was sad for them. Time to cheer them up.

He kicked in his heels. 'What about a nice cup of tea?' he called. 'My mouth feels like old Lobengolly's armpit. But if you don't want a *nice* cup of tea, *I* can make it.'

It did the trick. 'Perish the thought,' said Alice. 'But let's stop for a minute.'

They did so and stretched their legs, standing to drink from their tin mugs near a large kopje.

Mzingeli threw away the dregs and moved close to Fonthill. 'We are followed,' he said quietly.

'How long?'

'Last hour, perhaps. Now people ahead. Behind kopje. They watch us from top.'

'How many?'

'Do not know. Perhaps six, ten. Perhaps more.'

Fonthill nodded and took a last reflective drink from his mug. 'Thank goodness for your splendid eyesight, Mzingeli. Have you any idea who they might be?'

'Just Kaffirs, I think.'

'Very well.' He paused for a moment and walked to his horse on the pretence of adjusting the saddle cinch. From under his hat he scanned the top of the kopje, which was perhaps a quarter of a mile away and some sixty feet tall. He could see nothing. His gaze swept around. They were still on the plateau, although its undulations would have made it easy for them to have been followed and then overtaken. There was no sign of any other living thing.

Softly, he called Jenkins to him. 'Mzingeli tells me that we are being followed by natives who are armed,' he said. 'They have been observing us from that kopje up ahead – no, don't look! I am surprised, because I thought that if we were going to be attacked it would be when we were in the bush. But these people obviously didn't want us too near the security of the border, in case we made a break for it.'

'Is it that Portuguese swine, bach sir?'

'I can't think of any else who might want us dead. De Sousa must have learned of our mission to meet Rhodes and wants to stop us. The Matabele wouldn't attack the king's friends – and particularly his doctor.' He gave a grin to show a confidence that he did not feel. 'Now, the trail takes us quite close to the kopje. It is my feeling that they will attack us from its cover. So we will not give them that chance. I don't want them to know that they have been seen, so we will gently change course to take us away from the kopje, and then they will have to break cover to attack.'

'Do they have horses?' he asked the tracker.

'Not seen any, Nkosi.'

'Good. Tell Sando to climb into the wagon with Ntini. Alice, into the wagon too, please, with your rifle ready.'

Alice opened her mouth to protest, but he held up his hand. 'Only one general here today, my love,' he said. 'You must obey his orders. Hitch your horse to the side of the wagon away from the kopje, so that it is protected. Mzingeli, stay leading us from the front on foot but drop back a little, and as soon as the attack comes, get into the wagon quickly and fire from there.'

Jenkins frowned. 'What do we do then, bach sir?'

'We will act as a sort of cavalry screen. Drop back a little on the kopje side and I will do the same. They will have to run across open ground to get anywhere near us – I am gambling that they don't have horses and that's why they wanted to attack from the kopje. As soon as they leave cover, we charge at them, halt, fire two rounds and then gallop back to the wagon. We throw our reins to Ntini and then we climb aboard the wagon and fire from there. It will be our fortress.'

'Humph.' The Welshman's eyes lit up. 'You will probably fall off.'

'If I do, you will just have to pick me up.'

The tracker's face carried a faint smile as he tried to follow the exchange, but Alice's features were grim. 'Surely it is best to stay in the wagon, Simon? Make it a fortress, as you say.'

'No, my love. We can break them up at short range as they run towards us. Kaffirs can't shoot well and they certainly won't be able to do so on the run. They may not even have guns. No. We will do as I say. Make sure that your rifles are loaded, but do so surreptitiously. I don't want them to know that we are on to their game.'

He swallowed hard. His brain worked smoothly in assessing the situation, as that of a soldier should, but he knew that they were outnumbered and in great danger. No one in the little party betrayed open fear, not even the native boys, but he could see that faces were drawn and chins set determinedly. Everyone realised that they would need calm nerves and straight shooting – or perhaps a miracle – to survive the coming attack.

They mounted and set off again. This time Mzingeli led them slightly off to the right. Leaving the track was no hardship, for it was only faintly defined and the grassland was dry and the going firm. Fonthill put a handful of cartridges from their ammunition box into both his pockets, and he and Jenkins drifted out to the left. He tried not to eye the kopje too suspiciously, but he caught a flash of light as the sun reflected off ... what? It wouldn't be an assegai head, for the natives this far north had blades of beaten black iron. A rifle barrel? Possibly.

They had drawn level with the kopje, although not far enough away from it to satisfy Fonthill, when the first shot rang out. It came from the base of the rock and was the signal for a stream of spearmen to emerge at a fast trot and fan out and run towards them. Simon was reminded briefly of that terrifying moment at Isandlwana when the Zulu impis had poured down from the escarpment and spread out to surround the British camp. Except that this time there were fewer attackers – but even fewer defenders.

He saw Mzingeli and Sando climb into the wagon. He nodded to Jenkins, and the two of them galloped towards the natives. Good, they were not carrying rifles! The charging men were dressed exactly like Matabeles – monkey-tail adornments, ostrich feathers and little else – and carrying, in their left hands, the long hide shields behind which, in Zulu style, would be clutched a handful of throwing spears, and in their right, the short, stabbing assegais. They looked formidable enough and seemed completely unfazed by the approaching horsemen.

Fonthill reined in, steadied his horse and raised his rifle at a range of about two hundred yards. Jenkins, however, was even quicker, and his shot brought down the leading native. Simon's own missed. Cursing, he rammed another round into the breech and took careful aim, this time spinning round the third man in the line and bringing him down. Jenkins's next shot tore through the shield of the second man, whirling it away and causing the native to stumble. Then a puff of smoke came from the base of the kopje and a bullet whistled between the two horsemen. As the smoke began to clear, Simon saw a small figure in yellow behind it.

'Back to the wagon,' yelled Fonthill, pulling round the head of his horse.

They galloped back, wheeling around to the far side of the vehicle, where Alice's horse was already tied, and, throwing their reins to Ntini, scrambled aboard. Alice and Mzingeli had now lowered the white canvas canopy and were kneeling, their rifles levelled across the wooden side pieces of the wagon.

'Don't waste ammunition,' cried Fonthill. 'They will circle around us until we are surrounded and then run in. That's when we will need every bullet. We shall have to reload very quickly. I don't think they have realised yet that we have two Martini-Henrys. Old Gouela must have gambled that we only had light hunting rifles. But keep your heads down – he has a rifle himself and is taking shots from the kopje, although I think he's too far away to be effective.'

The natives now formed a loose ring around the wagon and stood for a moment, raising their spears and chanting.

'They not Matabele, not Zulus,' grunted Mzingeli.

'I don't care who they are, bach,' answered Jenkins grimly. 'I've just counted twenty-five of 'em left, an' if we let 'em close enough to come aboard, I'd say we're done for.'

'They're out of range of anything but the Martinis,' said Simon. 'See if you can pick off a couple before they charge, 352, and I'll do the same. When they come in, you fire over to the right, Alice. Jenkins, you go over the oxen to the front – it's the most difficult shot. Mzingeli, you take the rear and I will fire to the left.' He nodded to the tracker. 'Tell the boys to stand ready to fight with their spears if anybody gets through.'

The last was a superfluous remark, because Ntini and Sando were crouching by the wagon side boards, their spears at the ready. Their faces, however, showed the fear they felt. But that seemed to disappear when Mzingeli spoke quickly to them.

Fonthill raised an enquiring eyebrow. 'I tell them that these just Hottentots from the east, not Matabele,' grunted the tracker. 'Make them feel better. They afraid of Matabele.'

Further discussion was halted by the crack of Jenkins's rifle. Immediately, one of the natives crumpled. 'Good,' said the Welshman, reloading. 'Just in range.' He shuffled on to the driver's seat and sighted again. ''Ere. 'Ave another one, lads.' A second man in the ring staggered and fell, clutching his shoulder.

Fonthill now fired, and a spurt of dust sprang from just ahead of his target. 'Elevate, elevate, for goodness' sake,' cried Jenkins.

'Sorry, Sergeant,' murmured Simon. He adjusted his sights and fired again, this time hitting his man. This seemed to be the signal for the attack, for the rest raised their spears, stamped their feet and then began running for the wagon.

'Hold fire until I give the order,' cried Fonthill, then, in a lower voice to his wife, 'You all right, my love?'

Alice was nestling her cheek against the butt of her Westley Richards. She replied without looking up, 'I'm all right. Good luck, Simon.'

'Fire!'

The four guns spoke as one, and three of the attackers fell. Jenkins, closely followed by Fonthill, was the first to reload, and their second bullets also found their marks. Simon realised that Alice, firing from the right, was either out-ranged or her accuracy was wanting, so he added his firing to hers, but he could not leave his flank completely unprotected and it was difficult to switch position and fire accurately. Nevertheless, it was the Martini-Henrys, of course, that had the greatest firepower, and the warriors seemed to sense this, for they veered away from the guns of Jenkins and Fonthill and ran towards the weaker sides, those manned by Alice and Mzingeli.

It became clear to Fonthill that these 'Hottentots from the east', whoever they were, seemed to possess the courage and warlike skills of both the Zulus and the Matabele, and he took up his position at his wife's side, firing as fast as he could inject the single cartridges and jerk down the cocking lever behind the trigger guard. The bravest and fastest of the attackers had now reached within range of the wagon to launch their throwing spears, and one buried itself into the breast of the already injured Sando, who sank to the floorboards, feebly clutching at the assegai. Ntini plucked it out and threw it back, all in one movement.

'Nkosi!' The cry came from Mzingeli, whose slow-loading Snider was now being used as a club as he tried to fight off two natives who were stabbing at his feet and trying to climb into the rear of the wagon. Fonthill shot one and then stabbed the muzzle of his rifle into the face of the other, pushing him to the ground, where the thrown spear of Ntini penetrated his breast.

'Behind you, bach.' Simon whirled and saw a tribesman climb over the side of the wagon behind Alice, who was now kneeling to tend to the prostrate figure of Sando. He swung the stock of his rifle towards the man's chin, but this one was made of sterner stuff. He bowed his head to take the butt of the gun on his tightly curled hair, shook his head as though to get rid of a fly and then gave a short-arm stab in reply. The blade grazed Fonthill's thigh and its point stuck for a moment in the side of the wagon, giving a slight advantage to Simon, who brought the barrel of the gun strongly down on his adversary's neck. The crack could be heard above the firing and the screams of the attackers, and the man slumped to the floor of the wagon.

'They're goin'! They've 'ad enough.' Jenkins's cry came from the driver's seat, where he was standing, waving his rifle.

Fonthill wiped the sweat from his eyes and looked around. It was true. The remnants of the attacking force – now reduced to a dozen men – were running back towards the kopje, one of them limping. Behind them, in a ring surrounding the wagon and stretching back towards the kopje, lay the inert figures of those who had fallen.

'Alice, are you all right?' whispered Simon as he knelt by her side, putting his arm across her shoulder.

'Yes thank you,' she replied. 'But I am afraid Sando is not. I think he has gone. Oh Simon...' and she turned and buried her face in his chest, her shoulders shaking in sudden reaction. He swayed with her, gently patting her back and kissing her hair. Then the soldier in him re-asserted itself. 'Any more casualties?' he called.

'No, sir,' said Jenkins. 'All present and accounted for. I can't understand why they didn't spear the oxen or the horses. Why d'you think that was?'

'They too valuable.' Mzingeli was now squatting on the floor of the wagon, wiping his brow with the tail of his shirt. 'Take them back to Mozambique and sell them. Make money.' He looked sadly at Sando and shook his head. 'He good boy. Bad thing, this.'

Simon felt suddenly shamefaced. Still holding Alice, he said, 'I am so sorry, Mzingeli. This was not your fight. I don't know ... I am so sorry.'

The tracker looked up. 'Ah, it was our fight. If we don't kill them, they kill us. But why this man attack us?'

'It's a long story. Here.' Tenderly Simon put Alice away from him. 'Are you all right now, my love?'

She nodded.

'Good. Jenkins?'

'Sir.'

'You stay here just in case there is another attack, although I don't think for a moment there will be. They have clearly had enough.'

'Where are you goin' then?'

'Yes, Simon.' Alice's eyes were wide. 'Where *are* you going?'

'Mzingeli, break out our two horses and come with me. I may need your tracking skills. I am not going to let that Portuguese bastard get away with this. If I catch him, I will bring him back here and we will hang him. A bullet's too good for him.'

'I'll come with you, bach sir.'

'No. Do as you are told. Stay here.'

Fonthill dipped into the ammunition box, filled his pockets with cartridges once more, scrambled over the side of the wagon and mounted his horse. Waiting only for Mzingeli to join him, he set off at a gallop for the kopje. The remaining tribesmen had long since disappeared, but he paid no heed, setting his horse towards the side of the rock opposite to that from which the attack had been launched, in the hope that he could cut off the Portuguese if he was retreating.

They found nothing except a few empty cartridge cases at the base of the rock on the other side of the kopje.

Fonthill grunted. 'The man's a coward as well as a murderous swine. He set his men to attack but wouldn't join them. Now, which way have they gone?'

The tracker pointed to the north. Together they galloped to a rise and then stood in their stirrups peering ahead. The retreating group could clearly be seen, the warriors on foot gathered around a solitary horseman, who was setting a fast pace.

Mzingeli shook his head. 'I think, Nkosi, we do not follow. Still too many for us two. Kill him another day.'

Fonthill shot a sharp glance at the tracker. Then he relaxed. 'I suppose you are right. I think they have had a lesson and will not attack again. Anyway,' he shook his head, 'we should not leave the wagon. Even if he gets reinforcements from Bulawayo, I doubt if he can overtake us before we reach the border. And he would not dare to follow us into the Transvaal.'

He looked to where the trail wound around the kopje. 'Mzingeli,' he said, 'we all owe you a debt. If you had not seen them on the kopje we would have been unprepared and they would have swung round here and overwhelmed us before we could bring our guns to bear. It was quite a clever ambush, actually. Thank you.'

He held out his hand and the tracker shook it, a little self-consciously.

'Why this man hate you?' he asked.

'He thinks I am in the pay of Rhodes, in the Cape, and that I will stop him from signing a treaty with Lobengula to overturn the agreement the king has already made with Rhodes. Well...' he shifted in the saddle and looked again for the retreating figures, now almost out of sight, 'that's exactly what I now intend to do. After his two attacks on us, I intend to stop that man being involved in the development of Matabeleland. Come on. Let's go back.'

Back at the wagon – to Alice's great relief – Fonthill allowed his wife to fix a dressing on his grazed thigh, and he then joined the others in digging one shallow grave, into which they tipped the bodies of the attackers. Mzingeli gathered up all their assegais and looked at them carefully.

'They dress like Matabele,' he said, 'but they come from Mozambique border. Look.' He pointed at the spear heads. 'These from Portuguese land. They want us to think them Matabele. Strange.' Then he shrugged his shoulders. 'But they just as dead.'

Tenderly Sando's body was wrapped in a blanket and placed in the back of the wagon. 'Where does he come from, Mzingeli?' asked Alice.

'My father's village. My village. I know his mother, father. Sad.'

It was indeed a sad little group that set off to the south, Ntini cracking his long whip over his oxen and the three other men ranging out on horseback to the rear, right and left to ensure against another surprise attack. They camped that night without incident, and continued for another two and a half days along a track that had become a miserable mixture of rough stones and deep spruits with precipitous banks until eventually they entered Mzingeli's village. At first they were greeted with happy cries, for the carcasses of the lions had been found, of course, and their killings confirmed by the Matabele who had arrived from Bulawayo to collect the horses, wagon and oxen. Then, however, as Sando's body was lowered to the ground, a wailing began, soft at first and then growing in grief and intensity.

The party spent only two nights in the village, for Fonthill felt uncomfortable there: guilty, of course, for being responsible for Sando's death, however indirectly, and frustrated that he could not explain it to anyone's satisfaction, least of all his own. He was glad then when they said a muted goodbye to the *inDuna* and made for the river crossing into the Transvaal. Once across, the open veldt helped to restore a touch of tranquillity to them all, and they made good progress under the snowy-white balls of cloud that chased each other across the sky.

'What now, then?' asked Alice, as she rode companionably with her husband, Jenkins following alongside Mzingeli and Ntini at the rear.

Fonthill eased his buttocks in the saddle. 'Back to Cape Town, I think. I should pay my respects to Lamb.' Major General George Lamb, CB, the recently appointed army commander-in-chief at the Cape, had been the man who, as a colonel and chief of staff in Cape Town, had sent Simon on his first mission, to the camp of the Zulu king, ten years ago. He had then become his mentor in the second Afghan War on the North-West Frontier. Lamb had been away, up country in Natal, when Simon had called on their arrival in the colony.

Alice nodded. 'Of course. But then what do we do?'

'I must see Rhodes.'

'Do you have to? He's a strange character, as you know. He can ensnare people.'

'Oh come along, Alice. I'm no bloody rabbit.'

'I know that, darling. But, well...'

'I gave my word to Lobengula. Besides which,' he frowned and screwed up his eyes to focus on a distant kopje, 'I have a debt to settle. I want to do everything I can to make sure that the Portuguese and that blasted man de Sousa do not talk the king into giving them his country.' He turned in the saddle and looked directly at his wife. 'You know, Alice, once Matabeleland is settled, I wouldn't mind at all buying a tract of land there, up in the north, perhaps, where they say the country is magnificent for farming.'

Alice remained silent, so Fonthill hurried on.

'We would keep Norfolk, of course, but that

almost farms itself these days. It would be good to come out here in our winter, get some sun, sport and so on. We could well afford it, you know...' His voice trailed away as Alice's frown deepened, and then it became more plaintive. 'It would, well, make life more interesting, don't you think?'

She gave him a quick, rather forced smile. 'If that's what you want, then of course.' Slowly the smile faded. 'But I can see a lot more trouble developing before Lobengula gives away his land to us, the Portuguese or anyone else for that matter. He's no fool, you know.'

'That's true. But Rhodes does have an agreement with him, so that must be a head start. Anyway, it will be interesting to see what Lamb says about it all. He's no fool either.'

The five of them rode on in silence, some thinking of the sadness left behind in the village; others steeling themselves for the challenge that lay ahead.

Chapter 5

A little over three weeks later, Simon found himself waiting in a small anteroom outside the impressive office of Major General Lamb in Cape Town. He and Alice had dropped off Mzingeli and Ntini at their huts in the Boer farm in the southern Transvaal where they had first employed them. The parting had been unemotional, as befitted the bearing of the dignified tracker, but

Mzingeli had gripped Fonthill's hand and said in farewell, 'You call, whenever. I come.'

The door into the inner office was suddenly thrown open and Lamb exploded through it. Fonthill grinned and stood. Nothing had changed. Energy seemed to fizz and spark from the general's every movement, and now he bounced rather than walked towards Simon, his hand outstretched.

'Damned glad to see you, Fonthill. Knew you would call. Sorry to have missed you last time. How are you? Tell me, how are you?'

'Fit as a fiddler's fox, thank you, General. And you?'

'Couldn't be better. Come through. Sorry to have kept you waiting.' Then, over his shoulder, 'How's old 473?'

'Three five two, sir.'

'Dammit. Never could remember his number. Sit down. Sit down. Cigar?'

Fonthill regarded Lamb with interest. The general was diminutive – hardly more than five feet two inches – and his complexion, a ruddy nut brown, gave testimony to his years spent in India. They had last met outside the gates of Kandahar, after General Roberts's comprehensive victory over the Afghan army. Simon and Jenkins had played a not insignificant part in that victory but Fonthill's refusal to rejoin the army at Roberts's request had soured his relationship with the general. Lamb, then a brigadier, had tried to be ameliorative, but Simon had left the Frontier under a cloud. His relationship with Lamb, however, had remained one of mutual admiration.

The general walked from behind his desk to

light Simon's cigar. 'Delighted to see you awarded a GB after the Sudan. Joined the club, eh?' Fonthill nodded behind the cloud of blue smoke. 'My God, for a young chap you've moved around since we last met – Sekukuniland, that terrible Majuba business, then Egypt and the Sudan.' The general's bright blue eyes twinkled. 'For a feller who didn't want to rejoin the army, you've done a fair bit of soldiering, I'd say.'

Fonthill shifted uneasily. 'On my own terms, though, sir. But I should congratulate you on your promotion and appointment here.'

Lamb puffed at his cigar and shrugged. 'Not bad for an old India hand, I suppose. Lucky to get it under Wolseley, I have to confess.'

Simon grinned. The rivalry between the two best generals in Queen Victoria's army, Roberts and Wolseley, was well known. Lamb had always been a Roberts man, which meant that with Wolseley at the Horse Guards in London as adjutant general, he should have been doomed to spend the rest of his career in India, where Roberts was commander-in-chief. Somehow he had slipped through the net.

'Now.' Lamb leaned across his desk. 'You've been in Lobengula's kraal, I hear.'

Fonthill lifted his eyebrows. 'How did you know that? We only returned yesterday.'

'It's my business to know these things. Seen Rhodes yet?'

'How did you know I was going to see him?'

'I didn't, but I know that he wants to see you.'

'Why should he want to see me?'

Lamb pushed his chair back and let a spiral of

blue smoke curl towards the ceiling. 'Several reasons. Firstly, you have become almost famous, my dear fellow, with your exploits in various parts of the Empire, and Rhodes would admire that. He is, as you must know, first and foremost an Empire man.'

'Yes, I do know that. I met him in Kimberley some years ago.'

'Did you now? Secondly, Rhodes is always trying to recruit bright young men into his own empire – and my word, that empire has become almost as large as the Queen's. He owns all the diamond mines in Kimberley now, of course, and most of the gold strands too.'

'So I understand.'

'But the third reason is the most important. I think he has a job for you.'

'For me? Well, I'm not at all sure that I would want to work for him, thank you very much.'

'Ah!' Lamb let the silence hang after the word for at least twenty seconds. Then he waved his cigar and looked up at the ceiling. 'But my dear Fonthill, both Wolseley in London and I here rather hoped that you would, you see.'

'What, work for Rhodes? Why should you want that?'

'Well, here's the background.' The general let his chair crash to the floor. 'You know that Rhodes believes he has done a deal with the King of the Matabele ... what's his name again?'

'Lobengula.'

'Yes, that's the feller. Rhodes's agreement gives him permission to dig for mineral rights in Mata-beleland and Mashonaland. Now, young Cecil

John – dammit, the man can't be much older than you – would certainly want to pick out all the gold and silver that those two territories have, but he is really after settlement. He wants to open up the route to the north, beyond Mashonaland, and the best way to do that, he knows, is to settle the land. Let pioneers in. Of British stock, of course.'

'But that's not part of the contract with Lobengula, is it?'

'It certainly isn't, and from what I hear of the king up there, the old blighter would never agree to it.'

'Yes.' Fonthill put his hand to his mouth pensively. 'In fact, Rhodes is in some danger of losing the contract he has anyway.'

'What? Why is that?'

Fonthill proceeded to explain the mission he had been given by the king, and also the presence in Bulawayo of de Sousa and his own brushes with the Portuguese agent. 'I gather,' he went on, 'that the Germans, the Boers and other, independent British companies are all sniffing around the king's kraal, trying to persuade him to drop Rhodes and let them in. Bit of a mess really. But what's the British government's view of all this?'

Lamb smiled. 'Where Her Majesty's Government is involved, my dear boy, nothing is straightforward, but I will try and explain. The Government does not wish to venture into any further expensive acquisition of territory in Africa. It has enough on its plate as it is down here and with the Russians across the border on India's North-West Frontier. It certainly would not wish to become involved in another war with

103

the natives – another Zululand, if you like.'

'Would it try and stop Rhodes, then?'

'On the contrary. Despite what I have just said, the idea of settling the country north of the Transvaal – *at no cost to the Government...*'Lamb emphasised the phrase heavily, 'is quite attractive, because it could open up the north and even facilitate Rhodes's dream of a transcontinental railway from Cairo to the Cape, which, again, HMG would rather fancy if someone else pays for it and it doesn't involve another bloody great war. You talked about the hangers-on in Bulawayo. We would rather have the king locked into a firm and legal agreement with Rhodes than with anyone else.'

Fonthill wrinkled his brow. 'So what is the problem, then?'

'Ah. It is the character of young Rhodes, d'yer see? He is damned impulsive and even more damned ambitious. His riches give him great resources, and the Government and Wolseley – the AG because the army will almost certainly become involved if Rhodes gets into trouble – are worried that the bloody man will use force if necessary to take Matabeleland and Mashonaland. All those wet knickers on the Opposition bench in Westminster will raise hell if he invades the territory willy-nilly and causes Lobengula to unleash his army and let his men wash their spears. It could be another Isandlwana all over again – and we've only just got over paying for that lot.'

'I see. Well, I think I see. But what I don't see is how I fit into all of this.'

Lamb stubbed out his cigar, as though he was trying to push it through the bottom of the ash tray. 'Wolseley knows you well and he has huge respect for your capabilities. I had picked up the rumour that Rhodes wants you on his team, and reported this to the AG. As a result, Wolseley has asked me to beg you to accept whatever Rhodes is about to offer you – if this can possibly be made to work into whatever your own plans are down here – and see if you can exert a calming influence on the man. Don't let him antagonise Lobengula. You know the king and Rhodes does not. You will have influence as a result of this if nothing else.'

A silence hung heavily in the smoke-filled room. Fonthill shifted on his chair. 'Well, I don't exactly know what I–'

The general interrupted him. 'I don't mind admitting it's an appeal to your patriotic sensibilities, Fonthill. Look,' he leaned forward across his desk, 'this country – and I don't just mean the Cape Colony – is on the verge of something rather extraordinary. Our colonies here are going to become some of the most influential in the whole of the Empire. Dominion status is just around the corner. We are rich in mineral, agricultural and labour resources, and as these are developed, we shall be able to provide leadership for and set an example to these cock-eyed little states that the great powers of Europe have set up in the middle of the continent.' The blue eyes twinkled and then hardened. 'We don't want Rhodes going over the top, upsetting the apple cart and raising Europe against us.'

Simon opened his mouth to speak, but Lamb raised his hand. 'Rhodes loves to have able and promising young men around him, and we know that he listens to them, more, much more than to old warhorses like me, or, for that matter, to anyone in Whitehall – whom he calls, derisively, "the Imperials".You, with your comparative youth and your magnificent record in various parts of the Empire, will be just the sort of fellow that Rhodes will take notice of – not least because you have never toed the party line, so to speak, in imperial circles. You have always been your own man. Rhodes will like that.'

'I am not sure that doing what you and Wolseley ask is exactly being my own man, but...' Fonthill thought for a moment. 'Have you any idea what Rhodes wants of me?'

'No. I heard in the club that he had been singing your praises and that he had heard of your return to Cape Town. Knowing his interest in Matabeleland, I cannot see him not wanting to contact you.'

'Hmmm. From what I have read of Rhodes, and from what I remember of my meeting with him, I can't see him being nursemaided by anyone.'

Lamb rose to his feet, a touch of exasperation in the action. 'Of course you can't be his nursemaid. But if you feel that he is being impatient, for instance – and this is his abiding failing – then you can counsel caution. I rather fear that the fellows he has round him at the moment are caught under his spell and have become a bit sycophantic. He will respect someone who stands up to him. But you must judge for yourself how to act. Just stop the blasted man from charging in with guns blazing, if you possibly can. We can't exactly offer you a salary, by the way.'

'I don't want money.'

'Good. In any case, Rhodes has the reputation of rewarding his people well. Often in kind – land, for instance, in the new territory.'

Fonthill raised his head. 'Land?'

'Yes. Could you be interested? This is fine country.'

'Ah. I don't know. I must consult Alice, my wife.'

'Dammit! I knew there was something I had forgotten.' The little man extended his hand to Simon. 'You married that remarkable lady Alice Griffith. Congratulations, my dear fellow. Belated, I know, but sincere none the less.'

Fonthill stood and the two shook hands. 'Thank you very much, sir.'

'Yes, well, of course you must consult your wife. Call me if you need anything while you are here. I am completely at your service. But let me know what you decide as soon as you can. I have a feeling that Rhodes is very much on the march, so time could be of the essence.'

'Thank you. I certainly will.'

Fonthill chose to walk back to their hotel, his brain working hard. What could Rhodes want with him? He was intrigued, despite his cautious reaction to Lamb. The chance to work with a man who within a decade had risen from comparatively humble beginnings as a sugar farmer in Natal to become the most influential figure in the whole of South Africa and, if rumours were to be believed, the next prime minister of the

Cape Colony was intriguing, to say the least. It would be a new experience after four years of farming under the grey skies of Norfolk. And if it carried with it the possibility of acquiring new land of his own in this vibrant new colony – ah, now *that* could be of distinct interest!

Treading with a jaunty new step, Fonthill realised how much he was relishing this visit to South Africa. The business in Matabeleland had been disturbing, to say the least, but also exciting. It was good to be in action again after the sad, fallow years since the death of his son. Good to be here with Jenkins, too, reviving that unique comradeship that had been forged in danger and tempered under attack from so many different enemies. A gentle smile crept across his face as he reflected that even Alice, whom he loved more than life itself and whom he would never consciously put in harm's way, had subtly changed when the time had come to defend the wagon. He recalled her calmness in firing at the lion as it charged and the cool determination with which she had reloaded her rifle at speed and kept firing at the Portuguese Kaffirs. He gave a little shrug. Perhaps not so strange, though. She was a soldier's daughter, after all. But this country, with its wild, indigenous people, its wide vistas and its changeable, challenging climate, could well suit her.

He looked around him at the bustling streets. Cape Town was just his sort of place. In some ways it reminded him of Bombay: so many faces, so many characters and so many colours. The dark skin of the locals, with their bare feet and scraps of clothing; the scurrying Indians, wearing turbans and a determined air, as though anxious to get back to their stalls to make another couple of shillings; the patrician white men, aloof under their pith helmets – quite unnecessary headgear here, where the breeze from the Atlantic cooled the heat of the sun, and worn more as a sign of class; the mixed bag of sailors from the docks; and the black-bearded Boer Dutchmen from the high veldt, striding along on legs bowed by years in the saddle and looking as though they had just strayed from the pages of the Bible. Yes, this was a vibrant port, a city of empire and, undoubtedly, the gateway to a land of promise.

Alice was standing by the reception desk in the modest hotel into which they had booked. 'Ah, my dear,' she said. 'I am so glad you have come.' Her face was clouded.

'What is the matter?'

'Well...' Her voice trailed away. 'It's 352. I asked him if he would go to the post office to see if we had mail. It is only ten minutes away and he went off quite happily, but he has been gone about three hours now. I called at the post office to see if he was there, but he was not. I picked up several letters. It looks as though Jenkins has not been there at all.'

Fonthill sighed. 'Oh dammit all. He's gone drinking.'

'Yes. That's what I thought.'

Fonthill kicked himself for not realising that the Welshman would be building up for a thirst-quenching run ashore as soon as they had booked into their hotel. The problem was that one or two drinks would not be sufficient to wash away the dust in Jenkins's throat. Once the familiar taste and tingle had entered his system, he would continue until he was completely drunk – or left for dead in an alley with a knife in his back.

Simon turned to the Indian receptionist. 'Where would I go if I wanted to drink myself senseless?' he asked.

The man's jaw dropped. 'You would not wish to do that, sir, surely?'

'Yes, I would. I want a street with rough bars in it.'

'Ah, goodness. Well. Let me think. The docks, I think, sir. Turn left at the door here and walk–'

'Yes, thank you. I will find them. Alice, you stay here. I might be some time.'

His wife opened her mouth to argue, but Fonthill was gone before she could do so, whirling on his heel and heading towards the clouds of black dust billowing into the air from where several freighters were re-coaling. Between the black columns he caught a glimpse of the blue Atlantic.

The harbour, when he reached it, seemed vast and he realised that his search would be more difficult than envisioned. The first bars he met seemed comparatively respectable, with white traders in creased cotton suits, merchant navy officers, their peaked caps tipped to the back of their heads, and port officials drinking whisky. Jenkins would not feel at home here. He would want beer and the company of off-duty soldiers and sailors.

Eventually Fonthill reached a narrow street off one of the quays where every second doorway seemed to be the entrance to a bar. He turned into the first, where the atmosphere reeked of tobacco smoke, beer and cheap gin. It was crowded but there was no sign of the familiar black moustache and stubbled hair. In the second, he approached two British soldiers of a line regiment and, describing Jenkins, asked if they had seen him.

'Yes, mate. It was 'im all right. Drank about three pints, bought us one and then said that'e was on 'is way to the post office. Welsh bloke, old 24th, wasn't 'e?'

Fonthill nodded his thanks and continued his way up the alley. He doubted if the post office would have seen Jenkins that day, although he had certainly left his mark in six bars, where he was warmly remembered by the clientele. Simon gritted his teeth and continued the search. He knew the pattern. Jenkins would be affable to begin with, and then, on the slightest provocation, the Mr Hyde in his nature would surface, fuelled by the pints he had put away, until he would become argumentative, truculent and then violent – and violence in this quarter almost certainly meant the use of knives.

Leaving the seventh bar, he paused. This was proving pointless. The man could be anywhere in this thriving but seedy port. Perhaps he really had put down the last glass and made for the post office. Then he heard a crash and shouting from an open door under a swinging inn sign. He ran to it and turned inside.

If Landseer had painted the scene, he might have entitled it *Jenkins At Bay*. The Welshman, his shirt torn and perspiration pouring down his face, was holding a broken, jagged-ended pint glass and backing away to a corner of the bar. Facing him and moving irrevocably towards him were two large men in dungaree trousers and vests. Both were coal-stained, and under the black smudges it appeared that one was white and the other coloured, perhaps a Lascar. It was clear that they were stokers from the coaling freighters, and it was also clear that they were intent on causing serious harm to Jenkins, for they both had knives in their hands. Around the sides of the bar pressed a bedraggled crowd of onlookers, loose grins on their faces in anticipation of seeing blood shed. Two smashed tables were strewn on the sawdust floor, and beside them lay a third stoker, blood streaming from his nose and a cut above his eye. He appeared to be unconscious.

'That's enough!' Fonthill's voice cut through the anticipatory buzz and he strode forward. 'The police will be here in a minute. Give me those knives.'

'Ah, good to see you, bach.' Jenkins nodded in greeting. His eyes were rheumy but alert. 'Now don't you worry about this,' he said. 'You don't need to get involved, see. I can 'andle these gentlemen all right on me own, thank you very much.'

'Don't be ridiculous. Put down that glass. You men, give me your knives before someone gets hurt.'

At first his strong, upper-class voice and his air of command made the two men pause, glaring over their shoulders at him. Then the white stoker spoke, slowly and with a strong Scandinavian accent. 'Stay avay, out of dis. We cut oop this man. We cut oop you as vell if you interfere.'

He gestured with his knife.

Jenkins, with the experience of a dozen or more barroom fights behind him, sensed that this was his moment. Taking advantage of the Swede's confrontation with this unexpected stranger, he leapt forward and smashed the bottom of his pint glass on to the man's head, then, swaying to his right, swept a left hook into his stomach. In doing so, however, he left his back unprotected, and the Lascar swung back his arm to bury his knife into it.

Instinctively, Fonthill launched himself into a low rugby tackle and caught the Lascar behind the knees, crumpling him so that the man collapsed on top and then away from him, his knife spinning into the crowd. For a moment the two lay winded on the floor, and Simon felt the taste of sawdust in his mouth. Then he threw himself on to the Lascar's back, fighting to thread his arms beneath the man's shoulders to lock him into a half-nelson, dimly remembered from his wrestling days in the school gym. But the stoker was a quarter as big again as Fonthill, and with one convulsive heave he threw him off his back, as though he was tipping a sack of coal into the hold of his ship.

Simon cracked his face on the planking of the floor, sniffing the sawdust again and landing at the feet of the onlookers. Immediately many hands raised him, and with a cheer, he was pushed back to meet the giant Lascar, who advanced on him now, both hands outstretched, seemingly to embrace and then crush him. Involuntarily, Fonthill grabbed the shirt of the man in the crowd

113

nearest to him, whirled him round and sent him crashing into his opponent. The stoker was huge but he was also ponderous, and clutching the onlooker to him, he fell backwards. Simon leapt forward and kicked his boot into the stoker's face. It seemed to have little effect, however, for the man merely shook his head and rose to his feet.

Fonthill advanced and put three successive jabs with his left hand into the face of the Lascar. Cheers rose from the crowd, but he might have been hitting the wall for all the damage he caused the big man; he was merely a mosquito stinging an elephant. The stoker lumbered forward, his arms outstretched once more, and Fonthill ducked under the attempted embrace and hit the man as hard as he could in the stomach. The wheeze that the blow produced showed that the man was not as invulnerable as he seemed, and Simon danced in again to repeat the blow, but the bloodstained sawdust was no place for fancy footwork and, inevitably, he slipped. Immediately his hair was seized and he was locked into a bear hug, his nose pressed to the dirty grey vest. His senses became overwhelmed by the smell of stale beer, perspiration, cold dust and then fear, as his chin was pushed back by the palm of the Lascar's right hand, while the left arm held him tight and exerted pressure on his vertebrae. The bastard was trying to break his neck!

Fonthill knew that it would be only a matter of seconds before the giant would relax his grip on his chin and then jerk it up and under, so snapping his neck. In desperation, he wriggled his left arm down the Lascar's abdomen until he felt the softness of the man's testicles. His fingers sank in, then, with almost his last breath, he squeezed and pulled. The big man shrieked and relaxed his hold, allowing Simon to slip out of his grasp.

Sucking air into his lungs, Fonthill staggered away, gasping and holding his throat, as the Lascar doubled up in pain. He was dimly aware that one section of the crowd was screaming 'Unfair!' while the other was whistling and cheering. But they had not yet seen enough blood spilt, for someone threw back the Lascar's dagger, which the coloured man caught in one giant fist before advancing on Fonthill again.

''Ere, mate,' another shouted. 'Let's make it a fair fight.' And a second knife curved through the air and quivered in the floor at Simon's feet.

He picked it up. It was a knife fight now. He dared not spare a moment to see how Jenkins was faring, but it seemed clear that he would have to see this through on his own. Kill or be killed.

Fonthill realised that he was completely outranged by the Lascar's reach and that his only hope would be to use his greater mobility. The big man was holding the knife blade down, as a dagger. That meant that he would have to bring it upwards before slashing down – perhaps there would be a fleeting moment of opportunity there, if Simon could get close enough to thrust himself. His brain raced. Close enough, yes, but how to get in under the man's guard?

Then he remembered a technique he had seen Jenkins use many years before when the Welsh-man had been confronted by a giant Zulu. Simon took two quick steps forward and then pretended to slip, going down almost on one knee, except that the bent leg remained balanced on the ball of his foot. His left hand went to the floor, and as the Lascar stepped forward and raised his knife, he picked up a handful of sawdust and threw it in the coloured man's face, causing him to blink and turn his head away for a second. Almost in the same movement, Fonthill brought his own knife hand upwards and thrust the blade into the other man's forearm, twisting it and pulling it away as the blood spurted.

The giant howled, dropped his own knife and grabbed his arm, sinking to one knee. At almost the same moment, Simon glimpsed the blood-stained face of Jenkins materialise behind that of the Lascar, as he lifted a chair leg and brought it down with a thud on the man's head. For a moment the big man teetered, and then, like a forest giant felled by a woodman's axe, he toppled to the floor and lay still.

'Blimey,' said Jenkins, 'why did you choose the big one? You could 'ave 'ad my bloke, though come to think of it, 'e wasn't so small either. Eh, you all right, bach sir?' He threw away the chair leg and, frowning, inspected Fonthill. 'Blimey, your nose is bleedin' a bit...'

His voice tailed away as he saw the look of fury in Simon's eyes. 'Yes, well, sorry, bach sir.' His manner now was abjectly apologetic, and he fumbled to put a very grimy handkerchief to Fonthill's nose. 'I only slipped away for a minute, see, to 'ave one or two 'alves. Sorry if you've been ... er ... inconvenienced like.'

'Inconvenienced!' Fonthill staggered to his feet

116

and looked around. There were three stokers on the barroom floor, two of them now stirring and the third, the Swede, sitting and holding his head. 'You've broken up a bar, nearly killed three men, as far as I can see, and almost caused me to have my neck broken. And you call it *inconvenience!*'

The Welshman was interrupted by a very large barman, who advanced on them carrying what seemed to be a Zulu knobkerrie. 'Now, man,' he addressed Jenkins in the guttural tones of an Afrikaner, 'I want paying for two broken tables and three chairs. And you're not going till I get my money.'

A look of intense indignation alighted on Jenkins's sweat-stained face. 'Hey, bach, I didn't start it, look you. It's these three bastards you should get to put their 'ands in their pockets. I only...'

Fonthill put his hand on the Welshman's shoulder. He pressed a white five-pound note into the bartender's hand and tossed the knife he was still holding on to the floor. 'That should cover it,' he said. 'And if it doesn't, you'll just have to get the rest from these bruisers. Come on, Jenkins. I've had enough of this place.'

If the barman had thoughts of arguing, they were dispelled by the looks on the faces of the two men, who were given a rousing cheer from the onlookers, now pushing furniture back and lifting the wreckage of broken chairs and tables, attempting the impossible task of fitting the shattered pieces together again.

Outside, Fonthill pushed his own handkerchief to his nose to staunch the bleeding and seized Jenkins's arm. 'I know this sounds out of character,' he said, 'but I could use a drink. Is there a bar here that you haven't wrecked and is not full of ruffians?'

Jenkins's face broke into a grin and he attempted to push the remnants of his torn shirt beneath his waistband. 'What a good idea, bach sir. Yes. I think the first one I popped into might suit. Bit quiet it was. Down 'ere, sir.'

Once seated, Simon placed a pint of ale and a whisky chaser in front of each of them, took a deep draught of the beer and then sat gazing at his comrade in silence. At first Jenkins grinned happily and half drained his glass. Then he realised that the genial forgiveness that seemed to be linked to the drink was not, in fact, going to be on offer, and he began to shift uncomfortably in his chair. He sniffed and ran the back of his hand under his nose.

'Look, bach sir,' he began. 'I really am sorry, honest.'

Fonthill held up his hand and the Welshman fell silent. But Simon kept looking at him, his face expressionless. In fact, he was attempting to weigh up how it was possible for someone only five feet four inches tall to take on three men, all much bigger than him, without the slightest trace of fear. How was Jenkins able to do it – particularly having consumed enough alcohol to sink a battleship? He had laid out two of the stokers, and although it was difficult to conceive that he would have survived without Simon's arrival, it was quite possible. Fonthill shook his head, and Jenkins took the kind of tiny sip of whisky that would not been out of place in a rectory and

118

looked up at the ceiling, waiting for the storm to break.

But Fonthill was still trying to analyse the kind of fighting machine that had been at his side for the last decade. In idle moments in the past, watching the huge hands of his servant stitching back a button or ironing a shirt with dainty precision, he had wondered at the dual nature of the man. Not only patient batman/servant and disciplined infantryman, but also fierce barroom brawler, as good with his fists or a wrestling stranglehold as with a knife. Why did he always come out on top? Well, he was magnificently strong, of course, with the courage of a lion. Then he was light on his feet and always seemingly unaffected by the drink he had taken. He also possessed a very low centre of gravity, which enabled him to take on much taller men. Simon shook his head and gave up. Over the years, he had benefited hugely by his comrade's ability to fight in any situation. Best to be thankful for it and regard it as a credit on the balance sheet of a very complex character.

He leaned forward. Jenkins's eyes now switched to the floor apprehensively. 'I suppose I was able to help...' Fonthill began.

'Oh, you did, bach sir, you did.' Jenkins jumped in thankfully. 'And I'm very grateful, indeed I am. My word, I couldn't see much of what was goin' on because I 'ad me 'ands a bit full, like, but from what I could see you was fightin' a lovely dirty fight. Not like an officer at all, see. I was very proud...'

Fonthill held up his hand with a sigh. 'But I

would have lost out to that brute in the end, because he was too big for me. So thank you for knocking him over the head. Anyway.' He raised his glass to his comrade. 'If I did help a bit, then it came no way near to matching what you did in that tent with that damned snake. So, my dear old 352, thank you and cheers!'

Jenkins' jaw dropped for a moment, and then, with a relieved grin, he downed his whisky in one gulp. 'Cheers, bach sir. Shall we 'ave just one more, then?'

'No, we will not. And I want your word that you won't go on another drinking rampage while we are in Cape Town.' Fonthill shook his head and sighed. 'You must stay out of trouble for the rest of our stay because by the look of it we may have some work to do again before long.'

The Welshman's eyes lit up. 'Oh really? An' what would that be, then, bach sir?'

'I don't know yet. But I shall soon. Now drink up – although God knows where you will put it all. We must get back because Alice will be concerned.'

Chapter 6

The expected invitation came from Rhodes the next day. It was amazingly informal: a page seemingly torn from a cheap notepad and covered with strong, forward-sloping handwriting. It read:

My dear Fonthill,
We met in Kimberley some time back. Could you
spare me an hour or less tomorrow? Come to breakfast
at my rooms. Best bacon and eggs in the Colony. Shall
we say 8 a.m.?
Yours, Cecil J. Rhodes.

As an afterthought, Rhodes had scribbled the address of his apartment on the back of the page.

Fonthill grinned and passed the note to Alice. She read it with a frown and passed it back. 'Well,' she said, 'at least we can say that there are no frills about this particular millionaire. It seems he doesn't employ a lady with the new type-writing machine. Will you go? How stupid of me. Of course you will go.'

'Yes. Of course I will. I have a message to deliver to him, and in any case, I am bursting with curiosity to know what he wants of me.'

'Very well, but Simon, do be careful. Don't be bullied or blackmailed by Lamb and Wolseley. You have served your country well enough now not to owe it any more.'

Fonthill bent and kissed her brow. 'Have no fears, my love. The great ensnarer will not catch this rabbit – unless he wants to be caught, that is. In any case, I love bacon and eggs and this hotel does a miserable breakfast.'

Fonthill arrived a little early the next day for his appointment and found that. 'The Richest Man in Africa' lived in second-floor rooms in one of the busiest streets in the middle of Cape Town, accommodation typical of a youngish bachelor of moderate means. The rooms were wood-panelled and cosy, those perhaps of a don at the university of Oxford. Rhodes himself answered the door and led him to a table of some polished dark African wood set for breakfast.

'Sit down, my dear Fonthill,' he said. 'My man will have breakfast for us in five minutes or so. That gives me the chance to ask you about Gordon. I knew him well, you know. But you must have been the last white man to have seen him. Tell me about him.'

Fonthill studied the great man with interest. Rhodes had put on considerable weight since last they had met. He must now weigh about fourteen stone, but he carried it well, for he was tall and broad-shouldered. He was dressed carelessly in an old tweed jacket and cream cricket flannels, and the air of an undergraduate was enhanced by the auburn hair, now touched with grey, but flung loosely over his forehead. His eyes were bluish grey, dreamy and kindly and rather bulbous. They seemed to be those of a country parson – Fonthill remembered that he was indeed the son of a clergyman – and they certainly betrayed no trace of ruthlessness or commercial avarice. The moustache had been allowed to droop either side of his full lips, and his voice was high-pitched and had risen to a squeak at the mention of General Gordon. His appearance and demeanour were far from those of a determined businessman and political schemer.

'Ah, Gordon,' said Simon. 'I did not know you knew him, sir.'

'Indeed. We were great friends. Worked together in the early eighties when we were both members of the Losses Commission set up to decide compensation for those Basutos who had remained loyal through the rebellion at that time. Big difference in our ages, but we got on well and Charlie asked me to join him in the Sudan. But I was about to come on to the Cape Cabinet and had to decline. Tell me what happened at the end.'

Fonthill described the voyage of the two steamers sent up the Nile ahead of Wolseley's expedition in a desperate attempt to relieve the general in a besieged Khartoum, and their arrival just two days too late. To his surprise, Simon saw tears well up into Rhodes's eyes.

The big man fished out a red handkerchief and blew his nose noisily. 'Disgraceful,' he said. 'Disgraceful and tragic. I wish I had been with him. I do, you know.'

The awkward silence was broken by the arrival of a beaming black man carrying two tureens on a tray, which he placed on the table. 'This is Tony,' said Rhodes. 'Been with me for years. Couldn't do without him. Tony, meet Mr Fonthill, a great man of the Empire.'

To Simon's surprise, the servant gave a half-bow then extended his hand. Rising, Fonthill took it and they exchanged hearty handshakes before the man retired.

Rhodes took off the lids of both tureens. 'You know, Fonthill,' he said confidentially, 'these Kaffirs are great people. I like and respect 'em. When I was farming in Natal years ago, I lent a great deal of money to them when it was hut tax time, and they always came and worked if off for me... Kaffirs are really safer than the Bank of England. Two eggs or three?'

'Er ... two, please.'

Rhodes busied himself with adding bacon, tomato, black pudding, mushrooms and sausages to Fonthill's plate, and Simon realised why the man had put on so much weight since last they had met.

'Now, Fonthill. You have just returned from Lobengula's kraal, I hear. Tell me about him and conditions there.'

'I have, and indeed I have a message for you from the king.'

'Oh.' Rhodes looked up sharply. 'Pray tell me.'

Fonthill put down his knife and fork and first described the situation in Bulawayo – the supplicants at the court of the king and in particular the pressure being applied by de Sousa on behalf of the Portuguese.

'Ah, Gouela. I've heard about him. But what's the king's message?'

'It seems that in return for the king's signature on a concession allowing your company to develop the mineral rights in Matabeleland and Mashonaland, you would deliver to Lobengula a monthly retainer of a hundred pounds, a thousand Martini-Henry rifles with a hundred thousand rounds of ammunition and a steamboat with guns suitable for defensive purposes on the Zambezi river. But the king says that none of these promises have been met, and, to put it politely, he will consider the contract to be null and void unless he receives these payments soon.'

Rhodes nodded his head slowly and removed a

tureen cover. 'Do have another egg, Fonthill. They come from my house up towards Table Mountain outside the city. I have a little farm there.' He nodded towards the pale blue flowers arranged in a bowl on the table. 'Plumbago. My favourites. They're from there too.' He ladled an egg. 'Come along. I insist.'

Fonthill sighed and accepted the egg.

Helping himself to bacon, Rhodes nodded his head again. 'All true, my dear fellow. All true. Incidentally, how is the king's gout?'

Shifting uncomfortably on his chair, Simon resisted the temptation to cry, 'Oh do get on with it,' and carefully explained Alice's treatment of the king and of her champagne diagnosis.

'Quite right. Best thing is to give it up. I only drink moderately, you know. Much too much to do. Now, turning to the king's message...' He pushed his plate away from him and, turning his head, shouted, 'Tony. Toast and marmalade, please.' He fixed his big grey eyes on Fonthill. 'Yes, the payment. As you can imagine, my dear fellow, it has not been exactly easy to get together the contingent parts of that. But I have done so. At least, the steamer on the Zambezi is certainly not there yet – and more of that later – but the gold, the guns and the ammunition are all now gathered together and are waiting in Kimberly to go north.'

'I am glad to hear it, sir. Why do they not go now?'

'Because, Fonthill, I am waiting for you to lead the expedition to take them to Bulawayo. It will not be an easy journey – particularly in view of what you tell me of de Sousa and his behaviour, although I had already had some indication of the man's determination to undo my treaty. No. It needs a person of great resource and qualities of leadership, with knowledge of the country, and yes, someone I could trust. My dear fellow, you would do me a great service if you could take this precious cargo to Lobengula and secure from him his confirmation that he will accept a party of my people, who will march north to Mashonaland to develop the land. I had heard you were somewhere in South Africa, and knowing of the fine reputation you have earned since last we met, I have waited until we could meet here and I could explain to you my plans and beseech your help.'

Fonthill's eyebrows rose. 'Well, sir, you certainly flatter me. But I don't know...'

Rhodes silenced him by raising his hand and standing. 'Let me first of all fill in some all-important details. Do come over here, there's a good fellow.' And then, over his shoulder: 'Tony, where's the toast and marmalade? Stir yourself, lad.'

They moved to a large table set against the panelled wall and covered with documents. Selecting one of them, Rhodes untied the red tape that bound it and smoothed it flat with his hand. 'Here you are,' he said. 'One of the three original copies of the treaty of friendship that I persuaded the British Government to enter into with Lobengula last year. This is important because it precludes the making of any other treaty or ceding of land with any other foreign power. Got it?'

Fonthill smiled as he remembered from their first meeting the staccato questions that so often ended Rhodes's statements. He nodded. 'Got it.'

'Good. Now.' Rhodes threw aside the document and unrolled another one of similar size. 'Here's the treaty the king signed with me. Look, see, there's Lobengula's cross and his great elephant seal. It gives me, as you say, the right to prospect and dig for minerals on his land.'

'Quite so, sir. But has the British Colonial Office seen this and approved it? If so, I am a bit surprised that it was happy to arm the Matabele with rifles. You know that these people are fierce warriors, and I understand that a law was passed here some years ago prohibiting the provision of arms to the natives.'

Rhodes threw back his head. 'Ah, that only applied to the Basutos. And don't worry about the Imperials back home. The deal was done before they'd adjusted their pince-nez and I got them to rubber-stamp it, though they looked down their noses at it a bit. These rifles won't make the Matabele an armed force, because there's no one to train 'em to use 'em. But Lobengula wants them to frighten the Boers, who are his main worry in terms of invasion, and they will probably do that, which also helps our cause, y'see. Old Kruger in the Transvaal would love to get his hands on Matabeleland and Mashonaland, and these guns and this document will stop him, or at least make him pause, because the treaty has legal viability.'

Fonthill gave a half-smile. 'But not, of course, if Lobengula renounces it on the grounds that you have not carried out your side of the bargain.'

'Exactly. By Gad, Fonthill, that's where I need you. And not just in terms of delivering the cash and the hardware, although that's vital.' Rhodes seized Simon by the shoulder. 'There's two other vital things that I want you to do for me and your country. Firstly, I want you to get the king's permission to allow a column of my men to go through Matabeleland – in fact, I intend to skirt it more or less, but that's a detail – to Mashonaland to start prospecting...'

'Is there gold or silver there?'

'There may be, but it's important to get men on the land up there. Once they are there, nobody will get 'em off. Occupation is the thing. Got it?'

'Yes, but what's the point of occupying the land? What do you want the men there for, if not to dig for minerals?'

Rhodes pulled from the table a map of South Africa, extending from the tip of the Cape to the great lakes north of Mashonaland. 'A road to the north, and homes, my dear Fonthill, homes. Mainly for the British, but I don't mind providing for the Cape Afrikaners too, if they want to go north – although not those dull Boers of Kruger's in the Transvaal.' He spread his hand across the northern part of the map. 'I would like to see all of that red.'

He began to pace the room and his eyes took on a gleam that Fonthill again recalled from their first meeting. 'I contend, old chap, that we are the first race in the world, and that the more of the world we inhabit the better it is for the human race. I contend that every acre added to our territory provides for the birth of more of the English race who otherwise would not be brought into existence.' He stopped abruptly and stared sharply at Simon.

'You've fought in more wars than I have been near to. Do you favour wars, Fonthill? Do they serve their purpose, despite the cost?'

'Absolutely not, sir ... well, not most of the time.'

'Absolutely right, my boy. I quite agree. The absorption of the greater portion of the world under our rule simply means the end of all wars. A road and homes, Fonthill, a road and homes. Not more wars.' He walked back to Simon, and his messianic tone left him for a moment. 'Do you know, I believe that every man has his price. At this moment in Bulawayo, as you know, there is a veritable foreign legion trying to bribe Lobengula to renege on his treaty with me, including your nasty Portuguese piece of work. Ah. Thank goodness. Here's the toast and marmalade at last.'

Fonthill tried another tack. 'Lobengula seemed rather perturbed that you hadn't been to his kraal to negotiate directly with him. Wouldn't it be easier for you to talk to him personally? Every man has his price, as you know.'

'Can't get away.' Rhodes shrugged his shoulders. 'Just can't do it. I am the only man who can drive these company purchases on and I have to be here to do it. And I also have to be in the Cape Parliament.' He dropped his voice and growled. 'Something coming up there that will involve me. No. Just can't get away. I need you. Come and have some toast. Marmalade's made on my land too.'

Fonthill smiled slowly. The sheer energy, drive and brutal honesty of Rhodes appealed to him, he had to admit. It was like being in the presence of a charming steamroller. He joined his host back at the table and buttered some toast, as much to gain time to think as to satisfy a hunger long since sated.

'Rhodes,' he began, 'you mentioned that my task would not just be delivering the rifles and persuading Lobengula to confirm the treaty. There was something else...?'

'Indeed.' Rhodes, his mouth already half full, inserted another piece of toast and marmalade under his moustache. 'Look.' And again he was on his feet, walking to the map on the table. 'See here.'

He stabbed a finger on to where Mashonaland was marked, rather indistinctly. 'Once my pioneers are there, it will take time for them to develop the land to feed themselves, so every damned thing,' he paused to wipe his moustache with a finger, which he then put into his mouth to remove an errant fragment of marmalade, 'will have to be carried overland, probably from the Cape, as near as dammit over a thousand miles. I must find a path to the sea, to the east, so that I can supply them that way. If the Portuguese would let me, we could perhaps do it by steamer up the Zambezi, but they control the river mouth and I don't see the blighters letting me go that way into country they claim as their own. And I am not even sure that the Zambezi is navigable that far to the west – which is another reason, of course, why Lobengula has not had his damned steamer, although I did promise him five hundred pounds to compensate him if I couldn't manage it.'

'So...?'

'So, when you have settled things with the king, I would like you to explore to the east. Find a way through to the coast there, see if the tribes are friendly, then come back and meet up with the pioneer column that I intend to send off as soon as I hear from you that Lobengula has given his consent.'

'I see. I have to say, Rhodes, that that is quite an undertaking.'

Rhodes fixed Fonthill with his protuberant grey eyes and spoke earnestly. 'Indeed it is, but I know that you can do it, Fonthill. You were undoubtedly one of the finest scouts ever used by the British Army. You would be instrumental in opening up this vital route to the north, in extending this remarkable empire of ours and spreading the beneficial rule of the British to that huge unclaimed interior, the great plateau of the continent, stretching from the north of the Transvaal up to the equatorial lakes and then the Sudan. Think of it, Fonthill, cool under the equator, good farming land, a country for white men.'

Rhodes's eyes were now ablaze. 'Up in the north there is something to make up to England for the loss of the American states. He who holds the north holds the balance of the map. The north is the trump card, the key position, the bulk of the shares. If Kruger gets the north, he holds a solid block of claims from the Orange river to the Zambezi. If he gets the gold of

Witwatersrand, he could build his Delagoa Bay railway, which would make him independent of the British in South Africa.'

He made a dismissive gesture with his arm. 'I don't want gold. But I want the promise of it to lure people in and occupy the land. Remember what the great East India Company did? In India there was trade to bring people in. Here it could be gold. If the north was occupied by a British company, it must then become a British colony. The north would be in British hands, and one might therefore federate South Africa on British lines.'

In his head, Simon heard again the words of Lamb: 'Dominion status is just around the corner...' but Rhodes was continuing.

'This would be a wonderful opportunity, my dear fellow, to make your mark on history. You would virtually be treading in the footsteps of Livingstone and Stanley – opening up a vast territory.' Then suddenly the visionary disappeared and the pragmatic man of business replaced him: 'And of course you will be paid: ten pounds sterling for every day you are away and three thousand acres of good farming land in Mashonaland.'

Fonthill's mind raced. The task would be prodigious. Hauling the guns and the ammunition to Bulawayo would be daunting enough, especially with Gouela lurking on the edges of the expedition. But exploring a route to the sea, through – what sort of terrain? Probably jungle and swamp. He had heard that the country to the east of Matabeleland was a breeding ground for the tsetse fly and goodness knows what else, and of course it was probably all claimed by Portugal anyway. What on earth would Alice say? He looked closely at Rhodes. The man's eyes were still alight with his vision of developing the whole of southern Africa for the British and spreading the enlightenment of the Empire. Was he mad? Merely a fanatic aiming to stretch personal power further from his base here in the Cape? Or was he a man of his time, perhaps even ahead of his time, a genuine visionary who would bring a balanced rule to vast territories under the sway of barbarians? Simon remembered his own embarrassment at being formally introduced to Rhodes's black servant, and the man shaking his hand as a gesture of equality. Well, Rhodes was clearly no conventional, black-hating white colonist. A liberal? Perhaps in some ways, and yet in others he was a prototypical exploiter of land and people. Whatever he was, he was undoubtedly different. No wonder he was treated with suspicion in Westminster and Whitehall. The politicians and the diplomats in London would almost certainly see him as some sort of rogue elephant crashing through the undergrowth of southern Africa – a wild and rich entrepreneur who could do harm but perhaps some good, as long as he was kept on a leash. Yes, a leash. Had the British Government already slipped some sort of harness around him?

Fonthill cleared his throat. 'Well, sir, I must confess that it all sounds fascinating. But let me tell you now that if I did agree, I would not wish to be paid. I have private means, and I would wish to preserve my independence – although I would expect you to meet all reasonable expenses, and I must add that the land grant could interest me.' His thoughts turned quickly to General Lamb's injunction. Would Rhodes rush into Matabeleland with all guns blazing? 'However,' he went on, 'I am anxious to know under what authority you would mount what would seem to be virtually an invasion of Lobengula's land.'

'Yes. A fair question. Here, look at this.' Rhodes returned to the table and picked up yet another sheaf of documents. *'I* would not be marching into the king's land,' he said. 'A pioneer column would be entering Matabeleland under a charter – a *royal charter* – signed by the Queen herself, allowing the British South Africa Company, my company, to do so under the terms of my original agreement with Lobengula.' He waved the document. 'This is the charter. Once it has the Queen's signature – and I am informed reliably from London that it will be forthcoming very soon – the chartered company can make treaties, promulgate laws, preserve the peace, maintain a police force and acquire new concessions. Here, read it if you like.'

He thrust the document forward, but Fonthill shook his head. 'I will take your word for it, Rhodes,' he said.

'Very well. These powers are wide-ranging.' Rhodes resumed pacing around the room. 'We can make roads, railways and harbours,' he went on, 'or undertake other public works; own or charter ships; engage in mining or any other industry; make land grants; establish banks and carry on lawful commerce, trade and business. In fact, my dear fellow, this gives me all I want, virtually the panoply of a modern state under British law.'

Fonthill frowned. 'But does British law apply to Matabeleland?'

'Given that I have the king's original agreement, it does. We are a British company, answering to British courts if there is a contravention in any way.'

The frown stayed on Fonthill's forehead. This didn't sound a very effective leash. 'Are there no restrictive clauses?' he asked.

'Oh yes, usual sort of stuff. Freedom of worship and protection of native rights, of course – the Aborigines' Protection Society have a strong lobby in Westminster. But I don't mind that. I wouldn't dream of exploiting Kaffirs. As I've said, on the whole they are fine people. The Secretary of State for the Colonies has limited rights of supervision, and after twenty-five years, or sooner if the company abuses its privileges, the charter can be revoked. No, Fonthill, once Her Majesty has signed this piece of paper – and she will, I am assured – it will give me all I want. And it will be legally and morally watertight.'

Rhodes replaced the document and extended his arm expansively. 'The capital of the new company will be fixed at one million pounds in one-pound shares. I can tell you now that sub-scribers will pour in.' He smiled. 'But, my dear fellow, it all depends upon you. Lobengula has given me the right to develop the land, yet I must have his permission – however informally – to enter it with my men and start road-building. I need you to get it for me.'

Fonthill nodded slowly but did not speak. The silence seemed to present itself as a challenge to Rhodes. He spoke again, but softly this time. 'My greatest worry, Fonthill, is the Portuguese. Oh, the Boers of the Transvaal are anxious to move in, and they hate us after Majuba. Lobengula is afraid of 'em and detests 'em, so I doubt if he will listen to them. But the Portuguese are on the spot and have always claimed suzerainty over Matabeleland. De Sousa, the man who tried to kill you, will probably be pouring poison into the king's ear this very moment. Once the king has accepted the rifles and ammunition, though, and given you his word, I am sure that the old buster will not go back on it. I don't want the Portuguese to have this country, Fonthill, and the Matabeles will not be able to keep it for themselves. Better me than de Sousa. Don't you agree?'

Simon cleared his throat. 'Would you ... er ... attack the Matabele?'

'Of course not. Not unless I was unreasonably provoked.'

A silence hung over the room. It was broken, of course, by Rhodes. 'Do have some more toast and marmalade, my dear fellow.'

Fonthill grinned at the banality. He could not help liking the open roguery of this strange man – the reference to de Sousa was a sly piece of blackmail. He shook his head. 'No thank you, sir. You are quite right. You do serve the best breakfast in the Cape, but I have had more than my fill. Now, I would welcome a little time to think this over and to consult with my wife. How long can you give me?'

'Oh, plenty of time. Shall we say twenty-four hours?'

'Good lord.'

'I must get on, Fonthill. These great events don't wait upon the ponderings of men, you know.'

'Very well. I will give you my decision by tomorrow morning.'

'Good. Think carefully, my dear fellow. Much depends on your decision, for I have no one who could do this as well as you. So weigh my proposition very carefully. Oh, and give my regards to your wife.'

'I will, sir. Goodbye.'

Once outside, Fonthill took a circuitous route back to the hotel, to give him time to think before meeting Alice. Jenkins must be involved, of course, in making the decision, but he would go along with whatever Alice and Fonthill decided. Simon's own mind was already made up. The challenge was too great to resist. The chance to be in at the birth of a great country; the pleasure of ruining de Sousa and his government's plans for Matabeleland; the call to find a route to the eastern coast – they were all too strong and compelling to evade. He and Jenkins had been lying fallow for far too long. It was time to set off again and to follow their star.

He grinned at the thought. Then his features hardened into a frown, as he remembered his promise to Lamb. It would not be easy to keep Rhodes on that leash. And Alice, of course, would not be pleased. There was naturally no question of her accompanying them on this mission. It would be far too dangerous, and in any case, it was far from certain that she would approve of the purpose of it all. It was clear that she carried no banner for Rhodes and that she categorically disapproved of empire-building. She was wont to quote Gladstone's words from his Midlothian campaign – words that she had reported for the *Morning Post* – of his 'shame' in thinking of 'the events which have deluged many a hill and many a plain with blood' in pursuit of Britain's colonial ambitions in Africa. Would she not see a danger of this happening again if Rhodes was allowed to release his column of pioneers to 'develop' Matabeleland? And was Simon himself not being incredibly selfish anyway in proposing to leave her again to go adventuring? He sighed.

Alice, of course, was waiting for him at the hotel, as was Jenkins, who was cleaning shoes in his room, nursing a ripening black eye.

'Sit down, my dear,' she said, her eyes sharp, 'and tell me what the great man has offered you. Was it the throne of some mountain kingdom in the hinterland, or merely a seat in the Cape Cabinet?'

'Now don't tease, Alice. This is quite important.'

'Oh, I'm sure it is. Shall I pack now?'

Fonthill sighed. It *was* going to be difficult. He cleared his throat and began to tell her, as accurately as he could remember, all that Rhodes had related. She interrupted him almost at once to call in Jenkins to hear the details, then listened impassively and without further question until the end. Then: 'You have accepted, of course?'

'Certainly not. I told him I wished to talk it over with you.'

'Good. That was thoughtful. How much time did he give you?'

'Er ... twenty-four hours.'

'*Twenty-four hours!* How very considerate of him.'

Fonthill squirmed in his chair and caught Jenkins's eye. 'Now don't be unfair, my dear. You know yourself that Lobengula is becoming very restive. Time is of the essence.'

'And you wish to go?'

'Well yes, subject of course to your approval. I do consider it the most remarkable opportunity–'

She interrupted him quickly.

'And what do you think, 352? Do you wish to go exploring in deepest Africa?'

Jenkins screwed up his discoloured eye. 'Well, you know, Miss Alice, I'll go anywhere the captain goes.'

'Not quite *everywhere*, I trust.' Her tone was acerbic. 'Good. Then that's settled. I'm afraid we can't set off immediately, my dears, because I need at least one new pair of breeches. My present ones are virtually transparent. But I will only need a couple of days...'

Fonthill set his jaw. 'No, Alice. That is out of the question. I am afraid you cannot accompany us. This will be far too dangerous for a woman. You have seen already how de Sousa likes to play things, and goodness knows what other dangers will lie in wait once we start to head to the east. Please, my dear, stay here in the Cape and–'

'And do my knitting and embroidery while you

two are having fun in the bloody jungle? Certainly not. No. I shall have work to do.'

'Work? What on earth do you mean?'

She leaned forward, and Simon realised that her eyes were gleaming in anticipation. To the side, he caught a glimpse of Jenkins grinning. 'Simon,' she said, 'this will be a damned good story, don't you see? I shall cable Cornford, the editor of the *Morning Post* immediately. I'm sure he will take me on again. The birth of a new nation, or at least a new colony, that sort of stuff. Those damned jingoes back in London will lap it up, and I shall have an exclusive.'

'You can't do that. What would Rhodes say?'

'To hell with Rhodes. The man can't operate in a vacuum. The world outside should know what he's up to. Oh, when his column starts to invade – and that is what it means, a bloody *invasion* – the correspondents for the nationals down here will be on board, I expect, so I shan't have that to myself. But they won't be coming with you first, my darling, taking your guns and bullets up to the dear old king, but *I* shall and I shall tell the world, from deepest, darkest Africa.'

'You can't. There are no cable facilities up there.'

She sighed. 'What sort of journalist do you think I am, my love? I have been solving those kind of logistical problems for years. The cable in the north begins from somewhere in the Free State, if I remember rightly, and I shall instruct a bearer to take my stuff back to be sent from there. I shall arrange all this myself with dear old Mzingeli. I presume that you will take him with you?'

'Well, I don't know...'

'Then I shall take him myself.' She turned round and gave Jenkins the sweetest smile. 'Does all that sound logical and sound to you, 352?'

'Well, Miss, I must say that–'

'Oh for goodness' sake be quiet, Jenkins.' A scowl was now firmly settled on Fonthill's face. 'Alice, it is dangerous and you will be a hindrance. This will be no place for a woman.'

'Oh, really?' The scowl was reflected in Alice's features. 'And who was it that treated old Lobengula's gout? Who fired the shot that stunned the lion when it charged? And who took part in the defence of the wagon? Was I a hindrance then? Come along, my dear. Was I?'

Fonthill bent his head for a moment in silence, but when he looked up he was smiling. 'Of course not. You were and are the bravest woman in the world. What do you think, 352?'

'Well I must say, Miss Alice seems quite determined.'

'You would say that. Very well, my darling, you will come with us. But for goodness' sake, don't criticise Rhodes in your dispatches. If you do, he might well recall us.'

She beamed at him. 'Oh my love. He might recall you two but he has no power to recall *me* – and if he did abort your mission I would just have to tell the world about it, wouldn't I? Now, if you will excuse me, I must send a cable and buy a new pair of breeches. I won't be long. While I am away, why don't you two find a nice little bar and start another war with the locals?'

Chapter 7

It was not, in fact, until three days later that Fonthill, Alice and Jenkins were able to set off for Kimberley. There was no train link north to the Transvaal, but Rhodes insisted that they take a ship round the Cape to Port Elizabeth, where a rail network had been established between that port and Durban and from which a line north was being built to Bloemfontein in the Free State. It had only reached as far as the northern Cape border, but it would still be much quicker than going by wagon or horseback overland from Cape Town. Fonthill sent a message to Mzingeli at his farm asking him to meet with them at the Kimberley headquarters of the de Beers diamond mining company of which Rhodes was chairman. He then went shopping with Jenkins to acquire two more up-to-date Martini-Henry rifles and a brace of revolvers, before meeting with Rhodes for a final briefing.

The meeting was disconcertingly vague. Firstly, Rhodes mentioned – almost in passing – that the number of rifles and cartridges awaiting Fonthill in the diamond town had been halved, to five hundred and fifty thousand respectively. 'All the promised money is there, my dear fellow,' he explained, 'but it's been damned difficult to find all the shooters, et cetera, in the time available. But don't worry. Old Lobengula will never notice, and if he does, just explain that this is the first down-payment on account. Anyway, this will lighten your load. The original consignment would have been dashed difficult to manage in one go.'

Rhodes was also less than precise with his instructions about finding a route to the eastern coast. 'Just head east. See if you can come to an agreement with the tribes out there – get a treaty of friendship between the chiefs and the company. We may have to build a road through to the coast eventually. Take plenty of gifts for the chiefs – lengths of cloth, hatchets, mirrors, that sort of thing. You can get all this from old Fairbairn up in Bulawayo. Don't let him overcharge you. But he knows the territory a fair bit and he could be helpful all round. I have used him before. I have given instructions for you to be able to draw on the company's account in Kimberley. Use the de Beers office as a means of communicating with me. They can telegraph me from there. Got it?'

On the day before their departure, Alice received an enthusiastic cable from the editor of the *Morning Post* agreeing to her proposal, and Fonthill felt it honourable to inform Rhodes that she would be accompanying him and of her journalistic role. He seemed remarkably sanguine about it all. 'I'm open about what I do, Fonthill,' he said. 'Nothing to hide. As for her alerting the opposition, by the time she gets her reports back to London, you should have settled the whole business with the king, eh, what? Oh, and tell her to use my name in full, Cecil John, there's a good fellow. It's just a small vanity I have, you know.'

It only remained for Fonthill, this time with Jenkins, to pay a farewell visit to Major General Lamb. The little man had heard, of course, of Simon's decision – was there nothing that escaped his attention in Cape Town? – and he showed his pleasure also at meeting Jenkins again. 'The last time we met, 384,' he reminisced, 'was on the ramparts at Sherpur, just outside Kabul, when the Pathans were attacking. I remember you had blood pouring down your face then. Now you've got a black eye. Where'd you get it, eh?'

'Walked into a door, General.'

'Lord, the same old barrack-room excuse. Well, good luck to you both, and God speed. Remember, Fonthill, curb the beast as best you can.'

'I will do my best, sir.'

And so they set off the next day, just the three of them, for Alice was not the sort of woman to employ a lady's maid on a journey such as this. Within two and a half weeks they were in Kimberley, thanks to the new railway. The town had changed a little since Fonthill's last visit nine years before. It still sprawled out on to the veldt in surprisingly orderly rows of single-storeyed wooden shacks, with their sad veranda *stoeps*. But the centre had become more sophisticated, with two-and even three-storeyed buildings predominating, many of them now made of brick and offering financial and other commercial services. Most of these were set around the large market square at a crossroads, big enough to turn an oxen team without it outspanning, and which seemed to be an open-air meeting place for an eclectic mixture of dust-covered miners, bearded

Boer farmers and barefooted Kaffirs in overalls. The de Beers headquarters, however, seemed exactly the same: an unpretentious low wooden building, set, like most of those in Kimberley, under a corrugated iron roof. There was nothing to indicate that the company now handled ninety per cent of all the diamonds mined in South Africa, or that its chairman could airily promise to launch a steamer on the upper Zambezi for a native king to play with.

Fonthill booked them all into a modest hotel, then, with Jenkins, hurried to the de Beers office. He was half hoping to find Mzingeli waiting for them, but realised that the tracker would have to make his way by foot for perhaps three hundred miles to reach the diamond town. He would need more time yet.

The two were ushered into a dark, gloomy office and greeted by a small, fastidiously dressed man who addressed them in perfect English, overlaid with a slight German accent. 'Alfred Beit,' he said. 'I have been expecting you.'

Fonthill regarded Beit with interest. He knew little of his background, except that as the son of a Hamburg Jew, he had been sent to Amsterdam to study the diamond business and then out to Kimberley to work as a diamond merchant. What he had heard, however, was that Beit and Rhodes had set up a warm and informal business relationship and that the big man now trusted the little Jew implicitly. Beit, in fact, had become Rhodes's right-hand man, although he avoided the limelight whenever he could.

'You have, gentlemen, taken on quite an assignment,' he said, favouring them both with a distant smile. 'But Mr Rhodes tells me that he has complete confidence in you, and of course I shall give you all the help I can.'

'That's very kind of you, Mr Beit. Can you tell me how far advanced are the preparations for my departure?'

'Indeed. Everything is ready. The rifles, ammunition and gold for King Lobengula are locked away in one of our diamond vaults, and I can assure you,' his smile became more affable, 'that nowhere could be more secure than that.'

He began to enumerate points, with one finger dropping precisely into the palm of his other hand. 'The rifles are packed into ten wooden boxes, which are sealed and locked with steel bands, fifty rifles to each box. The cartridges similarly are carried in two boxes, with the rounds wrapped in greaseproof paper in batches of twenty-five each. The money is in gold sovereigns and is carried in one smaller but stout box. I will require you to inspect them all and give me a receipt for them before you leave. I have provided five Cape wagons for you, which I suggest should be sufficient for the load you carry and your own travel requirements. Each wagon will be pulled by six oxen, and another ten oxen have been supplied to accompany you as reserves.'

Fonthill began to open his mouth to deliver a question, but Beit, the accountant supreme and master of detail, was well into his dry delivery. 'I don't believe that you will need mules, for oxen are the most reliable form of locomotion in the territory you will cover. However, there are three good horses for yourselves and, ahem, your wife, plus two reserves. They are all salted against the tsetse. Your personal belongings, of course, will be carried in the wagons. These include four serviceable tents and, of course, cooking utensils.'

'Men?' Simon was able to interject.

Beit nodded. 'Yes. I have provided five good Kaffirs to drive the wagons and another five to carry out whatever tasks you require from them on the journey. You may well become bogged down in drifts and need – what shall I say? – direct muscle to push and pull you through, although it should not be too bad at this time of the year.

'Of course you will need an overseer, and I have hired a man for this purpose and another to act as his assistant. They are British and have had some experience, I understand, of taking wagons to and from the gold fields on the Rand.' The little cough came again. 'They are a little what you might call rough and ready,' he smiled, 'but I think that will be an advantage on your journey.'

Fonthill frowned. 'Do they know the nature of the cargo – in fact, do any of the men know the nature of the cargo?'

'No. They know that the boxes contain gifts for the king, but I have deliberately had it put about that these are the usual knickknacks that we have given to natives in the past.'

'Hmm. Won't they be rather puzzled that we have bound knickknacks in stout boxes with steel bands?'

Beit waved a well-manicured hand. 'Oh no. A wagon could well overturn crossing a dry donga or whatever, and it is important to protect these

147

things from rough treatment. The men will know that. You will meet these people at whatever time you wish. Perhaps tomorrow?'

'Yes please. If all is in order, I would wish to set off as soon as possible.'

'Of course. Now, let me think if I have overlooked something. Ah yes. Do you have rifles?'

'Yes. Do the overseers?'

'No. Do you think it might be necessary?'

'If they are trustworthy, yes.' Fonthill had a quick mental vision of de Sousa's Portuguese Kaffirs streaming round the base of the kopje. 'There are those in Matabeleland who have a vested interest in seeing that we do not reach the king with our cargo.'

Beit raised his eyebrows. 'Really? Well, Mr Fonthill, these are unsettled times, and certainly you are going into territory that has no conventional rule of law, to say the least. I will provide rifles for your two overseers, whose names, by the way, are Murphy and Laxer. May I enquire as to your route?'

'Yes. We will take what I understand is the now reasonably well-established northern road through Bechuanaland, paying King Khama a courtesy call at his capital at Palapye, before continuing up through the Tuli Block between the Shashe and Macaloutsi rivers and crossing into Matabeleland at Tuli. There is a little gold mining there, I understand?'

'Umph, yes. It's been going on for some time, before the recent finds on the Rand. But it's small and not very profitable. When last I looked, Tuli gold was worth about four pounds per

148

ounce. But a word about King Khama.'

'Yes?'

'I have not met him, but by all accounts he is a civilised man and an enlightened ruler. However, he hates the Matabele. His people are peaceful and non-aggressive, all the things the Matabele are not, and Lobengula's men still raid into his territory, even though Bechuanaland recently became a British protectorate. In fact you could say that a state of war exists between the two countries, so I advise that you keep the contents of your cargo secret. It would not do for you to be seen taking weapons through his country to give to the King of the Matabele.'

Fonthill nodded. 'I take your point, Mr Beit. Tell me about the area just south of the Tuli crossing. I understand that it is a bit of a no-man's-land, lots of cattle stealing and that sort of thing.'

'Indeed it is. It is really a disputed territory, but no one is actually prepared to go to war to possess it. It has the reputation of being a rather lawless place – although, indeed, one could say that every-where north of here fits that description.' The gentle smile had returned. 'Mr Fonthill, this may be ... what shall I say? ... a not exactly incident-free journey you are about to undertake. But I know of its importance and I do wish you well.'

'Thank you, sir. Perhaps I could see the overseers at eight tomorrow? Ah. Just one other point. I am expecting a tracker – a member of the Malakala tribe, named Mzingeli – to arrive here to join me within the next couple of days. I would be grateful if you would direct him to our hotel. Oh yes. He will need a tent, please, and a good rifle.'

Beit's eyebrows rose again. 'A tent and a rifle for a Kaffir?'

'Yes. This man will be vital to me on this trip. Now, may I see the cargo?'

'Of course.' Beit rang a small handbell on his desk and gave instructions in German to a young man who entered. 'Hans will show you. Please let me know if there is anything more you need.'

There were no signs of diamonds in the diamond vault but the boxes were as described: made of stout timber, with two bands of strip steel strengthening them, and padlocked. The young German gave them two keys and Fonthill unlocked the boxes and examined and then counted the contents. It was, of course, all in order. The Cape wagons waiting outside were new and of sturdy construction, the maids-of-all-work in South Africa upon whose stout axles most of the transport in the southern colonies rested.

Early the next morning, Fonthill, Jenkins and Alice visited the de Beers offices again to meet Murphy and Laxer, the two men who would be virtual managers of the expedition while on trek and overseers of the natives.

The first impression was less than favourable. Murphy, the senior of the two, was in his middle forties and carrying a full black beard and a stomach that hung well over the belt that held up his woollen trousers. His face was pockmarked but his eyes were bright enough. Laxer, a dark-countenanced man with a strong Cockney accent, was younger, small and thin, but seemed wiry and energetic. Both men were burned by the Transvaal sun and they were dressed, Boer style, in wide-brimmed slouch hats, check shirts and lace-up boots.

'Have either of you been to Matabeleland before?' asked Fonthill.

'No, your honour.' Murphy had kept his Irish accent. 'But we've bin just about everywhere else in this godforsaken land. Down in the Cape, in Zululand, 'ere in the Free State an' through the Transvaal.'

'Doing what?'

'Drivin' most of the time. We can 'andle any size of team you can yoke up. An' we're used to 'andlin' the blacks and can speak the Bantu lingo.'

'Fine. Have you seen the oxen and the Cape carts?'

'Sure enough. Good beasts an' well-found wagons.'

'And you've agreed terms with Mr Beit?'

'Yes, your honour. 'Appy about that.'

'There is one point.' The two men's heads turned towards Alice in some surprise at hearing her intervene. 'We do like to treat our boys well, you know,' she said. 'There will be no beatings or anything of that kind. Is that understood?'

The two exchanged glances and this time Laxer spoke. 'Well, missus, I'd 'ave to say that in our experience a touch o' the whip is what's needed to get the black fellers movin' properly. We've bin at this lark a long time, see, an' they're a lazy lot. I don't care where they come from.'

'Well, Mr Laxer, whatever your experience, there will be no whipping on this trip. Is that clear?'

'Er, yes, mum.'

151

'Good.' Fonthill spoke again. 'We shall be trekking through Bechuanaland and then north through some rather wild territory. Can you handle rifles?'

'Oh aye, governor. We've 'unted all our lives.'

'Good. There is a possibility that we may be attacked at some time by unfriendly natives who will be ... er ... covetous of our cattle. So you may be expected to help us defend ourselves. Do you have a problem with that?'

'Oh surely no, sir.' Murphy's accent seemed to have grown during the course of the meeting, as though he was curbing it deliberately at first. 'We don't mind pottin' at the black fellers at all, at all. Ah, that is, missus, when they're out of order, that is. An' only then, bless you.'

Fonthill nodded. 'Very well,' he said. 'I am hoping to leave just after first light tomorrow, if, as I hope, my native tracker arrives in time, so I will expect you to inspan before dawn and for us to be fully loaded by then. We have a long way to go and I don't want to waste any further time.' He shook hands with them both. 'Let's hope it's a safe and uneventful journey. You can expect bonuses if you perform well. Jenkins and I will be here to help you load the cargo.'

The two men nodded, touched the brims of their hats with their forefingers and shuffled away. Fonthill, Jenkins and Alice exchanged glances.

'What do you think?' Simon asked them both.

'I could have wished for more congenial travelling companions,' said Alice, 'but I suppose we must take what we can get. At least they seem experienced enough.'

Jenkins made a face so that his black eyebrows seemed almost to meet his great moustache. 'Tough birds I'd say, bach sir. Not completely to be trusted, either. Let's hope they can do their jobs. I will keep a close eye on them, look you.'

'Oh goodness.' Alice smiled. 'I do hope that doesn't mean punching them in the eye, my dear.'

'Oh no, miss. Unless they deserve it, that is, see.'

Fonthill's last pre-departure worry was removed when, just after noon, Mzingeli arrived. He came in covered in dust and riding a decrepit mule, so that his bare feet nearly touched the ground on either side of the animal's flanks. Behind him, grinning widely, walked an equally dishevelled Ntini. 'Sorry, Nkosi,' said Mzingeli. 'Long way. Am I late?'

'My dear fellow, no, not at all,' said Fonthill, pumping his hand. 'I am glad to see that you have joined the cavalry.'

The tracker allowed himself a faint smile. 'Too far to walk. Where we go?'

In his message to Mzingeli, Simon had merely said that he must be prepared to be away for at least a year and that they would journey to the north. He knew that the tracker could not read and that the message would have to be conveyed to him by the Afrikaner upon whose farm Mzingeli had his home. He therefore felt it prudent to betray as little as possible of their destination.

'Well, I'm afraid that it is back to Bulawayo to begin with...' the tracker let his face signify faint

153

disapproval, 'and then exploring out to the east, towards the coast.' He explained the reason for the trip, and Mzingeli's expression lightened a little at hearing of the contents of their cargo.

'King will be pleased,' he said. 'But not Gouela, I think.'

'Indeed. I fear that we may be attacked again and we must keep a very keen watch. That is one of the many reasons I am glad you are with us.'

'Ah. I bring rifle.'

'Good, but perhaps Ntini can be taught to use it. I have a modern army rifle for you – and it will be yours to keep. Oh, and the pay will be higher this time because Rhodes is providing every-thing.'

Mzingeli allowed one eyebrow to rise and his mouth to twitch a touch to show his pleasure. 'Thank you. Good.'

It was after dawn before the column set off. Although the Kaffir drivers and herdsmen seemed competent, the oxen were not fully broken in to the yoke and it took a little time – with many curses from Murphy and Laxer – before they could be inspanned. Fonthill had begged an extra horse for Mzingeli to ride, which did not set well with the two overseers, who had been allocated seats in the wagons when they were not required to walk with the oxen and the boys. The mule was handed down to Ntini.

Eventually the party set off in a cloud of dust that rose and then hung sparkling in the rays of the early sunlight. Fonthill rode ahead, his com-pass in his pocket, for the trail to the north out of the town was clearly defined. By his side rode

Alice and Jenkins. In the leading wagon sat Murphy by the side of the senior Kaffir driver, who handled his oxen team well. Behind them, under the white canvas sheeting that protected the cargo from the sun, sat the tents and the paraphernalia of camping. If there had to be a trial crossing of a particularly difficult-looking river or donga, Fonthill reasoned that this load was the one that could most easily be risked, so it should lead. The second wagon, the most heavily laden, carried the guns and ammunition boxes. Then came the gold sovereigns, secured in one box, although Fonthill had procured other similarly bound containers, filled with stones, to sit around it to mitigate whatever attention might be prompted by one box being carried in singular state. The fourth wagon contained their personal belongings and half a dozen barrels of water, plus a similar number of light *fatchies*, or water bags. The last wagon was used to spell the Kaffirs who were herding on foot the oxen and extra horses at the rear. Laxer – at least to start with – was walking with these boys, ensuring that no animal was allowed to wander. Set out ahead of the column at angles of forty-five degrees, like probing horns, rode Mzingeli and Ntini as scouts, each equally proud of his new mount.

It was, felt Fonthill, looking around him, a well-equipped, well-organised convoy, and, he reflected grimly, it needed to be. Their route lay over untrammelled territory that bristled with danger. Despite the sunshine and the crispness of the morning, he felt a sense of foreboding.

The first day was uneventful and easy riding, in

155

that the veldt surrounding Kimberley was a huge plain, level and virtually featureless, even boring. The air was good but the country was dreary: the plain broken only by small, flat-topped hills, with a few thorny mimosa and a little wild jessamine poking through the thin sandy soil. Away from Kimberley, this land was arid and empty, as though it had never been farmed or occupied, and so unlike the prosperous, burgeoning town that they had just left behind them.

And so it continued for the next ten days or so, until they were well into the kingdom of King Khama, where the land became dry and arid, with the surface terrain coloured a dark red and the fresh water sources becoming few and far between, forcing them to rely on their carried reserves. The travellers met no one. It was as though they had discovered a new land, undefiled by human beings or other living things.

While they were still within a couple of days' riding of Kimberley, Fonthill had set a surreptitious watch during the hours of darkness to ensure that the precious cargo remained untouched. He, Jenkins and Mzingeli took it in turns to remain awake under their blankets for three hours at a time, keeping the boxes under surveillance, until, on the second night, Alice insisted on being added to the rota. Neither Murphy nor Laxer, nor any of the Kaffirs, however, showed the slightest interest in the cargo, and after a week Simon ended the guard duty.

The two overseers, in fact, displayed every competence. They took it in turns to spell the native drivers on the wagons' hard benches and they supervised the workers genially and managed the daily tedious outspanning and inspanning rituals with efficiency. When a little game showed itself on the plain as they neared the heart of Bechuanaland, Murphy hunted down a duiker buck and took it with a shot fired from the saddle. That night they ate boiled rice and fresh meat, the latter roasted by means of a sharpened stick thrust through it and extended over the fire, the stick leaning on the V of a forked branch pushed into the ground. They drank Kaffir beer purchased from one of the native villages that had now begun to appear. The consistency of very thin gruel and a pinkish colour, it was made from local corn, the grain of which had been left to vegetate, dried in the sun, pounded into meal and gently boiled. Jenkins pronounced it excellent – sweet, he said, 'with a slight acidity in the finish, like'. Bowing to the knowledge he had acquired as mess corporal in the 24th Regiment, they accepted his wisdom and bought several *fatchies* of it to supplement their water supply.

Alice had come to an agreement with Mzingeli that Ntini should take her dispatches back to Kimberley, from where they could be cabled to the *Morning Post* in London. It seemed that the young man knew where the cable office was – he had been employed similarly by a London businessman anxious to keep in touch with share values while on a hunting trip led by Mzingeli in the Transvaal. He was also reliable and anxious to earn the extra money that Alice promised him for providing this service. If it became necessary for her to cable while Ntini was away, she was resigned to relying on her ability to acquire a similarly trustworthy runner from local sources.

She had filed a preliminary story from Cape Town describing the purpose of their journey, the nature of their cargo and the route they would take. It was, she confessed, only a 'colour story', with little hard news. But it was a necessary preliminary sketch for what she hoped would follow.

After three and a half weeks of slow but not unpleasant progress, they reached King Khama's capital. It was little more than a collection of shacks made of mud and some timber and peopled by several hundreds of the king's rather unprepossessing subjects.

Observing them, Fonthill could well understand why the Matabeles treated them with derision. They showed little of the northern tribesmen's fine physique and posture, being smaller and diffident in bearing and not at all warlike. Their king, however, was obviously made of a different fibre. In the past, as a comparatively young man, he had fought both his father and his brother and banished them, ruling ever since with justice and kindness, while showing a bold front to Lobengula, who ever looked for an opportunity to raid into Khama's kingdom.

On arrival just outside the dusty little town, Fonthill sent a respectful message to the king, asking for his permission to camp in his capital and to pay a visit. The next day, a tall, slim, white-haired black man strolled unaccompanied into their camp. His high-cheekboned face featured a clipped beard and moustache, and he wore a well-

158

cut European jacket, impeccably creased trousers and a wide-brimmed black hat, around whose high crown a white cloth had been wound. Khama, King of the Bechuanas, could not have cut a figure more different than that of Lobengula, King of the Matabele, had he worn the uniform of an admiral of the British fleet.

'Good morning,' he said to Fonthill. 'I am Khama. I heard that you were on your way. I trust that you have had a pleasant and safe journey,' and he extended his hand in greeting. 'I believe that you are on your way to Bulawayo?'

Simon, who had been oiling his rifle, hurriedly wiped his palm on a piece of rag, shook hands and allowed his face to slip into a momentary frown. Did *everyone* in Africa know his business? He composed himself. 'That is true, sir. Please, sit down, and may we offer you coffee or perhaps some tea?' He pulled forward a camp stool.

'Oh, I am quite happy to squat on the ground, you know. I am very much an African, you see.' He sat cross-legged on the beaten grass and, awkwardly, Fonthill sat beside him. 'But I would very much like a cup of tea. You do not have Darjeeling, by any chance, do you? I have quite acquired a taste for it, you know.'

'Darjeeling?' Simon was just able to prevent his jaw from dropping. 'I think we might be able to oblige you, sir. One moment, please.' He scrambled to his feet and called to Alice. She immediately assessed the identity of their visitor and, quickly adjusting her hair, strode forward to be introduced.

'Darjeeling?' she repeated. 'Of course, your

majesty. It is our favourite. It will not take a moment.'

A minute or so later, the three sat together on the ground, drinking their tea and discussing the weather, as though they were in a vicarage garden on a sunny morning in England. Then came the question that Fonthill had been fearing.

'May I ask what it is you take across my land to the King of the Matabele?'

Simon drew in his breath. He had decided long ago that he would not lie to the man, but he knew that to reveal that his cargo contained rifles could well bring a refusal from Khama to allow him to continue his journey through Bechuanaland, so adding many days to the trip. What to say?

'I hope your majesty will forgive me if I do not reveal the contents of my cargo,' he said. 'They are items agreed by Mr Rhodes and King Lobengula as part of the treaty recently signed between the two, and I must respect their confidentiality. However, I give you my word, sir, that these cases will not be broached during our passage through your land and that their contents will have no adverse effect on your relations with the King of the Matabele.'

He inwardly winced at the dissembling, but clutched to himself Rhodes's assurance that the Matabele army would be unable to use the rifles effectively without the sort of training that would be unavailable in this part of Africa.

A frown settled on the king's dignified features. Alice hurriedly stepped in. 'May I refill your cup, your majesty?' she asked.

'Thank you. Yes. Excellent tea.' A silence descended for a moment. Then: 'Very well. I accept your word as an English gentleman that whatever is contained in those wagons will not be used against the Bechuana people.' He gave a wistful smile. 'You know, Mr Fonthill, that we are a rather poor country, with few mineral resources, in that most of our land is a kind of desert. My people are not aggressive and, unlike the Matabele, do not take easily to fighting. We are pastoral, not warlike. I would not wish to have the uneasy balance between these two countries swing unfairly towards our militant neighbours.' The smile deepened. 'I am sure you understand me.'

Fonthill felt a wave of sympathy towards this urbane man. He also felt guilty. Could he relieve Khama's fears, at least slightly, without compromising his position? 'I quite understand, your majesty,' he said, 'and I echo your sentiments. As I understand it, if this cargo has any significance outside Matabeleland, it would lie mainly towards the Transvaal.'

'Mmm.' The king did not look exactly mollified. 'Excellent tea,' he said again to Alice. 'Thank you very much.' He stood. 'You may proceed, and I wish you a safe journey.'

'Thank you, sir.'

'There is, however, one further point on which I fear I can offer no indulgence.'

'Sir?'

Khama nodded, and his face was grave. 'Yes. Alcohol. We make our own very good beer, Mr Fonthill, but one must drink a substantial amount before it affects the senses, and on the

161

whole it does not produce drunkenness in my people. This is not true, however, with the white man's spirits. It is against the law here to sell such substances to the native people of Bechuanaland. It corrupts their health and their behaviour. Do you follow?'

Fonthill inclined his head. 'Of course, sir. We do carry some whisky and a little Cape brandy, but I will ensure that while we are in Bechuanaland it is consumed only by us – and then moderately.'

'Good. Now tell me the route you expect to take.'

'We shall follow the north road towards Tuli and cross there.'

'Umph. Dangerous country. Keep a good watch.'

'So I have been told.'

'Come and say goodbye before you leave.'

'We will, your majesty. Thank you for your visit.'

The tall man bent down and brushed a few strands of grass from his trousers, then he looked around, gave a cheery wave of his hand to the company and sauntered away.

'Wow,' said Alice. 'What an interesting man. He would grace any drawing room in London.'

Fonthill nodded his head. 'I feel a bit of a cad for misleading him – if I did, that is. I am sure he knew we were carrying rifles.'

'Well, you didn't tell him any lies and I think he respected you for that. We'd better be sure that Messrs Murphy and Laxer don't slyly sell the odd bottle of whisky, though.'

'Oh I think we can trust them now, but I will

warn them of course.'

That evening, after sharing a customary dram, Fonthill told his overseers of the king's request, and although the two exchanged glances, they seemed to accept the situation well enough.

The little party stayed for one more day in Palapye, resting the oxen and horses, replenishing their water containers and buying reserve stocks of biltong, the strips of dried meat that sustained natives and whites alike on long journeys throughout South Africa. Before leaving, Alice and Simon called on the king, but he was away from the capital. They left a scribbled note of farewell, together with their remaining bags of Darjeeling tea.

'I've only met two African kings so far,' mused Alice to Simon as they rode off to the north. 'One likes the finest French wine and the other the best Indian tea. Strange. Do you think they're all like that?'

'Why not? Why shouldn't they share the benefits of civilisation? Why should it be only English devils that sing the best tunes?'

As the little cavalcade journeyed further north, it became clear that the terrain was becoming drier, with the few watercourses they crossed completely bereft of any form of liquid. So on the second night after leaving Palapye, they made their camp early, near a small village that had settled around a waterhole. Here, Fonthill ordered Laxer to replenish a couple of their *fatchies*.

The little man had been gone more than half an hour before he returned, carrying the bulging water bags and, incongruously, a small elephant tusk under his arm.

'I bought it orf the black fellers, missus, fer 'alf a crown,' he explained to Alice. 'Not bad tradin', I fort, eh?' And he grinned, showing blackened teeth.

'Bloody good,' agreed Jenkins. 'Let's 'ave a look, then.' He took the tusk and scratched it with his thumbnail. 'Seems genuine all right,' he said, handing it back. 'Worth about thirty quid back in the Cape, I'd say.'

Shortly afterwards, as Fonthill was attempting to light a fire under some carefully husbanded dried oxen dung, Jenkins squatted down beside him. 'I thought so, bach sir,' he said. 'There's a whisky bottle missin' from the store.'

'What? Are you sure?'

'Oh, it's gone, right enough. I counted this mornin' an' we're one down since then an' we 'aven't pulled a cork today. That little bastard Laxer must 'ave pinched one and took it into the village to trade for that bit of ivory. 'E knows its value well enough. I thought 'is shirt was bulgin' a bit as 'e walked off. 'E's a sneaky piece of work, that one, look you.'

'Right. Come with me.'

Together they strode to where Murphy was pegging out the tent he shared with Laxer. The little Cockney was inside, unrolling their bedding.

'Laxer,' called Fonthill. 'Come out here.'

'Yes, guv.'

'How much did you say you paid for that ivory?'

A hunted look came into Laxer's face. 'Two an' six, guv.'

164

'No it wasn't. It was a bottle of whisky, wasn't it?'

'No, I promise yer. On me mother's deathbed. It woren't me.'

Fonthill sighed. 'Don't lie. Bring out that damned ivory. We will go together and take it back and recover what might be left of the whisky. I told you that on no account must we sell spirits to the natives.'

'Well, your honour,' Murphy interjected, 'I 'spect old Jim 'ere thought that just one little bottle wouldn't 'urt, so far out 'ere in the bush, bless you. We was goin' to share the proceeds o' the sale of the ivory with you all when we got back, sure we was.'

'Of course you were. Don't you bloody well lie to me as well. I'm not a fool. Now, Laxer, bring out that damned tusk and we will go to the village this minute, before the contents of that bottle has gone.'

They returned ten minutes later, a half-emptied bottle in Fonthill's hand. He threw it to Jenkins. 'Put it back in the store, 352.' He turned to the two overseers. 'I just hope the king doesn't hear of this,' he said, 'otherwise we'll be thrown out of Bechuanaland long before we reach the northern border. You have jeopardised this journey and I shall be taking ten pounds each off your wages at the end. Don't step out of line again on this expedition. Do you understand?'

Sullenly, they both shook their heads.

That evening, as the flames from the fire flickered across their faces, Fonthill took counsel with Alice, Jenkins and Mzingeli.

'With respect, bach sir,' said Jenkins, 'I don't think we can trust these two to stand by us if we run into trouble, see.'

Alice frowned. 'What do you mean by trouble?'

Jenkins squirmed on his buttocks and cast a quick apologetic look at Fonthill. 'Well, not *real* trouble, like, just if old de Sousie tries 'is 'and again, when we get into Matabillie land. O' course we can see 'im and 'is black fellers off quickly enough, but it might be a bit easier if we 'ad a couple more 'ands to back us up. Though, look you, there's not much point in 'avin' 'em if they're goin' to bunk off, is there now?'

'But it wouldn't be in their interests to flee if we are attacked, would it?' Alice looked at Simon. 'I mean, we are miles from anywhere. Where would they go?'

Fonthill sighed. 'Well, although they say they've never been here before, they've knocked about this part of the world for years and I would say that they know how to look after themselves. Anyway, they might be rogues, but I doubt if they would desert us. This is the first time they have fallen out of line. What do you think, Mzingeli?'

The tracker looked up, his face quite impassive. 'These white men no good,' he said and lapsed into silence again.

'Well,' Jenkins broke the silence, 'this Portuguese bloke – 'ow's 'e goin' to know that we're comin'? It's still bloomin' miles till we get to the border. 'Ow would 'e know we're on our way, like?'

Fonthill gave a sad grin. 'I'm afraid everybody in Africa seems to know where we're going and why, old chap. I think de Sousa will have picked up the vibrations by now. Anyway,' he sighed, 'I don't think we have much of a choice. We must soldier on but keeping an eye on these fellows.'

The next two days passed uneventfully, but progress was slow, for the wagons were now being forced to cross more and more dongas, where everyone – even Alice – was needed to manhandle them up and down the steep sides of the dried-up watercourses, as the oxen strained and pulled up ahead. The party was quite defenceless at these times, but Fonthill believed that they were too far away from the border – even from the Tuli Block – to expect trouble. Even so, he instigated a night watch, with all the white men taking it in turns to stand to throughout the hours of darkness.

Shortly before dawn on the fifth morning after leaving Palapye, Fonthill was shaken awake by Jenkins. 'They've 'opped it,' said the Welshman.

'What?'

'Both of 'em, gone, an they've taken two 'orses an' the mule with 'em.'

'Have they taken anything else?'

''Aven't looked yet.'

'Damn.' Simon pulled his shirt over his head. 'If they've taken the mule, it must mean that they have stolen part of our load. Oh hell. I shouldn't have put them on watch on the same night. Stupid of me.'

Together they ran to the wagons. The full complement of boxes containing the rifles and the cartridges remained, but two were missing from the wagon containing the gold. A slow smile crept over Fonthill's face.

'The fools have taken boxes containing nothing more than stones,' he said. 'Oh, I would love to be there when they open those.'

Jenkins returned the grin. 'Very clever of you to mix 'em up. But are you sure they've not taken the right one?'

'No.' Fonthill showed him a faint mark on the back of what seemed to be an identical box to the others. 'This one carries the gold sovereigns. They obviously thought they were all full of coins – as they were supposed to – but couldn't take the lot with just one mule. So they took just two to set themselves up for life. Well, well, well...'

'They'll be miles away by now, bach sir. Best to let 'em go an' good riddance, eh?'

Fonthill shook his head. 'They can keep their precious stones, but I'm damned if I'm going to let them get away with two horses, two rifles and old Mzingeli's mule. I'm going after them. Wake the others up, I don't want to waste a minute.'

'Right, I'll come with you.'

'No. I want you to stay here to protect the camp. I will just take Mzingeli – I may need a tracker.'

'Oh blimey...'

'No arguments, Jenkins. There is precious cargo here of all kinds. I want you here to protect it. I think we are too far away from the border to be in danger, but you never know. Put the wagons into a laager and keep a good watch.'

Fonthill and Mzingeli stayed just long enough to fill their water bottles, stuff biltong into their pockets and drink one cup of coffee each before they kicked their heels into the flanks of their mounts. The sun tipped the flat horizon and sent their shadows long over the red earth as they rode away.

Chapter 8

It was not difficult to follow the trail, for the hoofprints were clear on the soft earth of the desert, and Mzingeli's skills were needed only when patches of rock and the occasional spread of dry, wispy vegetation made the ground un-receptive.

'How far ahead are they, do you think?' asked Fonthill.

Mzingeli shrugged. 'Maybe two, three hours. But they don't go fast. Look.' He pointed to the smaller spoor of the mule. 'Mule heavy loaded. Sink into ground. Slows them. Maybe we catch up when sun is at highest. They stop then, I think, to eat.' He shot a quick glance at Fonthill. 'They know we come after them. Yes?'

Simon frowned. 'I don't know. It depends, I think, if they have been able to break open the boxes. If they do and they find just pebbles, then of course they will be furious, but they may well think we would not bother to track them, so they won't be on their guard.' He urged his horse on. 'But I think they will have difficulty in opening the cases, so we must be careful on our approach when we do catch up. They both have good rifles and Murphy, at least, can shoot.'

They rode on during what Fonthill felt must surely be the hottest morning of the journey so far. The heat forced them to allow their horses to find their own, plodding pace and perspiration dripped down from the sweatband of Simon's hat, making it difficult to see very far ahead. His head was down and his horse had almost collided with that of Mzingeli before he realised that his companion ahead had halted with raised hand. The tracker pointed to the ground. Small spots of blood, not yet dry, lay on the earth, melding in so well to the soil that they could only be discerned by a man with Mzingeli's skill.

'They worried,' he said. 'They want to go faster. They beat my mule. Near now, I think.'

'If they are hurrying, that means that they are expecting to be followed.' Fonthill stood high in his stirrups and concentrated on looking ahead. He could see nothing. 'Can you see them yet?'

The slim man raised himself similarly and shaded his eyes. For a moment he did not speak, and then, 'Ah yes. I think. Maybe half a mile or more. I think they stop.'

'Good. In that case, let us dismount so that there is less of a profile of us on their horizon.' Fonthill pulled out his compass and took a rough bearing. 'I would like to get round them while they are eating, so that we can approach them from the south. They will not expect us to come that way.' He looked hard at the black man. 'Mzingeli, I do not want to harm these men if I can help it. But if they do resort to violence, then we must both shoot to kill.'

The tracker nodded his head slowly but said nothing.

'Right. Let's go. I will rely on you to keep them in sight – but only just. I don't want them to know that we have caught up.'

They dismounted, slipped a round each into their Martini-Henrys, and set off at a tangent, leading their horses. It took them nearly an hour before Mzingeli nodded and pointed back to their left. 'They back there,' he said. 'I think they lie down under some sort of shade.'

'Good. Perhaps we can take them while they sleep.'

The two mounted and urged their horses into a quiet trot. It soon became apparent to Fonthill that Murphy and Laxer had indeed used their tent awning to provide them with shade from the midday glare. His lip curled as he noticed that the poor mule had been left tethered in the sun with the two heavy boxes, still unopened, strapped to its back and hanging down on either flank. The horses stood close beside the mule. As they neared, Simon could see two pairs of boots sticking out from under the awning. The overseers appeared to be asleep.

But they were not. At about one hundred yards away, Mzingeli pointed. The boots were unattached to human limbs and merely propped up against the edge of the awning. The whereabouts of their owners became clear as two shots rang out from behind the horses, where Murphy and Laxer had been taking cover. The bullets sang over the heads of the approaching horsemen and Fonthill made an immediate decision.

'Don't fire,' he cried. 'We'll charge at them while they are reloading. Go quickly, NOW!'

Remembering a technique used by Jenkins years ago, Simon let out a penetrating shriek and dug his heels sharply into his mount's flanks. Heads down, the two galloped towards the little group of horses, mule and men, with Mzingeli screaming his own tribal cry, dredged up, Fonthill presumed, from distant days when the Malakala were more warlike. The combination of the gunshots, the shrieks and the thunder of the hooves bearing down on them had the effect of causing the overseers' horses to rear and scatter, knocking the two men to the ground and sending spinning away their rifles and the cartridges they were clumsily trying to insert.

Fonthill reined in and pointed his rifle at the men as they tried to scramble after their guns. 'Stay down or I will fire,' he cried. 'Lie flat, I say.'

Murphy looked up over his shoulder. 'Don't shoot, your honour,' he cried. 'We're not armed.'

'I said lie flat. Go on. Faces on the earth.' Fonthill's voice was emotionless. 'You are liars as well as thieves.' He seemed now to address Mzingeli. 'Best thing is to put two shots in their spines and just leave them to the vultures. Save both of us a lot of time and trouble. No one is going to miss scum like this.'

'Now, now, sor.' Murphy's voice was high-pitched. 'That wouldn't be the action of a gentleman, so it wouldn't. You couldn't do that, now. I admit we did you wrong but we didn't cause you harm. Sure, we only took two o' the boxes now. We left you the rest, did we not?'

'You only took two because you couldn't carry more. I'm not a fool. Stay down! Faces to the earth. That's better. Mzingeli, get their rifles and bring back the horses and the mule.'

As Mzingeli busied himself with retrieving the horses and the mule – none had gone far, and the poor beast of burden had only trotted a few yards – the little tableau in the desert was maintained for five minutes or more, with the two overseers lying spreadeagled, faces down on the hot ground, and Fonthill remaining in the saddle, keeping the men covered with his Colt as his mount shuffled in a half-circle and then back again. Eventually the tracker returned, leading the horses and the mule, with the Martini-Henrys lying across his saddle. He looked expectantly at Simon, with a faint gleam of amusement in his eye.

'We kill them now, Nkosi?' he enquired.

'No, mate.' Laxer's voice was a whine, as he spoke with his nose pressed against the red soil. 'Don't shoot us. We never meant no 'arm, honest.'

Murphy's plea was almost a shriek. 'Don't shoot, your honour. I'm sorry, I really am. We're white men like you, so we are. You can't kill us in this terrible country. It would be an unchristian act, so it would.'

Fonthill grinned across at Mzingeli. 'Oh, very well.' Slowly he dismounted and gestured to the two with his revolver. 'Get up. You, Laxer, go and get your boots. Cover him with your rifle as he goes, Mzingeli, and if he moves sharply shoot him.

'Now,' he addressed Murphy. 'Do you have full water bottles?'

'What? Oh yes, your honour. More or less.'

'Right. We will top up your bottles from our reserves. Do you have knives?'

'Oh yes, sor. We have knives.'

'Good. You may need them if you are attacked, because I am taking back the rifles, your horses and the mule, of course. They are not your property anyway. I don't think this is lion country, but I know the beasts are about just a mile or two north, so you had better be prepared when you sleep. Oh, you can have your tent, of course. It will be a long walk back to Palapye, but if you keep the sun on your backs more or less, you will keep going south and you can follow our tracks. They are not going to be washed away by rain, that's for sure.'

Murphy wiped his brow with the back of his hand. 'Aw, yer not goin' to leave us unprotected in lion country, are yer? Yer can't do that, man.'

'Oh yes I can. If I give you the rifles, you could well come after us. No, my friend. As I said, I don't think this is lion country, but one or two could well come this far south. So thread the tent up tightly at night.'

Fonthill grinned. 'Got the boots? Good. Mzingeli, top up their water bottles, there's a good fellow, and give the horses, and particularly the mule, a drink from your hat.'

Five minutes later, Mzingeli linked up the three animals on a leading rein and slowly walked them away to the north. Fonthill mounted his own beast and looked down at the overseers.

'You've been dishonest and stupid,' he said. 'If your greed hadn't taken over, you would have

174

been well paid for this journey. As it is, you won't get a penny. Now, start packing that tent.'

The two men looked up at him with hatred in their gaze. Laxer was about to say something but, seeing the steel in Fonthill's eyes, decided against it, and the pair trudged back to the tent and began striking the awning. Without a backward glance, Simon rode away after his tracker.

The black man gave him one of his rare grins. 'You would not kill them, Nkosi?' he asked.

Fonthill smiled grimly. 'Only if it turned into a gun fight. Then there would have been no alternative. No, I just wanted to frighten them. I think it worked.'

'Oh yes. It worked. They frightened.'

It was after dark when the two returned to the camp to find a fidgety Jenkins on guard and a relieved Alice tending a fire within a loose circle made by the wagons. The oxen had been put to graze on whatever vegetation they could find on the unpromising earth, with a boy to watch over them.

'Why didn't you leave the boxes with the stones?' asked Alice.

'Because we may just need them again, to serve the same purpose.' Fonthill turned to Jenkins. 'We will need to stand guard from now on, 352,' he said. 'I don't think those two will bother us again, but you never know, and it won't be long before we are back in lion country, and our oxen and horses are precious.'

He turned to Mzingeli. 'Can we put Ntini in charge of the boys, do you think?'

The tracker nodded.

175

'Good. Then tell him he must put the boys on a guard rota for the animals through the night, and we three will do the same for the camp.'

'Not three,' said Alice over her shoulder. 'Four.'

Fonthill sighed. 'Very well. Four it shall be.'

The next few days proved uneventful as they resumed their journey north. The guard watch was maintained each night, with Alice taking her turn (and Fonthill struggling to stay awake on her watch to ensure her safety), and Mzingeli circled the camp each morning to look for signs of nocturnal visitors. It became clear, however, that the overseers had decided to leave well alone, and as the days rolled by, they felt able to relax their guard a little.

The going was now much more difficult. As they neared the Sashe river, which for a short way formed the border between this part of Bechuanaland and Matabeleland, the semi-desert gave way to more broken country, with tall kopjes standing up like broken teeth from terrain that had become more verdant, and thorny plants hindering their progress. Particularly annoying were the wagt-jen-betges, or 'wait-a-bit', a generic name for plants that had double thorns, one slender and outward-pointing and the other curled backwards from it. They caught and held the clothing and often reduced it to rags.

Fonthill's mind had been occupied for some time with de Sousa. Given the way news travelled in this barren country, it was likely that the Portuguese knew of their coming. Would he make an effort to stop the arms reaching Lobengula and so cementing his treaty with Rhodes? It was highly

likely, and after the first reverse, he would probably bring more men with him to attack this
second time. Once across the river, the expedition
would enter the densely wooded country of
southern Matabeleland, and this would be the
most likely place for the Portuguese to strike.
Simon confided as much to his companions.

'We know that country,' he went on, 'and it's
difficult to see through the bush for a hundred
yards. I think that's where he will hit us if he
does. What do you two think?' He nodded
towards Jenkins.

'Well, bach sir, the thinkin' bit is your department, but that sounds about right to me.' The
Welshman frowned. 'What worries me is that now
that them two rascals 'ave gone a-walkin', like,
we're a bit light-'anded in the fightin' department,
see.'

Fonthill nodded. 'True. Mzingeli, can Ntini use
a Martini-Henry, do you think?'

'Not good yet. Perhaps Nkosi can teach?'

'Good idea. Better Jenkins than me, though.
Can you teach him, 352?'

'Certainly. Would you care to join the class,
bach sir?'

'That will be enough of that. What about any of
the boys, Mzingeli? Could we trust them to use a
rifle properly?'

'Only one. Boers call him Joshua. Lead driver.
Good boy. He has fired the Snider. Give him
lessons too.'

'Very well. See to it, Jenkins. I think we are safe
until we are across the Sashe.'

But they were not. On the sixth day after losing

177

their overseers, Mzingeli, who had ridden on far ahead as usual, could be seen in the distance galloping back towards the wagons. Reining in, he called to Fonthill: 'Tree across track further up. Not blown down. Cut down by axe. Fresh marks on stump. Could be ... what you call it?'

'Ambush?'

'That is word.'

'Did you see anybody?'

'No.' He used his hands to gesture. 'Two kopjes close together, like this, about mile away. Trail narrow down. I see tree down on other side of kopjes. Other side is plenty bush. I think men hide there but I don't see.'

'Did they see you?'

'I think no. I get off horse long way off and take look, very careful. Keep hidden.'

'Good.'

'I think they expect us to ride through, stop at tree and then they come back and front, all around. We ... ah ... strung out. They kill us easy.'

'Mzingeli, you should be a general. Now, get Joshua to circle the wagons here in the open, and have Ntini get the boys to drive the oxen and horses inside the laager. It's going to be very crowded with the cattle in here, so we will have to space the wagons out a little and somehow fill in the gaps. We must be quick. They will come at us immediately they realise that we have sensed what they are up to, and we don't want them down upon us before we've laagered. Alice ... yes, what is it?'

His wife had taken out her notebook and her pencil was poised. 'Exactly how many are there of us to fight now?' she enquired.

'Er ... ten boys, Mzingeli, Ntini and the three of us.'

She scribbled in her book. 'And how many rifles?'

'Why do you need to... Oh well. We have five Martini-Henrys, the Snider and your hunting rifle.' Alice wrote down the figure.

A touch of exasperation now crept into Fonthill's voice. 'Since you are so interested in our firepower, perhaps you would break out the ammunition and distribute the spare rifles. Jenkins, you come with me.'

'Where're we goin', then? To fight 'em single-handed?'

'Not quite. If there are many of them, we could have our hands full keeping them off, given that our firepower has been sadly reduced. But I have an idea.' Fonthill looked around carefully. 'It's good that we're in a nice open spot, before the bush begins. Come on, we've got to work quickly.'

He strode towards the wagon that housed the bedding and tents and extracted from under the cargo two small kegs of powder. They had been taken along as an afterthought in case the expedition needed to manufacture its own cartridges. So far they had not been opened. Fonthill rummaged again and produced a small bottle of lamp oil and then a bottle of Cape brandy. Quickly he twisted out the cork and threw away half the brandy.

''Ere' bach,' wailed Jenkins. 'Steady on. That's good stuff.'

'If it is, it may save our lives.' He unstoppered the lamp oil and, again, threw away half its contents. Then he took two of their tin cups and filled one with brandy and the other with lamp oil, before pouring the contents back into the wrong bottles so that each contained a mixture of brandy and oil. He then tore his handkerchief in half, poured a little of the mixture on to each half so that it was thoroughly soaked and laid them to one side. As a puzzled Jenkins watched, Fonthill then withdrew the cork from one of the powder kegs and poured a little powder into each bottle so that it was completely full. His last act was to screw up the wet pieces of fabric and twist them into the tops of the bottles as substitute corks.

A slow smile spread across Jenkins's face. 'Ah,' he said, 'bombs, is it?'

'Not as such. I am not sure that they would explode when I want them to, or if the explosion would be effective. But I am damned sure that they will burn for a short while, and that's all I want. Pick up the kegs and come along.'

Down from the wagon, Fonthill pointed to the edge of the scrub, which stopped some two hundred yards from the trail and ran parallel to it on both sides of the camp.

'The oxen have beaten out all the vegetation from the trail to there,' he said. 'So a fire wouldn't cross these strips either side of our wagons. But it would take hold deeper in the bush. I want you to spread a thin trail of powder just inside the edge of the vegetation all the way round the camp in a rough circle.'

Jenkins frowned. 'What are we doin' with the

bottles, then? You can't 'ave wasted good grog for nothin', surely?'

'No.' Fonthill looked ahead down the trail. It twisted a little over ground that undulated, so that the distant twin kopjes could not be seen. 'Good. It looks as though they didn't spot Mzingeli. That means they're still waiting for us and we've got a few more minutes yet. But when we don't turn up, they'll send scouts out to look for us and then they'll attack. But at least we can face them in the open.'

'Yes, that's all very well, but what are we doin' with the bloody bottles, look you?'

'Don't worry about them. That's my department – until I call you in, that is. When you cross the open space, across the trail itself, make sure that you continue the powder line so that there's an unbroken circle of the stuff.'

Jenkins nodded. 'Just inside the edge of the bush, then?'

'Yes. Off you go, there's no time to lose.'

The Welshman pulled a face and, keg under each arm, set off. 'With respect, bach sir,' he called back over his shoulder, 'I do not approve of the use of alcohol in this way – even though I don't know what you're goin' to be doin' with it. It could set a bad example to the natives.'

Fonthill watched him go and then turned to observe Mzingeli directing the formation of the laager. The boys were cracking their long whips, and slowly, agonisingly slowly, the five wagons were being pulled into a small, very irregular circle within which the oxen and the horses were now being herded. It was becoming clear that

181

there were not sufficient wagons to form a tight circle big enough to enclose the beasts, and as the oxen were freed from their traces, Simon rushed to help Mzingeli tie the long boom of each wagon to the rear of that in front to extend the perimeter of the ring. Even so, a space had to be left between some of the wagons and the booms to stretch the ring and accommodate the animals.

'We have to fill these gaps,' he called to Mzingeli. 'Get some of the boys to cut thorn bushes and pile them under the booms and in the spaces. Bring bedding and whatever else they can carry.'

He turned and noted that Alice had carefully laid out the Martini-Henrys, her own hunting rifle and Mzingeli's Snider at intervals around the ring, with piles of cartridges beside each one. Her action, however, had only underlined the paucity of their firepower. Seven rifles – two of them of doubtful efficiency – against ... how many? He shrugged. Out in the bush, Jenkins had almost completed his circle. Well, they would soon find out how effective his plan would be.

He walked back to the wagon from which they had taken the kegs and picked up the two bottles. Carrying them carefully, he strode out into the bush and located the powder trail at an angle of ninety degrees to one side of the flattened circle formed by the wagons. There he found a thorn bush of the size he was seeking and which was just a touch away from the powder line. He smeared dust over the bottle so that it would not reflect light from the sun and would be, if not invisible, then at least difficult to distinguish.

Gingerly he placed the bottle at the base of the bush and partially concealed within it. With his knife he cut away a large branch and wedged it at the top of the bush, so that it stood out clearly. Running now, he took the remaining bottle into the vegetation on the opposite side of the wagons and repeated the same operation.

Back inside the laager he met Jenkins, smelling of gunpowder. 'Brush those trousers, for God's sake,' he said. 'If you get a misfire on your rifle, you'll go up in smoke.'

'Blimey, yes. Very good, sir.' Jenkins shielded his eyes from the sun and looked northward. 'Can't see a bleedin' thing,' he said. 'Nothin' movin' up there, as far as I can tell.' He turned back to Fonthill, brushing his breeches with a soiled handkerchief. 'Maybe old Jelly was mistaken, eh? You said yourself that these blokes wouldn't come at us until we were in Mattabellyland. Perhaps that tree just fell down because these bloody ants that creep under my blanket 'ad a go at it. What d'you think, bach sir?'

Fonthill shook his head. 'Mzingeli has a sixth sense for these things. I think they have come to get us here – if they are de Sousa's men, that is, and I think they are. He's crossed the river because we are in that disputed area of no-man's-land where nobody is going to worry about a fight. If he attacked us in Matabeleland, he could well upset the king, given the nature of our cargo. No. They are out there all right.'

He looked around. The formation of the laager was almost complete. Inside the ring, it was ridiculously crowded. The cattle and horses were pressed together into an almost solid mass. How would they react when the shooting began? He had read somewhere that oxen never stampeded, and the sensitive horses had been put in the middle of these placid beasts. But fire? Smoke and flames?

An additional thought struck him. 'Where the hell is Alice?' he cried.

Jenkins pointed. 'In that wagon. Writin' somethin', look you. Dunno what, though.'

Frowning, Fonthill pushed his way between the milling oxen and climbed into the wagon. 'What on earth are you doing, darling?'

She looked up, her pencil between her teeth, her fair hair straggling down from under her wide-brimmed hat. 'What the hell do you think I'm doing?' She glowered. 'I'm writing my story, of course.'

'Oh, lord!' Then he grinned, a touch soulfully. 'I wish I shared your confidence that we shall come through this so that you can write a piece about it all.'

She knocked back her hat so that it hung down her back, held only by the thong around her throat. Then she smiled and leaned across to plant a kiss on his chin. 'Of *course* we shall come through this, my love,' she whispered into his ear. 'We are led by those two Great Indestructibles, Fonthill and Jenkins, Soldiers of the Queen and Heroes of the Empire. And if we don't, I personally shall be very annoyed, because I have the germ of a great story here. What's more, it is exclusive and I am setting the scene for it now.'

He stayed silent for a moment, looking at her.

Then he cupped her chin within his hands. 'Oh, Alice,' he said. 'I am so sorry to put you in this danger.'

She thrust his hands away. 'Rubbish. Simon, you really must stop treating me like a china doll. It's true that I haven't gone through as many scrapes as you and 352, but there have been a few now and I have every confidence in you, my love. Now, kindly leave me to finish the first part of this masterpiece. But rest assured that I shall not be scribbling when these people attack.' She smiled up at him. 'I have my rifle here and, look, a pile of cartridges. I shall play my part in the defence.'

He seized her hand, kissed it and jumped down from the wagon. Some of the boys were tying the last boom and others were milling about among the oxen, pushing their way through, talking softly to each beast and scratching their ears as if to reassure them. Fonthill called Mzingeli.

'Do the boys without rifles have assegais?' he asked.

'Yes, Nkosi. But they frightened of Matabele.'

'Yes, I thought so. Please tell them that if we are attacked, it will not be by the Matabele. These will be Bantu from the Mozambique border, slaves of the Portuguese who are being pushed into this by their master. They are not warriors. The boys must fight with us. Spread them out to stand with their spears by the thorn bushes between the wagons. Those that fight well will be given an ox each when we reach Bulawayo. I promise that.'

Mzingeli nodded his head slowly. 'A good

thing–' he began. But he was interrupted by a shout from Jenkins.

''Ere they come at last, bach sir.'

Simon jumped on to a wagon boom and looked northwards along the trail. At this distance they appeared merely as a black blob, but as he focused his field glasses, he realised that – whatever he had told his own Kaffirs – these were indeed warriors. Each man carried a large shield, and he could see plumes nodding above them. They were too indistinct to count and he could catch no glimpse of any European amongst them, nor whether they carried rifles. But as he watched, they began to fan out on either side of the trail, trotting Zulu style, quite quickly. There were clearly enough of them to surround the ring of wagons.

He turned to shout to Mzingeli, but the tracker was already walking among the Kaffirs, quietly talking to them and dispatching little groups in turn to gather their assegais and man the gaps between the wagons where the thorn bushes, mattresses and boxes had been wedged to form very insubstantial barriers. He let the man be and turned to Jenkins, now at his side.

'Right, old chap.' He pointed to where a tall branch on either side of the laager marked the sites of the two bottles. 'See those branches?'

'Yes.'

'At the base of each bush I have hidden my fire bottles. When I give the word, I want you to fire at the base of the bushes – it will probably take a couple of shots or more – to hit the bottles and set them afire. I am gambling that they will fall on to the powder trail, spark if off and so set the bush alight. But it is important to wait until sufficient of the blacks are between us and the trail, so that the blaze will spring up behind them and put the fear of God into them.'

Jenkins's eyes gleamed. 'Ah, now I see. But 'ang on. What if I can't see the bleedin' bottles for the black fellers in between?'

'Then you must get into a high position on top of one of the wagons where you can see and fire downwards.' He grinned. 'You keep telling me that you were the best shot in the British Army. Hit the bottles and I will give you an ox for each one.'

'Oh thank you very much. What would I do with a bleedin' ox?' But he was already clambering up on to the side board of one of the wagons. He called down. 'It might just work.'

'Good.' Fonthill climbed up beside Jenkins and looked north along the trail. The approaching warriors were now running and spreading out further to encircle the wagons. He made a quick estimation: about fifty, perhaps fewer, but still no sign of rifles being carried. They had about four minutes.

He jumped down. The boys were now carrying their spears and running to the thorn bush barriers. He called to Mzingeli: 'Bring Ntini and Joshua here and interpret for me. Alice and Jenkins, join me here, quickly.'

The little circle gathered around him. 'Alice has already spread the rifles,' he said. 'Each of you take up position in one of the wagons, where you will find the rifles. Alice, I leave it to you whether you use Mzingeli's Snider or your own hunting rifle.'

'I will use my own,' she said. 'I will be more accurate with that.'

'Very well. You will each have a wagon. Pile up whatever you can find to fire behind. They may have rifles. I will stay more or less in the centre to reinforce whichever wagon is under most pressure. Do not fire until I give the order, and then ... shoot to kill. Oh, Mzingeli. Perhaps it might be a good idea to put two of the boys in among the animals to quieten them if things get ... er ... hot. Yes?'

Mzingeli, ever economical with words, nodded, interpreted for Ntini and Joshua and then ran off to find two herdsmen from the boys manning the gaps in the wagons. As the group broke up, Simon pulled Alice back. 'I will be right behind you, my darling.'

She gulped but regarded him steadily. 'Yes, thank you,' she said. 'I may just need that.'

Fonthill thrust a box of matches into his breeches and then climbed up again on to one of the booms and watched as the warriors halted, spread out across the track, some two hundred and fifty yards away. He could now see that they seemed to be wearing full warpaint, and that they had monkey's or cow's tails attached, garter-like, just below their knees and elbows and, from what he could see behind their shields, more across their chests, suspended from necklaces. They stood in silence, perhaps waiting for orders. Simon could see no European, nor any evidence that the warriors were armed with anything other

188

than spears, although these were not black-bladed like those of the Matabele, but shone silver in the morning sun.

'Who are they, Mzingeli?' he called. 'Where are they from?'

The tracker climbed up beside him. He was silent for a while. Then: 'Not sure. Not Matabele. Maybe Zulu.'

Fonthill's heart sank. Although they had been finally defeated by the British at Ulundi eleven years before, the Zulus remained among the finest fighting men in Africa. They were the bravest of the brave. 'They can't be, can they?' he pleaded. 'Their homeland is about eight hundred miles away.'

'Yes. You right. Not Zulu. Perhaps Swazi.'

Simon gulped. That was no improvement. The Swazis were fierce enough and he had seen how well they fought when they had joined forces with Wolseley to defeat the Sekukuni tribe some nine years before on the Transvaal border with Portuguese East Africa. But they too would have been forced to travel a vast distance to link up with – and be paid by – de Sousa. Unlikely.

His supposition was interrupted by a great cry as the warriors lifted their spears and shields and stamped their feet.

Mzingeli did not change his expression but spat. 'Not Swazi cry,' he said. 'Minor tribe from east. Look good but not fight well.'

It became clear that the cry was some form of salute, for Fonthill saw their front rank open for a moment and a pale figure in a familiar yellow uniform push through. He stood still for a moment as he surveyed the pathetic little laager before him, his outline reduced by the tall warriors flanking him.

'Can you see him?' Fonthill called softly to Jenkins.

'Just about, bach sir. Shall I try?'

'No.' Then into Simon's mind's eye came the image of the puff adder, poised to strike. He did not hesitate. 'Don't try,' he called. 'Kill the bastard.'

The shot rang out clearly and de Sousa staggered for a moment, clutching his shoulder, before the ranks closed around him once more. The warriors raised their shields and assegais again and shouted their war cry. Yet it seemed more a gesture of defiance than a signal to attack. They remained standing, waiting for something.

'Hold your fire,' shouted Fonthill. 'Wait until I give the order.' Then, quietly to Mzingeli, 'Back to your post, old chap. Quickly.' He gave a reassuring grin to the boys crouched under him behind the thorns, and remained standing on the boom. If there were rifles among the warriors he wished to draw their fire. No answering shot came, however, and he frowned as he looked at the ranks ahead of him, still bunched together. It was not an overwhelming force, but his worry remained that they would fan out completely, surround the wagons and then attack all at the same time. With one gun per wagon, and only three reasonable shots among them, it was highly unlikely that a concerted attack could be withstood. If, however, the natives attacked in a tight bunch on one side only, relying on overwhelming force concentrated on one target – which was a usual tactic – then he might be able to reinforce the attacked side.

He shouted to Jenkins: 'If they bunch and attack just one side, leave your post and join me in firing from that side.'

'Very good, bach sir.'

Then he heard a cry from among the line of warriors. It was not delivered in the normal guttural deep bass of the Bantu. More a high-pitched shriek – Portuguese? It was enough, and the warriors immediately broke into a loose run towards the north-facing wagon, in which crouched Alice. His heart in his mouth, Fonthill waited for a moment to see if the attacking line would deploy to spill around the little circle, but it did not. It came straight for Alice's wagon.

'On the north side, 352,' shouted Simon. 'FIRE!'

A ragged volley ensued and Fonthill rushed to the side of Alice's wagon. It brought down just two warriors, but that was enough to trip up another. 'Reload,' shouted Simon. 'Wait... FIRE! This time three attackers fell, and then Fonthill realised that Mzingeli was at his side. 'Reload,' he ordered, and then, again, 'FIRE!' This time the range was considerably shortened and four warriors fell, showing that Alice, too, was causing damage.

It was enough to halt the attack, and the line stopped at a distance of about one hundred yards as the warriors faltered and then stood, un-decided, waving their spears and shouting. Font-hill tasted again that familiar acrid powder on his lips and smelled the cordite as it entered his

191

nostrils. The old elation of battle, first savoured – albeit for only a tragically brief moment – at Isandlwana returned, and he grinned as he thumbed another cartridge into the breech. 'Let's give them another while they're standing,' he screamed. 'FIRE!'

It was impossible to miss at that range, and the line immediately broke, turned and fled, leaving ten bodies on the dusty ground, two of them slowly attempting to move. The boys at the thorn bushes raised their assegais and hurled derision at the retreating warriors.

'Are you all right, Alice?' Fonthill called.

'All is right in this wagon, sir. Although I have to say that this gun smoke is ruining my hair...'

'Good girl. Anyone hurt, Mzingeli?'

'No, Nkosi. They not really near enough to throw spears. Next time perhaps.'

'Hmm.' Would they come again? They had lost about a fifth of their number, and if they had any sense, they would spread out and attack from all sides at once. It depended upon whether there was leadership in their ranks. Had Jenkins finished off de Sousa?'

He called up to the Welshman. 'Good shooting, 352. It looks as though you got the Portuguese.'

'Oh yes, bach sir, I got 'im all right, but only in the bloody shoulder, see. It was a bit long range to be accurate an' he was partly covered by the black fellers either side of 'im. I wish 'e would do somethin' brave, like, an' lead a charge.'

'Fat chance of that.'

'Will they 'ave another go, then?'

'Oh yes. I think they will. But they might spread

out the next time and come at us from all around. That will make it difficult.'

'Do you want me to shoot the bottles?'

'Not yet. Only if we're hard pressed. I am worried about the cattle if we start a blaze. But we will if we have to. Can you see the bushes?'

'Just about.'

'Good. Wait for the command. Mzingeli...'

'Nkosi.'

'If the attackers reach the spaces between the wagons, do you think the boys will stand up to them and fight?'

The tracker's face remained expressionless while he considered the question. Fonthill marvelled once more at the man's imperturbability in the face of danger. He was, after all, not a fighting man, and this certainly was not his war. He had not even asked why they were being attacked.

'They not warriors, Nkosi,' he replied. 'We will see. At least oxen behind them means they cannot run.'

It was a point. Even if the attackers broke through, they would have precious little room in which to move. Unless...'

'But will these warriors kill the oxen?'

Mzingeli allowed the nearest that he ever came to a smile to steal across his features for a moment. 'No. Cattle are precious. Oxen not as good as breeding cows but still worth much. They want to take them when we are killed. They don't kill them—'

He was interrupted by a cry from Jenkins. 'They're doin' what you said, bach sir. They're spreadin' out to encircle us.'

'Right. Cross to the boys in the wagons on the other side. I'll stay on this side to support Alice.'

He saw the Welshman make his way through the oxen and climb into the wagon of first Ntini and then Joshua. Each was crouching, his long Martini-Henry balanced on the edge of the wagon side boarding. Jenkins patted each boy on the shoulder and grinned at him. They both smiled back, albeit distinctly nervously. Fonthill was not sure how effective they could be, even with Jenkins to back them up, for they had not been subject to the first attack. They would be tested now, though. And he thought again of Alice.

He called across to Mzingeli. 'Ask one boy at each of the thorn bushes to get into a wagon to help fight off any natives who get through.'

The tracker lifted his rifle in acknowledgement, and Fonthill felt some reassurance as he saw the boys, smiling broadly and waving their assegais, climb into the wagons. At least *they* seemed confident enough. But was this very thin line enough to resist an attack from all sides? He looked at the cattle. The oxen had been seemingly unfazed by the gunfire and were standing, heads down, quite passively. Even the horses in their midst were trying to graze in the tiny space allowed to them. The warriors were taking their positions now, spreading out on the edge of the bush, with the powder trail behind them. No, he could not afford to wait.

'Time to shoot the bottles,' he called across to Jenkins.

The Welshman waved his rifle in acknowledgement and climbed on to the side planking of his wagon, situated next to that of Joshua. There he paused, wobbling for a moment as he wrapped an arm around one of the steel roof hoops, now bereft of their canvas covers. He raised his rifle to his shoulder ... and paused. 'Can't see the bleedin' bush on this side,' he shouted. 'These bastards are in the way.'

'Damn! Try when they start running. I'll do the one on this side.'

'All right. 'Ere they come again.'

Balancing at the end of his wagon, Fonthill raised his rifle to find the bush with the tall branch, but Jenkins was right. The attacking warriors gave him no sight of it. Forgetting the need for translation, he shouted, 'No volleys. Fire at will. FIRE!'

Once again gunfire rang out from the wagons, but on the word 'Fire', the warriors had immediately plunged to the ground, so that the bullets hissed over their heads. Now they raised themselves and continued to run towards the wagons, shrieking and brandishing their spears above their shields. But not all of them. Hurriedly ramming in another round, Fonthill had time to see three of the warriors slinking away from the charge, clearly declining to risk their lives in the last few yards of the dash to the wagons. The others, however, came on.

Again, at such short range it was impossible for anyone to miss, and Fonthill, firing from Jenkins's old wagon, felled one man, reloaded and killed another before he turned to his left, where the line was almost upon Alice's wagon.

He brought down a third, who was attempting to reach up to Alice with his knobkerrie. But the boys in the wagons were now involved, and they stood manfully along the side boardings, thrusting and stabbing downwards. In his wagon, Simon joined them, swinging his rifle by the barrel as a club.

A thrown assegai thudded into the side of the wagon and he plucked it out and threw it back, swinging the gun again and smashing its heavy barrel on the head of a warrior who was attempting to climb on to a wheel. He thrust the muzzle into the face of a second, who fell back on to those behind, giving Simon time to look up. He could see the bush! Quickly – too quickly – he aimed and fired. Nothing! Before he could reload, however, there was an explosion from the other side of the compound. Turning, he saw a flame rise and then fall, before running along spluttering and dancing, virtually at ground level, as the fire took hold of the powder and then leaped into the dry brush all around. In seconds, the bush beyond the far side of the wagons was a wall of flame. It reached the edges of the vegetation but there, starved of fuel, it spluttered and died. Nevertheless, although it did not vault the barren trail, it continued to burn behind it, crackling and rising in a yellow wall, causing the attackers in front of it to run, screaming, away from the flames towards the northern part of the trail.

'Three five two,' shrieked Fonthill. 'Come over here and protect Alice. I'm going out to fire the trail. Cover me if you can.'

Without waiting for a reply, he rammed a round into the breech of his rifle and leapt down on the inside of the laager, pushing his way desperately between oxen and wagons until he reached the point nearest the end of the flame wall. He shot one attacker and then vaulted from the wagon and ran headlong through a narrow gap in the warriors until he reached the unfired end of the powder trail. There he turned, in time to swing his rifle at a large native, who took the blow on his forearm, causing him to stumble backwards. Fonthill was conscious that another attacker had been brought down by a bullet from the laager, and he crouched and fumbled for his matches, praying that one would strike first time. It spluttered into life and he just had time to roll away from an assegai thrust that plunged into the ground near his hip before the powder trail hissed and then broke into life. The fire immediately danced away until it broke into a wall of flame on reaching the vegetation, complemented by an explosion as the second bottle was reached. The laager was now in the centre of a fire storm.

Fonthill threw himself forward, away from the fire, and lay prostrate. He, however, was no longer of interest to the warriors nearest to him. The effect of the blaze and the explosion on them and the remaining attackers had been immediate. Those who had reached the wagons turned and fled, rushing into the warriors behind, so that the ground between the flaming bush and the laager became a maelstrom of black figures, silhouetted against the yellow flames.

'Keep firing,' shouted Fonthill, now crouching

and running back towards the wagons, but he could not be heard above the roar of the flames. It was a superfluous order in any case. The black figures starkly illuminated against the flames made perfect targets, and the firing continued from the wagons. The terrified attackers, not knowing which way to turn at first, had now found one escape route, however. The line of powder across the trail to the north had found no vegetation to feed on and had now spluttered to extinction, leaving a narrow gap between the fires. Through it ran what was left of the attackers, hurling away their weapons as they fled.

'Alice!' shouted Fonthill, hauling himself into her wagon.

'Yes, I'm all right.' She rose from behind the little barricade she had made, he face smudged black with cordite and her eyes looking at the flames in wonder. 'What on earth have you done?'

'Just a few fireworks. Thank God you're safe. Whoa!' The last exclamation came as the oxen nudged at the wagon, causing it to shudder. 'Boys.' He gestured to the black figures in the wagons and at the thorn-filled gaps, who were staring wide-eyed at the flames. He pointed to their two comrades who were mingling with the oxen, attempting to soothe them, and in dumb show indicated that they should join them. He bit his lip. If the beasts did stampede, then the wagons would be easily overturned.

He jumped down himself and joined the boys, who were all now thrusting their way between the horns, patting necks, talking quietly and gently calming the animals. The horses were wide-eyed, but Mzingeli and Jenkins made their way to the middle of the herd to quieten them too, and the compound was soon more tranquil, if still a little disturbed.

They were helped by the fact that the fire had run its course on both edges of the wide trail, where the vegetation ran out and offered it no fuel, so leaving the laager untouched. The flames still ran back a little into the bush, but there was no wind and it was clear that, amongst the stony outcrops, the fire was beginning slowly to burn itself out.

'Blimey,' said Jenkins. 'Just like bonfire night, bach. Bloody good idea.' He grinned broadly. 'I'm glad I thought of it.'

Fonthill turned to the tracker. 'Mzingeli, see if any of the boys have been hurt, and Jenkins and I will make sure that the varmints have actually gone. We must be careful.'

Treading carefully, their rifles at the ready, the two moved between the figures lying around the clearing. There were, in fact, no wounded, for the range had been too short to inflict light wounds and those seen moving on the ground earlier had obviously succumbed. Even Alice's hunting rifle seemed to have proved effective. They counted twenty-three corpses and then, horrifyingly, another three blackened figures where the flames had taken them in the bush. Nowhere was there evidence of a uniformed figure.

Fonthill climbed on to the north-facing wagon and levelled his field glasses up the trail. He could clearly see the last of the retreating warriors and ... was that a litter being carried, bearing a figure in yellow? He refocused but the distance was too great.

'Only two boys hurt little bit by spears,' reported Mzingeli. 'But they happy with fight. They think they now great warriors and are excited about the oxen promised to them.'

'Well.' Fonthill grinned 'That's one way of getting rid of the animals when we reach Bulawayo.'

'Will they try and 'ave another go when we cross into Mattabellyland?' asked Jenkins. 'Or even, look you, on the other side of those koppy things?'

Fonthill pursed his lips. 'I think we've hurt them badly enough. We must have killed almost half of them and I doubt de Sousa is paying 'em enough to persuade them to have another go at us. The fire, I think, would have really frightened them.'

Mzingeli nodded. 'They think you great witch doctors,' he intoned. 'Masters of fire. They don't attack again.'

'Good. Now...' Simon looked around. 'Where the hell is Alice?'

'She's scribblin' again,' said Jenkins. 'Would it be a letter to 'er mother, then, d'you think?'

Fonthill sighed. 'I doubt it, old chap. I rather feel she is recording for posterity what she will probably call the Battle of Tuli Gap. But whatever she names it, I'm damned glad it's over.'

He sank to the ground, all the fatigue and misery of warfare suddenly descending upon him and the adrenalin raised by the excitement of battle now drained away. He wiped his blackened face with what was left of his handkerchief.

For a moment the two men, one squatting on

the ground, the other standing protectively over him, were silent. Then Fonthill looked up and grinned sadly. 'Come on,' he said. 'We'd better organise a burial party.'

Chapter 9

It was late afternoon before the debris of the battle had been cleared away, and reluctant as he was to remain in this blackened, benighted spot, Fonthill decided that it would be best to stay in laager overnight before moving on. He sent Mzingeli and Ntini out to scout the other side of the kopjes and further ahead to the far bank of the little Shashe to ensure that the Portuguese and his men had retreated fully. They returned to say that the tracks of the attackers had ended at the Shashe Drift and then reappeared on the other side, heading north. They were, it appeared, quite safe. For now.

While the burial parties worked, Alice attended to the minor cuts sustained by two of the boys and then stayed in her wagon, head down, writing on her pad. She broke off only to stride into the blackened bush to estimate distances, speaking to no one, her brow wrinkled in concentration. Only on Mzingeli's return, when Simon broke open the whisky to celebrate, albeit wearily, the victory, did she join the others.

Later, as the boys cooked, she settled by Fonthill's side. 'I have written my story,' she said, 'and I must send it back to the cable station. May I have Ntini set off to do this tomorrow?'

Simon shook his head. 'Sorry. That's just not possible. Once we are in Bulawayo, I have to deliver the goods to the king and then persuade him to allow Rhodes to send off his pioneer column. When, hopefully, he has agreed, Ntini can leave to send my telegram to Rhodes and he can carry your cable at the same time.'

'Hell, Simon, this is a *news* story, for goodness' sake! I must get it off *immediately*.'

'Oh come along, Alice! Who is going to scoop you out here? I agree that news travels amazingly fast across this emptiness, but none of your competitors will trust native rumours, and anyway, you will have the kind of details that no one else could possible garner. I'm sure you can afford to wait.'

'No I can't.' Her eyes were cold and hard. 'You can surely spare just one man for me.'

Fonthill sighed. 'I am afraid not. I am sorry, my dear. You must wait. This mission is more important than your story.'

Alice's eyes came alight. *'Your mission.'* The words were a sneer. 'Do you really consider that taking guns to a native chief is an honourable mission? We have seen today another example of the criminal brutality that exists everywhere out here. By bribing tribes with guns – bloody *guns*, for God's sake – do you really think that Rhodes is peacefully settling this territory?' She grabbed her husband's arm. 'Of course he's not. He is just stirring the pot. It's not *his* country to settle anyway. It belongs to Lobengula. Why can't he leave the man alone? You are not on a *mission*, Simon. You are just running guns, like any other disreputable smuggler, although you seem to manage to kill more people in the doing of it. Don't talk to me about your *mission!*'

Simon tried to reach for her hand, but she withdrew it. He frowned at her vehemence. Then his own temper rose. 'Dammit all, woman. Only a few minutes ago I was being kissed as a hero of the Empire. Now I am being condemned as a murdering gun-runner. I think you had better make up your mind.'

Their voices had risen, and Mzingeli and Jenkins, washing their cups from a water bag, looked up in surprise, while the boys bent their heads to their tasks in some embarrassment. A silence descended on the little camp.

Fonthill swallowed. 'It's silly to quarrel like this, Alice,' he said, his voice low. 'I had not realised that you felt like this about this journey, and I am sorry that you are upset.'

She looked at him stonily for a moment, and then her face softened and she leaned towards him and took his hand. 'We were all very nearly killed today, Simon,' she said, 'and I have to confess that I am still trembling. Writing my story made me realise how stupid – how pathetically stupid – all this killing is. We could have been speared to death, and more than twenty of these tribesmen were killed by us. And for what? A tribal home that is not ours nor that of Portugal. You know,' she gripped his hand tightly, 'this man Rhodes is nothing more than a rich adventurer who has now turned his hand to land-grabbing.

He has become a despot whom I regard as being far worse than poor old Lobengula with his gout.'

Fonthill shook his head. 'No. I disagree. Rhodes may be a rich adventurer, but he is a man with a vision who is not after further pecuniary gain for himself. He has as much money as he wants.' He enfolded her hand in both of his. 'Alice, dear Alice, things are moving at a fast pace in this damned continent. Rhodes believes fervently that the Matabele – and particularly their subject tribes – would be far better off as part of the British Empire than under some somnolent European country represented here by that cruel bastard de Sousa. And that's really the choice, you know, with probably the Boers of the Transvaal thrown into the equation. Them or us. Slavery, or freedom under the British flag. Poor old Lobengula cannot stay sitting like a fly in aspic, guzzling champagne and brandy while the world moves on around him. I think he knows that too.'

Alice wrinkled her nose. 'Yes, but what if Rhodes has to kill the whole Matabele nation to give them this "freedom"? He's quite likely to do that, isn't he? He's a ruthless man. It's clear that Lamb, Wolseley and the British Government are worried about it too.'

'He has promised not to do that unless pro-voked, and I doubt if that will happen. But any-way, that's part of my job, don't forget. To stop the man going in with all guns blazing.'

'Hmm. So you won't object, then, if I take one of the boys and go back myself to cable my story?' She could not resist grinning.

'Yes I bloody well would. I can't spare another man, and most of all I can't spare you. Who is going to treat poor old Lobengula's gout? He may well treasure me as a dear and close friend of Queen Victoria, but he treasures his own personal witch doctor even more. If he finds that you are not part of the parcel I have brought, he's likely to slit my belly open and feed me to the crocodiles.' Her grin widened and he went on: 'And what about the bigger story about him conceding agreement for Rhodes to allow his column of pioneers in to start digging – or colonising – Mashonaland? If you are not with me, you will miss that, my love, won't you?'

She shook her head resignedly. 'Oh, very well. You win. I will wait until you have got your own story for Rhodes. But please, please, no more killing, darling. I have become so weary of it.'

'So have I.' They exchanged a kiss, and it seemed as if a collective sigh of relief ran through the whole camp.

They inspanned early the next morning, but, still cautious, Fonthill sent Mzingeli ahead to cross the river and ride ahead to the village of Makobistown, the 'gateway' to Matabeleland, where the task of the *inDuna* there was to report to Bulawayo the entry of strangers to the country from the south. On their first, unheralded visit, Fonthill and his party had crossed the border from the Transvaal over the Limpopo, much further to the east. Given the importance of his cargo, Fonthill instructed the tracker to request an escort from the border to the king's capital. This would remove once and for all the threat of

205

another attack from Gouela.

In the event, the progress to Bulawayo was uneventful, in fact almost regal, for the border *inDuna* was quick to recognise the importance of the party and he provided fifty plumed Matabele warriors, in full regalia, to act as escort for the journey.

'Blimey,' observed Jenkins, 'now I know 'ow our Queen feels.' To emphasise the point, he bestowed a wave of the hand, a gracious nod of the head and a regal smile on the many villagers who turned out to watch the procession go by.

The biggest crowd of all, of course, was provided in Bulawayo itself, where it seemed that many hundreds of people swarmed out to accompany the party on the last mile or so of the entry into the capital. Here, the escort took its duty very seriously, using spear and shield to keep the crowds away from the wagons as the little procession approached the outlying thorn *zariba* that enclosed the town. Now, however, there was no praise singing to precede the meeting with the king, for Lobengula was waiting for them outside his house, sitting under the shade of the great indaba tree, on an ox cart where, Fonthill was later told, he often preferred to sleep. Despite the heat, he was dressed in his European garb, complete with billycock hat, and carrying a short assegai. He descended with great care, for it was clear that his right foot was still swollen, and as his wooden throne was quickly brought from his house, he gestured with a broad grin and his spear for the visitors to sit on the goatskins laid before him.

No provision for interpretation had been made, so Fonthill nudged Mzingeli to translate as Lobengula began to speak.

'He say,' began the tracker, 'that his good friends are welcome once again to his kingdom. He does not care what they bring for it is their good company he wishes.'

Fonthill, Alice at his side, inclined his head. 'I too am delighted to see his majesty again and I thank him for his warm welcome.' He had agonised for days wondering how to address the fact that his cargo was not all that had been promised, and in the end he had decided simply to ignore the matter until it was raised. 'I bring warm greetings to the king from Mr Rhodes, who apologises for the fact that he could not come himself. This is because he is about to be made prime minister of the Cape Colony, and he was forced to remain in the great city of Cape Town to receive this honour.'

The king waved his assegai in acceptance. 'It is understandable,' translated Mzingeli, perspiration beginning to appear on his brow as he grappled with his unfamiliar and important task. Fonthill waited for Lobengula to make some reference to the cargo, but the king remained silent, beaming at Simon and his wife. It was obviously beneath his dignity to refer in public to the gold, guns and ammunition. Again Fonthill marvelled at the innate good manners of the man.

Simon cleared his throat, but Alice spoke first. 'How is his majesty's foot?' she enquired, with a sweet smile.

'Ah.' A comic expression of great suffering came over Lobengula's face. 'It is ... what you say?' enquired Mzingeli desperately.

'Hurting?' offered Alice.

'Yes, hurting.'

'Is the king still drinking much champagne and brandy?'

A frown descended upon the royal countenance, to be replaced by a look of petulant annoyance that in turn gave way to another of his face-splitting grins. 'Less than before but still too much. Does the Nkosana doctor bring with her the painkiller?'

Alice inclined her head. 'As before, I can help a little, but the main cure will come from the king drinking less of the white man's alcohol and eating less red meat. It is, I fear, the only way.'

'Good. Then the Nkosana perhaps will visit later to put the little spear into bottom...?'

'Of course.' The king's relief was clear.

Fonthill cleared his throat. 'We have brought with us, your majesty, the ... er ... goods that Mr Rhodes promised as his part of the treaty he signed with you–'

Lobengula interrupted the translation by waving his assegai across his face, as though brushing away impertinent flies. 'That is good but not of great importance. We can talk of this later. Now we have beer...'

''Ow very, very sensible,' breathed Jenkins.

'...and then, when you have rested from journey, you will eat with us.' He clapped his hands, and gourds of beer were brought by young Zulu girls, shepherded in by the great bulk of Nini, the

208

king's sister, who beamed on them all. This time, Fonthill noted with approval, Mzingeli, Ntini and all the boys were served also.

Small talk ensued for a few minutes as the king enquired about their long journey. Simon had decided that he would make no reference to the two attacks on them by de Sousa – at least not in public – and conversation quickly petered out. Then the king waved his assegai again.

'You go to huts now,' he said. 'Then, at sunset, we eat. Good meat,' he caught Alice's eye and finished lamely, 'with many berries. Can Nkosana come early and cure foot?'

'I will come, of course.'

With that the meeting broke up and the party retreated to their wagons, where Ntini presided over the unloading of the personal possessions, which were taken to the huts that had housed them before. Fonthill was glad to see that the hole cut into the back of his hut had been carefully repaired.

'What about the gold an' stuff?' enquired Jenkins.

'Look.'

Silently, six of the king's men had appeared and were quietly offloading the cases. 'He can't get into them until I unlock them,' said Fonthill, 'but it's clear that he is not so uninterested in them as he made out. At least everything will be under guard overnight and we won't have to worry about them.' He turned to Alice. 'Shall I come with you into the treatment room?'

'No. Witch doctors don't like to be watched when they're casting their spells.'

'All right. But take Mzingeli with you.'

'Of course. I shall need him to translate anyway.'

Alice carefully unpacked her medicine bag and checked its contents. 'Right, Mzingeli. Let's go.'

This time, however, they were forced to wait outside the king's house by a very nervous servant as loud voices came from within. Mzingeli frowned. 'King angry with someone,' he whispered. 'Man inside steal royal cattle, I think. Ah. Yes. Man is to have hand cut off and he thrown to crocodiles in river.'

'Oh my God.' Alice blanched. 'How disgusting. He can't do that.'

The tracker shrugged. 'It is the way here. He not always cheerful man. He very cruel.'

Alice took a deep breath. 'Then he can cure his own blasted gout.'

'No, no, Nkosana. Don't make him more angry. We all in his power here. He ... er ... value you. Perhaps if you make him angry, we all die.'

They were forced to remain silent, until a scream came from within. At that, Alice thrust her way past the servant and entered the smoke-filled interior. The sight that met their eyes was repellent. Lobengula had removed his European clothes and was standing, wearing just a loin-cloth. The black folds of his skin were glistening in the firelight and his eyes were aflame. Kneeling in front of him, writhing in agony, was a native, whose right hand had been hacked away by an axe. Blood was spurting from the stump.

As Alice watched, he was dragged to his feet by two men and hauled towards the door, presumably on his way to the river. She barred the way.

'Put that man down,' she cried, pointing to the ground. A silence fell on the room, broken only by the crackling of the fire. The two men stood, gripping the victim, who had now slumped into unconsciousness. Their jaws had dropped and their eyes, widened in surprise, were white spheres in the half-light. They turned in consternation, looking for direction from the king, but Lobengula stood immobile, frozen by surprise.

Alice turned. 'Mzingeli, bring my bag. Quickly now, or this man will bleed to death.'

The tracker shook his head. 'No, Nkosana. No interfere. They kill us.'

'Do as I say. Here, yes. Good, thank you. Now, hold the man's arm up. Quickly.' She unclipped her bag and fumbled inside. 'Higher than that. I don't want the bag filled with blood. That's better.'

Kneeling and working quickly, she produced a narrow strip of bandage, which she folded lengthways and wrapped around the stricken man's arm above the elbow, knotting it loosely. Then she looked around, plucked a knife from the girdle of one of the two executioners, thrust its handle into a fold of the bandage and twisted it to act as a tourniquet. 'Hold this, Mzingeli,' she said. 'Keep it tight until the bleeding stops, then, when it does stop, loosen it slightly, and tighten it again. Now...'

Alice rummaged in her bag once again and produced a large pad of cotton wool, which she screwed tightly, wrapped in gauze and drenched in antiseptic from a bottle. Perspiration was now pouring from her brow. Wiping it away with the back of her hand, she pressed the pad on to the bloody stump and looked around in some desperation. Her eye fell on the nearest of the executioners.

'You,' she cried. 'Yes, dammit, you. Come here.'

Uncomprehending and fearful, the man remained unmoving. Alice reached across and pulled him towards her roughly by his forearm. 'Here. Hold this. *This*, you bloody fool. Look.' She gently pressed her hand on to the pad. 'Hold it like this. Yes, well done, you great barbarian. Hold it still while I bandage.'

Kneeling awkwardly, Alice wound a bandage around the thief's forearm and then crossed it several times over the pad to hold it in place on the stump, before doubling it back to the forearm, cutting it off with her scissors, slicing the cotton into two strips and firmly knotting the two together to hold the bandage in place. She looked up and blew out her cheeks. 'Keep the tourniquet tight for the moment,' she ordered the tracker.

Then she caught the eye of the king.

There was no sign now of the grinning, genial monarch. Lobengula's face was contorted with rage. The King of the Matabele had never in all his life had his way thwarted when ordering an execution – and certainly not by a woman, whatever her colour. He opened his mouth to speak – or scream – but Alice interrupted him.

'Your majesty,' she said in a loud but precise tone that seemed to cut through the hot, smoky atmosphere like a jet of cold water, 'this man has suffered enough for his crime.' She turned to the kneeling Mzingeli. 'Go on. Interpret.'

The tracker did so, in a low, hesitant voice. 'I

have tried to staunch the bleeding,' Alice continued, 'but I am not sure I have succeeded. The
man may well die during the night. So it will
certainly not be necessary to feed him to the
crocodiles. If you are a wise and tolerant ruler, as
I am sure you are, the compassionate thing to do
would be to leave him to die in his bed, with his
family at his side. By severing his hand, you have
already punished him for his crime. I am sure
you agree.' She summoned up a smile.

It was clear, however, that the king did not
agree. He gave a shouted order and the victim,
now regaining consciousness, was roughly seized
again by his captors, so that Mzingeli was forced
to remove the knife from the tourniquet loop.

Alice took a deep breath. 'Ah, I see that your
majesty has lost respect for my healing powers. In
that case, of course, I can no longer treat your
painful foot. I wish you good evening.'

As Mzingeli translated, Alice bent down and
slowly began repacking her medical bag. Then
she stood, and with a deferential nod, turned and
began making her way to the door.

A shout from the king halted her. 'Why you
interfere with our customs and judgement?' he
demanded. 'Do I do this with Queen Victoria in
your country?'

There was a logic to the question that con-
founded Alice for a moment. 'Ah, but Queen
Victoria would never give two punishments to
one man for the same crime,' she said. 'The loss
of the hand would be considered sufficient in any
civilised country.' The criticism implied by the
use of the word 'civilised' put her on even more

dangerous ground, she realised, but she was determined to hold her position.

Mzingeli translated, though unhappily. 'Careful, Nksosana, please,' he pleaded. But the king was speaking again. This time he was addressing the *inDunas*, wives and others crowded into the room. The tracker continued: 'He say your words have wisdom and ask why no adviser said same to him in past. He say he cannot do all thinking himself. *InDunas* should advise like you. You clever woman. You heal and you speak well. Man shall go to his family.'

Alice felt relief flood over her. 'The king is gracious, wise and compassionate,' she said. 'If he will allow me to finish my work with this man, I will attend to his majesty's foot.'

Lobengula nodded, a touch petulantly, and Alice knelt again at the thief's side. The stump was still bleeding, of course, but less so. She applied a second pad, bound it more tightly, and retied the tourniquet, less tightly. Then she selected a white cotton sling from her bag and arranged it around the man's neck, so that the arm was held pointing upwards, close to the chest. Finally she nodded. 'Take him,' she said.

The king gestured with his assegai, and while the mutilated man was helped to his feet and escorted from the room, Lobengula lowered himself on to his couch. Alice asked for water to wash, and a bowl was brought. Then she inspected the royal foot. It was swollen, of course, and still discoloured, but not as enlarged as when last she had seen it. Perhaps the king was, indeed, reducing his indulgences. Certainly the pile of bottles had disappeared.

Alice returned to her bag. In Cape Town she had resorted to a pharmacy, and now she laid out on the beaten earth the fruits of her visit: a box of Blair's Gout Pills, 'The Great English Remedy', and a bottle of Clarke's World Famed Blood Mixture. She had been assured by a doctor she had consulted in the Cape that these, coupled with a restrained and balanced diet, would reduce the symptoms of the affliction and indeed help to remove it altogether. She was anxious to lessen the king's reliance on her injections of morphine, for she wished to keep the drug for more serious emergencies.

She doled out a week's supply of the pills and explained that one should be taken every day with water, supplemented by a teaspoonful of the Blood Mixture. Then she injected the king, as before, with morphine, this time reducing the dose.

Immediately the king's good humour was restored, although it was unclear whether this was because the drugs took immediate effect – which was unlikely – or because he had managed, narrowly, to keep face over the sentencing of the thief. The great beam came back.

'How long you stay this time?' he asked.

'I am not sure,' replied Alice, thinking quickly. 'I know that my husband is anxious to seek the king's agreement to a question he will put to your majesty, but certainly we are not anxious to leave Bulawayo. In due course, however, I understand that we intend to explore to the east, towards the Indian Ocean coast.'

'Oh! Very difficult country that way. Very dangerous. Why you go?'

'Er... I understand that Mr Rhodes is anxious to find a route to the coast, either by river or by land.'

'Why he want that?'

'Your majesty must ask my husband. I do not know.'

'Ah. Rhodes always want something.'

'Um ... yes.' She smiled, packed her bag, bowed and left, Mzingeli in tow.

The two walked together in silence back to the huts until, nearly there, Mzingeli spoke. 'You very brave woman,' he said. 'Very fine.'

Alice gave the tracker a sad smile. 'Thank you. The trouble is that I very much doubt whether it was worthwhile, for I am sure that the man will die, probably of shock or blood poisoning. Still, better he dies in bed than being dragged under by some foul-smelling crocodile.' And she gave an involuntary shudder.

Alice decided not to tell Simon of her intervention, and they prepared for their dinner with the king in companionable silence – broken, inevitably, by the arrival of Jenkins, who still perforce shared their hut.

'Been to Mr Fairbairn's,' confided the Welshman, 'just to see if 'e'd 'eard anythin' about the Portuguese bloke, look you.' The strong smell of whisky he exuded gave the lie to that, but apart from exchanging glances, neither Simon nor Alice decided to issue a rebuke.

'And what did he say?' asked Fonthill.

Jenkins gave a chortle. 'I got Gouela all right. In

the shoulder. 'E's walkin' about with 'is arm in a sling. An 'untin' accident, 'e's tellin' everybody.'

Simon nodded. 'Well,' he reflected, squatting on a stool and pulling his head through his best shirt, 'if there was any doubt about who was behind that attack, that settles it.'

'Do you intend to tell the king?' asked Alice.

'I think not. However...'

'Yes?'

Fonthill grinned. 'If Lobengula does make a fuss about being short-changed with the number of guns I have brought, I would be sorely tempted to say that old Gouela took half of them when he attacked us.'

'Oh, I don't think...'

'No, neither do I. It would be wrong to lie about it, and anyway, I could never prove it. So I will just keep quiet and see how things develop.'

Alice sat for a moment in silence, and then decided it would be wise to tell Simon about her intervention after the mutilation, and of her brief conversation with the king following her treatment of his foot. Jenkins and her husband listened with rapt attention as she unfolded her brief tale, and at its end, Fonthill shook his head slowly.

'My dear Alice,' he said. 'I don't know what to say...'

'I do,' said Jenkins. 'It was a very brave thing to do. I wouldn't 'ave pushed my nose in there, with the old bastard in 'is 'and-choppin' mood. You did very well, Miss Alice, if I may say so. But blimey. It just shows what these people are capable of, isn't it?'

Fonthill stood and wrapped his arms around

his wife. 'Yes, it does. So don't do anything like that again, my love. Will you promise?'

She pushed him away. 'Certainly not. I had him over a barrel and he knew it. I wouldn't have treated him if he had let the poor wretch be taken to the river. And that was that. I would do it again if necessary.'

Fonthill raised his eyebrows to Jenkins, shrugged his shoulders and resumed dressing. 'What did he say when you mentioned the exploration trip to the east?'

'He wanted to know why Rhodes wanted you to go, but I told him he had better ask you.' She grinned, her grey eyes sparkling in the gloom. 'I thought I had got into enough trouble for one day.'

'Ah.' Fonthill gave a histrionic sigh. 'Acknowledgement at last! But thank you for telling me. I had better think of a good reason.'

As the sun dipped away and the brief African twilight began to disappear, revealing the first spray of stars in the blue-black sky, the three walked together down to the king's hut. The heat had gone, taking the flies with it, and the evening was soft and delightful. After careful thought, Alice had decided to wear her only dress, having smoothed out the wrinkles with a sprinkling of water and the application of her hand. A touch of femininity, she had reasoned, would not be out of place after her show of masculine determination earlier.

Fonthill regarded her with approval as they strolled together, arm in arm. Alice had tied back her hair with her favourite apple-green silk scarf –

a treasure of much importance in her tiny wardrobe – and donned open-toed sandals. A touch of face powder and a little rouge had smoothed her sunburned cheeks, and her eyes were sparkling.

'How nice to go to an elegant dinner in the tropics,' she said. 'I wonder if the old boy will serve us champagne.'

'Hmm. Equally, he might decide to cut our hands off. Which reminds me.' He turned to Jenkins, walking amiably by their side. 'I know you've had a touch of whisky, 352,' he said, 'so do please behave yourself tonight. If somebody stamps on your foot, take it as a compliment. Don't punch him on the jaw, there's a good fellow. The family has been in enough trouble for one day.'

'I shall be 'ave with great property... propoty... prop...'

'Propriety?'

'That's the word, Miss Alice. On the tip of me tongue. Not a finger out of place, see. Oh, incidentally, old Fairbairn 'as been invited.'

Fonthill's eyebrows rose. 'Ah, so it's a kind of diplomatic party all round, probably to celebrate the fact that Lobengula's got his guns and gold.' A second thought struck him. 'I wonder if de Sousa will be invited. We shall see.'

They entered the large hut to find that, thankfully, the fire had been allowed to die down, even though the evening had become cooler with the descent of the sun. Benches of differing heights and provenance had been arranged in a great circle around the fire, with Lobengula's old wooden throne arranged on one side of the circle, facing the door. The king had not yet made his appearance, but all of the senior *inDunas* were there, including the man who had led them to the king on their first entrance to the country and who had been saved from punishment by Fonthill on their arrival at Bulawayo. He came forward with a grin, and made a great show of shaking hands, European style, with Simon, Alice and Jenkins, as though they were old friends. Fonthill took this as a good sign.

Nini, too, came bustling over, an ironmongery of copper charms and medallions cascading over her huge bosoms. 'How is you?' she enquired.

'We is ... ah ... we are very well, thank you, Princess,' said Simon, bowing over her hand.

The king's sister made an impatient gesture, and beer was immediately produced for all three. Receiving his, Jenkins gave an extravagant bow and immediately caught the attention of Nini. 'You not married?' enquired the princess.

'Ooh, yes,' the Welshman hurriedly replied. 'I 'ave three wives back 'ome.'

Nini immediately whirled round to Fonthill. 'He say you only allowed one wife at a time.'

Jenkins thought quickly. 'Ah well, you see, your majesty, two of 'em are dead an' buried, like. I've got one that is very much alive, look you. An' that's all I'm allowed, see. Great pity it is.'

The princess looked puzzled, but let it pass. Now she put her face close to Jenkins's and examined his great moustache, taking its end between plump finger and thumb and rubbing the hairs vigorously. 'Why you grow this?' she asked.

220

'Er ... to make me look pretty, see.'

At this, Nini threw back her head and roared with laughter, giving a lead to all of the wives and girl servers in the hut, who laughed along dutifully, although they could not have understood for a moment the meaning of the joke. Fairbairn now joined the party, bringing with him his distinctive aura of tobacco smoke and whisky, and he immediately engaged the princess in fluent Zulu, which relieved Jenkins of his duties as purveyor of pre-dinner small talk.

The Welshman caught a stir in the far corner of the room – was there another entrance? – and he immediately turned to Fonthill. ''E's 'ere, bach sir.' He jerked his head.

Simon followed the direction of the nod and caught a glimpse of the familiar yellow uniform. De Sousa was talking to a couple of *inDunas*, standing firmly and with his right hand nonchalantly tucked into his unbuttoned jacket, Napoleon style. No sling was evident. Fonthill grinned. 'He's not prepared to show us that he's been wounded,' he said. 'Well, well, well. I must go across and pay my respects and ... ah ... offer him the hand of friendship.'

He strode across and interrupted the conversation. 'Ah, Mr de Sousa,' he said, 'how good to see you again. I hope you are well.' He extended his hand, but the Portuguese ignored it.

'Perfectly well, thank you.'

'Good. I had heard that you had suffered an injury while ah ... out hunting.'

'It was nothing. Just a slight mishap. The beast I was hunting, however, was wounded.' He gave

221

a faint smile, revealing a gold tooth. 'He will die the next time. I always get the animal I am pursuing. Always.'

'Quite so. Sentiments I echo. I am the same.' And with exaggerated jocularity, he slapped de Sousa on the shoulder – the injured shoulder, of course – causing the Portuguese to wince and turn away in half-disguised agony. 'Oh goodness,' exclaimed Fonthill. 'Was that your bad shoulder? I am so sorry.'

Further exchanges, however, were prevented by the arrival of the king, who entered accompanied by his chief wife, a lady of proportions very similar to those of Nini but who carried herself with far less confidence than the princess. The king was dressed in his best European apparel, the billycock hat tilted at an audacious angle and his round face wreathed in a grin that indicated, perhaps, that Alice's new pills and potions, together with the morphine, were promising a pain-free evening.

Lobengula raised his fly whisk, which for social events seemed to have replaced his short assegai, and acknowledged his guests by pointing it to them all as he turned. Then he shouted an order, and everyone scuttled to take their places on the benches as more beer on wooden trays was brought in by the young girls. Significant gaps were left on either side of Lobengula's chair, and the *inDuna* who had greeted Fonthill on arrival now hurried over to indicate that Alice should sit on the King's right, with Fairbairn, rather surprisingly, at her side, and Simon, flanked by Jenkins, next to the trader. Disconcertingly, de

Sousa was placed on the king's left, with the chief wife on his other side.

Alice leaned across to the Scotsman. 'We seem to be honoured, Mr Fairbairn,' she said.

The trader gave a wry smile. 'Oh, you may be, ma'am, but I'm just here to interpret, y'see.'

Alice gave him her best smile. 'Well I am jolly glad that you are here, whatever your role.'

The king clapped his hands, and immediately great wooden platters were borne in containing mounds of beef, which steamed as they were placed on rough stools in front of all the guests. Alice sighed, as she could see no sign of vegetables or bread, but could not resist a smile when piles of berries were placed ostentatiously in front of herself and the king. Lobengula caught her eye and winked. She was, it seemed, forgiven for her intrusion of a few hours ago – at least for the moment.

The monarch leaned forward and grabbed a choice piece of meat, and fastidiously picking off the gristle, which he threw over his shoulder, he handed it to Alice. She nodded her acceptance and took it. It was the signal for everyone on the benches to bend to the task of selecting beef from the platters and begin wolfing down the prime cuts. Immediately a hum of conversation rose, and Alice could not but smile at the resemblance to a sophisticated dinner party in London, where the guests would wait for the host to begin before raising knife and fork and embarking on the tedious business of engaging in conversation with the person to left or right. The setting, though, could not have been more different. She looked around her with interest. The fire in the middle of the hut had been built up again, alas, and the flames cast a flickering glow across the half-naked figures that constituted most of the ring, their black skin glistening and the firelight reflected in the copper accoutrements of the women. White teeth and protuberant eyeballs shone in the half-light, and the murmur of conversation was low and guttural. There was no glitter of silver, no sparkle of diamonds, and the hum of voices certainly did not tinkle.

She could not resist grinning at the king. He leaned forward and spoke, his black eyes gleaming. 'The king says, eat your berries,' translated Fairbairn. 'Now what's that about?'

Alice nodded. 'A private joke,' she said. 'Tell me, Mr Fairbairn, why is that man,' she gave an almost imperceptible nod of the head, 'sitting next to the king?'

'Aye, the snake man. Well, Lobengula seems to like him, or to respect him at least. He knows that the Portuguese to the east have vast territories and wants to keep in with them. Gouela appears to have quite a personal bodyguard living here in the capital, and the king believes that the man is well regarded in Lisbon, which he ain't, ma'am, he's only an agent. But I shouldn't worry too much about all that. Lobengula has sat him there just to balance things a bit with your husband – to let him know that even though he has brought a box or two of lollipops from Kimberley, it doesn't mean that Rhodes can just walk into the place.'

'Ah, so you know about the cargo we have brought.'

Fairbairn nodded his head as he munched. 'Oh yes. Everybody does.'

Simon leaned across his wife to address the trader. 'Would you ask the king if I can call and see him tomorrow, please? I have some keys I must hand over to him and other things to discuss.'

The king nodded equably. 'Come before sun is highest.'

The evening meandered its way to a conclusion, with the pyramids of beef disappearing under the attacks from the ravenous guests. Nothing more was served – it seemed that the berries were only a gesture towards Alice – except flagon after flagon of beer. Fonthill was glad that Jenkins was sitting beside him, and the Welshman behaved impeccably, even talking endlessly to the friendly *inDuna* on his right, who had not the slightest idea what was being said, but kept nodding amiably.

'Well,' asked Alice, as the three wandered back to their hut, 'what was all that about?'

'Fairbairn seemed to think,' said Fonthill, 'that although the king pretends to be uninterested in the guns, ammunition and gold, he is pleased that Rhodes has kept his side of the bargain. He says that the Portuguese talk and promise a lot, but nothing happens. Now the British have shown that they keep their word...'

'Even though we've only brought five hundred rifles?'

'Well, he doesn't know that yet, and, anyway, that's still a hell of a lot of firearms. He could frighten even the Boers with them.'

'And the British, eh?' Jenkins chimed in.

'No. We are not looking for confrontation.'

225

Alice gave a cynical smile. 'We will just have to wait and see about that, my dear.'

The next morning Fonthill removed a parchment document from its oilskin covering and spread it out on his sleeping mat. He had had it prepared in Cape Town and it looked impressive enough, with Cecil John Rhodes's signature at the bottom, beside the chartered company's crest, and leaving space for Lobengula's mark and his great elephant seal.

'What's it say?' asked Jenkins.

'Oh, the content is simple enough. It states that the king has given permission for surveyors and engineers from the company to enter the king's domain and to build a road through Mashonaland to the north and prospect for minerals there.'

Alice sniffed. 'Does it say anything about settling the land?'

'No. That is not the purpose of the expedition.'

'I don't believe that. Anyway, I thought Lobengula had already signed a similar document.'

'Yes, but the point of this is that now that the king has received his guns and cash, he will permit the column to enter his land *now*. There was only a rather vague reference to the future in the original treaty. Rhodes wants it all watertight before he invokes the great expense of getting his column together and moving north.'

'Well, good luck.'

Fonthill took the precaution of asking Fairbairn to accompany him this time to act as interpreter, instead of Mzingeli. It would be sensible, he reasoned, to have another European present as witness.

The king welcomed them both with the inevitable beer, and accepted imperturbably the keys that Fonthill presented to him. He continued to give the impression that the cargo was of no importance to him. Then, with great care, Simon began the task of gaining the king's acceptance of the need for a column to enter his country imminently to begin the road-building work.

'Why we need this road?' asked the king.

'Because, your majesty, it is impossible to bring in the equipment needed to mine without having a road through to the north. There is a well-defined trail through Bechuanaland to your border, as you know, but not through Matabeleland.'

'Humph. How many men come?'

'I do not know, but it is likely to be several hundred.'

'Sounds like an impi.'

'No, sir. They will be pioneers, not soldiers.'

'I give permission already for Rhodes to mine. Why I have to sign new paper?'

'This will be more specific, giving him permission to enter your country very soon – as soon as he can form his column, that is.'

'My *inDunas* don't like me signing all this paper.'

'It is merely confirming your word, your majesty. It is normal in dealings between European countries. There is nothing sinister in it.'

Lobengula looked around anxiously, as though looking for some escape. But there was no one else present. Eventually he clapped his hands to summon one of his wives and then gave orders to

have his seal prepared. His face, however, remained heavy.

'I sign,' he said, 'because I trust you. You are
English gentleman and know the Queen of
England. I take your word I am not giving away
my country.'

Fonthill writhed internally. He could not take
responsibility for something over which he had
no control. Yet he could not be seen to dissemble.
That would throw even more doubt into Lobengula's mind. He cleared his throat. 'Your majesty,
there is nothing in this paper that gives away your
country, I promise. You are only allowing these
people in to build a road to the north and then
start mining.'

The king grunted but still looked unhappy. A
silence fell on the room, which was broken by an
inDuna bringing in a blob of still smoking wax,
together with the great seal, fashioned from
ivory. A quill and a small pot of ink was also
produced.

Lobengula ignored them for a moment, and
then directed his gaze at Fonthill. He did not
speak, but looking into the man's black eyes,
Simon could see a bewilderment, an uncertainty
– even a touch of fear – that plucked at his own
heart. It was like confronting a caged animal, a
beast that had great power and was used to
striking fear into everyone with whom it came
into contact, but which realised that it was now
confronted by something intangibly more powerful. Lobengula had the innate intelligence that
sent warning signals to his brain, yet he did not
know how to evade this all-pervading pressure.

His look now to Fonthill was almost an appeal. Then he shook his head and very slowly reached for the pen.

'Just there, sir,' said Fonthill, pointing to the space left for the king's mark. He felt like a crooked solicitor, forging a will.

Lobengula scratched his mark and then, sighing, reached for the wax. He scooped a little out with a broad finger, spread it on the paper alongside his cross, and then firmly impressed his seal on to the still warm wax, with a finality that seemed to express relief. The deed was done.

'Thank you, sir,' said Simon, sharing the relief. 'I will see that this is taken directly to Cape Town.' He looked up at the king. 'As this is an important document and,' he coughed, 'I believe there are people near here who would wish to see that it is not delivered, may I ask your majesty if he would provide a guard to see that, at least, it gets to the border safely?'

The king waved a hand airily. 'You shall have fifty warriors,' he said. 'They shall leave to-morrow.'

Fonthill inclined his head. 'The king is most kind.'

Lobengula nodded. 'I am told you want to go to the east. Why?'

'Ah yes, sir. Mr Rhodes is anxious that once the road to the north is established, some way is found to make a passage to the Indian Ocean, so that a supply route is set up and it will be easier to trade with Matabeleland and Mashonaland by sea from the south. He has asked me to explore to examine the possibilities. I intend to begin this journey as soon as I am equipped, with, I hope, the help of Mr Fairbairn here.'

'You go so quick?'

'I fear so, sir.'

'You take your wife with you? It is dangerous country that way.'

Fonthill gave a rueful smile. 'As I think you ... er ... know, sir, she is a strong woman. She insists on accompanying me, and I must confess, I will find her support and company on this difficult expedition of great value.'

'Umph. Matabele men don't take women with them when they go to war.'

'Well, I am not exactly going to war. I hope that I shall not encounter violence where I go.'

A grin came over the king's face. 'You will. The tribes that way are fighting people, not...' his lip curled, 'like the Bechuanas the other way.'

There seemed little more to be said, so Fonthill inclined his head. Then he rose. 'If the king will excuse me, there is much to be done.'

Lobengula dismissed them both with a wave of his hand, and they left him disconsolately picking shreds of wax from the bottom of his ivory seal.

Once outside, Fonthill let out a sigh of relief. He rolled the parchment up and tied it firmly with a red ribbon. 'I'm glad that's over,' he confided to Fairbairn. 'I was never sure that he would sign it.'

'Come back to the shop and have a dram,' said the Scotsman. 'In celebration if you like – and you'd better tell me about this expedition of yours and how I can help.'

'Thank you, I could do with a whisky. Yes, I

shall need your help with provisions, and rather more than that, I fear.'

The two trudged up the hill towards the trading post. 'It sounds as though you will have to go through de Sousa's province,' said Fairbairn. 'You will walk into trouble there.'

'Not if I can avoid his land, or if I can leave him behind here. Slip away before he knows about my departure. I intend to travel light and fast, if I can.'

'Huh, that depends on the terrain. There is some pretty thick bush that way – and Gouela is not the only one you have to worry about. This is slavers' country.'

'What, this far south? I thought they did not come further down than the Sudan.'

'Good lord, no. The Arabs are all over central Africa, including the Congo. They stop short at Mashonaland, though. The Matabele would be too much of a handful for them. But they are a fierce lot. They employ mercenary tribesmen who can fight, and they have their raiding down to a fine art. It doesn't do to tangle with them. They raid down to the east here, next to Portuguese East Africa and Matabeleland, although there is no precise border – just a jumble of small tribes – ideal hunting ground for them, of course.'

They reached the store and ducked under the low lintel of its doorway. 'Here, sit down,' said Fairbairn. 'I'll bring us a wee dram – on me. Take a look at this.'

Fonthill sank into a cane armchair that creaked with his weight and picked up the old map that

Fairbairn flung at him. He spread it out on his lap. It showed the east coast of southern Africa, accurately, as far as he could see, with the formidable block of Portuguese East Africa dominating the coastline north to south for about a thousand miles. No getting round that. The blue line of the Zambezi snaked its way down from the north, eventually curving to debouch into the Indian Ocean. But it was far too far to the north, perhaps some four hundred miles away from Bulawayo, to offer the convenience of a riverside road. And what good would a steamboat be for Lobengula at that distance? Fonthill had brought with him from the Cape a couple of maps that charted expertly the Indian Ocean coast but did little to help inland. Now this map shared the same fault. It too showed no distinct frontiers between Matabeleland/Mashonaland and its northern neighbour, a kind of no-man's-land round Lake Nyasa, nor to the west towards Portuguese Angola or the east and the huge Portuguese possessions along the coast. What was more disturbing, however, was that the map was virtually blank between Bulawayo and the nearest point to the Portuguese eastern territory: just a reference to 'swamp' and the brown shading of a mountain range. It was, without a doubt, a wilderness.

'Have you been out this way?' he enquired of Fairbairn.

'No fear,' said the Scotsman. 'No real reason to go, and wouldn't want to anyway. Not much more than tsetse fly, swamp, spears and slavers. I wouldn't recommend it to anyone.'

'Where is Gouela's territory exactly?'

'Exactly, I don't know. But I think you can expect it to be pretty much due east of here. Just in the Portuguese eastern territory, of course. Border country. The dagoes claim all the land west of there to be under their control, or "protection", of course. The British Government disputes this. But neither side seems really anxious to do much about it, though de Sousa huffs and puffs here.'

At that point a Matabele crept deferentially into the shop and bent to whisper in Fairbairn's ear.

The Scotsman nodded and looked up. 'You should know this,' he said to Fonthill. 'I've just heard that de Sousa decamped before daylight this morning. Gone, with his little army. The word is that he has returned to his territory. Just the way you are planning to go, I'm afraid, old chap.'

Chapter 10

Fonthill returned to his hut, the map and his signed agreement with Lobengula under his arm but his brain a-jumble with conflicting thoughts. He had to go east to explore the possibilities of finding a route to the sea, but that way would lead him right into Gouela's arms. To detour would obviously be sensible, but he had no idea of the precise location of de Sousa's province, the better to avoid it. Before leaving the Cape,

Rhodes had told him that he intended the road to continue the well-established trail through Bechuanaland, then, after crossing to the border, to skirt well to the east of Bulawayo – 'to keep out of trouble with the old boy' – and then curl north and east into Mashonaland proper. But where exactly? First, however, there was the task of getting the new agreement back to Rhodes and Alice's story back to the cable station.

Simon did his best to give answers to the many questions with which Alice plied him on his return, and was able at least to assure her that Ntini would be protected by an escort to the Transvaal border, beyond which the Portuguese would not dare to go, even if his leaving of the king's kraal did turn out to be a ruse.

Alice immediately set about writing a separate story – to follow on from the battle at the border – confirming Lobengula's agreement to the entry of the road-builders, and Fonthill began to sort out his requirements for the exploration to the east. He wanted at least five of the ten Kaffir boys with them as bearers on the new journey. Would they agree to come, leaving behind their newly acquired oxen and accepting instead the promise of good cash payments at the end of the journey? He would certainly need Joshua, who had proved himself to be a good right-hand man to Mzingeli.

He asked Mzingeli to pick out the five who had fought the best at the Tule kopjes and offer them £25 each to make the journey. The tracker advised mules, salted against the tsetse fly, as the best means of carrying their loads through the heavy bush, and undertook to see if there were any locally that could be bought to supplement his own animal. The wagons and the surplus oxen Fonthill decided to present as a gift to the king.

The tracker returned to say that he had been able to persuade only four of the Kaffirs to accompany them on the journey and had been forced to increase the payment offer to £30. Fonthill shrugged. There was no alternative and they would have to make do. The good news was that bright-eyed Joshua had been eager to come.

Alice completed her story early that afternoon, and Ntini was instructed to travel south with it together with the escort and the other boys, and then return to wait for them at Bulawayo.

Shortly after dawn, the fifty plumed and armed warriors reported for duty and they all set off: the oxen herded by the six boys, now returning home with the cattle as prizes, Ntini proudly astride his horse, carrying his precious documents – the signed agreement, Fonthill's telegram to Rhodes and Alice's long message in cable form – strapped behind him, and his escort walking, assegais and shields in hand, on either side of him.

That evening Alice, accompanied by Mzingeli, called on the king to treat his painful foot. She found him relaxed and, as ever, delighted to see her.

'You should not go with husband on stupid journey,' he said. 'Stay here until he come back. You safe here. We all look after you. Good food, no work, except to treat foot. Plenty beer...' he giggled, 'and a little champagne if you like – too much bad for you, you know.'

She smiled. 'You are very kind, sir, but where my husband goes, I go.'

'You got no children? I have many – too many.'

'Yes, but you have sixty-three wives. No, we have no children. Our only child died in childbirth. I was lucky to survive but we lost our son.'

'Yes, but you still young. Don't you try no more? Is husband no good on sleeping mat?'

The question was put without embarrassment, although Mzingeli hesitated to find words to reduce its coarseness. Alice looked away for a moment but realised it would be ridiculous to take offence. This was not genteel Norfolk.

'He is splendid there as elsewhere, your majesty. It is just that we have not been blessed. So we accept it now.'

'Ah.' The first sign of empathy crossed the king's broad features. 'King is sorry. Now, stick little spear into bottom. Pain not so bad today.'

'Have you been taking the medicine and pills?'

'Yes. As you say.'

'Then I think that is helping you as much as the morphine. Now, please roll over.'

That evening after dinner, as the firelight flickered outside their hut, Fonthill called on Mzingeli and Joshua to join Alice, Jenkins and himself in a whisky – heavily laced with water for Joshua – and a briefing on the journey ahead. The tracker, who had returned with the good news that he had procured five good mules, interpreted in a low voice for Joshua.

Simon spread out Fairbairn's map. 'This is the best chart I've got,' he said, 'but as you can see, it doesn't tell us much.' He took out a small ruler. 'I estimate that it's about two hundred miles as the crow flies between here and the Portuguese border. Firstly, we are not crows, and secondly, I understand that it is very rough ground indeed – swamp, heavy bush and mountains, or at least very big and awkward hills. That is why we are not taking oxen or wagons. Count the distance, in fact, as the equivalent of four hundred miles on easy going.'

No one spoke, and in the near distance two dogs howled their frustration. Simon continued. 'However, I don't wish to go out on a route directly to the east. Again, there are two reasons for that. Firstly, old Gouela's territory lies that way, and although he would love to see us again, I wouldn't want to experience his welcome. The second reason is that the route to the ocean – if we find a way, that is – should link up with Rhodes's projected road coming up to Mashonaland from the south, and I think that that will terminate somewhere north or north-east of here.' He stabbed at the map with his ruler.

'So...?' asked Jenkins.

'So, we set out from here in a north-easterly direction, before turning to the right and making for the Mozambique border. If we get that far, our journey in fact will be much longer than two hundred miles anyway.'

Alice frowned. 'Why don't we go further north and use the Zambezi as a river road, so to speak?'

'Because Rhodes knows about the Zambezi. He is not convinced that it is the best way to the east. There could well be problems with the Portuguese at its mouth, on their territory, and there are other, navigational problems about using it as the main entry into Matabeleland. No. Rhodes wants a road. A proper land road.'

'Blimey!' exclaimed Jenkins. "E doesn't want us to build the bloody thing too, does 'e?'

Fonthill grinned. 'Well, if I had offered, no doubt he would have accepted the idea. But no. What he wants is to find a way that is roughly geographically suitable in the long term and politically acceptable in the short term.'

'I don't understand,' said Alice.

'He wants us to link up with the local tribes, once we are out of Lobengula's sphere of influence, and get them to sign treaties with his chartered company, which will offer them protection under the company's flag and be the first step in the road-building procedure.

'What Rhodes wants is a progression like the one he has achieved with Lobengula: a basic agreement, a payment of sorts and then a road-building programme that will lead inevitably to some sort of settlement – small at first but larger later. Maybe one that will not even take place properly until the twentieth century.'

A silence fell on the circle once more. It was broken by a question from Mzingeli. 'How long we away?'

Fonthill nodded at the question's relevance. 'I just don't know,' he said. 'Maybe six, maybe nine months. I can't be sure. It depends upon so many things, in particular the terrain and our welcome or otherwise from the tribes.'

Mzingeli translated quickly for Joshua.

'Is this all right for him?' asked Alice.

The tracker smiled his slow smile. 'He say he go where I go.'

'Oh, there's cosy then, isn't it,' said Jenkins. 'I'll come with you as well.'

'Now,' Fonthill pointed again at the map, 'it's a hell of a long way, but I have worked out what we need for provisions, and by the look of it, Fairbairn can provide virtually all we want, particularly native presents.' His face slipped into a frown. 'I am afraid that we must be prepared for anything, and the man has some old Sniders that should be all right for the boys to use if they have to, so I have bought them. Can you give them shooting lessons, 352?'

'Of course.'

The silence returned, to be broken, inevitably, by Jenkins. 'Do you think you could spare just a drop more?' he asked, holding out his empty mug. In fact, they all – except for Joshua – took one more drink before, deep in thought, they retired to sleep.

The next three days were spent in steady preparation for their journey. Thinking of the possible dangers, Fonthill ensured that every morning Jenkins took Joshua and the four Kaffir boys, together with their Sniders, away from the kraal to teach them target practice, speed reloading and rifle care. Their new skills could be vital in the weeks to come. As he watched, however, he became more concerned than ever about the perils that almost certainly lay ahead. So few riflemen against Gouela – and who else? He shrugged his shoulders. They were committed now and they must just prepare as best they could.

Alice continued her evening visits to the king. Concerned that rheumatism was affecting the royal joints, she added sweet spirits of nitre and quinine to Lobengula's daily dosage. She had also acquired a second patient. The cattle thief had made a good recovery and was now taking his place in looking after his family. Alice showed his wife how to change the dressing on his stump, left her a precious supply of bandage, padding and a little antiseptic, and recommended, through Mzingeli, that they leave Bulawayo to be away from the king.

On the eve of their own departure, she found Lobengula in a particularly melancholy mood as she completed his treatment.

'You don't go on this bad journey,' he said.

Alice, methodically packing away her bottles, shook her head and smiled. 'I must,' she said. 'I am not really a doctor, as you know, and I must accompany my husband.'

The king growled. 'I need you here. I am getting better. You help me. You stay. He not need you as I need you.'

'No, sir. I must go.'

'I pay you to stay. I give you cattle and little house. Wait here until Fonthill come back.'

Alice frowned. There was a note of angry anxiety in the king's tone, and a warning light flashed in her brain. She remembered only too clearly the blood gushing from the thief's forearm. The jocular, beaming monarch could change into a despot immediately he was crossed. She must be careful.

'Your majesty has sixty-three wives,' she said slowly, anxious that Mzingeli should translate every nuance. 'That means that you have much love and care. Because of our custom, my husband only has one wife. He needs me and I must be with him. Now, I do believe that your condition is improving and that your foot will recover if you take the medicine I leave with you and change your diet and drinking habits. The choice is yours.'

She allowed herself a smile after this homily. 'We expect to be away only about six months. Then I shall return to see how you have progressed. It will not seem long. But then, of course, I must return with my husband to our own homeland. The king will understand that, I know.'

But there was no answering smile from Lobengula. 'You go now,' he said shortly.

Bowing, Alice picked up her bag and left.

Outside, she mopped her brow. 'I think that the sooner we leave, the better,' she said to the tracker.

Mzingeli nodded. 'King is now ... what is word ... depending on you. That is bad. He has everything he want here. Now he want you.'

'Well he can't bloody well have me.' She tucked away a stray lock of blond hair. 'He is a petulant bully. He has to learn that he can't have everything he wants in this world. Good God – he's got sixty-three wives already. He mustn't be too greedy.' A sudden thought occurred to her. 'Mzingeli, I have never asked you. Do you have a wife or ... er ... perhaps more, at home?'

The tall man shook his head slowly. 'One wife,'

he said, 'but she die ten years ago.'

'Oh, I am sorry. Children?'

'Two. They die also.'

'Oh dear.' She felt a warm surge of affection for this quiet, resourceful man with whom they had already shared moments of great danger. She touched his arm. 'I think I know how you must feel.' They walked in silence for a moment. Then, 'Come on. If we are leaving tomorrow, we still have much to do.'

The next morning, the expedition was ready to leave and Fonthill, Alice and Mzingeli called on the king early to bid him goodbye. They found him clothed only in his waist circle of monkey skins, sitting on his cart under the great tree and in a surprisingly avuncular mood. Bowing, Simon asked him if he would accept the wagons and the remaining oxen as a parting present.

'Good,' said Lobengula. 'I add to my herd. You come back soon and we drink beer together.'

'How is the foot this morning, your majesty?' enquired Alice.

The king gave an airy wave. 'Ah, foot is nothing. I can live with bad foot.'

Alice and Simon exchanged glances. 'Then,' said Simon, 'I will bid the king goodbye and thank him for his hospitality and many courtesies.'

'Good travel. Go well. My heart is white for you.'

The couple nodded their heads low at this traditional, warm farewell and left the king's dwelling – perhaps for the last time.

They set out as the sun crested the hill above the kraal, sending their shadows stretching along the ground to their left as they headed to the northeast. Fonthill had decided reluctantly that the rough nature of the terrain ahead precluded the use of horses, and he left them behind in the care of Fairbairn. He and Mzingeli now strode ahead in the lead, followed by Alice and then Jenkins. Behind them came the five mules, heavily laden with their provisions and kept moving by the urgings of Joshua and the four Kaffir boys.

It was a fine, bright morning, but Fonthill felt no elation. To Mashonaland – but then where? To slavers, swamps and, somewhere, the Portuguese, de Sousa? He gulped, but set his jaw and lengthened his stride.

Chapter 11

Initially, Fonthill set off aiming for the range of high hills that sat on the horizon to the northeast of Bulawayo. These formed the watershed for a fistful of rivers flowing north into the Zambezi and also south into the Limpopo, but they looked formidable so he tacked to the north to avoid them and skirted around until on their fifth day they approached a singular mountain called, by some lone Englishman years before, Mount Hampden. Here he set course due east, and then they felt that they were in Mashonaland proper.

Now the country was indeed magnificent: league after league of rolling plain, a grassy vista

243

dotted with clumps of trees and bush, interspersed with the mighty baobab tree, whose pods, Alice had earlier established in Cape Town, contained liquid that was both thirst-quenching and fever-curing. The visibility was clear and the air was good, despite the heat.

The little party's demeanour had changed gradually as the journey had progressed. As Bulawayo, with its potential threat from de Sousa, the king and his impis, dropped well behind them and the country opened out, so their mood lightened. The few Mashonas they met were curious but diffident and clearly offered no threat. Game, if not exactly plentiful, was on offer and they feasted for two days on the meat from two impala that Jenkins shot.

They did not press hard, for in anticipation of hard times ahead, Fonthill was anxious to preserve their energies. So day followed pleasant day. 'If Rhodes wants to build his road this way,' Simon confided to his wife, 'then I can't see what there is to stop him. But more to the point, we could farm here, darling,' he added. 'Good soil, plenty of water from these little rivers and the grass looks sweet. What do you think?'

Alice tried to prevent a smile, but her husband's enthusiasm was infectious. 'Well,' she said, 'I have to agree that it all looks very fine, and the air is good, too. But settlements here would very much depend upon the king, surely. Building a road and making the odd excavation for gold or copper is one thing. Letting in people to farm is very much another.'

Fonthill reached across and seized his wife's

hand. 'Oh don't be such a grouch, darling. Old Lobengula would certainly let *you* in. One wave of your hypodermic thingummyjig and thousands of acres would be ours. But one thing is certain. There is no one else here farming the land or making the most of it. It's just lying gloriously fallow.'

And indeed it was. The local Mashonas lived in small, isolated villages and the few cattle they seemed to possess grazed in enclosed paddocks close to their wickerwork houses. Only wild game roamed the open plateau.

'Lions,' said Mzingeli quietly. But no one heard him.

As they pressed on to the east, however, the terrain became less hospitable. The land was now an ochre red, and as they dropped down from the plateau, the going became less hard underfoot. They had to cross more sprints and, importantly, the bush became thicker. For the first time, they decided to set up some form of protection for their camps overnight.

Mzingeli explained that, in addition to lions, this could be buffalo and elephant country, and showed them how to make a scarum for the camp. This involved cutting large boughs or stakes and driving them into the ground on the windward side to form a semicircle capable of containing the whole party, mules and all. Then small bushes were cut and interwoven into the boughs, making a hedge some nine feet high, capable of withstanding a large shock, on three sides of the encampment. At the open end, wood was stacked and fires lit at night. They all slept out of doors, cutting grass to form a mattress with a blanket laid on top. Saddles or spare clothes were used as pillows.

Some four weeks after leaving Bulawayo, as they sat near their roaring fire, Fonthill consulted his compass and the map that Fairbairn had provided. 'I have no scale for this damned thing,' he confided to Alice, Jenkins and Mzingeli, 'but I reckon that we have left the Matabele kingdom now and are well out of Mashonaland. We should be somewhere in this area of small tribes and therefore not far from the border with Portuguese East Africa.'

'Strange that we have not seen any natives,' said Alice.

'They here,' murmured Mzingeli.

'What?' Jenkins looked perturbed. 'I 'aven't seen a damned thing.'

'No.' The tracker nodded to the bush pressing in on them all around. 'They watch us. I see. I think they frightened of us.'

'Why?'

'Perhaps they think we slavers.'

Fonthill frowned, mindful of Rhodes's injunction to befriend the tribes. 'Well I would like to make contact. Can you speak their language, do you think?'

'Not well, but I try if they come.'

'How can we make them come?'

The tracker shrugged his shoulders. If he had nothing to say, he rarely spoke.

'Right.' Fonthill stood. 'We will stay here all tomorrow. Tonight we will put a few of the trade goods just outside the opening. Let's see if that will induce them to come forward, although...' he looked around and wrinkled his nose, 'I don't think this is the best country for laying down a new road, I must say. But perhaps we can discover if the terrain is better elsewhere, if they will talk to us, that is.'

Before retiring to his blanket, Fonthill hung a few brightly coloured lengths of cotton fabric, two axes and some copper trinkets on the edge of their scarum.

The night was dark when something woke him. Immediately awake, he reached for his rifle and sat up. The fires at the edge of the scarum were still guttering and the low flame was reflected in the copper amulets hanging from the hedge. So they had not been taken. What, then, had woken him? He narrowed his eyes the better to see through the opening, and as he focused he made out several large grey shapes, as tall, it seemed, as the scarum, moving slowly, ponderously, past the opening.

'Elephant,' said Mzingeli from his blanket. 'Stay quiet. They don't harm us.'

By the morning, both the elephants and the trinkets had gone.

'Good,' said Fonthill. 'Joshua' – the boy had now picked up a serviceable knowledge of English – 'put some more of those things outside. Then we must just sit and wait.'

It was well past midday when Mzingeli nodded. 'They come now,' he said. 'Don't show rifles. They frightened if you do.'

Gradually, as they watched, three men emerged from the bush and stood tentatively just beyond

247

the ashes of the fire, at the opening of the scarum. Very slowly, Mzingeli rose and ambled towards them, his arm lifted in greeting. He spoke a few words but there was no reply, so he squatted on the camp side of the ashes and silently regarded the natives. After a while, they lowered themselves to the ground and sat cross-legged.

'Is it goin' to be a card game, then?' enquired Jenkins quietly of Fonthill.

'Shush. Let's leave it to Mzingeli.'

Simon looked at the natives. They were of far less impressive stature than the Matabeles, and seemed unwarlike, in that they were not painted and carried no weapons. They were naked except for loincloths of some animal skin, and their hair was plastered down with red earth. The middle of the three now spoke hesitantly to Mzingeli. The tracker responded, picking his words as though only partly understanding the language. Then he stood nonchalantly, handed down the trinkets and gave them to the three.

As a result, the conversation improved considerably, although it was clear that Mzingeli did not speak the language fluently. The tracker stood, walked back into the compound and, turning, beckoned the men to follow him. Reluctantly they did so until they stood facing Fonthill and Jenkins. Simon immediately made a gesture towards the ground and the three, followed by Mzingeli, squatted before him.

'There's cosy now, isn't it?' said the Welshman, grinning.

Jenkins's ability, proven in so many different countries and continents, to break through all kinds of linguistic barriers worked again, and his grin was immediately returned by the visitors, who revealed great yellow tombstone-like teeth.

'Who are they?' enquired Fonthill of Mzingeli. 'Can you communicate?'

'Yes, but not fluent. They Manica people, ruled by king called Umtasa. Their land goes up to Portuguese land. But Portuguese claim their land too. They heard of English and are glad we not Portuguese.'

'Good. How far away is their king?'

The tracker directed the question to the man sitting in the middle of the trio, who seemed to be senior. He had taken the gifts to himself and now sat with the cloth draped over his shoulders and the copper artefacts hanging around his neck. He replied at some length.

'He say that Umtasa is at kraal, say a day's march to east. He can take us to his village nearby and then come with us to Umtasa.'

'Good. Thank you, Mzingeli. Have Joshua offer them some food and we will make ready to go. I think we will leave Joshua, Alice and the boys here – they should be all right within the scarum – and the three of us will go to the king's kraal. It will be quicker that way.'

'Thank you very much, but I am not going to be left behind.' Alice had quietly approached. 'Simon, will you stop treating me as some kind of fragile supernumerary who is to be perpetually excluded from the more exciting parts of this expedition. Really, I am tired of it, my dear.'

Fonthill sighed. 'Very well, Alice. We will leave Joshua in charge. We will be away overnight so we

249

must go prepared. Quickly now. I would like to be there by nightfall.'

As soon as the visitors had eaten their rice and biltong, the party moved off, taking one mule, laden with presents, food and their bedding, with them. The bush was now very thick and the going soft underfoot, deteriorating now and then to semi-swamp. Mosquitoes were accompanying them step by sodden step, and Alice was glad that she had brought quinine with her. To them all the unspoken thought occurred: this is no place for road-building.

They reached the village after a four-hour trudge. It was a poor affair, just a few huts set in a small clearing by a stream, but so hidden by thorn bushes and low trees that even invaders knowing the territory would have difficulty in finding it. It was clear that the man leading the trio was the local headman, and Fonthill prevailed upon him that they should not pause at the village but press on towards the king's kraal. He was retrospectively anxious that their scarum, containing most of their possessions, had been left so lightly defended, and wished to return to it as soon as possible.

They passed several other villages on the way to the Manican capital. The people were shy but friendly, not at all militant and more pastoral than the Matabele. They possessed few cattle – indeed the land did not encourage grazing – but they grew maize and grain where they could. It was clear that if they decided to come this way, Rhodes's engineers would have no trouble with the natives. The terrain and climate, however, could be another matter. It was hot, and the dreaded tsetse flies seemed to be as numerous as the mosquitoes. Fonthill kept a concerned eye on the mule, but, having been treated with salt, it seemed to be impervious to the insects.

It was nearly nightfall before they came to King Umtasa's kraal. It was set in clear land on a slight rise that took it away from the swamp and the worst of the mosquitoes and tsetses. It was not as large as Bulawayo, but was similar in shape and style, with thorn bushes providing a series of enclosures that led to the king's own house, a circular construction of wickerwork and red clay only slightly larger than those that surrounded it. The usual chorus of barking dogs and excited children ushered them into the heart of the town. Unlike in Bulawayo, however, the adult Manicans hung back.

The headman prostrated himself before a large man who appeared from the house, and taking their cue, Simon and his entourage bowed their heads before the king. The man was dressed inconspicuously in a loincloth of some animal skin and little else, except for a necklace of animal's teeth – lion's? – around his throat. His skin was very, very black and glistened in the reflection of the flames that danced from several fires lit outside the entrance to his house. Unusually, he affected a short white beard that contrasted strangely with the tight black curls of his hair. His frown on first seeing the Europeans disappeared as the headman, still prostrate, spoke.

'He say we not Portuguese,' murmured Mzingeli. 'That good.'

251

The king grunted to the headman, who rose to his feet, and raised his forearm, the palm of his hand facing Fonthill, in greeting.

'Please tell him,' said Simon, 'that we bring greetings from the Queen of England and from her representative in Africa, Mr Cecil Rhodes.'

'Huh,' grunted Alice. 'That's a bit much.'

Ignoring her, Fonthill continued. 'We come to offer a treaty of friendship between the British and the Manican people. We would like to present some small gifts as a token of our goodwill. Jenkins, please...'

The Welshman turned back to the mule, whose load he had begun unfastening on their way through the township. From the packs he produced lengths of cloth, several knives and axes, more of the copper decorations, two small hand mirrors, and – to gasps from the spectators who had now gathered near – two Snider rifles. He laid the gifts at the king's feet, gave a cheery nod and said, 'Merry Christmas, your worship.'

The king immediately picked up a rifle, weighed it in his hand, sighted along the barrel and spoke to Mzingeli.

'He say good, but no good without bullets.'

''E's no fool,' breathed Jenkins, who turned back to the packs and produced three small boxes of cartridges and laid them on the ground with the other gifts.

The king nodded and spoke again, flashing a sly glance at Alice. 'He say we are welcome. We come a long way, so stay with him to recover from journey. Lady particularly welcome. He not seen white lady before. Eat with him tonight.

Take beer now.'

A signal was given, mats were brought for them to sit on, and after a slight delay, the inevitable gourds of beer were produced by smiling women. Fonthill noticed that the gifts were left lying on the ground, as though they were of no importance, although everyone was eyeing them. He liked that. It showed good manners.

They were given one hut for them all to share, and then joined the king and some of his *inDunas* – no wives – at a meal around the fires. Seated on logs, they ate meat that had a strangely fishy taste and which was served with mealies. On asking, Simon was told that it was crocodile. He decided to keep the news from Jenkins, who was conversing merrily but one-sidedly with an *inDuna*. Jenkins did not like crocodiles.

Through Mzingeli, whose proficiency in the language seemed to have improved considerably, he asked the king about the nature of the terrain throughout his kingdom. Did the semi-swampland continue to the north and south?

The king shook his head. 'Better land to the north. Firmer. Take wagons easily. That is best way to Mashonaland. But further. He take you there tomorrow.'

'Thank you. We must return to our camp first, but with the king's permission, we will return immediately with our mules and people to look at that land.'

'King want to know why you interested.'

Fonthill cleared his throat and felt Alice's gaze on him. 'If the king is prepared to sign a treaty of friendship with the Queen's company in South

Africa, then one day it could be that a road will be built – with his permission, of course – through his country to link Mashonaland with the Indian Ocean.'

'That Portuguese territory.'

'Yes. An agreement would also need to be reached between the Queen of England and the King of Portugal.'

'You know the Portuguese?'

'Er ... yes. I have met one of their agents.'

'They say that they own my country. They do not. Would your Queen give me protection from Portuguese?'

'If you reject the Portuguese claim to your land and sign a treaty with the South African charter company, which has powers under the British Government, then this can be done.'

'Are you sure, Simon?' The question came very quietly from Alice, but he was forced to ignore it because the king was speaking.

'He say that he will sign it but he will need more guns.'

'I will pass on his request to Mr Rhodes in the Cape, who is the chief of the company.'

'Then he sign.'

'Good. I have a copy of the treaty back at my camp and I will bring it to him for his signature tomorrow.'

The evening ended early, for Simon was anxious to set off back to the camp at dawn the next day. Predictably, before turning in, Alice raised the question of the treaty.

'Have you really brought a proper document with you?'

'Yes, of course. In fact I brought three with me from Cape Town, duly signed by Rhodes. We didn't know the tribes then, of course, because we didn't know whom we would meet, but all I have to do is fill in their names and those of the kings and get them to sign.'

She screwed up her features. 'Gracious, this all sounds so ... tawdry. And what on earth could Rhodes – let alone the British Government – do if the Portuguese came here and started to throw their weight around? Think of Gouela. A bit of paper isn't going to stop him.'

'One thing at a time, Alice. The process has to be started somewhere, and it starts with this bit of paper, as you call it. Once the charter company is established in Matabeleland – and that means the road – then Rhodes can extend his protection to outlying provinces like this.'

Alice sniffed but said nothing more.

The next morning they set off back to their scarum even before the king had risen, although the village headman and his two villages kept their promise to accompany them. As always, the return journey seemed quicker than the outgoing one, and it felt like only a couple of hours before they reached, and passed through, the village, dropping off the natives there. In the early evening they caught sight of the tall tips of the scarum fence. Everything seemed quiet and peaceful as they approached. Perhaps too quiet.

'Joshua should have been keeping a lookout,' said Fonthill testily. Then he held up a hand to restrain the party. 'Wait,' he said.

From the fringe of the bush cover they studied

the makeshift stockade. Nothing could be seen through the opening and no sound came from within it. Their mule brayed, but no answering call came from the animals that should have been inside. Fonthill withdrew his rifle from its saddle holster and slipped off the safety catch. He signed for the others to do the same. Then, cautiously, they began to advance, only to be halted by Mzingeli's hand on Simon's arm.

The tracker nodded to marks on the floor of the clearing. 'Big party been here,' he mouthed.

'Damn! Do you think there are any still inside?'

'Think no. They move out. See spoor.' He pointed to where the marks went off through the bush to the south. Now the trail was there for all to see: broken branches and scuffed earth, winding away.

'Inside, quickly,' cried Fonthill and they moved into the scarum, their rifles at the ready. It was, however, a ghost camp. There was little sign of a struggle, except that their packs had been slashed away from the mules and left, unopened, on the ground. Of Joshua, the boys and the mules there was no trace.

'They couldn't have deserted and gone back to Bulawayo, surely?' asked Alice.

'No.' Mzingeli pointed to the ground to their left, by the exit from the scarum. 'Look. Blood.'

The stains were splattered in a strange, uneven sequence that led off into the bush. Everyone looked at the tracker in horror. He glanced up, his face expressionless as usual. 'Slavers,' he said. 'They whip.'

'Oh dear God,' murmured Alice. 'The boys.

They've taken the boys.'

'How long ago, Mzingeli?' asked Fonthill.

The tracker kneeled down and rubbed his finger in the marks. Then he walked to the broken foliage and examined it, fingering the broken twigs and branches with his thumb. 'Maybe five hours ago. Maybe six.'

'Blimey.' Jenkins spat on to the ground. 'They'll be miles away by now.'

'Not necessarily.' Fonthill joined the tracker. 'How many were there, do you think, and could they move fast in this bush?'

Mzingeli squatted and examined the tracks carefully. Eventually he looked up. 'They have captured slaves with them, walking in chains like this.' He gestured with his fingers to show a single file. 'Gun has been fired here. See marks of powder. Old gun. Like Arabs use.' Simon's brain immediately conjured up the picture of an old musket or *jezhail* that he remembered the Pathans using in the North-West Frontier of India – and he winced as he recalled a butt smashing into his nose.

But Mzingeli was continuing. 'No one killed. See, here they kneel to have chains fitted. Blood only from whip marks. Whips used to make them move.'

'Yes, but how many?'

The tracker shrugged. 'Cannot say. Cannot tell difference between slaves and slavers. Say thirty or forty. But party on foot – no hoof marks except our mules at end of train. They many people for this bush and mules slow them. They don't move quick.'

Fonthill drew in his breath and looked around

carefully. 'Strange, they have left our packs. Why?'

Mzingeli shrugged again. 'They don't want to carry. They would like to move quick, though they don't.' He looked up at Fonthill, his face showing concern for the first time. 'Good spoor,' he said. 'We follow, yes? Get our boys back?'

'Of course. But we must be careful. There are only four of us, and they are used to fighting.'

'So are we, bach sir.' Jenkins spoke quietly and looked around, his gaze lingering on Alice as he added, 'All of us.'

Alice smiled, although it did not hide her anxiety. 'Couldn't we get help from the village?' she asked.

'No.' Fonthill was emphatic. 'That would slow us down, and even if some of them came, they would be useless. They are not fighters.'

'No,' agreed Mzingeli. 'They all frightened of slavers.'

'Then we will go as quickly as we can,' said Simon. 'Alice, please check on our rations and see if we need to supplement them from those packs over there ... and,' he forced a grin, 'before you plead to be left behind, let me tell you now that you are very much part of this party. We need someone who can shoot.'

'Yes,' grunted Jenkins, 'that will make two of us.'

'Don't be insubordinate. Check the ammunition, 352, and fill up the water bottles. Mzingeli, hide the packs. We leave in five minutes.'

They set off in less time than that, in single file, with Mzingeli treading softly some way ahead, followed by Fonthill, then Alice and Jenkins bringing up the rear. Surprisingly, they had found two of the boys' Sniders, buried under their blankets in a corner of the scarum. They took them, one each slung over the shoulders of Simon and Jenkins, to supplement their firepower.

As they walked, Fonthill's brain was busy. Once they caught up with the slavers, they would be heavily outnumbered. Mzingeli had estimated that as slaving parties went, this one was comparatively small, made up of perhaps only five Arabs, armed with their *jezhails*, plus maybe twenty warriors, carrying spears and whips. They were not accustomed to opposition, for they inspired terror from the natives wherever they went and deliberately did not plunder nations of warriors, like the Matabele. Nevertheless, they moved stealthily and fell upon a village before their presence was detected. They did not take all the villagers, for this would denude them of further pickings, only selecting the healthiest men and women. Joshua and the four boys, big and strong, would have been a welcome bonus. Fonthill's jaw tightened. A small party – but still big enough! How to tackle it?

The trail was, indeed, easy to follow. Even though the slaves were walking in single file, the column had pushed its way through the bush heedlessly, leaving broken stems and torn foliage. Footprints were easy to see, even in the fading light, and the mules, of course, had left their droppings.

'Don't they care about being followed?' Fonthill asked Mzingeli.

'They don't care. People don't follow them. Everyone afraid of slavers.'

'Good. We shall be the exception.'

The four were striding quickly, and they stopped only once, for just five minutes, to drink water and eat biltong and berries. Fonthill had not worked out his tactics, for they would depend upon the deposition of the slavers, but he was sure enough of his strategy. They would reach the slavers' camp before dawn and attack at once, using surprise and the cover of darkness to reduce their enemy's advantage in numbers.

Accordingly, after four hours, he sent Mzingeli much further ahead to ensure that they would not all blunder on the camp itself or a rearguard. The prizes at stake – and the danger involved – were too high to make a stupid mistake. Slave traders struck terror into the hearts of those upon whom they preyed, not just because of the disgusting nature of their predations, but because they could fight. They could defend themselves. Care was needed.

The forest – for that was what the bush had become – was thick and the trail was becoming difficult to follow when Mzingeli could be seen approaching, running softly and weaving his way between the trees.

'They about five minutes' walk ahead,' he said. 'They make camp. Built fires.'

'Good. Take me there now. You two stay here. I won't be long.'

The slavers had made their bivouac for the night in a little clearing, near a stream, and Fonthill followed Mzingeli, treading softly as they approached the edge of the bushes and trees. The Arabs had made no attempt to build a scarum, and seemed confident that an irregular ring of fires, now burning low, would keep out predators. Two small 'Crusader' tents had been erected, presumably to give the Arabs comfortable night quarters, and two spearmen, huddled in blankets, had squatted at either side of the circle and appeared to be dozing. Inside it, the slaves lay in an irregular line.

It was they who caught the eye, presenting a sight of such misery that Simon felt a lump rise in his throat. There were perhaps thirty of them, men and women, linked together in single file by straight wooden yokes, the Y-shaped end of which encircled the throats and was closed at the back of the neck by chains. Their ankles were shackled, and links of chain attached them to the person behind. The chains and the yokes prevented them from finding comfortable postures for sleep, and they half sat, half sprawled. Bowls at their side, however, showed that at least they had been given food.

'Can you see our boys?' hissed Fonthill.

Mzingeli indicated with a nod of his head. There, at the end of the line, were Joshua and the four bearers, all stripped naked like the rest. Joshua's back carried four whip marks, from which the blood still oozed.

Suddenly, some of the women in the line began singing softly. It was a song the like of which Fonthill had never heard before. It was clearly a lament, a slow ululation that bespoke desperation and the realisation of a great, consuming sadness.

Tears were in every syllable, and as others joined in, the melancholy rose and settled above the little clearing like a thundercloud.

Then an Arab, a trim figure with a pointed beard, emerged from one of the tents, shrugging on his white burnous. He barked a command, and from out of the shadows appeared a huge, very black man – probably a Nubian from the Sudan, speculated Fonthill – wielding a long whip of buffalo hide. Immediately the whip cracked and hissed through the air, singling out the women and lashing their backs and bowed heads. The song died and silence of a sort descended on the clearing. Fonthill winced. His mind flashed back for a moment to a whipping post in Omdurman and the beat of a drum.

'If we can't kill 'em all, I know which ones we *will* kill,' he whispered. 'Now, Mzingeli. Please go and bring the others up. No. Wait a second. Am I right that the wind is coming this way,' he gestured, 'from the north?'

The tracker twisted his face to catch the breeze, and then nodded. 'Not much, though.'

'Good. Go now.'

As the tracker glided away, Fonthill began to move with great care around the edge of the camp, to the south. One rash move now could lead to disaster and upset his plans. He found the spot he was looking for, fringed on the camp side with bushes and low trees, but behind this foliage was another small clearing, its edges strewn with dead wood and dry grass. He hurried back, treading carefully. All was quiet in the camp now that the women had been silenced. Only a distant growl and then a bark showed that they were not alone in the forest.

A rustle presaged the appearance of Jenkins, Alice and Mzingeli out of the darkness. They gathered around Fonthill.

'Right,' he whispered, 'the plan is simple. We will take up various vantage points around the camp under cover but close enough to open fire when I give the signal. Alice and I will stay here; 352, you will go directly opposite us on the other side; Mzingeli, you go down ahead there to the south. You will find a little clearing behind a fringe of bush. Once there, I want you to gather some brushwood – dry tinder wood, to make sure that it will burn. There is plenty about. I want it to be big enough to frighten the camp but not big enough to set the whole damned forest ablaze. The wind is coming from the north, so if the blaze does spread, it will go away from us and the camp. But I hope that in the panic, none of these bastards will realise that.' He pressed a box of matches into the tracker's hand.

'When do I light?'

'Once you are in position, give us a good ten minutes – 352 has the furthest to go – and then light it.'

'Then what do we do, bach sir?' Jenkins's eyes were glowing in the semi-darkness.

'Wait until I fire from this side. I will take out the two guards.' He turned to Alice. 'I am sorry, but this will be cold-blooded killing,' he said. 'We must take advantage of surprise. If we don't kill quickly, they could overwhelm us. But I shall quite understand if you do not wish to fire.'

Alice's face showed white. 'I will do whatever you want me to do,' she said. 'I quite understand the need. These men are depraved.'

'Very well. Now, 352, as our best shot, you will have the key role. Here, take one of the Sniders as well as your rifle. The blaze will raise the alarm, of course, and then my shots. There are Arabs sleeping in those tents there, I don't know how many. The openings are on your side. They will turn out, of course, when the alarm is given. Kill them – or as many as you can. Mzingeli, you shoot as many of the natives as possible, but of course avoid the slaves, as we will on this side.'

He looked at them in turn. 'I am banking on the fact that the fire will cause initial alarm; then, when the shooting sets in from different sections of the forest, panic should ensue. Key to this, of course, is the killing of the Arabs. I want the natives to be leaderless. I will try and pick off any that you miss...'

'I'll not miss, bach sir.'

'Of course you won't. If you are attacked, duck and run and try and make it back to Alice and me here. Understood? Any questions?'

Alice cleared her throat. 'Where are the mules?'

'Good point. I have to confess that I don't know. Did you see them, Mzingeli?'

'No.'

'I suppose they will be somewhere in the compound. If they get excited, they might break their tethers and run about; that should help us. Cause a bit of panic. Just be sure we don't kill any of them. We will need 'em. Anything else? Good. Now go to your posts, and good luck.'

Jenkins and the tracker slipped away. Fonthill looked at his wife anxiously. 'Would you rather use this Snider instead of your own rifle?'

'No thank you. I am happier with this. It may not kill but it will cause a nasty wound. The Snider is too heavy for me.'

'Very well. Alice, let me take the guards, then you shoot at the Kaffirs who are nearest as they rush out. Is that all right?'

She nodded. She seemed completely calm, yet Fonthill knew that within she would be apprehensive at the prospect of having to kill. Oh, she had shot men before, but not like this, in cold blood. Nevertheless, he wished he had her composure. He licked his lips. The waiting was the worst part. He raised his Martini-Henry and sighted it on the guard furthest away. Then he realised that the muzzle was beginning to sway and he lowered it. Mustn't get tired. He frowned and wished – not for the first time – that he was a better shot.

Then, at last, about a hundred and fifty yards away down the trail, a thin flicker of light appeared in the bush. It danced tantalisingly in the darkness for a moment and almost went out, then it took hold, and suddenly that area of the forest was illuminated as a sheet of flame licked upwards.

Fonthill waited for a moment, and then, slowly, he raised his rifle. 'Now,' he muttered, and squeezed the trigger. The bullet took the sleeping warrior fully in the chest, and he sighed and then toppled over. Quickly Simon jerked down the extractor handle behind the trigger guard, inserted another round into the breech and aimed again. Almost inevitably, he missed the second guard as the man rose to his feet quickly, too quickly.

'Damn!' he cursed under his breath. Then Alice's Westley Richards barked at his right elbow, and the man staggered and fell. 'Good girl,' said Fonthill as he inserted a third cartridge and fired it into the figure of the guard, who, wounded, was now trying to totter to his feet. The man went down again immediately.

The sleeping camp suddenly became a scene of hectic activity. The Kaffirs appeared as if from nowhere – in reality, from their sleeping mats on the far side of the camp – and stood waving their spears and pointing, first to the fire and then to where Fonthill and Alice were now shooting at them systematically. To their shouts were now added screams as two, three and then four of them fell to the ground, clutching at gunshot wounds that sent blood gushing from between their fingers. The confusion was heightened as Mzingeli's rifle opened fire from the south.

'Why doesn't Jenkins fire?' hissed Fonthill.

'He's probably waiting to get a shot at the Arabs but the Kaffirs are in the way,' muttered Alice as she methodically loaded and fired, loaded and fired.

This seemed to be proven as two of the white-robed Muslims now came running into view from the side of their tents, bent low and carrying their *jezhails*.

'They're coming towards us,' cried Alice.

'Pick 'em off before they get near enough to use their muskets.'

Fonthill pulled his trigger, but the bullet only spurted dust from in front of the feet of the nearest Arab, who immediately knelt, levelled his *jezhail* and fired. The ball took Alice in the thigh, and she gasped, dropped her rifle and fell to the ground, clutching at the wound. Simon, quickly reloading, had time only to glance down and then fire at the first slaver, who was almost upon him. The bullet took the man in the chest, and he sprawled forward on to his face, his momentum taking him skidding along the ground until he lay still.

Fonthill knelt down quickly at Alice's side. The action, almost certainly saved his life, for a second musket ball sang over his head and buried itself into the trunk of the tree above him.

'Behind you,' hissed Alice, her face contorted with pain. Fonthill just had time to turn and avoid the butt of a musket as the second Arab swung it at his head. The momentum took the man around, and Simon clenched his right fist and hit him hard in the ribs, following it with a left hook to the face. But his half-kneeling posture meant that he could get no power into either blow, and the folds of the man's unravelled turban softened much of the impact of the punch to the head. He staggered back, regained his balance and swung the *jezhail* again. Fonthill ducked under it but caught his foot on a tree root and sprawled forward, rolling on to his side to avoid the butt of the musket, which thudded into the earth beside his temple. He grabbed the stock to help him regain his feet, and for a matter of seconds he and the Arab fought for possession of the gun. The

Muslim was taller than Fonthill, but he was also older, and years of being indulged by slaves had done nothing to toughen his body, whereas the last few months of trekking had left Simon with not an ounce of superfluous fat on his frame. He pulled the Arab towards him, then hooked his leg around that of the other man and pushed hard. The Arab twisted and then sprawled backwards on to the ground. Fonthill picked up the musket and brought it down on the slaver's head. This time the unwound turban did nothing to protect him, and his skull cracked with a sickening sound.

'Simon...'

Fonthill whirled and threw the *jezhail* at a native who, spear upraised, came at him from out of the forest. Then in one quick movement he bent, picked up the Snider, cocked it and fired from the hip at the native, who collapsed with a bullet in his stomach. Gasping, he picked up his Martini-Henry and looked about him quickly before crawling to Alice's side.

'Where are you hit, my love?'

'In the leg.' Perspiration was pouring down her face as she held out her hand. 'Help me up. It's only a flesh wound, but the rest of them will be on us in a moment. I must be standing.'

'Yes, but can you?'

'I can. Let me lean on this tree. Reload, for goodness' sake, Simon. They know where we are.'

Fonthill picked up his rifle and thrust another round into the breech. He could now hear shots coming from both Mzingeli's and Jenkins's positions, and pandemonium seemed to reign within the slavers' camp. One Arab was standing within a circle of Kaffirs, attempting to direct operations – were there others? Had Jenkins got them? The man was pointing towards the positions of the three rifles, obviously attempting to divide his force into three to launch separate attacks on the source of the fire. But the Kaffirs were clearly reluctant to move. The blaze that Mzingeli had created had taken hold and seemed to be threatening the camp; the rifle fire from three different points was now bringing down a man with each shot; and panic, as Fonthill had hoped, was beginning to set in.

First one man, and then two and three began to slip away from the edge of the group surrounding the Arab, and suddenly the rest threw away their spears and ran to the only point of the compass, the south, that offered them escape. They ran as fast as their legs could take them and disappeared into the bush, leaving the slaver standing, waving a curved sword and cursing them. He stood, however, for only a few seconds more before Jenkins's shot shattered his head.

Fonthill looked anxiously towards where the slaves lay. It looked as though none had been hit in the affray, for they all had remained as close to the earth as possible as the gunfire sounded all around. They were now lifting their heads cautiously to look around, and Simon could see that Joshua, at the end of the line, was attempting to stand, although the wooden yoke, attached to the next man, still lying, was preventing him.

It seemed that all the slavers had fled, but then he saw the Nubian slave master. The man, distinguished by the long coiled whip hanging from his cummerbund, had emerged from the edge of one of the tents and was crawling towards the line of slaves. He had a knife in his hand.

Alice had seen him too. 'My God, Simon. He's going to kill the slaves!'

Fonthill raised his rifle to his shoulder and took careful aim. But the Martini-Henry, so terrible a man-stopper, was never happy at being fired consistently without being allowed to cool – as the defenders at Rorke's Drift had found – and now it jammed.

'Damn!' Simon threw the rifle to the ground and ran forward, crashing through the under-growth and leaping over the embers of the perimeter fires. He was too late to save the first man in the slave line, who succumbed with a slashed throat, but he threw himself on to the assassin, landing on his back as he crouched, preparing to continue his grisly work. The man lurched forward, arms outstretched and spread-eagled across the second slave, who screamed in terror. Fonthill recovered quickly, and straddling the two, he slipped his arms under the slave master's shoulders and locked his hands together at the back of the neck in the classic half-nelson hold. The Nubian, big and strong, hunched his shoulders and flung Simon to and fro, but was unable to break the lock as Fonthill hung on like a terrier clinging to a fox.

Then the man went limp as Jenkins's rifle butt thudded into his head.

'Sorry, bach sir. Couldn't shoot the bugger because you was 'uggin' 'im so close. Didn't know you fancied 'im, like.'

'Thanks, 352,' Fonthill gasped, scrambling to his feet. 'Search him for a key to the chains and unlock these poor devils. I must get back to Alice.'

He found his wife now sitting at the base of the tree, her face completely white, hacking away the cloth of her breeches with a knife.

'Here, let me do that.' He took the knife from her and slit the seam of the breeches. She gave a little gasp and bit her lip. The musket ball had buried itself into her thigh, leaving a neat, plum-coloured hole from which blood was oozing.

'Lucky it wasn't a rifle cartridge,' said Fonthill. 'That would have gone through and done a lot of damage, but I think we shall be able to get it out without too much trouble.' He looked up, his eyes moist. 'You are a strong, brave girl.'

'No I'm not.' Alice's voice seemed to come from far away. 'I really want to have a good cry. At this moment, Norfolk seems a very nice place to be. I've had enough of bloody Africa...' Then she slumped forward.

As Simon knelt and gathered her in his arms, he became aware that Mzingeli was at his side. He stood, lifting Alice, and adjusted her tenderly to avoid putting pressure on the wound. 'Have they all gone, Mzingeli, do you think?'

The tracker nodded. 'We kill many. Only maybe nine or ten left and they run. They don't come back. All Arabs killed.'

'Good. Pick up the rifles and please go on and find somewhere where I can lay Alice and build up one of the fires. We shall need to get this musket ball out of her leg.'

Carrying Alice into the clearing, he found

Jenkins unlocking the big padlock that secured all the chains at the head of the line. He acknowledged the cries that came from the slaves as, one by one, the chains were threaded through and they were freed. Fonthill exchanged grins with Joshua and the other boys at the end of the line, and then the women began to sing again. This time it was no lament.

Alice had regained consciousness as Simon lowered her on to a divan of sorts within one of the tents. He tipped water from his bag on to his handkerchief and wiped her brow, and then gave her some to drink. Although beads of perspiration were beginning to fringe her hairline, he wrapped a blanket around her. Delayed shock and perhaps fever, he knew, would be a danger now.

'Three five two,' he hailed through the tent opening. 'Did you get the rest of those Arabs?'

'Yes, bach sir. I couldn't get a bead on 'em to start with, because of the black fellers in between. Then I got the first one, you got two and I eventually put away the last. There was only four, see.'

'Good. Now stand guard just in case any of the other bastards try to come back. Oh – and get Joshua to see if he can find clothes for the slaves. There must be some somewhere, and they should have their dignity back.'

Mzingeli had now joined him. 'I've left my pack by the tree over there,' said Fonthill. 'Please fetch it.' He lowered his voice. 'Then I shall need your help in getting this musket ball out. I'm no doctor, blast it.'

The tracker nodded and ran off. Simon returned to his wife and knelt by her side. 'We will soon have this damned thing out,' he murmured. 'Did you bring your first-aid bits and pieces with you by any chance?'

She nodded. 'I thrust a small bundle into the top of your pack before we left,' she whispered, her eyes heavy. 'Not much. Just a bandage or two, a little morphine, some antiseptic. Had to leave my bag hidden where we camped. Too heavy...' Her voiced tailed away.

'Splendid. Hold on. Won't be long now.' But he did not share the confidence his voice expressed. He held his wife's hand tightly until Mzingeli returned carrying his pack. Fonthill foraged inside it and produced the little bundle, wrapped in oilskin, that Alice had prepared. He unrolled it and laid the contents carefully on a blanket at the side of the divan: three tightly rolled bandages, some lint and a cotton pad, a jar of antiseptic cream, a small bottle of painkilling pills – and a broken bottle of morphine, its precious liquid long since drained away.

Hurling the bottle away with a curse, he fumbled once more in the pack and produced a half-bottle of whisky, now containing only a little of the spirit. He beckoned Mzingeli outside. 'Let me see your knife,' he said. The tracker produced it. 'Good. Better than mine. Thinner and sharper. Now, go and put the blade into a fire until it glows completely red. Let it cool – but don't touch it or let the blade touch anything else. It's got to be completely clean. Then bring it back here.'

273

Fonthill re-entered the tent, his wife's anxious eyes following his every movement. He took the cork out of the whisky bottle, put his other hand behind Alice's head and lifted it up. 'Now,' he said, 'drink a little of this, my love, please.'

Her wide eyes on his, she took the bottle and swallowed, spluttered and handed it back. 'I hate whisky,' she coughed.

'I know, my darling, but you must finish the bottle. Come along now. Do what Dr Fonthill says, there's a good girl.' He gave a mirthless smile and handed her the bottle again. 'Do it in your own good time, but drink it all, please.'

Pulling a face, she raised the bottle to her lips again, and eventually drank all the amber liquid. Her head sank back on the sheet that Simon had folded for her as a pillow. 'Oh God,' she whispered, 'I feel awful.'

'Lie there for a moment, my darling. Sleep if you want to.'

He put down her hand and left the tent. All of the slaves were now unshackled and were standing or lying, rubbing their ankles and necks where the chains and yokes had chafed their skin. Jenkins, rifle cradled, was talking to Joshua, and Mzingeli was gingerly holding his knife blade in the flames of a rekindled fire.

'Ready yet?' called Fonthill.

The tracker held up his free hand to quell Simon's impatience, and Jenkins came hurrying over. 'I didn't realise she'd been 'it,' he said, his face showing lugubrious concern. ''Ow bad?'

'She has a musket ball in her thigh. I am going to try to dig it out as soon as Mzingeli gets that knife clean.' He pulled a face. 'I'm not looking forward to it.'

'Excuse me if I don't come in. I'll be sick if I do.'

'No. Stand guard and make sure that none of the Kaffirs return. Oh.' He nodded to the slave master. 'Tie him up. We have unfinished business with him for the morning.'

Jenkins gave a puzzled look, then nodded. 'Very good, bach sir.'

The tracker held the knife up into the night air to cool it. Behind him, the fire he had started in the bush began to flicker and die as it ran on to the stony ground of the clearing. He strode towards Fonthill and offered him the knife, handle first. 'Still bit warm,' he said.

'Yes. Perhaps better to wait a minute anyway. I've given her some whisky. It's the only anaesthetic I had. She's not used to it, so I hope it does the job.'

The tracker nodded sympathetically. Then they both re-entered the tent. Alice was lying back, half unconscious, her head rolling from side to side.

Simon licked his lips. 'Right. Might as well start. You hold her leg very tightly and make sure that it does not jerk. Press down. I expect it will start to bleed again when I fish for the bloody ball, so staunch the bleeding with this felt. I want to be able to see what I am doing.' He shook his head. 'Oh dear. My poor Alice.'

As Mzingeli crouched on one side, Fonthill settled on the other and began very slowly to peel back the skin surrounding the wound. 'Forceps is what we want,' he breathed, 'not this damned butcher's knife.'

At first Alice seemed to feel no pain, but then, as Simon began gently probing to locate the ball, she jerked and then moaned.

'All right, darling,' he mouthed, 'won't be long. Nearly there. Ah, found it!'

With as much care as he could muster, he pushed the tip of the knife around the side of the ball and then, very slowly, worked it underneath the lead. At this point, Alice opened her eyes and then screamed. 'Hold her,' breathed Fonthill, 'nearly there. Now...' He levered the ball upwards until, in a welter of blood, he could seize it with his thumb and forefinger and flick it away.

As he did so, Alice sat upright and, eyes staring, grabbed his shoulder. 'Brave girl, brave girl,' he soothed. 'It's out now. Clean as a whistle. Lie back, my darling.' He pushed her gently back on to the bed. 'Just got to clean it up now. Lie still, there's a good girl.'

He seized the whisky bottle and emptied the last drops of the liquor directly on to the wound, before pouring a little water around the edges and wiping them gently. Then he opened the antiseptic cream and – all the finer points of hygiene lost in his anxiety – scooped a little out with the tip of the knife and spread it on the cotton pad. Handing the knife to Mzingeli, he pressed the pad down firmly on the wound and began winding a bandage around it to keep it in place. As he finished with a knot, he realised that Alice was watching him.

'Oh my love,' he whispered, 'I am sorry to have

hurt you.'

She shook her head slowly and summoned up the palest of smiles. 'Don't be silly. Couldn't have done better myself. Do you know, I might take to whisky.' Then she closed her eyes and her head sank back on to the folded sheet.

'Can we find another blanket?' Fonthill asked Mzingeli. 'Shock is a danger now. We must keep her warm.'

The tracker nodded and stole out of the tent, to be replaced by Jenkins. 'Oh blimey, bach.' The Welshman's face was as white as Alice's. 'I was outside listenin'. I couldn't 'ave done what you just did. Do you think she will be all right?'

Fonthill wiped the perspiration from his brow and shook his head. 'I don't know,' he said. He looked around. 'It was just so ... so bloody primitive. I only hope I did the right thing and that infection hasn't got into the wound.' He looked unspeaking into the Welshman's eyes for a moment. 'You know, 352, I don't know what I would do if I lost her. Bringing her out here, exposing her to all this violence... She fought as coolly as a Guardsman and certainly saved my life by shooting one of those spearmen. And now, if I've botched this up... Oh lord!' He put his hand over his eyes.

Jenkins patted his shoulder. 'You've done all you could, bach,' he said. 'A bloody wonderful job, I'd say. Now it's up to the man upstairs, see. I think you need a rest. Just you lie down on that bed thing there. Go on now. You'll be near 'er if she wants anythin'. I'll watch over the camp.'

Reluctantly Fonthill nodded and sprawled on

to the other divan. Then he rose, pulled the bed so that it was next to Alice's and lay down on it again, reaching across so that he could take her hand. He was already asleep when Mzingeli crept in with two blankets, one of which he added to Alice's covering; the other he laid across Simon, before tiptoeing out.

Chapter 12

When Fonthill awoke, sun was streaming in through the tent opening and the camp was clearly active, for he could hear the sound of mules braying, the clanging of cooking utensils and voices singing. He had cramp in his arm from where he lay awkwardly, still holding Alice's hand. He looked across sharply at her. She lay peacefully asleep, her breast rising rhythmically to her breathing, colour now back in her cheeks. He smiled in relief, gently disengaged his fingers from hers and threw back his blanket.

Outside, fires had been lit and the wooden neck yokes were proving to be excellent fuel underneath two cooking pots. Some of the women, now chastely wearing brief garments that seemed to have been roughly fashioned from the Arabs' white burnouses, were stirring the contents of the pots, and others were helping the men throw earth into pits that had been dug on the periphery of the camp. Away to his left, the mules grazed. It was a scene of pastoral activity.

'Ah, good mornin', bach sir.' Jenkins hove into view, chains wrapped around his shoulders and arms. 'You got a bit of sleep, then? 'Ow's Miss Alice? I looked in about an hour ago an' she was sleepin' like a baby.'

Fonthill yawned. 'Thank you, yes. She's still asleep, thank goodness. Are you going to start an ironmongery business?'

'Ah, this lot. Thought I'd throw 'em all in on top of the bodies I've 'ad the lads bury up there, see.' He gave a theatrical shudder. 'These irons – awful bloody things.'

'Good idea. How are the boys?'

'Joshua's back is still a bit sore but 'e's all right really – at least now. So are the others, although, as you know, we lost one of the slaves. I've 'ad 'im buried separately.' He sniffed and then grinned. 'Everybody's very relieved to be free again. We would 'ave the freedom of Africa if they could give it to us.'

Fonthill returned the grin. 'Where's Mzingeli?'

''E went out early and shot us a bit of meat, an' that's what's stewin' now. Now 'e's in the other tent, rubbin' some leaf stuff into Joshua's poor old back. It'll probably kill 'im.'

'Well I'm glad I'm not being asked to do it. I don't think I'm much of a doctor.'

'Don't say that. Miss Alice is goin' to be all right, look you. Right as rain, I tell you. You can see to my 'angovers any time.'

Fonthill yawned again and stretched. 'Well, she will need rest. I think we had better stay here for at least two days. Can Mzingeli feed us all with his rifle, do you think?'

Jenkins munched his moustache. 'Should think so. What are you goin' to do with this slave lot?'

'Give them the choice of coming back to the local village with us or making their own way back to where they were taken.'

'An' what about 'im?' Jenkins jerked his head to the side of the tent. Fonthill turned and saw the slave master lying on the ground, shackled in his own chains.

Fonthill's face seemed to be set in stone. 'Oh, *he* will be no problem,' he said.

'Yes, but what will we do with 'im?'

'We shall hang him.'

'What! Just like that?'

'Yes. The sooner the better.' Fonthill spoke slowly and decisively. 'The man is a slaver and a murderer. I saw him cut the throat of a defence-less slave. If any of the Arabs had survived, they would have met the same fate. Let us do it now, before Alice recovers. We will take him a little way into the bush, drape those bloody chains around him, string him up by his whip and leave him there. Anyone who comes this way – and it seems to be a slavers' route – will see him and know him for what he was. He will be a warning to others. Fetch Mzingeli and Joshua and we will do it now.'

Jenkins's eyes narrowed. 'Are you sure, bach sir? I mean, killin' a bloke in cold blood – even if 'e is evil – isn't like you, now is it? I mean, an officer an' a gentleman?'

'To hell with that.' Fonthill's expression had not changed. 'The British made slavery illegal eighty-three years ago. One day, perhaps sooner than we think, this territory will be under British rule, and I want these people here,' he gestured to the ex-slaves, 'to know that wherever we are, we will always strive to exterminate this filthy trade. It will be a lesson to them too. Come on. Let's get on with it.'

The Welshman, surprise still on his face, shrugged the chains to the ground and went to fetch Mzingeli and Joshua. Fonthill strode to the centre of the clearing, clapped his hands and waved everyone towards him. The singing stopped and he was soon surrounded. He waited until they were joined by the tracker and Joshua and then he asked Mzingeli to translate his intention.

The announcement, made hesitantly by the tracker, who seemed to share Jenkins's surprise at Fonthill's decision, was greeted by a low hiss and then, when the import of it sank in, by a fierce shout of approval. Immediately the men ran to the Nubian, picked him up, chains and all, on their shoulders and bore him out of the clearing.

Simon yelled to Jenkins, 'Stay with Alice!' and followed, with Mzingeli and a grinning Joshua. The execution was carried out with dispatch. A large baobab tree with a sturdy branch extending out some ten feet from the ground was found, and a man shinned up and secured the base of the slave master's whip to the branch. Within seconds the end of the whip was tied securely around the Nubian's neck and willing hands launched him to swing, weighed down by the chains that only hours before had marked their own captivity and passage into slavery.

Fonthill experienced a sudden, reactive surge of disgust as he saw the man's frozen expression of

281

terror before the drop broke his neck. Then he turned on his heel and walked quickly back into the camp.

During the two days that they remained in the clearing, Fonthill and the others learned of how Joshua and the boys had been taken. They had stood guard in turns through the night, as Simon had instructed, but the guard had stood down with the dawn and they were all taking breakfast within the scarum when, without warning, the slavers had struck. The spearman had come running quickly into the camp, and it took only seconds to herd the five boys together within a ring of steel. The slave line had followed and they were immediately shackled and yoked. Only Joshua had tried to escape, and he had been flogged for his audacity. The slavers, it seemed, had come from the north, from a port called Bagamayo (meaning in Kiswahili 'lay down your heart'), and the slaves were destined to be exported from there. They had been captured from villages on the slavers' march to the south. Some had been in chains for two weeks. Listening to the story, Fonthill felt exonerated for hanging the slave master. Killing wasn't easy, but in some cases it was the only means of justice.

Alice continued to recover, and to Simon's huge relief, it became clear that his rough and ready surgery had proved effective and that no infection had entered the wound. Nevertheless, she still found it difficult to walk. The unpleasant associations of the clearing – the grave pit and the swinging, enchained body in the forest, although Alice knew nothing of the execution –

began to press in on them all, however, and Fonthill decided that they should set off on the third day and make their way back to the scarum, where they had left their tents, supplies and, most importantly, Alice's medical bag. A litter was constructed for Alice from one of the divans, and they set off shortly after dawn.

It was an uneventful journey, made long by the necessity to put the litter down every hour to allow Alice some respite from the jarring, irregular movement she was forced to endure. They found their camp untouched, however, and were able to retrieve their possessions from where they had been hidden in the bush.

Once inside their tent, Simon examined Alice's wound. The antiseptic ointment seemed to have done its job well, for there was no sign of infection, but the hole made by the musket ball remained gaping and there was some suppuration. Fonthill caught Alice's eye.

'I'm afraid it needs stitching,' he said. 'Mustn't leave the hole like that in this climate.'

'Hmm.' Alice's face was white under her tan. 'Who is going to do that, then?'

'I ... er ... don't suppose that you...'

'No. I couldn't quite face that, and anyway, I am not as good a needlewoman as I claimed. I am afraid, my love, that it must be you. It isn't saying much, I fear, but you are far and away the best surgeon in our little group. You have already proved that.'

Fonthill gulped. 'Do we have a needle and some gut?'

'Yes. In my bag.'

'So I just...?'

'Yes, dear.' She gave a wan smile. 'You just pierce the skin and draw the edges together. Neatly and tidily. While I scream.'

'Oh lord. Do you have any morphine in your bag?'

'Yes. And a syringe. Might as well get on with it, darling, while I have faith in you. I don't want people staring at a nasty hole in my leg while I bathe in the North Sea off the Norfolk coast, now do I? And if you do well, you can take on the task of mending your socks when we get home.'

Gloomily Fonthill opened up her precious medical bag, laid out a towel on a collapsible stool and placed upon it the necessary implements. He stuck his head out of the tent and called Joshua to bring soap and hot water and to summon Mzingeli.

'What's up?' enquired Jenkins.

Simon explained. 'Ah yes.' The Welshman's face looked drawn, then he nodded his head in appreciation of the task ahead. 'I'll just see to the lightin' of the fires for the night, then,' he said. 'Important, this fire-layin' business, see. Got to be done right. You won't need me in there.' And he strode away very quickly.

Alice, her jaw set squarely, supervised the injection of the morphine and then threaded the needle before lying back, waiting for the drug to take effect. 'Remember,' she said, her head on the pillow, 'you must make the edges of the flesh meet. No gaping gaps, please.' Then she nodded. 'I think the morphine has taken effect now. Stitch away.' And she took a deep breath and looked the other way.

Once again Mzingeli took on the task of holding down Alice's leg, and staunched the bleeding while Simon made the incisions. It took about fifteen minutes before he was able to draw the needle through for the last time, snip off the end of the gut and tie it in a knot to prevent it slipping back.

'There,' he said. 'Not a bad job.' He looked up at his wife, who had made no sound during the operation, but her face was wet with perspiration and blood was flowing from where she had bitten her lip. She was quite unconscious. It was clear that the anaesthetic, clumsily applied, had not been as effective as had been hoped. Cursing, Fonthill bandaged the wound, gently tucked Alice's leg beneath the blanket and, kneeling, began to wipe her brow with a cloth dipped in cold water.

Within a minute she had come round. She gazed at him dreamily. 'I don't suppose there is any whisky in the camp, is there?' she enquired.

'There is just one bottle left,' Simon breathed, 'and you can have all of its contents, my love. You have been a brave, brave girl.'

'Oh good.' And she went back to sleep.

Mzingeli allowed himself one of his rare smiles. 'Nkosana like a warrior,' he said.

They all stayed within the scarum for the next three days while Alice recovered, but the problem of what to do with the ex-slaves began to be pressing. They were becoming fractious, and yet were timorous of leaving the camp on their own. They still feared that the slavers, in some form or other, might return, although Mzingeli tried to assure them that this was most unlikely. The question was: where should they be taken? Most of them seemed to have come from outside the Manican territory. Could they find their own way back to their villages?

Fonthill called a meeting, and he, Jenkins, Mzingeli and Joshua, whose English had now improved to the point where he could understand most of what was said to him, sat around Alice's bed. It was Mzingeli who stated the obvious.

'We no nursemaids,' he grunted. 'Take them to nearest village. Then they decide what to do.'

Simon looked at his wife. 'I don't think you will be able to walk for a time,' he said. 'And I don't want to leave you here.'

Alice waved her hand. 'Don't worry about me. I want to start writing the story of the fight with the slavers anyway, and will need a bit of peace and quiet to concentrate. You must take Mzingeli with you to interpret and Jenkins to help you keep them all moving. I have a feeling that you will have to herd them like cattle, so you will also need some herdsmen.' She smiled. 'Just leave Joshua with me, with a couple of Martini-Henrys and that whisky you promised, and we will be as right as rain.'

'Well I don't know about that.' Fonthill looked at Jenkins, who shrugged his shoulders, and then Mzingeli, who gave an almost imperceptible nod of assent.

He sighed. 'All right. We will go tomorrow. If we make an early start, we should be back well before nightfall–'

Alice interrupted. 'No. It's pointless rushing. When you get to the village, you are virtually halfway to the king's kraal. Why don't you push on to see him and get him to sign your treaty? He will be so happy that you have sent the slavers packing that he will give you anything you want. Probably make you deputy king or Prince of Wales. Strike while the iron is hot. Joshua and I will be right as rain here for two days if you leave us food and drink. Eh, Joshua?'

The boy grinned, not quite comprehending the conversation but glad to be included, and nodded his head.

'Very well. But we won't be away longer than two days. Joshua, you keep a good watch and look after the Nkosana.'

Joshua's grin widened and he nodded again.

In truth, Fonthill was happy to accept Alice's suggestion. Her leg was healing well, but she would need to rest for at least another three days or so, and he did not relish the prospect of kicking his heels idly in the scarum for that time. He was anxious to pull King Umtasa into his bag, prospect a little to the north for firmer terrain for a road, and return to Bulawayo as quickly as possible before going south to meet Rhodes's column on the march. It would almost certainly be on its way now, and he was eager to march with it and look for possible farming land in Mashonaland. For Alice's safety he had no fear. The Manican people were not warlike and would cause her no harm, and Mzingeli had assured him that no slavers would come through

287

this way now for a year or more after the rebuff the last party had received.

It was with a happy heart, then, that he, Jenkins, Mzingeli, the four boys and the chattering band of ex-slaves set off for the Manican village. Surprisingly, it seemed that two of the natives, a pair of brothers, were from the king's kraal and were anxious to return there. They had been taken when they had strayed too far to the west on a hunting expedition. Bringing them back safely would surely cement Fonthill's relationship with the king, and thus confirmed the good sense of pressing on to his kraal as soon as possible.

And so it proved. The majority of the ex-slaves were left at the village, and Fonthill, Jenkins, Mzingeli and the two Manicans continued their journey, arriving at the kraal just before nightfall. They were met with cries of joy and dancing as the two brothers were welcomed back from the dead. Chattering children, singing adults and barking dogs formed an avenue through which they all marched to the king's hut. It was, Simon reflected, rather like the return of the prodigal son.

That evening they were once again the guests of King Umtasa at an outdoor feast. The king had insisted on interrogating the two brothers on their capture and learning how Fonthill and his party had rescued them. He nodded his head in particular approval at the hanging of the slave master. The man, it seemed, was known to the tribe, and although the king's own kraal was too large and well defended to be a target for their depredations, the slavers had raided other villages in Umtasa's territory and the big Nubian had earned a reputation for cruelty. It was good, said the king, that his new British protectors had already showed that they would and could keep their word.

Fonthill swallowed hard at this. It would be some time, he knew, before a British presence could be extended directly to the Manican people – and what about the Portuguese claim to their land? Through Mzingeli, he gently probed Umtasa on this. Was the king forced to pay allegiance to the European power?

The king shook his head. 'No. They want money. They come sometimes and want me pay taxes. I give little grain but nothing more. Their man comes with his men from the south. He used to take slaves and particularly women from my villages. But I say I complain to Mozambique so he don't no more.'

'What man was that?'

'His name de Sousa,' Mzingeli allowed himself a ghost of a smile as he translated, 'but everyone call him Gouela.'

Fonthill nodded. 'This man is known to me,' he explained. 'He is an agent for the Portuguese government in territories just over the border in Portuguese East Africa. But he has no claim on your country. He also makes claims on the land of the King of the Matabele, but King Lobengula does not accept them. You are right to reject him. He is no better than the Arab slavers who come from the north.'

The king listened impassively. 'Will your Rhodes protect me from him?'

If your majesty will sign the treaty of friendship between your country and the charter company of Mr Rhodes, as has King Lobengula, then the company will be able to extend protection. Mr Rhodes has now begun building a road through Matabeleland and Mashonaland to the west that will bring him and his influence close to you. I must first return, of course, with the treaty signed by you.'

'And he will give me guns?'

'I shall relay your request to him.'

'This treaty don't take my country from me?'

'No. This is a treaty of friendship between your country and the British Government, as represented by the charter company. It will give the British the right to oppose the Portuguese claim to your land.'

'Ah.' Umtasa pulled at his trim beard for a moment. Then he nodded his head. 'Your words are good. You fight slavers already and bring back two of my people. You show you can fight. You bring me treaty. I sign it now.'

Fonthill gave a quiet sight of relief. He was growing weary of the strain of picking his words carefully and delicately balancing his answers. He was, he realised, tiptoeing between the truth and the near truth. It was a role he did not relish.

Jenkins, who had been listening, immediately rose and retrieved the carefully rolled piece of parchment from Simon's pack. He also brought a pen and a sealed bottle of ink. Umtasa called for a table to be provided, and then he spread out the document and, following Fonthill's pointed finger, laboriously made his cross. Simon scrawled his own name, on behalf of the charter company, and a frowning Jenkins, his tongue poking out from under his moustache, scratched his signature as a witness. Sprinkling a little sand on the signatures, Fonthill extended his hand, and he and Jenkins shook the king's hand as the last seal of goodwill.

The *inDunas* sitting around the fire, not quite understanding what had just taken place but realising that it was a ceremony of some importance, set up a brief ululation in approval.

Jenkins carefully rolled up the document, put away the ink, pen and sand, wiped the back of his hand across his moustache and confided, 'Well, as we've just got married, so to speak, shall we 'ave another little drop of beer to celebrate, eh, your worship?' And he raised his empty cup in genial supplication.

The king grasped the meaning, nodded and ordered more beer, and the drinking continued until the fires were guttering low.

Fonthill rose the next morning with a throbbing head, although Jenkins and Mzingeli appeared to be completely unaffected by the night's carousing. During the evening, the king had repeated his claim that the country to the north offered more open and firm going, right through to the Portuguese border, but Simon resisted the temptation to detour on the way back to the scarum to see for himself. He was already feeling guilty about leaving Alice, and he decided that they would make all haste back to her and explore to the north-east as soon as she was able to walk.

They set off early, carrying with them a pair of medium-sized elephant's tusks that Umtasa had presented to Fonthill for freeing the slaves, and which the four boys carried slung between them.

It was, however, a long trek, and it was almost dark before they reached the scarum. The camp seemed quiet enough, with the mules grazing peacefully outside the stockade, and Fonthill raised a loud 'hello' as they approached. There was no reply, however, and Simon exchanged a puzzled glance with Jenkins. Then he broke into a run.

Alice's tent was empty, and there was no sign of Joshua either. Alice's travelling pack, her few clothes and her medical bag had gone, yet there was no evidence of a struggle. The two Martini-Henry rifles and her Westley Richards stood leaning in a corner of the tent. Alice and Joshua had disappeared without a trace.

Fonthill looked wide-eyed and despairingly at Jenkins and Mzingeli.

'P'raps they've just gone to pick berries or somethin',' offered Jenkins.

'Don't be bloody stupid, man. She can't walk.'

'Ah yes. Sorry, bach.'

In desperation, Fonthill looked around the interior of the tent once again. Something else was missing... Ah yes. 'The divan has gone!' he exclaimed. It was true. The bed from the Arabs' tent that had been converted into a rough litter to carry Alice had disappeared. So too had her blankets. 'Why the hell should she want to take her bed with her? Or, for that matter, who else would want to take it?'

Mzingeli had quietly walked outside. Now he re-entered the tent. 'Nkosana taken,' he said. 'Many men.'

Simon crashed his fist into an open palm. 'Oh my God! Who? Where?'

The tracker shrugged. 'Don't know. They go that way.' And he pointed to the west.

Chapter 13

Fonthill noted the direction of Mzingeli's pointed finger and ran outside the scarum and looked hard to the west. At first his unskilled eye could see little to help him. Then, on bending and examining the ground, he perceived the crushed grass and broken twigs that betrayed the passage of a considerable number of people. He turned to find Mzingeli and Jenkins at his elbow.

'Can you see anything that would tell us who they were,' he demanded of the tracker, 'and how long ago they struck?'

Mzingeli bent and put a long black finger into the disturbed grass. He wrinkled his nose. 'No, Nkosi. Not sure. But I think yesterday. And they don't wear shoes. Native men. Going fast. Look how ... what is English? Yes, heel of foot don't show. Only ball. They running.'

Fonthill nodded, although he could detect nothing of the sort. 'Running? Why on earth should they do that?'

Jenkins sucked in his moustache. 'I suppose

they'd be worryin' about us comin' after them, like.'

'Well they've got at least a day and a half's advantage on us anyway.' He bit the knuckles of his fist and tried to think rationally. He turned back to Mzingeli. 'Is there any sign of anyone being hurt?'

'No. No fight. No blood. Guns not moved. Bed gone. Blankets gone. They look after her. Take Joshua, too.'

'So they definitely wanted Alice,' mused Fonthill. 'They saw that, obviously, she couldn't walk, so they took her bed and probably carried her on that. Who would do that? Perhaps someone who wants to have a hold over us so has taken her as some sort of hostage. But who...?' Then his eyes lit up. 'Of course, why didn't I think? De Sousa!'

He turned to the others, anguish showing in his face. 'This is virtually his territory anyway, and he has a score or two to settle with us. He obviously saw the scarum and swept in. It was just his luck to find us gone but Alice remaining. Oh why did I leave her?'

'Don't think about that, bach sir.' Jenkins was at his most pragmatic. 'Just think about gettin' 'er back, which we will, as surely as God made little apples. Now, look you, do we go after 'em right away, or wait until morning?'

Fonthill deflected the question to Mzingeli. 'Can you follow the spoor in the dark?'

'Perhaps, but can't go quick at night.'

'Very well.' Fonthill spoke quickly. 'Let us have something to eat and drink. We will have to leave the mules because they will slow us down, and

294

we take only what we need: dried biltong, water bags; no tents, just blankets. Leave the ivory tusks. But we take Alice's Westley Richards and the other rifles. I want to be well armed and on the way before darkness falls.'

They all bustled about, unhobbling the mules, stuffing their packs with essentials, filling extra water bottles and then, squatting briefly, eating a quick supper. Fonthill was careful to ensure that the document he had signed with King Umtasa was safely stowed in his pack. They were still chewing when a crashing in the undergrowth made them grab their rifles and brought them to their feet.

From the direction in which they had come only a few minutes before, a figure emerged. He was a native, dressed only in loincloth and monkey-skin calf bands and carrying nothing except a water bag. Perspiration poured from his face and chest and he was gasping for breath. Fonthill raised his rifle but was restrained by Mzingeli.

'He from Umtasa kraal,' said the tracker, and he moved quickly towards the tribesman, who looked on the verge of exhaustion. Mzingeli seized the man's water bag to slake his thirst, but it was empty. Instead he raised his own bag to the runner's mouth and urged him to sit. They then engaged in conversation, conducted between the Manican's gasps.

'What does he say?' interrupted Fonthill.

Mzingeli lifted his hand for silence and continued to interrogate the runner. Eventually he rose. 'He come from King Umtasa,' he said. 'After we leave kraal, de Sousa arrive with men.

He tell king that he heard we in area and want him to produce us for him to kill. King say we left day before. De Sousa go off to find us. This man sent by king to warn us. He been running all day.'

'Ah.' Fonthill clenched his fist. 'That settles it. The bastard arrived here before us and took ... Wait.' He frowned. 'Ask him how long after we left the Portuguese set off.'

Mzingeli translated. 'He not sure but think about one hour. He run around Gouela and men and then come straight here. They not far behind him now.'

Fonthill's frown deepened. 'That means that de Sousa could not have got here before us and taken Alice. I just don't understand this, at all.'

'Well,' sniffed Jenkins. 'Do we wait 'ere an' give old Saucepot another bloody nose, or do we bugger off after Miss Alice? Not much time to decide, bach sir.'

Fonthill raised his hand. 'Let me think. Now, if Gouela had been able to overtake us in some way, by design or accident, and taken Alice, then he would have waited here to surprise us. That means that he hasn't taken her and someone else has. Right. We go after Alice, and we start now before that greaser and his men arrive. Here.' He delved into his pack and pressed two golden sovereigns into the messenger's hand. 'Mzingeli, please give him our thanks and ask him to pass our gratitude on to the king. Give the man one of our spare water skins and tell him that if he can hide them from de Sousa, the mules are his. We leave now.'

Leaving the young man standing in the

compound clutching his sovereigns, Fonthill and his party broke into a trot and set off into the bush, following a trail that was now only slightly discernible in the dusk. They alternately trotted and walked for about an hour, stringing out in single file with Mzingeli in the lead, followed by Simon, Jenkins and the four boys, before the tracker was forced to admit that he could not follow the spoor any longer in the growing darkness.

'Right,' grunted Fonthill, perspiration trickling down his face. 'We get off this track and bed down in the bush. No fire. No light. No talking...' He paused. 'Wait a minute, we are missing a boy.'

Indeed they were. Only three of the young men who had journeyed with them from Bulawayo had gathered around him. 'Mzingeli – find out what's happened.'

A quick conversation ensued between the tracker and the three boys. Then Mzingeli reported: 'Boy was last in line. Slow runner. Boy in front of him not realise he fall behind and disappear. Maybe he come soon.'

Fonthill shook his head. 'If you can't find the track in the dark, then this lad can't.' He sighed. 'All right. You and I had better go back and look for him. Jenkins, stay in charge here, and for goodness' sake don't let any of the boys stray.'

Jenkins pulled a face. 'Better I come with you, bach sir, with old Saucepot on our trail. Just in case you run into trouble.'

'No. You stay here with the boys. We don't want too many bodies wandering around in the bush in the dark. Keep a guard rota. We won't be long.

I only hope we can retrace our steps.'

'It was difficult, but they did so – at least for some forty minutes. Mzingeli was well in the lead and hardly visible in the darkness when a movement in the bush to his right caught Fonthill's eye. Something was swinging from a branch. Rifle at the ready, he took a couple of paces into the thicket before he stopped, his mouth opening in horror. Hanging from the branch by his neck was the young man who had fallen behind. Swinging at his side and equally dead was Umtasa's messenger. As Simon watched, the man's hand twitched and the two gold sovereigns slipped to the ground.

Fonthill was turning to shout to Mzingeli when something crashed on to his head and blackness descended.

Fonthill came round with excruciating pain consuming his mind and body. The throbbing in his head was as nothing compared to ... what was it? He opened his eyes and realised that somebody, very close to him, was slowly cutting into the flesh of his chest with a knife. There was a strong smell of pomade, highly scented hair oil. He struggled but realised that his wrists were bound behind him and his ankles were similarly tied. The black eyes of de Sousa looked into his at a distance of some twelve inches, and then, realising that he had regained consciousness, the Portuguese held up a knife, from the end of which dripped blood.

'Ah, Mr Fonthill,' he said. 'I thought that a little surgery without the benefit of anaesthetic might bring you round. I was just carving my initials in your chest to while away the time until I could talk to you.'

Simon winced but refused to cry out. 'Where is my wife?' he demanded.

De Sousa indicated genuine puzzlement. 'Don't tell me you have lost her? Well I haven't got her, nor do I want her. But you, my dear friend, I do want. Oh yes. I want you. You have a debt to pay, do you remember?' And he dug the end of the knife into Fonthill's pectoral muscle, this time bringing a cry.

The Portuguese sat back. 'It's been quite a chase catching you, but I thought that getting the boy would bring you back. And here you are.'

Fonthill gritted his teeth at the pain from his chest. He realised that the shirt had been torn from his body and blood was dripping down on to his breeches from the cuts that had been made. He looked around. They were in a clearing of sorts and it was still dark. But fires had been lit, and some dozen large natives, some with spears at their sides, others with rifles, were lounging on the ground near the flames, devouring meat. There was no sign of Mzingeli.

'What the hell do you want with me?'

'What do I want?' Gouela revealed a gold tooth and, at very close observation, his pockmarked yellowish skin. 'Well, firstly I want to cause you pain. Then I want to kill you, rather slowly. But given my responsibilities for this area—'

'Neither you nor your government has any claim to this territory.'

The Portuguese ignored the interruption. 'Given my responsibilities for this area, I must make an example of you. I intend therefore to set

299

off in the morning to take you back to Umtasa's kraal, and there, before his *inDunas* and his people, I shall roast you slowly over a very large fire, but not until you are dead. No. When we have turned this ridiculously white skin of yours into a fine piece of pork crackling, I shall hang you, Fonthill.'

Fonthill tried to summon up a dismissive grin. 'You won't do that. You know that I am a representative of Rhodes, and through him of the British Government. Your country and mine have a pact of non-aggression. The news would get back and you would have to answer to your government for my death.'

'No. I don't think so. This is a faraway, primitive country, Fonthill, and I have found that I can do more or less what I like here. I shall tell my friend King Lobengula that you tried to kill me and that I was forced to defend myself. But, of course, to Umtasa I shall demonstrate how the Portuguese crown treats those who attempt to persuade its subjects to defect to another colonial power. So you will roast for a while and then hang. Now,' he raised the knife again, 'where was I? Oh yes...'

The pain began again, and Fonthill clenched his jaw to prevent himself from screaming. Then came oblivion.

The fires were burning low and the darkness beyond the clearing seemed to have grown blacker when he regained consciousness. The pain was still burning his chest, but he forced himself to sit upright and look around. De Sousa seemed to have disappeared, but was probably sleeping in the small bivouac tent that had been erected in the centre of the clearing. Most of his men had wrapped themselves in blankets and were asleep, strewn around the ground. One guard, however, carrying a rifle of some make that Fonthill could not determine, was slowly, sleepily patrolling the perimeter of the camp, coming into and out of the light cast by the fires. Again Simon looked for Mzingeli, but there was no sign of the tracker.

Fonthill's mouth tasted as if it had been force-fed on ashes and it cried out for water, but he forced himself to check his bindings. They remained tight, and the effort nearly made him black out again, but he breathed deeply and sought to clear his head. He must consider his position rationally. The fact that Mzingeli had not been exhibited to him as a corpse surely meant that the tracker, with his innate sensibility in the bush, must have escaped, for there would be no particular kudos for de Sousa in taking him back to the king's kraal. He would be just another native to the Portuguese. Escaped, though, to do what? He pondered. Mzingeli, superb tracker and resourceful man though he was, was no soldier. If he had got away, then surely he would have made his way back to Jenkins.

Fonthill tried to roll over, and stifled a groan as the cuts burned into him and began to bleed again. Looking down at his blood-drenched torso, he rationalised that at least the wounds seemed to be only superficial, for if the knife had cut deeply, then surely he would have bled to death by now. He forced a grin. Small mercies!

301

Just then his hands, foraging around in the dust of the clearing, found a stone – a sharp-edged stone. He grasped it in his fingers and tried to force it backwards to saw the edge of the vine that bound him, but he could not reach. He looked around. A few feet away was a small grouping of stones. Could he inch his way towards them and wedge the base of the sharp stone into the middle, firmly enough to use it as a saw? He jerked his knees upwards, and again the pain flooded through his body, but he gritted his teeth and persevered. Gradually, inch by agonising inch, he moved towards the stones. He swivelled his head. Was he being watched? No. He continued the movement, scraping his bottom along the ground. There! Now. He turned his back and thrust the base of the stone among the others. Yes – there was a hole. Would the base hold? Would it stay upright and firm enough to saw away? Somehow, clumsily, he inserted the bottom of the stone into the gap. Thank God, it stayed upright. He began sawing.

Almost immediately the stone toppled over. Damn! Fonthill fumbled again, this time managing to move one of the base stones a little to enable more of his cutting stone to wedge into the resulting gap. Yes, firmer this time. Much firmer!

He had been sawing away for perhaps three minutes with seemingly little effect, except to cause the blood to seep more strongly from the cuts in his chest, when a sound made his head jerk upright. It was a high-pitched scream, of a malevolence that Simon had never encountered in his life, and it seemed to emanate from the western side of the clearing. As he listened, it increased in intensity, and was joined by similar screams from the bush on the other three sides of the camp. The sleeping men in the centre of the clearing started awake and sat upright, their eyeballs showing white in the half-light, fear in their faces. The banshee cry was like that made by a handful of lost souls, bewailing their descent into hell, and Fonthill felt the hairs stand up at the base of his head. He saw a half-dressed Gouela scramble out of his tent and stand erect as his head swivelled round to detect the source of the sound.

The consternation caused by the wailing, however, was as nothing compared to the next development. As Fonthill watched in wonderment, two fires, some fifteen feet apart, sprang into life a little way back in the bush, on the western side. They were small, but the light they shed was effective enough to illuminate two grotesque figures, each hanging above one of the fires, swinging gently from branches some twelve feet above the ground. The heads of the figures were twisted to one side, but they were unmistakably the two boys who had been killed and strung up further back in the forest.

Fonthill's jaw gaped as the bodies swung like pendulums, first into view as they moved into the yellow firelight and then back again into the darkness. And the screaming continued, now ululating, but still seemingly having no source.

Now the noise was supplemented by a single, sharp cry that seemed to come from the solitary guard who had disappeared into the blackness of the forest. It was enough to send the Kaffirs rushing into a terrified group in the centre of the clearing, their mouths agape, their eyes like white marbles set into their dark faces. Their heads twisted, for they seemed not to know which way to run, because the banshees were all around them.

De Sousa snarled and shouted an order, but he was ignored, for the fear that gripped the men was greater than that they held for their master.

Then: 'Lie flat, bach.'

The words boomed from the western end of the clearing, from where the apparitions were still swinging, although the fires were now flickering low. Simon flung himself on to the dusty earth, just before a fusillade of shots came from scattered points on the perimeter of the bush. Much of the firing was inaccurate, either whining over the heads of the men bunched together in the centre of the camp or burying itself into the ground at their feet. But that which came from two separate places was deadly, and within seconds, five of the Kaffirs had staggered, doubled up and lay prostrate. Immediately, the rest turned and fled towards the east, the only point of the compass that did not seem to belch flame. They ran, throwing aside spears and rifles, their legs pumping as they weaved in and out of the trees and bushes until they had disappeared from sight.

De Sousa, however, turned towards where Fonthill lay and, crouching, ran towards him, knife in hand. A bullet took him in the upper arm, sending the knife spinning away and causing him to stagger and fall. He was struggling to rise when two of the fleeing Kaffirs, leaders of the group, or so it appeared from the traces of grey in their hair, doubled over to him, seized him under each armpit and dragged him away until he was able to regain his feet and stumble after the others, holding his arm.

For a moment, silence descended on the clearing, and then there was a whoop and Jenkins appeared, rifle in hand, and ran to where Fonthill lay.

He knelt at the side of the still pinioned man and reeled at the sight of the blood on Simon's chest. 'Good God, we didn't 'it you, did we? Our lads can't shoot for toffee.'

'No, and it's not as bad as it looks. Can you cut away this damned binding? The bastards may return when they get their nerve back.'

Jenkins produced a knife and sawed through the thick vine that bound his wrists and ankles. 'No, I don't think they'll be back. We've killed 'alf of them, look you, an' the others are frightened out of their nappies, see.' He helped Fonthill to stand. 'Bloody 'ell, man. What 'ave they done to you?'

Simon staggered for a moment and put a hand on Jenkins's shoulder. Then he summoned up a smile as the three boys, grinning and with their Martini-Henrys proudly shouldered, emerged from various sides of the clearing. 'Gouela cut me up a bit, but not deeply. My, 352! Your show scared the life out of me. Was it your idea?'

'As a matter of fact, it was, bach sir. Not bad, was it?' He gave a reciprocal grin to the boys.

'*They* all enjoyed it, anyway, though I thought they'd shoot old Jelly and me before they 'it the black fellers. 'Ere, drink this.' He held a water bag to Fonthill's lips. 'Now lean on me and we'll get out of 'ere.'

'No. Wait a moment.' Fonthill nodded his head towards the two corpses, now clearly to be seen in the light of dawn, hanging inert, no longer swinging. 'They've served us well and we must not leave them there for the hyenas.' He looked over his shoulder to where de Sousa and the remnants of his band had disappeared, but there was no sign of them.

They were joined by Mzingeli, now wearing the half-smile that was as near as he ever came to showing pleasure.

Fonthill held out his hand. 'Thank you, Mzingeli. I didn't know you could sing so well. And you, lads.' He shook hands with them all before turning back to the tracker. He nodded his head in the direction taken by the Portuguese and his men. 'Do you think they will be back?'

'No. These men very soppos ... what is English word?'

'Superstitious?'

'That is it. They think this bush haunted. They no come back.'

'Good. Then please ask the boys to take down our two old friends up there,' he nodded to the hanging corpses, 'and burn them. I'm afraid we have no time to bury them. Jenkins and I will wait here with our rifles just in case those men return.'

'Yes, Nkosi.'

While they waited, Fonthill learned of how Mzingeli had melted into the bush when Simon was attacked, and of how he had followed the two men who had taken him back to the Portuguese camp, which had been set up about half an hour's march from the scarum. Then he had returned to an anxious Jenkins and together they had plotted the attack.

'It was old Jelly who really gave me the idea,' said Jenkins. 'He told me that these Kaffir blokes don't like being in the bush at night on their own – not just because of the animals, but because of the spirits of people killed in the place, y'see. I felt that an outright attack would 'ave been a bit chancy because only two of us could shoot – as you saw. I did think of your fire trick, but knowin' me, I would get it wrong and 'ave us all burned to death.'

Simon gave a weary smile. 'I have to say that the shooting was a bit haphazard, but that was the boys, I guess.'

'Ah yes. Sorry about that – an' I was worried that we might 'it you an' that's why I shouted. Mind you,' he sniffed, 'my shootin' wasn't the best it's ever been. I managed to pot quite a few of the black fellers, see, but I missed old Saucepot again, dammit. Only got 'im in the arm, so that's two lives 'e owes me. I'll get 'im next time, though.'

'No. I think he's reserved for me.' Fonthill looked up as smoke once again drifted down across the clearing. 'Right. It looks as though the lads have done that job. Let us go. We must find Alice.' Jenkins laid a hand on his arm. ''Ere, 'alf a

307

mo. What if old Yellow Pants 'as taken 'er?'

'I've thought of that. If he had got her, he would surely have exhibited her to me in delight. And if he had...' he gulped, 'already killed her, he wouldn't have taken her bed. Above all that, as I've said before, there is no way he could have overtaken us in the bush and arrived at the scarum before us. If he had, he would have waited and ambushed us on arrival. No.' He shook his head wearily. 'Someone else has taken her. But they have left a good spoor and we must get on our way and catch them.'

Jenkins sniffed. 'That's all very well, but you've been carved about a bit and 'ad a fair old bump on the 'ead, an' with respect, bach sir, I don't see you doin' much forced marchin' for long, see.'

'Nonsense. I can march. Come on.'

But Jenkins was right. They made what progress they could through the bush, yet everyone was tired, and when eventually Fonthill collapsed, there was almost an air of relief. They carried him into a glade and made him as comfortable as possible, and took turns to stand guard through the day. The next morning, Simon was clearly delirious and moving into a fever. Mzingeli carefully examined the cuts on his chest and declared that there would be no marching that day. Instead, he dug into the earth until he found what he wanted, some strange-looking, bulbous roots. He made a small fire, carefully disseminating the smoke, and boiled the roots in the only kettle they had. Then he mashed them into a paste with a rifle butt, spread them on to a couple of leaves from a baobab tree and tied them to his patient's chest. Lastly, he took a couple of baobab buds, crushed them and forced Fonthill to drink the resulting liquid.

The next morning, Simon awoke clear-eyed and with no sign of fever. 'You're a bloody marvel,' said Jenkins, and patted the tracker on the back. Mzingeli just shrugged.

During this enforced stop, Jenkins had posted guards on a rota back in the bush the way they had come, but there was no sign of pursuit. It looked indeed as though the Portuguese and his men had been forced to flee and lick their wounds. So they set off again, this time at a slightly reduced pace to allow Fonthill time to recover fully.

However, they were soon confronted with what seemed a virtually impossible hurdle. The trail, so clearly marked and which they had been following so assiduously, now suddenly branched into three. 'Clever bastards,' cried Fonthill. 'Mzingeli, can you tell which one would have been carrying the litter?'

The tracker frowned. While the rest of the party waited impatiently, he carefully and slowly walked down each of the three spoors a little way, sometimes bending to inspect a piece of grass or the edge of a footprint in a patch of dust. Then he returned.

'Cannot tell,' he said. 'I go a longer way now down each spoor. This will take time. You wait.'

Fonthill shouted a curse. 'We are already behind by about four bloody days,' he cried. Then he regained his composure. 'Yes, of course, Mzingeli. Do what you can and take your time.

We will wait here.'

But the tracker returned within ten minutes, holding out his hand and indulging in his joyful half-smile. 'Nkosana leave these,' he said. 'Very clever lady.' And he handed three gout pills to Simon.

'What...?' Fonthill examined the little white capsules. 'Gout pills. What the hell could they... Ah!' He slapped his thigh with delight. 'Of course. Why didn't I think of this before? It's old Lobengula! He's sent half a bloody impi or whatever to take her back to Bulawayo to treat his damned gout. It all fits – not caring about the rifles, the tents or the mules, but taking her bed and Joshua to look after her. The old devil!'

Jenkins nodded. 'His worship might have left us a note or somethin'. It would 'ave saved us a lot of worry an' trouble, wouldn't it?'

Fonthill's relief was etched into his face. 'Well, Alice left us a note of sorts. It means that she's being looked after and she will be safe with his men, even with Gouela on the rampage.'

'Do we take it a bit easier, then?' asked Jenkins. 'Now that we know which way we're goin', like.'

'No. We carry on following the trail. I want to catch them up. And when we get to Bulawayo, the king is going to get a piece of my mind and...' He broke off as a disturbing thought struck him and he turned to Mzingeli. 'Could somebody just have taken her bag and the pills simply dropped out, do you think?'

The tracker shook his head. 'Don't think so. Pills not in little pile. Dropped regular. A trail to show us way. Clever lady. Perhaps she do this earlier but we missed in dark.'

'Yes. Bless her. Now, you found the pills on this trail?' He pointed.

Mzingeli nodded his head. Fonthill produced his compass, squinted at it and consulted the much-folded map from his pack. 'Yes, it is to the north-west, roughly in the direction where Bulawayo lies.' He nodded his head, relief etched into his face. 'That settles it. They are taking her back to the king.'

'So we don't need to rush about like blue-arsed flies tryin' to catch up, then?' Jenkins's question was more of a plea for mercy.

'Oh yes we do.' The frown had returned to Fonthill's face. 'Knowing Alice, she might very well tell the king to go to hell, and he could lose his temper and ... and ... anything might happen. I want to catch them up, if we can, before they reach Bulawayo.'

'But think about it, bach sir. They've got about five days' start on us, you said so yourself. We'll never catch them.'

'We might. If they've taken Alice's bed, then she'll be on it and they'll have to carry her and it. Whether she's able to or not, she will not leave that bed. She'll do everything she can to delay them. We should be able to move faster. Come on. Up, everybody. Take the north-west spoor.'

So they pressed on, no longer attempting to increase their pace by breaking into jog trots from time to time, for Fonthill, at least, could not sustain that effort. But they made good time, particularly once they had broken out of the bush country into the more open high veldt of what

311

was now clearly Mashonaland. Here the signs of the passage of the Matabele party were less distinct, but Fonthill had set a compass course for them, removing the necessity to rely on Mzingeli's tracking skills, and he estimated that they were covering perhaps twenty miles a day. They must, he argued, be closing the gap. The pace could not be maintained, however, not least because Simon had by no means completely recovered from his treatment at the hands of de Sousa, and they were forced to take longer spells of rest at midday.

Fonthill was also showing the signs of the deprivations of the last two months. The years of peaceful farming in Norfolk had added flesh to what had always been a rather sparse frame, but all that had disappeared shortly after their arrival in Africa, and the recent fighting and forced marching had now left him gaunt and as taut as a bowstring. The threat of losing Alice had weighed heavily on his imagination and his conscience, and he was now hollow-eyed and drawn – a driven man, pushing himself and his party to the limits.

Nevertheless, they were now nearing the end of their stocks of biltong, and most of one day had perforce to be devoted to allowing Mzingeli to stalk and kill an impala. It gave them not only fresh meat and the chance to replenish their biltong, but also a blessed day's rest. The enforced break impelled Fonthill to consider his position vis-à-vis Lobengula and Cecil John Rhodes. He did so even while realising that his mind was perhaps not in its most balanced state to rationalise and draw conclusions. But his chest still hurt like hell and the muscles of his legs told him that there was now a limit to how fast and how far he could walk in a day.

So, sitting and chewing on the last of the biltong, he resolved that if the king had harmed Alice in any way, then he would kill the man. Life would not be worth living without his wife, and his act would show to the world that even the most powerful despot in Africa could not behave like a barbarian without attracting the consequences. If, however, he found Alice alive and unharmed, then he would have no more of this surrogate adventuring for Cecil John Rhodes. This strange millionaire would have to do his own exploring in future. Alice had never wished to come on this journey, and now she was being forced to suffer because of her husband's own arrogance and selfishness. No, he resolved, she would do whatever she wished now, and he would meekly follow her desires, even if it meant going back to sowing more wheat in flat bloody Norfolk!

The next day, their stomachs full and hopes renewed by the promise of another day of blue sky and scurrying snowball puffs of cloud, they set off as soon as the sun appeared over the hills behind them. It was towards the end of the day when they glimpsed a party of warriors trotting across the plain towards them.

Fonthill ordered a halt and they formed a square, their rifles at the ready. 'Who are they, do you think, Mzingeli? They don't look like Mashonas.'

The tracker shielded his eyes from the sun. 'They black blades,' he said. 'Matabele. They coming straight for us.'

Chapter 14

It was Fairbairn who told Alice that her husband had been found and was at that moment approaching the king's kraal. She immediately hurried to wash her face and comb her hair, then ran – for her leg had now completely healed – to meet Simon. She saw the party walking slowly down the hill, past the first thorn hedge, still accompanied by the platoon of warriors, who were anxious to reap the approval of the king for so successfully accomplishing their mission, but also by the usual cacophony of dogs and children barking and singing.

Alice strode forward to meet them and opened her arms in greeting. She could not help but release a sob, for Fonthill, Jenkins and Mzingeli now resembled scarecrows, their clothes torn, their bodies thin and, in the case of Simon and 352, wearing unkempt beards. Their eyes, however, were bright, and Simon, holding her close, whispered, 'Are you all right? They've not hurt you?'

'No, of course not. Now you are back I am perfectly fine.'

She made them all break away from their escort and walked them to her hut, where Joshua – and

314

Ntini also – greeted them with a warmth that only diminished when they realised that just three of the boys, their friends and contemporaries, had returned. Alice made the two build a fire and she busied herself with boiling water so that they could all wash, including the boys. Then she made tea and they sat around the fire drinking it while she and Fonthill exchanged their stories.

Simon and his party had only been gone an hour, she explained, when about sixty warriors had descended on the camp. They had been led by an *inDuna* and at first she had been terrified, helpless and crippled as she was, because they were painted as for war and carried assegais. Joshua had whispered that they were Matabele, and when she shouted – through the boy – that her husband and his party would be back within minutes, their purpose became clear. They had gently pushed her back on to the bed, put blankets over her, bundled a change of clothes into her pack, picked up the bed and her medicine bag and jogged away into the bush, Joshua being forced to trot with them.

She was clearly being kidnapped, for there had been no attempt to take her rifle or other items that would have been attractive to natives. But the medicine bag had been a priority, and it was now being carried with care by a warrior just ahead of her litter. Her attempts to put a foot to the ground had been firmly resisted, but no extreme force had been used and it was evident that she was not to be harmed.

It did not take long for her to speculate that she was being taken to Bulawayo so that she could continue her treatment of the king's foot. She had been sure that Mzingeli could follow the signs that so large a party would make through the bush, but she had been able to take a few of the gout pills from her bag and drop them to indicate where they would be heading. She had saved her last three pills, and it was well that she had done so, for she had used them to indicate which of the three trails she had taken when the party split up.

Simon nodded. 'Clever girl,' he said. 'This finally confirmed to us where you were heading and who had taken you. We felt much better after that. But you must have been in great pain being jolted about on that litter.'

'It was not as bad as all that. They were very gentle with me, and later, I was able to wash and change the dressing.'

'What happened when you reached Bulawayo, and why did the king send a party to look for us? If he wanted me back here, he could simply have waited for our return.'

Alice grinned. 'I refused to see the old rascal. I was not going to let him think that he could just send his warriors and drag me back here. So when he summoned me, I told him to go to hell.'

Jenkins nodded his head approvingly. 'Good for you, Miss Alice.'

Alice's smile had disappeared, however. 'Yes, well, he sent his sister to fetch me, but I insisted on talking to Fairbairn first. It was he who told me that Rhodes had sent a huge column that had already crossed into Matabeleland, that the king was in great pain and that his relationship with the white men had worsened.' She pulled a face. 'I realised that it would do no one any good for me to continue playing the Great White Lady, so I struck a bargain with his majesty.'

Fonthill frowned. 'What sort of bargain, for goodness' sake?'

'Oh, don't worry. Your position has not been compromised and I haven't sold bloody Rhodes short. I said that I would treat his foot if he would send a party out to find you and bring you back here. Eventually,' her smile returned, 'after we had exchanged a few choice words through Fairbairn, he agreed. And here you all are at last, my darlings, though you look as though you could do with a good bath and a hot meal – which shall be forthcoming, I promise.'

Simon took her hand. 'And your leg...?'

'It has healed perfectly well. Now, when you have eaten, I think you should go and see the king.' Her expression was now very serious. 'And I should be very careful about what you say to him, my dear.'

'To echo you, to hell with him.'

'Yes, well, you won't find him very contrite, I fear. He is not a happy monarch. Rhodes's column of pioneers has crossed over the Shashe into Matabeleland at Tuli and is building a fort there.'

'Rhodes has moved remarkably fast.'

'Yes, and I understand from Fairbairn that it's quite a crowd. The king thinks he is about to be invaded. This is a dangerous time, Simon.'

Fonthill lowered his brows over the edge of his cup. 'But he signed the agreement. He knew that

317

a column would be coming sooner or later to build the road.'

Alice smiled wanly. 'Yes, but it's very much sooner rather than later, and it sounds as though it's a virtual army. Fairbairn tells me that there are some two hundred prospectors, a hundred and fifty native labourers and, would you believe it, five hundred "police" – they're really soldiers – together with the usual paraphernalia of about one hundred and twenty wagons and two thousand oxen. They have even brought along a giant naval searchlight, which they shine into the bush at night to deter attack. Fairbairn is drafting a letter of protest from the king.'

Fonthill nodded and then looked at her sharply. 'That still doesn't excuse the bloody man from abducting my wife.'

Alice reached across and gripped his knee. 'I think, darling, that you must be very careful how you handle Lobengula. He has not harmed me and he did agree to send men to find you. To repeat, my love, these are dangerous times. In fairness to the man, remember that he has about twenty thousand warriors who are just dying to wash their spears in British blood. He is trying to restrain them.'

Jenkins, who had been listening, pulled at his moustache. 'Sounds a bit to me like Zululand all over again, isn't it?'

Fonthill nodded. 'Hmm. I think we have all done our bit for Rhodes now. You, my love, have had a bullet in your thigh, I have had my chest used as a carving block by this Portuguese mad-man and we have all tramped more miles than I would have wished over this bit of Africa. I have no intention of doing any further exploration to the east. I think we now make our way back down to the Cape, don't you agree?'

''Ear, 'ear,' growled Jenkins.

There was, however, an awkward silence from Alice, who looked away with an air of embarrassment.

'What?' Fonthill frowned in puzzlement. 'You never wanted to come on this expedition in the first place. Whatever is the matter?'

Alice gave him a weak smile. 'You will see that Ntini is back,' she said. 'He arrived just a few days ago. He came with this cable for me. I think you had better read it.'

Simon took the cable form. It was from the editor of the *Morning* Post in London, and it read:

SPLENDID COPY STOP UNDERSTAND PIONEER COLUMN HEADING NORTH-WARDS STOP TROUBLE EXPECTED FROM LOBENGULA STOP OPPOSITION PAPERS WITH COLUMN STOP CAN YOU JOIN IT SOONEST AND REPORT TROUBLE AND PROGRESS STOP CONGRATU-LATIONS STOP LIKE OLD TIMES STOP CORNFORD

Fonthill looked up in astonishment. 'You don't mean that you are going to join the column, surely?'

At this point, Jenkins rose and ostentatiously walked to where his pack lay. There he began

319

unpacking it. Alice followed him with her eyes before replying.

'I must, Simon.' She spoke softly and slowly. 'When I agreed to accompany you on this expedition, I did so on the understanding that I would report it for the *Morning Post*. You know that. I made a commitment to Cornford.'

'Yes, but this thing could develop now into a full-scale war, another Isandlwana for all I know. You can't be involved in that, my darling. It would be far too dangerous.'

She blew out her cheeks. 'Well, my love, let's see.' She began counting on her fingers. 'So far on this trip I have been involved in a close-up encounter with lions; two attacks by Portuguese mercenaries; a fight with slavers; and I have been abducted. Now, a bit of old-fashioned campaigning with a British invading force – for that's what it sounds like – should really represent only a touch of light relief, don't you think?'

Fonthill's face was thunderous. 'Don't be flippant, Alice. We agreed that you would report for the *Morning Post* only on our expedition, not some bloody invasion of the whole territory.'

'Yes, but...' Alice now gave her husband her sweetest smile, 'did you not wish to see for yourself this wonderful farming country in Mashonaland that the prospecting column will discover? And didn't Mr Rhodes offer to give you some of this prime land – even though it wasn't his to give? Don't you think you should look at it?'

'Oh come along, Alice. You know that I never wished you to become involved with the column.

320

I really thought that your journalistic days were over – with the exception, that is, of reporting on our particular expedition.' He held up the cable. 'Cornford speaks about "the opposition" accompanying the column. This means that you will be in it again up to your neck, trying to get scoops and all the rest of it. I know what you are like. You will be sticking your neck out, taking risks to get exclusives and so on. You will be well and truly back in the profession. And I shall lose you, I know it.' He floundered for a moment, lost for further words. 'Dammit all, it's not right, you know.'

Alice's face lost its expression of sweet cynicism and she reached out and took his hand. 'My darling, you will *never* lose me, you know that.' She paused for a moment and then spoke softly again. 'When I look at you, my love, I see a nose broken by a musket barrel in Afghanistan, a back terribly scarred by a Dervish whip in the Sudan, and now a chest cut horribly by a Portuguese knife. You have sustained all of this in the service of the Empire, although you haven't served formally in the army for years. Yet I do not begrudge you your adventuring, although I worry about you terribly. But I must have a life too, you know. It would perhaps be different if we had a child, but...' her voice faltered for a moment, 'we do not, so one half of us can't be off adventuring for the Queen and the other sitting at home knitting. Well, not this half anyway.'

Fonthill gripped her hand tightly in return.

'You see,' she continued, 'I have made a commitment to Cornford and he was kind enough to take me on. Now I don't anticipate for one moment returning to the *Morning Post* as a full-time correspondent, even if they would have me. But to be *here*, on the spot, so to speak, of this remarkable expansion of the Empire – even if I don't approve of it, perhaps particularly *because* I don't approve of it – and not write about it would be a terrible waste of the talent I know I have. I must report on what happens to this column and see it through. Then I can stop. Do you see?'

Simon sighed. 'Very well. I shall come with you, of course. But I must give 352 and Mzingeli the chance to opt out, if they wish.'

'Of course.'

Wearily, Fonthill stood and called Jenkins and Mzingeli over. They sat around Alice while Simon explained the situation. 'So,' he concluded, 'we cannot ask you to accompany us – nor the boys, of course – and I can understand why you in particular, Mzingeli, would want to return to the Transvaal. It is up to you.'

'Well.' Jenkins looked affronted. 'I go where you go, you know that, bach sir. But if you don't want...'

'Don't be silly. Of course we both want you. Please come with us. There will be plenty to do. What about you, Mzingeli? I would continue to pay you, of course, but we shall quite understand if you have had enough of danger and fighting.'

The tracker gave an almost imperceptible nod of the head. 'I come,' he said. 'You want Ntini and Joshua?'

'Oh yes please,' interjected Alice. 'I would like them to come and run my cables back for me.'

'Yes. Then they come.'

Simon gave a weary grin and rose to his feet. 'It seems,' he said, 'as though Fonthill's private army stays in being, then. Thank you both. Well done. Now, I suppose I ought to go and see the bloody king.'

'Not before you have shaved,' said Alice. 'And you, 352. You look like a pair of pirates. But you, Mzingeli, have managed to preserve your essential elegance and dignity. I am proud of you.'

She received the tracker's slightly embarrassed half-smile in return.

Later, Fonthill and Mzingeli walked down the hill to the king's house. Simon's anger at Lobengula's abduction of Alice had abated somewhat, not least because he had sensed a change in mood by the Matabele towards him and his party. The men who had met him out on the high veldt had been surly and had not engaged in conversation with Mzingeli, merely stating that they had come to fetch the white man back to his wife. In Bulawayo, there was now an undoubted air of hostility. Warriors were sitting outside their huts, ostentatiously sharpening their assegais and bending new hides around the framework of their shields. If Simon caught their eye, he received a scowl. It was not a good time to attempt to rebuke a king whose people were itching to go to war, to wash their spears in the blood of white men.

He found Lobengula standing, for once, and talking to his *inDunas*. The king whirled round and indicated that Fonthill and Mzingeli should sit, and then walked slowly to his couch.

Simon inclined his head. 'Tell the king,' he said to Mzingeli, 'that I hope I find him in good health and that his foot is causing him no pain.'

Lobengula ignored the pleasantries. 'I take back your wife because my foot bad,' he said, through the tracker. 'If you there when my men found her, they would explain that we borrow her. But you gone. We not harm her. Treat her well. And then send my people to tell you we have her safe here and bring you back.'

'I have to say, your majesty, that in my country it is a criminal offence to abduct someone's wife.'

At this, Lobengula stood and advanced on the seated pair, so that he loomed over them, his face like thunder. 'You not in your country,' he shouted, 'you in mine. I do what I want here. But I no harm your wife. I ask her to do service for me. If white men respect king, she should do that service.'

Fonthill kept his voice level and looked the king in the eye. 'You will know that my wife is not a doctor, and that in England, as in Matabeleland, her duty is to her husband. But she believes in trying to reduce pain with the drugs at her disposal. How is your foot now?'

The directness of the question and the refusal of Fonthill to be bullied slightly disconcerted Lobengula. He raised his eyebrows and then lifted his right foot and replaced it again. 'Foot better,' he said. 'King is grateful to Nkosana. What you do now?'

'Er ... I understand that the prospectors that your majesty has kindly allowed to enter your country have arrived on the southern border. We intend to join them.'

'Ah!' The king pointed his assegai blade towards Fonthill. 'I agreed for men to come and make road and dig. Now I have foreign impi at my border. Guns and big witchcraft light. It is too much. There is a wall around the word of a chief. But white men always lie.' There was a murmur of approval from the *inDunas*.

'Well...' Fonthill began, hesitantly. But the king was speaking again, quickly and with vehemence.

'Look,' he said, putting aside his spear and using his hands to illustrate his words. 'England is like chameleon stalking a fly. Chameleon changes colour to go into background. It rocks to and fro on feet,' he cupped his hand, palm down, and imitated the actions, 'and advances so nobody notices. Then flashes out tongue and eats fly.' The fingers of his hand leapt forward. The king's eyes stared into Simon's. 'I am fly. England is chameleon.'

As if exhausted, Lobengula sank down on to his couch. 'When you go?' he asked.

'As soon as we are able to buy provisions for the journey.'

'Good. You take letter for me to chief of this impi, man called Jameson. I know him. Like you, I thought him friend. At one time.' The last three words were heavily emphasised, and Mzingeli translated them faithfully.

Fonthill chose to ignore the innuendo. 'Of course,' he said. 'I will take the letter.'

The king spoke to one of his *inDunas*, and an unsealed envelope was produced containing the letter. It was addressed, Simon noticed, to Dr

L.S. Jameson. The king rose, indicating that the audience was over, and Fonthill and Mzingeli also stood, then bowed and left the hut.

Outside, Fonthill wiped his brow. 'Phew. That was not easy. Do you think they will go to war, Mzingeli?'

The tracker shrugged his shoulders. 'People and *inDunas* want to,' he said. 'But king knows power of white man and he afraid to throw assegai. He know you beat Zulu. Pot is boiling and he wants to keep lid on it. But maybe he don't.'

Back in their own hut, Alice and Jenkins had prepared a meal. Before eating, the four of them drank a little beer and Simon recounted what had happened at his meeting. As the envelope was not sealed, he took out its contents and read it. It was written in English, in a hand accustomed to writing bills, and Fonthill recognised the long loops and crossed Ts of Fairbairn. Its message was a simple repetition of the king's complaints already expressed to Simon, but it ended on a note of diplomatic insolence that he could not resist reading out: 'Has the king killed any white men that an impi is on the border,' it ran, 'or have the white men lost something they are looking for?'

Alice slapped her thigh in delight. 'Good for him,' she said. 'The old devil has guts and also a good sense of humour. I can't help liking him, you know.'

'So it seems.' Fonthill sniffed. 'But you seem to have forgotten that he lops off his subject's hands and noses at the pop of a champagne cork. Speaking for myself, I shall be glad to get out of his kraal now. I must say I worry for Fairbairn if trouble breaks out.'

'Well,' said Jenkins, 'I'd wager that that old Jock can look after 'imself. 'E's well in with the king. Where else would the old boy get his grog, eh?'

Alice nodded. 'Quite. But Simon, I think you would be wise to go and see Fairbairn. He has his own source of contact with Rhodes, it seems, and he is well informed about the column and the politics involved there. I gather it is a bit of a witch's brew.'

'Good idea. He might be able to help me get this agreement document with King Umtasa safely back to Kimberley. You will need Ntini and perhaps Joshua for your dispatches. And we must get our horses back from him anyway. I will go after dinner.'

The smell of stale tobacco and personal functions met Fonthill as he walked through the trader's door (did his shop never close?). Fairbairn, his pipe in mouth, came from behind his counter and extended his hand.

'Welcome back,' he said. 'I've heard you had a few knocks down in that swamp country, but at least you didn't get the fever.' He gestured to a rickety cane chair and picked up a whisky bottle. 'Rest your weary body. Care to join me in a wee dram?'

'Ah, that would be very kind of you. Thank you very much.'

'It'll only cost you two shillings.'

'What? Oh ... er ... yes, of course.'

Fairbairn poured out two minuscule measures and set them down on a dusty table before pulling up another chair. 'You'll have heard that the column has arrived, down in Tuli?'

'Yes, so I understand. We shall be setting off to join them once we've settled things up here. We will need some supplies from you and, of course, our horses.'

'That will be no problem. Cheers. Here's to the Queen, the poor lassie.'

'Er ... yes. The Queen.' Fonthill tasted the whisky, coughed and replaced the glass. 'Lobengula has asked me to take the letter you presumably wrote for him to a Dr Jameson. Who is he?'

'Aye, I wrote it. I usually write the king's letters now. He knows what he wants to say, so I just put it into English. Jameson, you say? Ah, quite a character. He's become virtually Rhodes's right-hand man – outside business, that is. He was the first doctor to set up practice in Kimberley, and Rhodes took a shine to him. He's a little Scotsman and as tough as nails. Great horseman and traveller and even better talker; he's been up here several times and the king likes him. Makes him laugh. Now he seems to handle all the dirty work that Rhodes can't do himself.'

'These five hundred "police", or whatever they are – where do they come from and what's their purpose?'

'Well, Cecil John's original idea was that the settlers would be able to protect themselves. They would be stiffened, so to speak, with a few regular officers, and Frank Johnson, who has organised the column and is in charge of the workmen and settlers, himself has the rank of major. Rhodes would provide weapons and ammunition. There would be no line of communication stretching back because these chaps would be self-sufficient, able to look after themselves along the way and in Mashonaland. You get the drift?'

Fonthill nodded.

Fairbairn grinned. 'Well, the powers that be in Whitehall didn't like the sound of a bunch of amateur soldiers heading into a country bristling with natives just itching to get their assegais into their bellies, and they insisted that Rhodes should organise proper protection for the column, otherwise they'd cancel his charter. So Rhodes gave in. He's now got these police – so called so as not to upset his majesty here – with the column, armed to the teeth and under the command of a regular soldier from the Inniskilling Dragoons, a Colonel Pennefather. And they've got to leave a chain of forts behind them.'

'Good lord,' said Fonthill. 'So who is in command of the whole column, then?'

'Ah, that's just the point. It was obvious that there would be trouble if the major who had organised the whole thing was outranked by a colonel. So Rhodes has sent his very canny Scots doctor along, with no obvious rank or position but with his power of attorney.' Fairbairn giggled into his pipe stem. 'That means that nobody can do anything without Jameson's approval, because he's the moneybags. Rhodes's company, of course, is paying for everything, so Jameson is in effective control.'

Fonthill frowned. 'It sounds a ridiculous situation to me. Very complicated and tortuous.'

Fairbairn leaned forward and slapped Fonthill on the knee. 'Ah, you know what Rhodes is like. Everything is done on the run, on the back of an envelope sort of thing. But it seems to work in the end. And that's true of this expedition. They've all worked harmoniously together through Bechuanaland, so I hear, and built a damned good road.'

'Yes, but the difficult bit is about to start. What happens if Lobengula attacks? You know his people are looking for a fight.'

'Aye, you're right there.' The Scotsman looked rueful for the first time. 'But Rhodes certainly doesn't want a fight. That's why the route for the road has been taken so far away from Bulawayo. The colonel will be looking to gain a medal or two by taking on the Matabele, but the civilians are in charge of the column, and Jameson and Johnson will be out to avoid bloodshed.' Then his face lit up. 'And it's my view that dear old Lobengula wouldn't want to unleash his warriors. He just wants a quiet life.'

Fonthill nodded. 'I hope you are right. But tell me, Mr Fairbairn, I believe you have a fairly regular means of communication with Rhodes.'

'Yes, I do. I've got a reliable set of laddies who can travel safely up and down to Kimberley. In fact, your wife has used me to get one of her stories back down to the cable station. There'll be a charge, o' course.'

'Of course. Let me know what it is. There is an important document that I wish to send back to Rhodes. I will bring it tomorrow. Now, can we talk about provisions for our trip to the Tuli...'

They set off two days later. There was no opportunity to say goodbye to the king, for he had left Bulawayo to visit one of his villages to the north. However, it seemed that he had had a pang of conscience about his abduction of Alice, for he gave Fonthill a farewell gift of a wagon and six oxen to carry them on their journey. His contrition might also have extended to the letter of complaint addressed to Jameson, for he asked Simon to tell the doctor that he would be dispatching one hundred and fifty native labourers to expand the work force of the column – 'Although,' said Fairbairn, who had passed on the message, 'whether he actually does so is entirely another matter, o' course.'

The party consisted of Simon, Alice, Jenkins, Mzingeli, Ntini and Joshua. The three boy bearers who had come with them on the long journey from Kimberley, out east to the forest and wetlands of Manica and back again to Bulawayo had been released, with a handful of gold sovereigns and a Snider rifle each.

The journey was uneventful and even enjoyable, for the weather was pleasant, the trail well defined and for once they all felt free from danger or the need to hurry. Alice's wound had long since healed, leaving hardly a trace of a scar, which produced much ribaldry between about Simon's prowess with needle and thread. Good food and the healing powers of Mzingeli's herbs had hastened Fonthill's recovery from the effects of de Sousa's knife-work, and all in all, the party was in good spirits as the oxen plodded over the low veldt towards the Sashe river. Simon had dispatched his document signed by King Umtasa back to Rhodes with a letter explaining all that had happened in that region and telling the millionaire that he was about to join the column of pioneers. His disillusionment with Rhodes's expansionist ambitions and Alice's return to hard-nosed journalism had diminished with the promise of exploring the fine farming land of Mashonaland.

The further they rode south, the more they realised that this mopane woodland, which stretched throughout southern Matabeleland to the Macaloutsi and Shashe rivers at the border, was ideal country for an ambush. Although it was the height of the winter dry season and the thorn trees had lost their foliage and their bark had turned black, presenting a kind of charred, dead forest appearance, visibility was remarkably restricted. A man standing amidst it could only see for about one hundred yards. The impression of crossing burned-out country after a fire was heightened by the sun beating down day after day from a clear sky as the temperature soared, and heat seemed to bounce back from the dry soil, turning their nostrils into hot, acrid channels.

'If the Mattabellies want to come at this column thing,' sniffed Jenkins, 'this is the place for it. The blokes cuttin' trees and all wouldn't see a thing until the black fellers were on 'em, see.'

His view was more than confirmed when, at last, the party mounted a hill and saw below them the column at work. A party of pioneers –

all white men – led the way, cutting down trees to the stumps with their axes, while a second group used horses and mules to pull the trunks away. Out ahead and on either side ranged horsemen, presumably of the 'police', acting as scouts to warn of potential attack. But as Fonthill watched from his high vantage point, he saw that some of these outriders were clearly lost, for they were slowly making their way in circles, often blundering back into the tree-cutters before turning and venturing back into the bush again. Behind the pioneers snaked a long column of wagons and oxen, stretching back for at least two miles. Halfway along the line, Simon picked out a large, low-slung trailer, carrying the searchlight, with its own steam engine, dynamo and battery. He shook his head. It was clear that it would take at least two hours for this clumsy line to form into a laager if it was attacked.

'God, they're vulnerable,' he muttered. 'If the Matabele attacked now, it would be a massacre.'

Jenkins cocked a quizzical eye. 'Best to tell 'em, then?'

Fonthill frowned. 'I don't want to get off on the wrong foot with this Jameson, or with the other two so-called commanders. But you are right. They can't go on like this.'

The little party allowed their horses and oxen to pick their own way down the side of the hill until they drew level with the first of the wood-clearers. Dr Jameson, Fonthill was told, was back in the leading wagon, and there they found him, sitting on the driver's seat, scribbling on a pad. Simon looked at him keenly. He was a little man, dressed for the trek in rough boots, old trousers and a flannel shirt, opened almost to the waist in the heat. His bush hat had been thrown aside to reveal a balding head and a moustached face that showed character: a fine forehead, full lips, a firm chin and eyes that were as bright as a monkey's.

Diffidently Fonthill introduced himself, with apologies for his intrusion. Immediately the doctor's face lit up and he took in the members of the party in one swift, appraising glance: Simon, slim and weathered, with experience lining his face; Alice, her features tanned by the sun and dust-covered, but presenting a refreshingly feminine figure in her jodhpurs, cotton shirt and soft blue neckerchief; Jenkins with his immense moustache, width of shoulder and black button eyes; and Mzingeli, as dignified as a native chief with his erect posture and white hair, but holding back discreetly.

'My word, Fonthill,' said Jameson, jumping upright and reaching across to pump Simon's hand. 'I was hoping that we would meet up.' He spoke with only the softest of Edinburgh accents. 'I've heard so much about you and,' he gave a small bow to Alice, 'your wife and the rest of your party. Rhodes told me all about you, and I've been reading with fascination your pieces in the *Morning Post*, Mrs Fonthill. Och, what a time you seem to have had of it.'

Alice summoned up her sweetest smile, and relieved by the warmth of their welcome, Fonthill introduced her formally and then Jenkins and Mzingeli.

'Right,' said Jameson. 'Hitch your horses to the

end of my wagon and pull yours in behind it, if you can get in. We only progress, of course, by fits and starts as the way is cleared up front, but we are still travelling at the rate of about ten miles a day, which I think is pretty good given the workload and this heat. Then you must all come and have a cup of tea with me and meet Johnson and Pennefather, my ... er... colleagues.'

Fonthill was pleased that the invitation clearly included Mzingeli. It looked as though Jameson was one of the new breed of colonists who were relaxed about relationships between black and white – and that was a relief. Within minutes they were all sitting at the side of the column drinking tea from primitive and distinctly pioneering tin mugs. Johnson and Pennefather, it seemed, had ridden on ahead with the scouts in the van.

'Congratulations on your good work with Lobengula,' said Jameson. 'I can well imagine that getting him to agree to our entry was not easy. How is the old boy's gout?'

Fonthill gestured for Alice to speak. 'Oh, I'm only a first-aid practitioner,' she said quickly. 'I have been plying him with morphine injections and anti-gout pills. They seem to have begun to work, but the real problem is his drinking, his diet and his lack of exercise.'

'Oh aye.' The doctor nodded. 'I did exactly the same when I was up there and came to the same conclusion.' He turned back to Simon. 'But how did you get on out in the east? Last I heard formally was that you were setting out, and then of course I read Mrs Fonthill's account of the attack on the slavers. Marvellous stuff.'

Simon inclined his head, then related to Jameson his securing of a 'first stage' treaty with King Umtasa. He decided to omit the story of Lobengula's abduction of Alice, but described in full the clash with de Sousa and the man's claims to territorial suzerainty over Umtasa's kingdom, and also his persistence in cultivating Lobengula.

'The problem,' concluded Fonthill, 'is that whatever he has signed, the king is very uneasy about the size of the column here and particularly the police you have with you. I think he is coming to the conclusion that this is a virtual invasion of his country. Here, I have a letter for you from him.'

Jameson read it impassively, until giving a wry smile at the concluding questions. 'Aye,' he said, tapping the envelope against his moustache. 'I understand his worries and I can well imagine the pressures he's been under from all those supplicants at his court. What's more, I know that his *inDunas* think he's giving away too much and all his warriors want a fight. But, you know,' and he shrugged his shoulders, 'this is not the eighteen sixties. We're nearing the twentieth century now and the old boy has to move with the times. Civilisation will come to Matabeleland whether he likes it or not. And he has signed those treaties with us. We have the right to make our road and dig for minerals in Mashonaland.'

Alice leaned forward. 'But do you have the right to settle his land?' she enquired.

'Oh.' Jameson waved the envelope dismissively. 'That will come inevitably. Matabeleland will become a British protectorate sooner or later, just like Bechuanaland.'

Alice gave the little man the full benefit of her smile. 'Yes, but your treaties with the king acknowledge his ownership of both Matabeleland and Mashonaland. You cannot just ride roughshod over him and colonise the place, now can you?'

Jameson frowned, and seemed to recall the fact that Alice was not just Fonthill's wife but also a journalist for one of Britain's most influential newspapers. He was seeking a reply when Simon, uneasy about the direction the conversation had taken, intervened.

'When we left Bulawayo,' he said, 'the atmosphere was very uncomfortable. The warriors seemed to be preparing for war: there was much spear-sharpening and new shield construction, and the women were making sandals for their men, always a bad sign. And, of course, Lobengula has the five hundred rifles and the ammunition that I took to him, although I must say I have seen no sign of them practising with the guns. But do you expect to be attacked?'

'It is certainly a possibility. So, in the end, I am glad that we have the soldiers with us, although,' he gave a wry smile, 'Rhodes didn't want 'em. Soldiers, he said, always end up looking for a fight. But we do take good precautions. We laager every night, set off firecrackers at intervals in the bush through the hours of darkness, and we have this damned great searchlight, which,' his smile broadened into a grin, 'I borrowed from the British navy at Simonstown. We use it through the night, sweeping the bush. So far, it has frightened to death every Kaffir we've met.'

Fonthill acknowledged the ploy with a smile. 'The trouble, though,' he said, 'is that you are in ideal terrain for ambush – and you are likely to remain in it for another hundred miles or so. Your line stretches back for two miles. By the look of it, your scouts out in the bush wander a bit – and I don't blame them for it, because you can't really see your hand in front of your face out there – so you will get precious little warning of an attack. Like the Zulus, the Matabele like to attack at dawn. You would never have time to pull the wagons into a laager.'

Silence fell on the little gathering. It was broken eventually by Jenkins, who munched his moustache and nodded. 'The captain's right, sir,' he said. ''E knows about these things, see.'

Jameson glanced at them both. 'Look,' he said eventually. 'I'm really just a general practitioner from Edinburgh, so I wouldn't dream for a minute of arguing with two distinguished ex-soldiers who I know have fought at Isandlwana, Kabul, Kandahar, Majuba, El Kebir and Khartoum. What you say sounds sensible to me, but I shall have to put it to Pennefather. He should be back soon. Now, tell me what your plans are. I do hope you are joining us.'

Fonthill explained that Alice had been instructed by her editor to join the press contingent on the column (it turned out to be small – five only, all men, of course) and that they would indeed like to stay until some sort of settlement had been established at the end of the trek. He added that Rhodes had promised him land in the new territory and he wanted to see it for himself.

'Then you're most welcome. We can certainly use your knowledge of the country and your military expertise.'

At that point two men on horseback joined them. The first, a lithe figure, deeply tanned and dressed like a Boer, was introduced as Frank Johnson. Fonthill was surprised at how young he looked (he later learned that he was only twenty-four) for a man who had such a record. He had, of course, hunted and prospected through the country since his teens and he had the skill to put together the logistics of this remarkable operation, which was, so far, working well. The second man was easily recognisable as Colonel Pennefather, in that, despite the heat, he was wearing the uniform of a colonel in the Inniskilling Dragoons. A tall man, with a white moustache, he regarded Fonthill steadily.

'Heard about you,' he said abruptly. 'Who were you with?'

'Originally the 24th of Foot, Colonel, and then the Queen's Own Corps of Guides on the North-West Frontier.'

'Must say, you look damned young to have a CB.'

'Oh, that came up with the rations after the Sudan,' said Simon airily. 'The DCM of Jenkins here was far more important.'

Jenkins stood immediately and shook the hands of both men, bestowing on them his great moustache-bending smile. Johnson took this act of equality with equanimity, but Pennefather's jaw dropped momentarily, although he gave Jenkins's hand a firm enough grip.

'Er ... Fonthill here has a point about our defences,' said Jameson.

'Ah.' Simon tried to look uninvolved. 'It was just something that occurred to Jenkins and me as we breasted that hill up there. It's probably not quite got home to you because you've not had the benefit of our vantage point. If you have a minute, perhaps I could show you.'

'Certainly,' said Pennefather, with a quickness that surprised Fonthill. 'I would be glad to have your view. Let's go now.'

At the top of the hill, Simon swept his hand back along the wagon line, the end of which was out of sight to the west. 'It's a single line, of course...' he said.

'And stretching about two miles,' Jenkins pointed out helpfully.

'...and I don't see how you could laager it in time if the Matabele attack.'

'Probably won't be necessary.' The colonel pulled on his moustache. 'We've got ample fire-power, you know. Five hundred rifles should be able to stop any kaffirs coming at us, I'd say.'

Fonthill stifled a sigh. 'With respect, Colonel, Pulleine had one and a half thousand seasoned professional infantrymen at his disposal at Isandlwana – *and* he was on a plain and could see the Zulus coming at him for at least a mile. Yet he and his men were still massacred. Lobengula has about twenty thousand warriors, all descended from the Zulus. In this bush they could be on and through you in two minutes.'

Pennefather scowled and Simon took a deep breath, prepared to continue the argument. The old soldier, however, stiffened in the saddle, turned to Jameson and said, 'He's right. We *are* vulnerable.'

Jameson lifted his eyebrows and addressed Simon. 'What do you propose we should do?'

'If the colonel agrees, I would suggest that you change the method of advance. Instead of having your wagons in single file, you should have them in two parallel lines. This will reduce the length of the column and enable you to close the two lines at front and back in the event of an attack by just drawing over the leading and rear wagons. This could be done quickly, and although it would be a hell of a long laager, it *would* provide cover for the men to fall back into. And I believe you should have the scouts riding much further out from the wagons. The officers in charge don't seem to have sight of the column because of the thickness of the bush and are getting lost as a result. They should be given compasses so that they can plot their courses and range wider. This should give you more time to laager if there is an attack. And don't forget that like the Zulus, the Matabeles like to attack at dawn, so the pickets should be out during the night in extended order.' Fonthill paused, suddenly realising that he was sounding like a senior officer talking to three juniors. 'I ... er ... hope that this is helpful.'

Jameson, Johnson and Pennefather exchanged glances. Johnson spoke for the first time. 'This would halve your rate of progress, Doctor, and consequently cost more money,' he said. 'Can we afford it?'

The diminutive doctor looked across at

Pennefather. 'Colonel?'

'It's a good idea,' said the tall man. 'But it will cost you.'

'We'll do it,' said Jameson. 'Johnson, you arrange it with the wagon master, and Colonel, I will leave the matter of the scouts to you, of course. Thank you, Fonthill and ... er ... Jenkins. Now, let's get back.'

When they returned, they found that Alice had gone to find her fellow journalists and Mzingeli was erecting a tent for Simon and Alice, Jenkins having already elected to sleep in the wagon with the tracker.

'I don't mind tellin' you, bach sir,' said Jenkins, 'that I'm glad they've accepted what you suggested, like. I'd 'ave felt very, very exposed, see, sleeping in this long thin line with blokes out in the bush gettin' lost. Even I could see that this was barmy.'

Fonthill shrugged. 'Well, I must say, Pennefather took it well. I have a feeling that he hasn't seen much active service, so I hope these police chaps know what they're about.'

The night was not exactly passed tranquilly, for little landmines of gelignite, spread all around the laager and fired from the searchlight's battery, exploded throughout the dark hours. The searchlight itself stabbed the bush like some ghostly probing finger. Fonthill wondered if the column had the facilities to continue this nightly practice throughout the rest of the long trek, but had to confess that he could well understand these defences working against the superstitious Matabele.

The next morning, he found that the 'police'

were, in fact, actual policemen, in that they were composed of five troops of the British South Africa Police and three troops of Bechuanaland Police, more militia cavalrymen than gendarmerie, but experienced horsemen who were used to putting down isolated instances of skirmishes with natives in the bush. He also learned that Pennefather had served in the Zulu and Boer campaigns. The puzzle of why the pioneers themselves were doing the labouring – an unheard-of thing in Africa, where black labour was plentiful and cheap – was explained when he was told that the original one hundred and fifty black labourers had been lent by King Khama in Bechuanaland, but had been withdrawn once they had left their own country.

Fonthill realised that he had not passed on Lobengula's verbal promise to provide his own detachment of workers for the column, but when he confided this to Jameson, the doctor nodded and seemed unimpressed. 'I'll believe that when I see 'em,' he said. Simon's lingering doubts about discipline within the column, however, were dissipated to some extent early that morning when the pioneers assembled to begin their labours at the head of the line.

Setting off on their duties, they looked more like elite cavalry than labourers. They wore brown corduroy uniforms, yellow leather leggings and bush hats and had waterproof coats strapped behind their saddles. They carried Martini-Henry rifles in gun buckets, Webley revolvers in holsters at their waists and long-handled axes slung across their saddles. Fonthill could see that they were

343

mounted on fine, well-salted horses and he could not help speculating how much this had all cost Rhodes. Later he learned that they were earning seven shillings and sixpence a day, with the policemen receiving five shillings, and that they had been promised a grant of five thousand acres of land each and the right to peg fifteen mining claims. He decided that he would not offer these details to Alice. She would only point out that the land was not Rhodes's to give. Once at the head of the column, the men stripped off and worked with a will, although their weapons were at their sides and their mounts tethered nearby, ready for them to join the police in defending the column at the sound of a bugle. The thud of axes cutting into wood and trees falling was soon to become a constant companion to Fonthill as the days passed.

He rode to meet Jameson, who was already out and about. 'I have written back to the king,' said the doctor. 'Tried to reassure him by saying that we have no militaristic ambitions at all and that the police are with us purely for protection, as insisted on by London. All of which is true, of course, although I don't suppose he will believe me.'

Fonthill nodded. 'Thank you. By the way, I would like us to be useful to you,' he said, 'but I don't think we would be much good wielding axes. What if my chaps and I scout ahead every day and even do a little shooting for the pot?'

'Excellent idea,' said the doctor. He reached out and caught Simon's arm. 'Look here,' he said. 'I am most grateful to you for your suggestions yesterday.' He nodded to where the wagons had been lined up in two rows. 'It's no good me saving Rhodes and the company money if we all end up disembowelled. And I was delighted to see the way Pennefather accepted you. It's a relief to me to have you on board, I must say.'

Fonthill smiled. 'Delighted to be of service.' He looked around at the busy scene. It still looked vulnerable. 'Tell me, Jameson. You know Lobengula. Do you think he will attack?'

Jameson frowned and lowered his voice. 'To be honest, my dear fellow, I don't see how he can resist doing so. As you know, we've deliberately mapped our route to keep as much distance between him and us as possible, but I know we offer such a juicy target that, considering how his warriors are jumping up and down and anxious to go to war, I don't see how we are going to get away without blood being shed.'

Smiling his thanks, Fonthill pulled at his bridle and rode away. Unbidden, terrible memories of Isandlwana and Rorke's Drift flooded into his mind as he made his way back towards the column. He saw again the Zulu warriors – 'Here they come, as thick as ants and as black as hell!' a terrified sentry had shouted – streaming across towards the red-coated defenders; he smelled the cordite and the blue smoke of battle; and he heard once more the screams of the wounded and the dying. Was it going to happen again – and this time with Alice amongst it all? He shook his head. He could not envisage how this attenuated and vulnerable column could escape the sort of massacre he had seen in Zululand eleven years ago. Surely it could not survive?

345

Chapter 15

Three months later, Simon, Alice, Jenkins, Mzingeli, Ntini and Joshua stood amongst cheering pioneers in the shade of jacaranda trees as the Union Jack was hauled up a very crooked pole and fluttered at the foot of Mount Hampden. The end of the trek had provided a rather embarrassing anticlimax, in that, having reached the high kopje, outspanned and declared the terminus Fort Salisbury, in honour of the Prime Minister of Britain, Johnson, as nominal leader, had sent a scout to the top of the kopje who had then seen the *real* Mount Hampden ten miles to the west. The ceremony had to be repeated at the new site, but this time the embryonic township was firmly declared to be the capital of their new country, which was then and there formally annexed in the name of Queen Victoria.

'Why don't they call it Fort Rhodes and have done with it?' whispered Alice.

'Probably will within a week,' grunted Simon. He was almost right, for it took only a few days before it had become common practice to call the new territory 'Rhodesia'.

The journey from the border to their destination, some two hundred miles to the northeast of Bulawayo, had not been without incident, for it had been a gruelling task to cut a road through the wooded territory of the south and

346

then up over the mountain ridge that ushered them into Mashonaland. But despite all the threats and alarms along the way, Lobengula had not attacked. When the column reached the Lundi river, he had sent a message saying, 'Go back at once and take your young men,' but nothing ensued. Every night the searchlight had probed the bush, and every morning, from three a.m. until dawn, the column stood to, waiting for the attack that never came.

'Why didn't he come, eh, Fonthill?' asked Colonel Pennefather just after Mount Hampden had been reached. 'He could have taken us at any time, you and I know that. Why didn't he do it?'

Simon shrugged. 'I presume because he just didn't want to. For all his faults, Lobengula is a shrewd man. His spies were observing us all the time as we plodded and cut our way through the timber country in the low veldt in the south, and he knew that a couple of impis could have overwhelmed us at any time. Yet he also knew that a terrible retribution would come afterwards, which would mean the loss of his country. He remembered that eleven years ago, Ulundi followed Isandlwana. He doesn't want to take on the British Empire.'

'Hmm. Suppose you are right. Pity, in a way. I wouldn't have minded a bit of a scrap, don't you know.'

Along the route, Jameson had dutifully followed the instructions from Whitehall that the column should leave a string of forts behind it, with small garrisons, to protect the lines of communications to the south. The last one had been called Fort

Charter, and the one preceding it, Fort Victoria, had been sited just after Providential Pass, the 1,500-foot-high passage through the escarpment that marked the entry into Mashonaland. From this vantage point, the pioneers had looked down across the rolling, lush plains of what was, literally, their promised land. Here, the high veldt offered long grass and distant views, merging into mauve hills on the far horizons. This was what they had been straining to reach as they chopped and sawed their way through the humid bush of the low veldt. Here, stretching before them, were the farmlands and rich mineral sites that would make all their labour worthwhile.

After the pioneers had finally been dismissed as semi-soldiers under the flagstaff at Salisbury, it was not at first the threat of war that caused them problems as they spread out across the thinly populated land of the new Rhodesia, looking to stake their claims. The Matabele was not the enemy as they ranged through the high veldt, anxious to stake and then register their precious acres. Fonthill, together with his little party, was among them. And he, like the others – prospective farmers and miners alike – suffered as nature turned on them all, as though she had decided that if Lobengula would not protect his own, she would.

The worst storms that the region had seen in many years swept across the high veldt in late 1890 and the early months of 1891, turning dried-up dongas into swollen rivers and washing away the early diggings that the miners had begun. After the rains came mosquitoes and the

348

blackwater fever, and rough burial grounds sprang up, almost outnumbering the wooden shacks that formed the early townships.

Fonthill, with Alice, Jenkins and Mzingeli – plus Ntini and Joshua, who had agreed to stay and help establish the farm – suffered less than some of the others, in that Simon had staked his claim in the north of the territory, far away from the diggings in the foothills of the mountains of the south, which had been so badly affected. They rode out the storms in the little huts the men had built. The members of the press contingent had returned home, of course, after Mount Hampden had been reached, and Alice had contentedly stepped down from her assignment with the *Morning Post*, clutching to her the congratulations from her editor on the quality of her reporting and a request that she should contribute the occasional colour piece about life on the high veldt in the new country. She retained her indignation that Rhodes had succeeded in riding roughshod over Lobengula and had, as she had predicted, settled land that was not his. Within a year, some fifteen hundred settlers had followed the pioneers and were living in the old Mashonaland. But there was nothing, it seemed, that Alice or the king could do about it. She had long since acquiesced in Simon's determination to twin their land in Norfolk with a farm in the new territory, and they had all decided to grit their teeth and ride out the frightful weather to establish their holding, although it meant living the rough life of pioneers for a couple of years.

Fonthill had always known that it was Lobengula's practice to send out raiding parties among the Mashonas to keep them in line – to maintain his sovereignty over them, at least, if not on the ground they trod. He also knew that Jameson, who had been appointed by Rhodes administrator of the new territory, had attempted to keep the king sweet by giving him the ownership of a gold reef and even equipping the mine with a steam engine, with the king's initials picked out on the green paint of its boiler. It was Jameson who told Simon of the first dark shoots of unrest.

'The trouble is,' he confided, 'the Mashonas are perfectly happy to have white people living among them and don't see why they should pay tribute to old Lobengula any more. This has gone to the head of a Mashona chief called Lomagundi, who has refused to pay his dues to the old tyrant in Bulawayo. I am trying to soothe things down a bit and I don't think it will get out of hand.'

A Matabele troop was sent and Lomagundi was killed. Jameson protested, but Lobengula was evasive in his reply. Soon the incidents began to mount. Another Mashona chief cut five hundred yards of Rhodes's newly laid telegraph wire and was promptly fined by Jameson and ordered to pay the fine in cattle. He did so – but with Lobengula's cattle, which had been sent to graze on the chief's green land as part of his tribute. The king promptly sent his warriors, and this chief, too, paid the price for attempting to shield behind the white settlers. Once again Jameson's protest was met by the bland and not altogether illogical answer that while all the white men must abide by the laws of Mr Rhodes's company, the natives of Mashonaland and Matabeleland remained subject to the king's laws. Nothing in any of the treaties that had been agreed between him and Rhodes, Lobengula pointed out, negated that fact.

'I don't like any of this,' said Alice. 'The fundamentally immoral nature of Rhodes's position here is being exposed all the time. Things are building up. Rhodes must not push Lobengula too far. If he does, the lid really will come off the pot.'

There had been so many false alarms, however, both on the long journey to the north and in the petty skirmishes since the farmers and miners had become tentatively established, that few of the white folk in the tiny townships or out on the veldt believed that the explosion would come. For the Fonthills, the news was brought by a Kaffir on horseback, who arrived at their remote holding with a message from Jameson. It was terse and to the point:

Big trouble with Matabele around Fort Victoria. Can you come right away?

Simon had come to respect the little Scotsman, and such a request could not be resisted. With Jenkins and Mzingeli, therefore, he prepared to ride south. His intention was that Alice would stay with the two boys and look after the cattle. Inevitably, though, she insisted on joining them. Whatever the rights and wrongs of the 'big trouble', this would be too good a story to resist, and the arrival of the telegraph at Victoria meant that she could cable a dispatch to the *Morning Post* immediately. Simon's protests were easily overridden, and the four arrived to find that the situation around the little town had become critical.

They rode through country just outside Victoria that was littered with the corpses of killed and mutilated Mashonas. The Matabele impi had taken this opportunity to wash their spears, and it seemed that few had been spared, including natives working on the new farms, some of whom had been pursued into the farmhouses and butchered under the horrified eyes of the settlers.

Fonthill found Jameson in a determined but unfazed mood.

'Glad you could come with your private army, old chap,' he said, rising from the chair in a little hut near the ramparts where he had set up his headquarters. He bowed gallantly to Alice.

'How did it start?' asked Fonthill.

'Usual thing. The local Mashona chief here refused to bend the knee to Lobengula. In his time-honoured fashion, the king sent two and a half thousand warriors to carry out what he felt was some well-deserved disembowelling. This time, though, the chief lived close to the town. The arrival of an impi in full war regalia was frightening enough to our folk here, but then the Matabele proceeded to kill *all* of the Mashonas in the area, including, as you have seen, many who worked for the white men. Settlers from around have flocked into the town behind our rather flimsy walls and the war drums are beating.'

Alice looked up from her notebook. 'Have any white people been killed?'

'Not yet, although cattle have been stolen.' Jameson removed his spectacles and vigorously polished the lenses with his handkerchief. 'I certainly don't want war and I am sure that Lobengula doesn't either. If we do have a little skirmish here, then I think the king might even be glad that we have relieved a bit of the pressure on him by thrashing some of his young warriors.'

'Depends upon whether his foot is achin' or not, I should think,' murmured Jenkins, but no one seemed to hear him.

'The trouble is,' continued Jameson, 'the settlers here have put up with a lot over the last few days. This impi is composed of very arrogant young bloods who undoubtedly have behaved extremely badly. I am afraid that, uncharacteristically, so has Lobengula.' The administrator leaned forward. 'He has sent a most brusque letter to the magistrate here, demanding that the Mashonas who are sheltering within the walls of the fort should be handed over to Manyao, the *inDuna* who is leading the impi. He has offered one insolent concession: he says that they will not be killed near the river, where they might pollute the water, but would be finished off in the bush.'

Fonthill frowned. 'It sounds as though things have gone too far.'

'Yes. The other complicating factor is that the settlers here, having been frightened out of their lives, are just itching for a fight, and are talking about dealing with the Matabele "now and for

353

ever". So I've got two lots of hotheads on my hands, so to speak. Even so, I think I can handle it.' He sat back in his chair, his bald pate gleaming.

'What do you propose to do?' asked Fonthill.

'I have rushed a very polite but firm letter by special messenger over to Lobengula in Bulawayo, asking him to withdraw his impi at once. In the mean time, however, I have summoned Manyao to a meeting on the banks of the River Tokwe. As you know, I have always believed that talking is better than fighting. I think I can calm everyone down.'

Alice looked up from her pad, her face flushed. 'I do hope so,' she said. 'Lobengula has been pushed pretty far already in my view. I don't think anyone back home – and particularly in the government – wants another native war. It's Lord Salisbury in Number Ten now, you know. Not Disraeli.'

'Aye, I understand that. But if the members of the House of Commons could see the bodies that you saw when you rode in, then perhaps they might have a different view of things. But as I say, I am going to try and cool things down. You're welcome to come to the meeting.'

The following morning, Jameson took his kitchen chair down to the banks of the river and sat with his back to the fort, with a handful of settlers and Captain Lendy, the officer in charge of the modest detachment of soldiers based at Victoria. Fonthill, Alice, Jenkins and Mzingeli joined them.

As Fonthill arrived, he drew in his breath at the

Matabele ranged opposite the little doctor, a small group of *inDunas* at their head. He had never before seen so many of Lobengula's men arrayed for battle. One hundred and fifty of the two and a half thousand massed on the other side of the river formed a semicircle in front of Jameson. They were splendid specimens. Tall and muscular, and naked except for their loincloths and monkey tails at calf and biceps, they wore warpaint on their faces and chests and their black skin glistened in the morning sunlight. Plumes nodded from their heads, and most carried assegais and shields, though some were proudly nursing new rifles. They were restive and their postures exuded hostility, most of the warriors jigging up and down. It was as if their killing spree had released a long-pent-up savagery within them.

'Blimey,' murmured Jenkins. 'I don't like the look of that lot. 'Ow many men 'ave we got to fight 'em, if it comes to it?'

Fonthill spoke softly so that Alice could not hear. 'About forty or so soldiers, I think, with probably the same number of settlers who can handle weapons. Not exactly an army. Let's hope that Jameson can talk them out of more killing.'

The doctors raised his hand for silence. For a moment all that could be heard was the buzzing of the thousands of flies that had decided to attend the conference, probably still gorged from feasting on the bodies that surrounded the fort. Then Jameson began to speak. He did so observing the etiquette that members of the Zulu race espoused at meetings of this sort: welcoming

Manyao and his *inDunas* with compliments but suggesting that they had gone too far by indulging in the mass slaughter in the country that he, Jameson, now controlled.

Manyao was an elderly man, with the *isiCoco* ring of the *inDuna* woven into his grey hair, and he spoke with equal politeness and dignity. Through his interpreter he pointed out that the original treaty with Rhodes had acknowledged that Lobengula was king not only of Matabeleland but also of Mashonaland, and that the only powers given to the white men had been to dig for minerals, not to erect forts or settle the land. For more than a century the Matabele had collected tribute from the Mashona, and the law decreed that default was punishable by death. The action taken had been within the law and following precedent. No white people had been hurt.

Alice put her pencil in her mouth and tugged at her husband's sleeve. 'I don't approve of the killings,' she whispered in his ear, 'but if this was a court of law, old Manyao would have won the verdict hands down.'

The *inDuna* finished speaking, and it was clear that, for once, Jameson had no reply. The silence hung on the air like a blanket of embarrassment as the doctor sought uncharacteristically for words. Then one of the minor *inDunas*, named Umgandaan, stepped forward. He was much younger than Manyao, tall and well muscled, a warrior in his prime. But while Manyao had been rational and elegant, Umgandaan was truculent and loud. His king, he said, was paramount in his

356

own country, and he had been sent to perform the king's will. No white man would stop him.

His aggression produced a murmur of dissatisfaction from the small group of settlers behind Jameson's chair and gave the doctor his prompt. He cut the young man short and ordered Manyao to withdraw all of his impi across the river before sundown, or his white soldiers would drive them across.

'With what?' asked Jenkins sotto voce. 'Three blokes on 'orseback?'

The meeting broke up in surly disarray. Jameson picked up his chair and strode towards Fonthill, who blew out his cheeks in consternation. He remembered hearing that the doctor had earned a reputation in Kimberley as a hard-nosed poker player. 'You're taking a big risk, aren't you, Jameson? What will you do if they call your bluff? We're outnumbered by about fifty to one. And they've got rifles.'

The little man seemed completely unfazed. 'They'll go,' he said. 'I know these people. They think they're Zulus but they're not really. They will move back by tonight, you'll see.'

But they did not.

Looking down from the flimsy mud ramparts of the fort as the sun sank towards the horizon, Jameson, with Lendy and Fonthill, realised that the Matabele impi remained firmly encamped on the Victoria side of the river. Many of those who had remained on the far side for the morning's meeting had obviously crossed during the day and were now either sitting cross-legged on the bank or milling about, quite unperturbed, under the walls of the township. Fonthill noted, however, that all carried their weapons. In the distance, he saw that another kraal had been set on fire and more of the company's cattle were being rounded up.

'Well, I was wrong,' admitted Jameson.

'What are you going to do?' asked Fonthill.

The little Scotsman looked up sharply. 'Do? Why, disperse them, of course. Send 'em back across the river. Off you go, Lendy. How many men do you need?'

The captain looked down on the milling throng below. 'Well, it would be unwise to take all of my troop,' he said. 'Should keep some in reserve back here. I'll take forty. That should do it.'

Fonthill gulped. Forty against two and a half thousand! 'Jenkins and I will come with you,' he said.

'Rather you didn't, Fonthill,' said Jameson. 'I would be grateful if you two stayed back here with me and organised the manning of the walls. Haven't got too many chaps, you see, who know what they're doing in these matters.'

The doctor still seemed quite unconcerned. Simon's brain, unbidden, recalled the words to him of the British commander at Isandlwana when warned that twenty thousand Zulus were about to descend on him: 'I hope Johnny Zulu does attack. I'll give him a bloody nose...'

Captain Lendy strode away and Fonthill heard him giving orders to his little troop below. Simon exchanged glances with Jenkins. 'Right,' he said. 'We have little time. Come with me. We'll run through the streets calling for every fit man to

358

bring his rifle and gather in the square below. Quickly now.'

The two ran down and took to the streets. Within the eight-foot-high mud walls – not high enough, thought Fonthill – the township was more of a hamlet, with insubstantial wooden huts radiating out from the square behind the wooden doors guarding the only entrance, and forming only four streets. It took barely five minutes, given that many men were already on the ramparts, for the main population of the town to gather around them. Fonthill counted: some seventy men, old and young, but all of them carrying rifles, some more than one. Almost as many women and children had accompanied them. To one side stood the ten troopers that Lendy had left behind.

Fonthill looked over his shoulder. Lendy and his men had not saddled up yet. 'Right,' he shouted to his little group. 'Ladies, go and fetch whatever spare ammunition you have. Bring it back as quickly as you can, then take the children and lock yourselves and them in the houses.'

'I'm not doin' that,' one amply proportioned woman called from the back. 'I'm stayin' with my man. And the little 'uns will do the same.' A chorus of approval rang out from the rest of the women.

Simon glimpsed Alice arriving and joining the crowd at the back. He sighed. 'Very well, but please don't get in the way. We may have some hard fighting to do. Now.' He gestured with his hand to segregate about twenty men. 'You men stand over here with Sergeant Major Jenkins. You

359

will be in reserve and when I call will double to whatever part of the wall looks under pressure. The rest of you, space yourselves around the ramparts – but don't fire until I give the order. Troopers, come with me. I will spread you out among the civilians,' he lowered his voice, 'to give a bit of stiffening if it is needed. Right, go to your positions. Quickly now.'

He realised that Alice was at his side. Her eyes were pained. 'I have just used the telegraph to send my story,' she said. 'Oh, I do so wish it hadn't come to this.'

'So do I, darling.' Fonthill pulled her to him briefly. 'Look. I really can't see forty men dispelling two thousand. Where do you want to be?'

She looked up at him unflinchingly. 'With you, of course. I shall go and get my rifle.' And she turned on her heel and strode off.

'Strong lady, the Nkosana.' Mzingeli was at his shoulder, carrying his rifle.

'Are you going to fight, old chap?'

'Of course. Matabele long time enemy. They kill my people. Now I kill them. I stay with you.'

Fonthill nodded and looked across at Jenkins. 'You understand, 352? Hold your men back until I shout and tell you where to go on the wall.'

'Very good, bach sir.'

'Good. Come on, Mzingeli. Let's see what's happening on the other side.'

They scrambled up on to the ramparts. The natives below seemed to have sensed that battle was imminent, for those of them who had been seated had now risen and all were flourishing their spears at the men on the walls. To Fonthill, they seemed to stretch almost as far as the river and they presented a frightening sight, their plumes nodding as they danced and chanted and their painted faces contorted with derision.

He gulped. 'Throwing forty horsemen out into that lot is going to be suicide.' He spoke to himself.

Slowly the big wooden gates to the fort creaked open and Lendy and his men, their bush hats buttoned up to one side and the butts of their carbines resting on their thighs, trotted out in excellent order in two columns. Immediately the cries of the Matabele rose in a crescendo, but they did not attack. Instead they fell back a little, as though surprised at the audacity of the little group of horsemen who had come out calmly to face them.

Fonthill realised that the gates had been left gaping open. 'Close those bloody gates,' he called down. He was, of course, cutting off whatever chance of retreat Lendy's men might have, but he could not risk allowing the Matabele to cut through the horsemen and run on unimpeded into the heart of the settlement.

The troop split and wheeled to right and left, so that each man had a clear view of the enemy. Then Lendy shouted: 'Select your target. Take aim. Even-numbered troopers, FIRE!' Twenty rifles cracked as one and the same number of natives, standing at pointblank range, crumpled and fell. Lendy's voice, clipped and clear, rose up again to Fonthill. 'Reload. Odd numbers, FIRE! Reload. Even numbers, FIRE! Reload.'

Among the first to fall was Umgandaan, who

ran forward brandishing his spear. Perhaps it was his loss or the steadiness of the volleys, but immediately the mass of warriors broke and ran as fast as they could back to the dubious safety of the river. Only a handful of young, brave men followed Umgandaan's example and ran towards the troopers, only to die in their turn. From a phalanx of threatening warriors, the Matabele had splintered within seconds to become hundreds of frightened individuals, turning their backs on the enemy and running away from the guns. It was a complete rout.

'Fire at will,' screamed Lendy. Then, 'Canter, follow them up. Fire as you go.'

A single shot rang out from the wall of the fort. 'No firing from the walls,' shouted Fonthill. He realised that the men on the ramparts, only a few of whom could be called good shots, were more likely to hit the troopers than the tribesmen. Even now, as the soldiers urged their horses forward, they were in great danger, for if the Matabele rallied and counterattacked, they could surround the troopers and engulf them before the horsemen could reload. Then the fort would be virtually at their mercy, for the mud walls could be easily scaled.

But the warriors continued their headlong race towards the river, spreading out in a black mass, their truculence, like their pride, melting away as their strong legs took them from the fearful firepower of the forty white men on horses.

'Oh, thank God. Lendy is bringing them back.' Alice was at Simon's side, her rifle held listlessly at her side and tears pouring down her cheeks as her gaze took in the figures sprawled on the ground below. At least fifty of the tribesmen lay dead. All forty of the troopers, however, were trotting their horses back, their bush hats thrown back, their faces beaming with triumph. In the distance, a host of black figures could be seen wading and swimming across the river.

'It's the most amazing turnaround,' gasped Fonthill. 'Forty routing two and a half thousand. God, Lendy and his men were brave to ride out there. I am not sure I would have done it.'

'What's 'appenin' outside, then?' Jenkins called up from the square. ''Ave we won the war? Can we come up and 'ave a look?'

'Yes. Let all of them come up. The Matabele have fled.'

'Blimey. An' I didn't fire a bleedin' shot. Amazin'.'

Fonthill dropped down to order the opening of the gates and was met there by a sombre-faced Jameson. Simon shook his hand and congratulated him.

'Humph,' grunted the doctor. 'It's Lendy we must congratulate. It was the surprise, you know. The Matabele just didn't think *we* would attack *them*. They thought we would stay holed up behind these walls. Then the old fears about our guns stirred up among them when the shooting started and they just took to their heels.' He took off his hat and wiped the sweat off his pate with his handkerchief. 'Trouble is, Fonthill, I'm sure that this is not the last of it. I can't really see Lobengula accepting this. I shall have to tell Rhodes to prepare for war now. Dammit, it's

363

going to cost the company a packet.'

He hurried forward to meet Lendy, while the settlers raised a cheer to welcome back the troopers as they rode through the gates. Fonthill and Jenkins joined in the applause, but Alice and Mzingeli watched silently.

'So Rhodes is going to have his war, then,' murmured Alice.

Fonthill sighed. 'It looks like it.' His face was sombre. 'I suppose it was inevitable, once Lobengula's men began all this killing.'

'No,' she said coldly. 'It was inevitable once Rhodes sent in his damned column to invade the king's country. And I shall say so in my dispatch.' She turned away, her face tear-stained but determined, and strode off to the telegraph station.

Just before dusk descended, Jameson had Lendy send out patrols to see if the Matabele were forming up again, but the horsemen returned to report that the shattered impi had remained broken and was limping back, in small groups, towards Bulawayo. It looked as if the danger to Fort Victoria was over – at least for the time being. The doctor, however, was convinced that the Matabele threat was not ended. He confided to Fonthill that Rhodes had been advised by military men in Cape Town that a force of at least seven thousand well-equipped troops would be needed to subjugate the Matabele nation if things got out of hand.

'The company can't afford that,' he said. 'Rhodes is very strapped for cash as it is. I've got to get a second opinion – one that knows these

Kaffirs better than the colonels and generals in the Cape. I'm going to talk to the Boers.'

There were a handful of Dutchmen from the Transvaal who had moved north into Mashonaland and taken shelter in the fort. Most of them had had brushes of one sort of another with the Matabele in the past, and Jameson set about getting their advice. The next morning he took tea with Fonthill, Alice and Jenkins and told them the result of his soundings.

'These chaps say that seven thousand is ridiculous,' he said. 'They believe that a force of between eight hundred and a thousand men, well mounted and armed, will do the job.'

'Sounds light to me,' said Fonthill. 'They would need Maxims and cannon if they're going to take on all of Lobengula's impis. Where are those going to come from?'

Jameson sipped his tea and gave a rueful smile. 'That's the point. Rhodes abhors the thought of what he calls the Imperials – that's the redcoats in the Cape, with the Colonial Office behind 'em – getting involved. As it is, we've now got a high commissioner appointed by the government in Salisbury to oversee the colony. But of course, he's got no money. It's the company that will have to raise the force and pay for it.'

He fished in his pocket. 'I cabled Rhodes late last night to put the situation to him. Here's his reply.' He handed the cable to Fonthill, who read it aloud.

'"Read Luke XIV: 31." Is that all? What does it mean?'

Jameson produced a battered pocket Bible. He

read, '"Or what king, going down to make war against another king, sitteth not down first, and consulteth whether he be able with ten thousand men to meet him that cometh against him with twenty thousand."'

Fonthill frowned. 'I suppose he means that you've got to think carefully about expenditure.'

'Exactly. But Rhodes is down there and I am very much here. I have told him that I can do the job with a thousand men but they must be well armed and he will just have to find the money.'

Alice put down her cup in exasperation. 'Surely this war is not inevitable. You have always said, Doctor, that neither Rhodes nor Lobengula wants to fight. Can't you make a last appeal to the king? I am sure he would listen.'

'Hmm.' James smoothed his moustache. 'It's not quite as simple as that, Mrs Fonthill. Y'see, time is not on our side. In a few weeks the rains will start, and mounted troops – our main weapon – will be immobilised. The settlers will be cut off from the south and the Matabele, in their own good time, could swoop down on the settlements and destroy them piecemeal. We would not be able to move our men about to protect them. Plus I've got idiots among the settlers who want to form their own militia and set off now to burn Bulawayo. To go off at half-cock would be equally disadvantageous.'

He smiled. 'So, I really have to strike while the iron is more or less hot. Having said that, the High Commissioner is making one last appeal to Lobengula from the British Government to restrain his troops. But I think things have gone too far for that, and I can't afford to wait. I must make preparations now and I have told Cecil John that he must find the horses and arms right away.'

'But 'alf a mo,' intervened Jenkins. 'I thought you said 'is cupboard was bare.'

'Oh aye.' Jameson's smile was now mirthless. 'The company's cupboard is as empty as a Scotsman's wallet. I understand that Rhodes is going to sell forty thousand of his own chartered shares. They're at rock bottom just now, with all this trouble, so he won't be pleased about that, but we can't afford to wait. So we shall get our mounts and weapons. I only hope they are in time.' He shook his head. 'I also hope that we won't have to use 'em, but that, I fear, is a forlorn hope. Now you will have to excuse me. I must begin the business of organising our men to fight. We want volunteers, and we don't want the Border Police coming in from Bechuanaland.' He smiled wanly. 'This has got to be a company fight, you understand. No Imperials.'

His departure left the little group in silence. Eventually Alice spoke: 'Will you fight, then?'

Fonthill looked at the floor, then met her gaze. 'I will have no alternative–' he began.

'*Of course you will!*' Her anger made her stamp her foot. 'You don't have to go to war just because Rhodes wants his little empire. It's a terrible shame he's had to sell some of his shares, and my heart bleeds for him. But that does not mean that you must risk your life,' she shot a glance over her shoulder, 'and that of 352. If the company wants to fight, then let the bloody

367

company fight!' Her voice and took on a more conciliatory tone. 'It's not *your* war, darling.'

Fonthill shook his head. 'I'm afraid it is, my love. Having invested in this territory, I cannot turn my back on the people here. You heard what Jameson said about the rains. Things have gone too far now, and Jenkins and I cannot walk out on the settlers and leave them at the mercy of the Matabele. You saw what Lobengula's impi did to the Mashonas here.' He reached across and seized her hand. 'We couldn't move aside and watch a series of massacres. You must understand that.'

'Oh, I understand all right.' She turned her head away. 'More butcherings – this time of natives by machine guns.' Her voice fell away to no more than a whisper. 'It's too high a price to pay, even for the best farmland in the world.'

Chapter 16

The bitterness that had coloured her reply stayed with Alice that night and through the next day. She received a cable from Cornford in Fleet Street congratulating her on her story of the clash at Fort Victoria and asking her to file further dispatches as and when the crisis escalated. But this did little to ease the agony in her mind and soul. She had agreed with Simon that the four of them should return to Salisbury, which was nearer to their land and to where Jameson had ridden to organise the forces needed to face Lobengula. So her morning was spent in packing their few belongings, but as she did so, her mind was racing.

Her years as a journalist and then with Simon had consigned her to a role as observer and housewife. True, her reportage had been proactive and might even have altered conceptions back home about the campaigns she reported upon, although she doubted it. And as chatelaine of their home in Norfolk, she had been a dutiful and hardworking supervisor of the house who helped Simon sometimes with the estate. Nevertheless, she had never become involved with things that mattered. As a war correspondent, she had watched and noted, never integral to the events she was describing and about which she often harboured such strong feelings.

In the little wooden house they had rented in Victoria, there was scant privacy, and having packed the last of their meagre belongings, Alice slipped out, climbed on to the ramparts and sat, chin in hand. Below her, native working parties were collecting the dead on wagons and cracking their whips over the oxen to pull them away. It must have been very like this, she pondered, during the great plagues in medieval Britain, when cries of 'Bring out your dead!' echoed throughout the land.

Thus prompted, her mind dredged up memories from the past of so many similar scenes she had observed: the Zulu bodies, rigid in their death postures and stacked in front of the mealie bags at Rorke's Drift; the dead Pathans, who had

369

had the audacity to defend their country, spread out on the plain before Kandahar; the blazing houses of the bePedi tribe, set afire by Wolseley's troops at Sekukuni; the white-clad Egyptians, poor troops, their scattered corpses strewn across the parapet protecting the guns of El Kebir... Alice shook her head. What carnage!

She slapped away a fly that had settled on her dusty riding boots. Boots ... breeches, shirt, wide-brimmed slouch hat. When was the last time she had worn a dress, for God's sake, or used cosmetics? She spent her time dressed as a man but she did not do a man's work – not *real* work. What had she ever done to try and stop the wars she had reported on so diligently? Nothing, of course. Nothing. And here she was again, observing the beginnings of another conflict and reporting on it. Just damned reporting. Oh, she tried to describe in her dispatches the blunderings and stupidity of the politicians and generals who had created the conflicts she wrote about, but there was no *real* evidence that this affected the course of events. Now it was happening all over again, the relentless, unstoppable march towards war, while she watched, an impotent observer.

But *was* it unstoppable, and was she quite so impotent?

She stayed for another ten minutes considering several courses of action, her eyes watching the disposal of the bodies down below but her brain recording nothing of it. Then, her mind made up, she stood, brushed away the flies and strode back to the hut. She found herself trembling. Was she afraid of the prospect? Dammit, yes!

They set off that afternoon riding as quickly as they could in the heat, watching warily for any sign of remnants of Lobengula's impi who might decide to take revenge on this vulnerable party. But they met no one, except one or two Mashona herdsmen, who waved cheerily at the white people who were freeing them from the Matabele yoke. Alice spoke little and Simon humoured her, realising her distress at the turn of events in this country where she had never really wished to be. But Alice's mind was active. She knew what she had to do, but how, and when?

By the time they reached Salisbury, she had decided upon the answer to the first part of that question, and circumstances provided the answer to the second.

They found the town agog with news of the happenings at Victoria and preparations for war. Rhodes's horses, rifles, machine guns and ammunition were being rushed up from the Cape, and the settlers were flocking to join units to march on the Matabele. They heard that a column was being formed at Victoria and placed under the command of a Captain Allan Wilson, who had earned a reputation for competence when serving in the Cape Mounted Rifles and the Basuto Mounted Police. Jameson himself had hurried off to Tuli in the south to arrange for more volunteers to be enrolled and led by Commandant Pieter Raaf, a Dutch Colonial who had served with distinction in the Zulu War and who was now a magistrate at Tuli. Rumours had it that the High Commissioner of Bechuanaland had moved a contingent of the Bechuanaland Police to the Matabele border in support of the Tuli column, and that King Khama himself had contributed a force of tribesmen to fight in the cause.

More to the point for Alice, however, was the fact that Jameson had left a message for Simon asking for his help in raising a column in Salisbury. Would he move out on to the veldt and 'borrow' as many horses as were suitable from the scattered farms? It would be at least a couple of months before Rhodes's mounts would arrive from the south.

'I shall be gone for at least two weeks, darling,' said Fonthill. 'I will take Jenkins with me, but Mzingeli will stay with you on the farm. There should be no danger there. We are away from things in the north, and in any case, I don't think hostilities will really get moving yet. Some sort of last-minute peace moves are still being made towards Lobengula, I understand, although I doubt if they will come to anything. Anyway, you will be safe enough.'

If Simon was surprised at his wife's ready acceptance of his departure without insisting that he take her with him, he showed no sign. They rode back to their little house on the veldt and parted there, Fonthill having readily agreed that Alice and Mzingeli should keep their horses for the time being.

As soon as Fonthill and Jenkins had disappeared over the swelling grassland, Alice made Mzingeli a cup of tea, strong and black, just as he liked it, sat him down and put to him her proposal.

He listened, his eyes growing larger by the second, then shook his head and said, 'No, Nkosana. Too dangerous.'

Alice sighed, shifted her position on the stool and tried again, but the tracker was obdurate. 'Nkosi don't agree so I don't agree. Sorry, Nkosana.'

Nodding, Alice played her last card. 'I need you very much for this, Mzingeli,' she said. 'I do not know the way and I do not speak the language. I need you also to protect me. But if you will not come with me, then I shall go alone. I am determined. I have to say, though, that I do not know what my husband will say to you when he finds that you have let me go.' She sat back, her face flushed and feeling rather ashamed of herself. There was a long silence while Mzingeli stared at the floor. Then he looked up.

'I go,' he said.

By noon they had set off, each riding a horse – for Alice decided that to take a wagon would slow them down too much – and with spare water bags, one small bivouac tent, blankets and one change of clothing all carried on the back of the sprightliest of mules from the farm. This was one trip, Alice resolved grimly, where a dress would *not* be needed.

As they rode in silence, she felt more and more guilty at using blackmail on Mzingeli. After all, she was probably putting him in more danger than she would be in herself, for there was less chance of a white woman being killed than a member of the Malakala tribe, so despised by the Matabele. She reached across and touched his arm. 'I am sorry, Mzingeli,' she said. 'I have been

373

unfair. I am putting you in danger.'

His features relaxed for a quick second; it was hardly a smile. 'Nkosana strong lady,' he said. 'I once married to strong lady.'

'Ah.' She gave him her best smile. 'Then you know what hell it can be. You will feel sorry for my husband.'

This time he acknowledged her with a brief nod, but his eyes were dancing. Having re-established relations, Alice felt able to ask him: 'How long will it take us to get to Bulawayo?'

'Maybe bit more than two weeks. If we not killed on way.'

'Oh lord, I do hope that things don't get worse before then. If war is declared before we arrive, I will have no hope.'

'Not much hope anyway, Nkosana.' Then, rather surprisingly: 'You leave message for Nkosi? He not like come back and find you gone. He very upset. Not know which way to turn.'

She nodded her head in appreciation. 'It is kind of you to think of it. But yes, I did leave him a note. I have not told him where we have gone because I do not want him to come pounding after us, although,' she pursed her lips, 'I suppose he will guess.'

In fact, the message had been as non-committal as she could make it. It ran:

Dearest Simon,
I just could not sit back any longer without doing something to try and stop this senseless war. Don't worry, I have blackmailed Mzingeli to come with me to look after me (don't blame him). Please don't

374

search for me. We will be back within the month.
I love you.
Alice.

Would he guess that she had gone to Bulawayo
to plead with the king? Probably, but she would
have a two-week start on him if he decided to
follow, which, she concluded glumly, he almost
certainly would. By then, she might be on her
way back – if, that is, they had not been disembowelled. Ah well. She set her jaw. At least she
was at last doing something positive!

Considering that Alice and Mzingeli were riding
into the heartland of the enemy, their journey was
surprisingly uneventful, although the terrain did
not make for easy going. It followed a ridge of
high hills that was very heavily wooded, so reducing visibility and causing Alice to worry about
sudden ambush. Towards Bulawayo, the ground
levelled off somewhat, but it was cut by river
valleys, with small kopjes all around. Underfoot,
the soil was sandy and grey. Yet they made good
progress and met no one until they neared the
king's kraal, when they glimpsed many groups of
warriors, armed and painted, heading in the same
direction. They received puzzled looks, for they
had made no attempt at disguise, but they were
not accosted nor questioned.

It was nearly dusk as they rode down the
familiar hill and passed by the first ring of thorn
zariba, but Alice decided against attempting to
see the king that night. Instead, she pulled her
mount round and urged him towards Fairbairn's
store, hoping desperately that the Scotsman had

375

not upped and left for the border in the face of the coming hostilities.

She was, then, vastly relieved to see the familiar curl of blue smoke coming from his chimney, in complete disregard of the inflammable thatch all around it.

The Scotsman's jaw sagged when she walked through his door. He took out his pipe. 'Where on earth have you come from, woman? Don't you know that everybody here's talking about murderin' all white folks?'

She smiled. 'Yet you're still here, Mr Fairbairn.'

He waved his pipe stem dismissively through the smoke haze. 'Och, they'll never turf me out and I'm not going to leave. But where have you come from, and where's your husband?'

She explained. 'I decided to come here to try and talk the king out of going to war. I think he knows that it would be suicide for his people and his country. I am serious, Mr Fairbairn. Someone has got to stop this senseless slide towards more killing. There is just a chance that because I helped to ease the pain of his gout, he might listen to me.' She gestured to Mzingeli, standing diffidently by the door. 'There's just the two of us and we've been riding hard all day. Do you think we might have a seat?'

'What? Oh goodness yes, my dear.' He pushed two old wooden chairs forward. 'Would you like a wee dram? It'll only cost yer two shillings.'

She gave a weary smile. 'Why not? And one for Mzingeli, please. I believe I have four shillings here.' She threw the coins on his counter. The trader poured three small measures and pulled up a chair to join them.

'Lassie,' he said. 'You've got an awful lot of guts, and it's just possible that if you'd arrived, say, a week ago you might have had some chance of success, for surely to God the old boy doesn't want to fight. But something's happened that has pushed peace right out of the window'

'Oh lord.' Alice passed a weary hand across her brow. 'What is it?'

'You know that Mashonaland – or Rhodesia or whatever the damned place is called now – has got a new high commissioner, appointed by the government in London?'

'Yes.'

'Well, he wrote to Lobengula in one last plea for peace, inviting the king to send three of his most trusted *inDunas* to Cape Town to discuss peace terms down there. The old boy agreed, and dispatched one of his half-brothers and two *inDunas* immediately. James Dawson, one of the traders here – I don't think you met him – went with them to interpret and make sure that they reached the Colony without trouble. I refused to go. Well,' Fairbairn spat on the floor, 'the idiot went off to have a drink when they reached Tuli, leaving the three black fellers in the care of a mine foreman.'

'I don't like the sound of this,' said Alice.

'Nor should you. It just happened that a feller called Gould-Adams had arrived in Tuli with a detachment of the Bechuanaland Police. Gould-Adams had heard that there had been trouble up north and shots had been exchanged, so on learning that Dawson had arrived in Tuli, he presumed that he had escaped from Bulawayo. I don't know what he thought Dawson was doing with three Matabele *inDunas*, but he immediately treated 'em as prisoners of war. One thing led to another, with no one to interpret; the *inDunas* resisted, there was a scuffle and two of the chiefs were shot and killed. The king's half-brother didn't get involved, and when things were sorted out, he was allowed to return to Bulawayo with – you'll never guess.'

'What?'

'A note of apology.'

'Oh, how pathetic – and how typical!'

'He has just returned and told his sad tale. This is the last straw for the king. He is convinced now that all white men are liars and cheats and has declared war. The impis are being called in from across the nation.' He leaned forward. 'Lass, it's no time for you to be interfering, I assure you.'

Silence fell on the little room. Alice stole a glance at Mzingeli, but the tracker refused to catch her eye. He stared straight ahead, expressionless.

'Not exactly propitious, I do agree,' she said at last. Then she drew in a deep breath. 'But I have ridden two hundred damned miles and I am not going back without seeing the king and making one last attempt to stop this killing.'

The trader shook his head sadly. 'It's taking a big risk, you know, for it's not just the king you have to worry about. It's all his *inDunas*, who have been spoiling for a fight for so long. You might not even get as far as his front door before they turn on you.'

'I will just have to risk that I ... er, I mean *we* will.' She turned her head to the tracker, who was listening silently. 'Will you come these last few yards with me, Mzingeli? You have heard it will be dangerous, but I shall need you to translate.'

The man's face remained expressionless. 'I come.'

Fairbairn nodded in approval. 'Good for you,' he said. 'But, lassie, there's one last thing you should know.' He paused, as though for effect. 'De Sousa is back.'

'Oh no!' Alice put her hand to her face and then withdrew it quickly, as though it was an admission of weakness. 'How long has he been here?'

'About two weeks. He's been pouring poison into the king's ear every day, trying to persuade him to attack and provoke the British. He wants Rhodes to invade, y'see, so that his government can protest to London, perhaps stop the invasion, and then he can take the credit with Lobengula and so take over the mining and other rights that Rhodes has negotiated. At the moment, he won't know you're here, but as he virtually lives at the king's elbow, he will find out soon enough. And lassie, as soon as you leave the kraal, he'll be after you, that's for certain.'

Alice gulped. 'Well, that's one development I hadn't foreseen, I must confess.' Then she shrugged. 'There's not much I can do about it at the moment, so I will worry about him tomorrow.'

'Where are you sleepin' tonight? You won't be gettin' your little hut back, I'm thinking.'

'No, nor will I ask for it. We will sleep as we

have on the trek, out of doors – at least, I have a small bivouac tent.'

Fairbairn sucked in his breath. 'No. That will never do. You will find a puff adder slipped under your tent flap just before dawn if you do. No. You must sleep here. I'm just at the back there,' he indicated with his pipe stem, 'and you two can bed down here, in the shop.'

Alice sniffed in a little of the tobacco smoke and coughed. 'That's very kind of you, Mr Fairbairn. Yes, perhaps it would be safer. Thank you very much.'

She slept little during the night and arose well before dawn to make notes about what she would say to the king. It was important, having risked so much to see him, that she should present her case as persuasively as possible. Then she remembered that de Sousa could well be there. Would he shout her down? And once she was out on the veldt, making her way back to Salisbury, having won or lost, would he pursue and kill them both? They would be virtually defenceless out there in the bush. She tried unsuccessfully to prevent a shiver. She would just have to deal with that if and when it occurred.

Alice waited until the sun was well up before setting off down the hill towards the king's inner kraal. As she walked, medicine bag in hand, with Mzingeli at her side, she could not but help noticing an air of surprise and then hostility rising towards her on all sides. When she had made that same journey regularly only five months before, she had been greeted by smiles and waves from the Matabele. Now, the smiles were scowls and the waves were derisive gestures, with the sharp points of the assegais turned towards them.

'Be careful what you say, Nkosana,' growled Mzingeli. 'Don't be ... ah ... hard to king. He different man this time, I think.'

'Thank you. I know what you mean. I will try and be careful.'

As they neared the inner kraal, a howl rose from within it. Their approach had been observed. Immediately, a crowd of natives – warriors in warpaint, women and small children – emerged from the entrance to the thorn fence and surrounded them, shouting and gesticulating. Alice continued to stride forward, however, her gaze fixed ahead, her head held up. She hated herself for feeling fear, yet she knew that the perspiration pouring down the small of her back and staining her shirt was not just caused by the heat of the sun. It was probably the presence of her medicine bag, which she carried like a symbol of authority, that prevented their progress being barred. Was she coming again, as once she had, to work her magic on the king's foot, perhaps at his bidding? The crowd fell back and gave her passage.

Lobengula was holding court out of doors, under the shade of his indaba tree, and the usual smell of goat dung rose to Alice's nostrils as she approached him. The king was sitting on his wooden chair, clutching his assegai. This time, however, there was no air of indolence about him. Stripped to his familiar midriff skirt of monkey tails, his glistening face and body were daubed in slashes of red and white paint and a tall ostrich feather had been thrust into the back of the *isiCoco* ring in his hair. By his side was a large white and black shield, almost as tall as himself. This was a king welcoming Armageddon, a monarch of war. Except that, endearingly, the sandal on his left foot was not matched by his right, which wore that familiar open-toed carpet slipper. This leader of great impis was still suffering from gout.

The king was surrounded by *inDunas* similarly painted for war. As she neared the great tree, Alice thought she glimpsed a face she knew among the rank and file of the natives watching her. But she could not bring his relevance to mind. Not so with the yellow-uniformed and red-braided man who squatted at the right hand of the king. Gouela was in town, and he was clearly in favour.

Lobengula's jaw dropped when he saw the two approaching, then he scowled and, as they drew near, indicated sharply that they should sit. They squatted on the floor of beaten goat dung.

'Why you come?' asked the king, through Mzingeli. 'You not welcome here.'

'I come from the White Man's Mountain,' said Alice. It was the term the Matabele employed when speaking of Mount Hampden, now Fort Salisbury. 'I come for two reasons. Firstly, I wish to speak to your majesty about this war, and secondly, I hope that perhaps I can be of help to you, briefly, in treating your bad foot.'

Before the king could reply, de Sousa spoke to him quickly in Matabele. The king grunted and turned back to Alice. 'He say you work witchcraft with your box. That why pain returns when you go. And what can you say about war when British soldiers kill my warriors?'

'I do not indulge in magic and I have always told you that my injections' – Mzingeli paused at the difficulty of translating the word – 'would only give you temporary relief. If you want to get rid of gout for good, you must stop drinking the white man's brandy and champagne and eat less meat. Your majesty,' Alice leaned forward to emphasise the force of her words, 'you must not listen to that man. He is evil. He makes slaves of black people and he is a rapist.'

'Humph. I have slaves. My *inDunas* have slaves. Some people not good for anything else. And women like to lie under men. Eh?' He turned to the women among the crowd surrounding him and they all giggled. Some nodded and others, more forward, shouted in acclamation. The king grinned at Alice. 'See?'

Alice realised that the debate was going against her. She swallowed and tried again. 'Your majesty, I have always argued with others – including my husband – that it was not right for the white man's column to invade your country. But you allowed it to do so. The white men are now well established in Mashonaland and I am afraid that you will never get rid of them. All over the world, my people have populated countries like yours and have stayed there–'

The king interrupted. 'Why they want these lands? Why they don't stay in their own country? Why they want my country as well?'

Alice thought quickly. Why indeed? She was uncomfortable in this role of devil's advocate.

Better to be honest. 'I do not know the answer to that question. Perhaps it is because we are great traders and roam the world to find new goods, or because we are great farmers who like to bring our modern ways of agriculture to make better use of land everywhere. But that is not the point.'

'What is point, then?' The king's posture had softened somewhat, and when, several times, de Sousa had tried to interrupt, he had gestured to him to be quiet. Lobengula was obviously beginning to enjoy the debate.

'The point is that, in addition to being great traders and farmers, the British are great warriors. You majesty, I am the daughter of a general, as you know, and I have seen fighting in many parts of the world. Always the British have won.' She began counting on her fingers. 'In Zululand, India, New Zealand, Egypt, Canada...'

'I do not know these places.'

'You know Zululand. You know that the Zulus won a victory at Isandlwana, but that the cost of that victory was so great that King Cetswayo said an assegai had been plunged into the bowels of his people. Then the British came again and the Zulus were scattered at Ulundi and the king was forced to flee. The Zulus are fine warriors but they were beaten. I was there. I saw it all. The British now rule Zululand.'

For the first time there was a pause in the confrontation and the onlookers, who had shouted in support of each of the king's responses, fell silent. A look of sadness came into Lobengula's eyes.

'Yes, I know that place,' he said. 'Zulus my ancestors.' He paused again, then leaned forward, and his voice was lower this time, as though begging Alice to understand. 'I try everything with white man. I give English everything they ask for. I let them come into my country to dig holes for their gold and they come and spread everywhere and make homes, not dig. I punish Mashona people because they do not pay tribute, as is custom, so English kill my warriors. I agree one last time to talk peace and send *inDunas* to Cape country. They kill them at Tuli.' He stood and his voice rose. 'The chameleon has struck. It is too late to talk more. No time for talking now. I call in my impis. It is time for war.'

A great roar rose from the crowd as the king finished his peroration by raising his assegai high above his head.

Mzingeli spoke softly to Alice. 'We go now, while we can. Eh?'

But Alice shook her head and looked up at Lobengula in supplication. 'Your majesty, I beg you not to fight the British. I know your warriors are brave and strong, but the British have mighty weapons of war – the new machine guns, cannon and many rifles–'

'Ah.' The king interrupted her again. 'Not like Zulus this time. This time I have rifles and many, many more men than British. This time we throw British out of my country.'

Another roar went up and the people began to ululate, swaying their hips and slowly jogging from one foot to the other. De Sousa had stood, too, and was clapping his hands in time to the rhythm. Then he smiled, turned and said something into Lobengula's ear.

The king relayed it to Alice. 'My friend here offers to take you back to the mountain. Keep you safe on journey. Country not safe for white woman to cross it alone.'

Alice shook her head. 'No. Twice before he has tried to kill me and my husband. He is a murderer and would butcher me and my servant as soon as we were on the veldt.' She thought quickly. How to buy time? 'Your majesty, allow me to treat your foot once more.'

The frown reappeared on Lobengula's features. His uncertainty was obvious. The choice lay between showing his rejection of the white witch and of her people's ways by openly dismissing her, or submitting and gaining some respite, at least, from the pain that nagged at his foot. Eventually he mumbled something very quietly to Mzingeli.

'He say come back when sun is at highest,' translated the tracker.

Alice rose and bowed her head, and she and Mzingeli walked away, to the derision of the crowd. As they made their way back up the hill, she heard Lobengula shout a command.

'He tell his people not to harm us,' said the tracker.

Alice hardly heard, for her head was spinning. She had travelled two hundred miles all for nothing. Her mission had been a complete failure. It had been a gamble, of course, but she had hoped that the strange half-friendship that had been forged as a result of her ministrations to the royal foot might have gained her a longer hearing. The killing of the *inDunas* at Tuli, of course, had sealed the matter. Now she had put her life and Mzingeli's at risk once again. How to avoid de Sousa on the long ride back to Fort Salisbury?

She put the question to the tracker.

Mzingeli was silent for an unusually long time while he pondered the problem. Eventually he said, 'Don't know, Nkosana. Could go long way back, to Tuli, and ask for help from soldiers there. But Gouela will have trackers with him. They will pick up trail and follow. Kill us before we reach Tuli. Perhaps king will give us men to protect us on way.'

'I doubt it. But I will ask him.'

On her return at noon, the atmosphere inside the king's house was cold, despite the fire that he habitually kept burning. Lobengula hardly spoke, and the pile of empty champagne and brandy bottles seemed to mock Alice as she once again injected him. As she packed her bag, she raised the subject of de Sousa's threat.

'He don't hurt you. I tell him. Now you go. King is grateful for you taking pain from foot. But go back to your own people and tell them that my impis coming to eat them up. Go now.'

Alice bowed, and with Mzingeli made her way back towards Fairbairn's store. The pair were just outside the inner *zariba* when a native appeared from one of the huts and gestured to them.

'What does he want?' asked Alice.

'He say one of *inDunas* has news about your husband.'

Alice paused, a frown on her face. 'What? Simon – oh goodness. He has followed us and been captured. Oh no! Come on, Mzingeli.'

'No, Nkosana. No.' But Alice was already running towards the man and following him down a steep incline into a little copse of trees. The tracker ran after her, and burst into the shade of the thicket to find two assegais at his throat. Alice was struggling in the grasp of a large black warrior of indistinct origin – not a Matabele – while de Sousa, resplendent in gold uniform, nodded in delight at both of them.

'Welcome, Mrs Fonthill,' he said. 'I am sorry you refused my offer of protection because,' he gestured with a cheroot, 'this place can be dangerous, as you see.'

Alice's mouth had suddenly become dry, and it seemed as though her tongue had swollen and made it difficult to speak. 'You will not harm either of us,' she gasped. 'The king has promised us his protection.'

'Ah, but you have said goodbye to the king, and he has other, more pressing matters on his mind than to worry about a silly Englishwoman who has set off across the very dangerous veldt.' He nodded to where a thin, elderly native held a sack well away from his body. It was tied at the neck but something was wriggling inside it.

'This is not exactly puff adder territory, but some of them do get this far north, and this one certainly has, as you can see.' He allowed a thin spiral of smoke to climb into the air.

The realisation of what de Sousa intended made Alice tremble with a mixture of fright and disgust. She struggled, but the man who held her strengthened his grip. 'Mzingeli...'she began. The tracker's eyes were wide and glowing yellow, but with two spearheads at his throat, he could not move.

'Mrs Fonthill!' James Fairbairn's voice rang out clearly from the track above. 'I saw you go down there. The king wants you urgently, I fear. Can you come right away, please? Are you all right?'

Before a hand could be clapped to her mouth, Alice shouted, her voice cracking with relief, 'Yes, Mr Fairbairn. Please hold on to help me up the hill, if you would be so kind. I am coming now.' Then, equally loudly, 'Come, Mzingeli.'

The man holding her looked quizzically at de Sousa, who snarled and made a dismissive gesture with his hand. Alice, her eyes on the sack, grabbed Mzingeli's hand and they both ran out of the thicket to meet the most welcome sight in the world: Fairbairn, pipe clenched in his mouth, coming crabwise down the steep track, his hand extended towards her.

Alice grabbed the trader's hand so tightly that the Scotsman winced. 'Don't worry, lassie,' he said, 'that bluidy man can't hurt you now. I am too close to the king for him to tangle with me.'

The three scrambled up the slope to the track above. 'How did you know...?' began Alice.

'I saw you follow that man down. I knew he was one of the Portuguese's little troop and I smelled trouble. So I came after ye. The king doesn't want you, of course, but he wasn't to know that. Now, don't worry, you'll be safe enough with me.'

'Oh, Mr Fairbairn, we are so grateful.' And she told him about the snake.

Fairbairn wrinkled his nose in disgust. 'Aye.

He's a bit handy with the reptiles. I remember how he tried to kill your husband. I'll have my lads take extra precautions around my place.' He gestured towards his store. 'We're nearly there. We'll all have a cup of tea – I'm only charging thruppence a cup now.'

Alice forced a smile. 'Cheap at the price, dear Mr Fairbairn.'

Once inside the store, the three sat together to drink their tea. 'I'm afeared that you've got a problem now, lassie,' mused Fairbairn. 'I know Gouela. He'll stay with the king to show he's not following but he'll send his men after you if you set off. You can stay here if you like.'

Shaking her head, Alice said, 'That's kind of you, Mr Fairbairn, but it would just enrage the king. He has told me to go. No. I suppose we shall have to take our chance out on the veldt.' She squared her shoulders. 'We have guns, after all. We can fight. We will need to buy provisions from you for the journey, and if you will allow us to stay overnight, we will set off before dawn and ride as fast as we can and to hell with them.'

The Scotsman grinned. 'You've got courage, lassie. I will spread the word that you're riding to Tuli. That might send 'em off on the wrong track for a wee while and give you a bit more time. Now, what will you be needing for your trek?'

Later that afternoon, Alice had finished her purchases and was taking a mournful second cup of tea with Mzingeli – 'Have this one on me,' said Fairbairn – when a Matabele and a woman, presumably his wife, came into the store and began speaking quietly to the trader. Alice noticed that the three kept looking at her as they talked, and then the Scotsman walked to his entrance, looked about outside and closed the door.

'Do you ken this man, Mrs Fonthill?' he asked.

'What? Oh, I don't think so.'

'I think he's a friend of yours.'

Alice rose and walked over to the trio. The man was thin and looked silently at the floor as she approached, as did his wife. She remembered glimpsing his face when she entered the inner kraal and walked to face the king. She felt then that she had seen him before but, as now, she could not remember where or when.

'He says you saved his life and he wants to help you now.'

'Why? I don't understand...'

Then the Matabele looked into her face and raised his right arm. His hand had been severed at the wrist and only a stump remained.

'Ah. The thief!' Immediately she felt ashamed of herself for so condemning him and involuntarily added, 'I am sorry, forgive me.'

Fairbairn grinned and waggled the pipe between his teeth. 'Don't worry. He can't understand. But he has heard that the Portuguese is planning to send some of his men out after you as soon as you leave tomorrow. And he has a plan, of sorts, to help. He's grateful to you, you see, and so is his wife here.'

'How kind of him to want to help us. But what can he do?' Alice was suddenly conscious that Mzingeli was by her side, listening intently.

Fairbairn nodded to the man, who looked over his shoulder nervously, then, seeing that the door stayed firmly shut, began speaking quickly.

The trader translated. 'He's seen your mule grazing outside and has asked if you have horses. I've explained that you arrived late yesterday and that I've put your horses in my stables just behind the house, where hopefully nobody has seen them. He's happy about that because his plan is this. You will set out after dark tonight, before the moon comes up, leading your horses and leaving by that dried-up watercourse at the back of the store. You will take a less direct course for Fort Salisbury, going due east rather than north-east. It will be difficult for anyone to pick up your spoor among the stones in the donga. At the same time, he and his wife will take your mule and head directly to the fort. They will go as fast as they can to give you time to get away. The idea is that the trackers will follow the spoor of two people and a mule, thinking that it's you two, of course. I have to say it's an ingenious scheme, so it is.'

The trader took out his pipe long enough to send another column of smoke to the ceiling. 'What you've got to do now is to be seen outside the store, ostentatiously loading the mule. I can give you sacks we can stuff for that purpose. You put your real provisions on your horses, of course, keeping them out of sight in the stables. It'll mean you'll have to travel very light, you ken. No tent, for example.'

Alice regarded the two Matabele, who were standing before her diffidently, almost sheepishly, as though they were about to be put on trial. She turned to Mzingeli.

'What do you think?'

The tracker gave his usual pause. 'Could be good way of stealing mule,' he said expressionlessly. 'Man is thief, remember. But if honest, good plan.'

She thought for a moment. 'I am prepared to trust them, Mr Fairbairn. Will you say that I am very grateful and I hope they find the mule useful.' She put out her hand and shook the left hand of the man and then that of his wife. They both allowed themselves to look into her eyes and returned her smile. 'Ah, Mr Fairbairn,' Alice exclaimed. 'I feel I can trust them. Anyway, it seems our only hope. I realise that they are also behaving very courageously. They could well be killed when de Sousa catches up with them.'

The trader nodded. 'You're right. It's damned unusual for a Matabele – let alone his wife – to go out on to the veldt after dark. And as for finding the mule useful, they will if they are left with it after de Sousa's men catch them. I agree with you that they are being very brave. They've got guts.'

The man and his wife left the store carrying several pots and pans – which Alice of course paid for – so giving a reason for their visit to any spying eyes. Half an hour later, Mzingeli began loading the mule, taking his time about it, before leading the animal round to the back of the store.

The night was black when they set out. Alice embraced Fairbairn at the stable entrance, somewhat to his embarrassment, and shook the hands of the two Matabeles before they began leading the mule away to the left as Alice and Mzingeli dipped down into the donga to the right, feeling their way awkwardly on the stones that lined its bottom. Then darkness swallowed them all.

Alice had plotted her course roughly. She had a compass that glowed dimly in the dark, and she planned to walk and then, as soon as the terrain allowed, ride through the night and the following days on a course that took them due east. When she judged it safe, they would turn to the north-north-east and follow a more direct route to Fort Salisbury. It was, she hoped, a course that might even take her into the path of Simon, if, as she fervently prayed, he had deduced on his return that she had gone to Bulawayo and followed her. The thought of that wriggling sack impelled her and they travelled quickly.

On the sixth day after leaving the king's kraal, and when they had broken out of the bush into a stretch of open country, Mzingeli's sharp eyes picked out the tiny figures of two horsemen riding across the high veldt far to the north of them. Cautiously they wheeled their horses round and put them to the gallop towards the riders, keeping low in the saddle. As they neared, the figures turned to meet them, and within minutes, Alice was in the arms of her husband.

Chapter 17

After that first embrace, each clumsily reaching out to the other from their horses, the reunion was not as warm as Alice would have wished, although she had expected nothing less.

'You've been to Bulawayo, of course?' asked Simon, his brow like a low-veldt thundercloud. Their fidgety mounts circled each other as though they too were sparring.

'Yes, I have. I wanted to make one last appeal to Lobengula to hold back his impis.' She tossed her head. 'And I might have succeeded if those fools in Tuli hadn't murdered two of his *inDunas* he was sending on a peace mission.'

'Yes, I heard about that.' Jenkins and Mzingeli had discreetly moved away. Fonthill's face remained set in stone and he spoke quietly but with vehemence. 'Alice, there are times when I think I should throw you across my knee and spank you. You have been thoughtless, foolhardy and downright silly. Things have gone too far for one single person – journalist, politician, woman or man – to have the conceit to think that she could stop this war by arguing. You have put your life at risk and that of Mzingeli, and you have worried me to death. You should be ashamed of yourself.'

Alice flushed. 'I may have been the other things, but I have not been thoughtless. I thought long and hard about what I believed I ought to do before I decided to do it. I am sorry that I had to force Mzingeli to come with me, but I couldn't have reached Bulawayo without him. I am also sorry that I caused you worry, but I knew that if I told you of my intention you would prevent me from going.'

She felt the tears begin to well up and gulped to hold them back. 'As for everything else, I have no regrets. I failed, but I would do it again if there was a chance of success. Simon, for God's sake!' Her voice rose and she stood in her stirrups. 'We are going to war, and hundreds, perhaps thousands of lives are going to be lost because of the ambition of some half-mad millionaire in Cape Town. It was worth risking my life and even that of Mzingeli to try and prevent that.'

Jenkins chose this moment to ride up. He put out his hand, seized that of Alice and gave it a clumsy kiss. 'Thank goodness you've come back safely, Miss Alice,' he said. 'We've both been very worried, look you. You must excuse us all if we're a bit exisp ... exagg...'

'Exasperated?' offered Alice.

'I was just goin' to say that, miss. But anyway, it's lovely to see you without a spear stickin' out of your ... er ... chest.'

'Oh dear.' The warmth of Jenkins's words, the genuineness of his welcome and the long-suppressed fear of the snake finally released the tears, and they poured down her face. She reached a hand out to both men and clutched theirs. 'I ... am ... so ... sorry,' she sobbed.

'That's a relief.' Fonthill allowed his frown to

disappear. 'I didn't fancy putting you across my knee. You're far too heavy now.'

She aimed a playful blow at him and the tension was released.

'Mzingeli,' called Simon. 'Can you make us all tea?'

'Yes, Nkosi. No milk. Black.'

'Oh very well. Now, Alice, tell me what happened.'

They squatted around a makeshift fire while Mzingeli boiled his billycan and Alice told her story. When it came to de Sousa, Fonthill's jaw dropped in horror. 'My poor love,' he said and took her hand.

Jenkins's face set into a scowl. 'I should 'ave put that shot through 'is 'eart,' he said. 'But I shall get 'im next time.'

'No you won't,' said Simon. 'As I keep saying, he's mine. And we might have a chance yet. If Gouela is in Bulawayo this late in the day, that means he is going to fight with Lobengula. The king said that he was gathering his impis?'

'Yes. We saw groups coming into the kraal from all parts, and Fairbairn told me that a large impi was due to arrive any day from Barotseland. It's probably there by now.'

Fonthill frowned. 'Hmm. Major Patrick Forbes is about a day behind us with his force from Fort Salisbury, and Allan Wilson is coming up to join them from Victoria with a second, slightly larger column. I gather they are hoping to meet up at Iron Mine Hill, just over there,' he jerked his head in the direction from which they had come, 'near Umvuma. We must get back there pretty quickly, because Lobengula will know exactly what's happening in his country and we don't want to be caught out here by an impi trotting in to attack. Pack up and let's mount.'

As they rode, Fonthill reluctantly conceded to Alice that even at this late stage, Rhodes was playing politics. 'This has got to be his war, you see. If he lets the column from Tuli engage with the Matabele, that means that the Imperials are involved, because the Tuli lot have regular troops with them, and Whitehall can dictate terms. So it's a race between the two forces to see who takes on Lobengula first: our settlers from Salisbury and Victoria or the regulars and policemen from Bechuanaland. If we get there first and beat the king, then Rhodes can make it a company peace and keep out the government back home.'

Alice tossed her head. 'Typical!'

They rode as hard as their horses could go, pausing occasionally to rest them, when Fonthill rose in his stirrups and searched the horizon behind them – they were still in open country – for any sign of a Matabele force coming up to confront the settlers' army. Nothing moved on that plain, however, except for the occasional quick-darting ostrich and guineafowl. Towards dusk, they met the combined forces from Salisbury and Victoria.

'My, they've moved fast,' murmured Fonthill, as the column's outriders rode towards them.

The reason, of course, was that this small army was comprised completely of cavalry, and it presented a fine sight as it moved across the veldt in a jingle of harness, with two columns riding side by side. Rhodes's personal fortune had provided not only the rifles, ammunition and horses, the latter scoured from all parts of Rhodesia and the Cape, but also uniforms for this citizens' militia. Each man wore a jacket – many of them ill-fitting, but who cared about that? – crossed at the chest by a bandolier, with riding breeches, leather leggings, and a broad-brimmed bush hat, pinned up at one side in jaunty colonial style. Underneath virtually every hat stretched a bushy moustache. Rattling along in the middle of the columns were light provision wagons and carts carrying five Maxim machine guns, and bouncing and banging further back were two Hotchkiss seven-pounder cannon. Light on artillery and numbers, yet still a formidable, fast-moving unit.

'How many, d'yer think?' asked Jenkins.

'About seven hundred, now that the two columns have joined together,' said Fonthill, his chin resting on his hand as he watched them approach. 'Mobile, which is good. But not so good if we have to fight in the bush. Horses will be useless there.' He sighed. 'And it's not many men compared with Lobengula's impis.'

''Ow many 'as 'e got, then?'

'Don't know exactly.' Fonthill frowned. 'Between eighteen and twenty thousand, I am told.'

'Blimey. Let's just 'ope they don't all come at once, then.'

Alice drew her horse alongside and shielded her eyes. 'Can you see any press people?'

'Well, they don't stand out. If they're there, they'll be dressed just like the rest.' Fonthill gave a cynical smile. 'They like to think they're soldiers too.'

Alice sniffed.

Riding at the head of the columns were Jameson and his two senior officers, Majors Allan Wilson (newly promoted) and Patrick Forbes, a Sandhurst-trained regular officer who had distinguished himself in brushes with natives in the east and who Jameson had put in overall command of the force. Fonthill and his companions rode forward to meet them.

'Fonthill!' Jameson raised his hat. 'And Mrs Fonthill. Glad to see that you are all reunited.' Alice flushed and wondered what they had been told, but the doctor was introducing his officers.

Wilson and Forbes seemed to be in competition to see who could grow the widest moustache in South Africa. Wilson, perhaps, shaded the contest, for his stretched down and stood out on either side of his chin. He was the younger and much the slimmer of the two, and had come up through the ranks. He carried an air of brisk confidence about the clash to come. Forbes was heavily built, stolid in demeanour and spoke little.

'Already had a brush with the Matabele,' said Jameson. 'They came at us on our way up from Victoria, before we'd joined Wilson's column. Came out of the bush without warning.' Fonthill marked that the doctor's tone was solemn and utterly without delight at having had the first encounter with the enemy. 'We hardly had time to lift a rifle. We got a few of them, but not many. Alas, Campbell, our ordnance officer, was badly speared in the leg. I had to amputate, but he died the next day. We lost Ted Burnett, too, one of the transport officers with the column. You remember him, Fonthill?'

'Yes, I do. I am so sorry. He was a good fellow.' It quickly occurred to Simon that this was probably the first time that the doctor had had to revert to his original calling and operate on a wounded man after a clash with an enemy force. Would it be the last?

Forbes grunted. 'Not easy to put out pickets in the bush. I'd much rather fight them in the open.'

'If they'll let us.' Fonthill tried to keep the note of warning from his voice. This was not his campaign. Nevertheless... 'What are your plans for the campaign, Jameson?'

The doctor removed his spectacles and polished them violently with his handkerchief. 'We are going to sweep round and attack Bulawayo from the north. We will cross the Shangani river and hopefully catch Lobengula napping and capture him, of course.'

Simon frowned. 'If I remember rightly, Doctor, that means you will have to go through some sort of forest called...' He turned his head. 'What's it called, Mzingeli?'

'Somabula, Nkosi.'

'Heavy woodland, is it?' The question came from Forbes, whose mouth under his moustache was set in a grim line. He sought the answer from Fonthill, rather than Mzingeli. Was it beneath his dignity to address a native? Simon dismissed the thought. Forbes had campaigned with native troops and would know their worth.

Fonthill diverted the question. 'Mzingeli?'

401

'Thick, Nkosi. Good place for ... what is that word?'

'Ambush.'

'Yes.'

'Well, if it's there we shall just have to push through it.' Jameson spoke quickly, as if anxious to get on. He turned to Alice, who had been listening quietly. 'May I ask, Mrs Fonthill, have you come from Bulawayo?'

The two majors swung round in surprise. It was clear that they had no idea why she and the three men with her were riding vulnerably out on the veldt on the brink of war. Alice was not anxious to inform them. 'Yes,' she said.

'And was the place preparing for war?'

'Oh yes. Very much so. Even Lobengula was stripped down and painted. He told me he had called his impis in and I understand that the last of them were due in several days ago.'

'Really. Thank you. In that case, gentlemen, the sooner we get on and tackle them, the better. Oh, by the way, ma'am, there are no journalists with us. I understand, though, that some may be with the Tuli column – if that lot get here in time, of course.'

He gave a grim smile, but Alice did not return it. She was not inclined to join in, however peripherally, with Mr Rhodes's little games. Nevertheless, she was pleased that this was one war that, by the look of it, she could report without competition. She gave a brief nod of acknowledgement and fell back a little as the three officers urged their mounts forward.

Jameson called back over his shoulder, 'You'll

402

stay with us, of course, Fonthill? We would all be glad to have the benefit of your experience.'

'Of course, Doctor.' Fonthill turned to his wife. 'Alice, I would much prefer it if you would continue on to Fort Salisbury. Jenkins and Mzingeli can escort you, and you should reach there in less than a week.' He smiled, persuasively he hoped. 'Jameson will be sending messengers back there to cable Rhodes and you will be well informed. What's more, you can send your own reports to the *Post* from the cable station there without delay.'

Mindful of the worry she had caused him, Alice bit back the derisory response on her lips and instead smiled winningly. 'Thank you, dear,' she said, 'but I would much prefer to stay with the column. So much more comfortable, and I do so like the fresh air.'

Jenkins smothered a grin, but Simon just frowned.

It was quickly decided that it was too late for the troops to advance much further, and Jameson resolved to take advantage of the open nature of the terrain and camp then and there. Fonthill noticed that despite the fact that Forbes was nominally in command, the force of the doctor's personality – or was it his command of Rhodes's wallet? – ensured that he took the main decisions, at least when the enemy was not present. Pickets were pushed out, guards were mounted, campfires were lit and the force settled down for the night.

For five days the two columns advanced, eagerly and yet nervously seeking action but finding none. Their scouts, with whom Fonthill and Jenkins ranged for much of the journey, could find no trace of the Matabele host, even though they rode through bush country that would be ideal for an attack. It seemed that Lobengula was holding his troops back to defend his capital – perhaps in Somabula Forest.

As the weather worsened, with mist and light rain descending, the British outriders reached the beginning of the forest and halted. It seemed, in fact, not particularly worse in terms of density than any of the more thickly wooded bush country through which they had already ridden, but Fonthill confirmed with Mzingeli that this would be the last and probably the best place for the Matabele to attack before Bulawayo, now only some fifteen miles away.

'What d'yer think, Fonthill?' asked Forbes as Wilson and Jameson joined them at the head of the column.

'Well, in one way it is tempting to push on through the forest during the night,' said Simon. 'The Matabele, like the Zulus, would never dream of launching an attack at night, so we might be able to reach the open ground on the banks of the Shangani on the other side. But I fear that with no moon, and this mist about, we would probably lose our way. The column might break up and we would end up dispersed all over the bloody place.'

He eased himself in the saddle and wiped the damp mist from his face. 'My advice would be that we should camp here for the night, wait until there's decent visibility after dawn and push on.

The forest is too big to go round, I understand.'

He shot a sharp glance at Mzingeli, who nodded.

'Oh, we don't want to make a diversion,' exclaimed Jameson. 'I want to get straight on to Bulawayo and have it out with Lobengula as soon as possible. If you agree, Forbes, I think we should do as Fonthill recommends.'

Fonthill stifled a smile. The race against the Imperials was never far from the doctor's mind.

'Quite so. We will make camp and push on in the morning.'

The morning, however, was almost as unpromising for riding through thick woodland as the night would have been, for a thick fog descended on the forest, leaving tendrils of it, like a spider's web, hanging from the tallest of the thorn trees and making the temperature drop by nearly twenty degrees.

'Rains will be here soon,' growled Jameson, wiping his glasses. 'Come on, Forbes. We don't have time to wait about. Let's get on.'

They set off again, their horses stepping delicately through the dripping, shadowy glades and every sound beyond the gloomy greyness of the tree trunks making the outriders twitch their rifles and lick their already moist lips. Fonthill, who rode with Jenkins in the van – Mzingeli had been sent back to stay close to Alice – had no idea how long it took the two columns to pass through the forest, but every minute spent in that fog made him curse the more that his wife was back there in the gloom. If the Matabele came at them here in force, emerging from the undergrowth without warning, dodging and screaming, hurling their throwing spears, then he knew that the little army would be overwhelmed. There would be no time to form a square or create a laager. The warriors would be on them before an order could be given. It would have been much wiser to take another three days, or whatever, and skirt this wet, dripping labyrinth. Damn this childish, dangerous race against the Imperials!

At last they were out of the wood. The country was now more open, although still carrying sufficient timber to provide cover for an attacking force. In the distance could be seen the bulge of the banks bordering the Shangani river. Of the Matabele there was still no sign.

'I don't think they were ever in there waiting,' said Wilson.

'Probably not,' agreed Fonthill. He caught Mzingeli's eye and saw the faint negative shake of the head. He rode over. 'Do you think they were there?' he asked.

'They there,' said the tracker, his face expressionless as usual. 'I heard them and see some. But they go.'

'Why didn't they attack, for goodness' sake? They had us at their mercy.'

Mzingeli sniffed. 'That fog. They think it white man's magic, brought down to stop attack. They frightened in wood – like us. But they go.'

'What? Do you mean they have given in and run back to Bulawayo?'

'No. They attack. Soon, I think.'

Simon rode back and shared Mzingeli's view with Forbes. The big man nodded. 'Probably right,' he said. 'Feel it in me water.' He jerked his head towards the Shangani. 'River will probably be low and the banks high, so we'll have to cut a defile down to get to the water and then lay down brushwood and what-have-you to stop us sinking into the mud. Just as well we haven't got too many wagons. Won't be able to get across today, so...'

Wilson had moved away a little to chide a man who had dismounted. Now he returned. 'What's the plan, then, Forbes?' he asked. 'Straight across, eh?'

'No. We'll laager on this bank while we cut a path down and up the other side. Safest. Cross tomorrow.'

The younger man tugged at his moustache and shot a questioning look at Fonthill. 'I would have thought we could easily get across today. There's no sign of the Matabele. We need to press on, you know. What do you say, Fonthill?'

Simon sighed. He had no wish to intervene in what seemed to be incipient rivalry between the two officers. 'I rather think Major Forbes is right, Wilson,' he said carefully. 'There's still plenty of cover for an attack, and we would be more or less defenceless if they came at us as we were trying to get across in the mud. One more day shouldn't make much difference, I would have thought.'

Wilson gave his cocky grin and indicated where Jameson was spurring his horse on to get a first glimpse of the river. 'I know someone who thinks that a day would make a hell of a difference,' he chortled. 'But you're in command, Forbes, though you may have trouble in convincing the medical department.' He raised a forefinger to the rim of his hat and rode away, to hurry along the last remnants of the columns emerging from the forest.

Jenkins had observed the conversation, although he was just out of earshot. 'What was all that about, then?'

'It was all about whether we should cross the river today. Forbes has decided better not, and I agree.' Fonthill raised himself from the saddle and looked about him. 'I must confess that I don't like this place. Mzingeli feels that the Matabele are out there near us now and are poised to attack.'

'Well,' sighed Jenkins, flicking the moisture from the end of his moustache, 'I wish they would bloody well get on with it. I'm catching pneuman ... newinia...'

'Pneumonia?'

'No. No. Influenza. I can feel it in me bones.'

The two columns redeployed and a rough laager was made from the wagons, carts and cut thorn bushes, curling out in a semicircle from the northern bank of the Shangani. The river itself was wide, sixty yards or more, but not deep, and mud banks thrust up from the water in the centre to glisten in the sunlight, now burning away the last of the morning mist. From within the protection of the laager, men worked to level down the high banks of the river and then to cut branches and strew them to provide a firmer base for wagons and horses in making the crossing. Forbes sent out patrols on the other side of the river, while work began on the further bank.

The task was completed just before dusk and the camp settled down for the night. Extra guards were mounted at dawn but still the Matabele did not attack.

The crossing began at once, and a very makeshift laager was created on the southern bank. It all took time and it was late afternoon before the two columns had squelched and slipped their way across the deep mud and re-formed on the far side.

'If you think this is bad,' Wilson confided cheerfully to Fonthill and Jenkins, 'just wait a few weeks. This place will be impassable. Once the rains come – and I mean real rain, not this bit of damp – the river will be in full flood. Almost impossible to cross.'

'Crocodiles?' asked Jenkins, his eyes wide.

'Not when the river's in spate. They don't like fast-flowing water and they'll head for high ground. But always keep your eyes open for the beggars.'

'Oh, I'll do that all right, bach. I'll do that.'

'We'll laager for the night on this side and set off again early in the morning,' called Forbes. 'Jameson is anxious to push on, of course.'

Fonthill nodded. The terrain on the south bank was very like that on the north – still suitable for a dawn attack. 'You'll be putting out patrols early tomorrow?'

'Of course.'

'Mind if Jenkins, Mzingeli and I go with them?'

'Of course not. But my feeling is that the Matabele have retreated to Bulawayo and are going to make a stand just north of there.'

Fonthill nodded. 'You're probably right.' But he was unsure. He pulled Mzingeli to one side. 'I thought you said they would attack on the north bank,' he said, 'once we were out of the forest.'

'No, Nkosi. They frightened of wood and ghosts so rush across the river. Did you not see their marks in mud?'

Fonthill shook his head. 'So they have retreated to Bulawayo after all?'

'No. They come tomorrow. I think they out there.' He indicated the bush with a broad sweep of his hand. 'They come at dawn.'

Jenkins gave a histrionic gulp. 'And you want us to go out early on patrol, bach sir?'

Simon shrugged. 'To be honest, I don't think too highly of these scouts that Forbes is sending out. They're noisy and too sloppy riding in this bush. Not proper soldiers. Perhaps we can stiffen 'em up a bit. Show them how to do it. All right?'

'Very good, sir.'

It was still dark when the three saddled up. The morning was overcast and dampish, with no stars to bid good night to the darkness and no moon to pave the way for the sun. The patrol consisted of twelve troopers, all good farmers, fine horsemen and keen shots, under the command of a sergeant, who had been chairman of their local community outside Fort Salisbury. As they fanned out to pick their way between the trees, Fonthill hung back a little.

'We will stay together,' he said. 'A bullet in your rifle breech but keep the safety catch on. We don't want any accidents in this rotten light. We will stay in the centre and try and keep those two chaps ahead in sight.'

The dawn seemed to be taking its time coming,

and very soon they had lost sight of the two troopers ahead of them. To their right, they could hear two of the troopers calling to each other, and to their left, the crackle of broken branches as horses were pushed through the undergrowth. Fonthill frowned. Did they have to advertise their presence so obviously? Ahead, however, there was silence. Riding on slowly, Simon felt the perspiration start to form on his upper lip.

Suddenly the bushes in front parted and a horse came crashing out, its eyes yellow and wide. On its back swayed one of the troopers, an assegai piercing his chest and its blade tip emerging from his back. At the same moment, Jenkins's rifle rang out and a warrior fell on the right, in the act of hurling his spear. Two more came running fast and softly between the trees, and Fonthill aimed quickly and fired, seemingly without effect.

'Back!' he shouted. 'Don't let them get behind us. Back to the laager.' He pulled on his bridle and his horse swung round as a spear hissed by over his right shoulder. 'Ride low,' he screamed.

He became aware that he was riding in the middle of two Matabele who had appeared as if by magic. One of them seized his bridle while the other jabbed at him with a stabbing assegai, catching the edge of his coat with the spearhead and becoming entangled with it. Lashing out wildly with his boot, he raked the spearman's face with his spur and swung the barrel of his rifle into the head of the man holding his bridle, sending him crashing to his knees. His horse surged forward and he heard the crack of Mzingeli's rifle off to his right. Where was

Jenkins? 'Three five two!' he yelled.

'Comin'.' The cry came from his left, and Jenkins emerged from the trees, his head low along his mount's neck and his heels raking its sides. Behind him came a group of natives, all seeming to run almost as fast as Jenkins's horse and sending in its wake a hail of assegais, before they halted, panting. To the right, Mzingeli rode on a parallel course, blood streaming from a cut on his left thigh. Fonthill, clinging on for dear life as his horse took the bit between its teeth, stole a precarious glance over his shoulder. The Matabele had disappeared as quickly as they had appeared. But had they been able to get behind the patrol? He filled his lungs. 'Troopers,' he yelled. 'Back to the laager. Ride for your lives.'

The three horsemen broke out of the brush at the same time and saw ahead of them, in the half-light, the rather pathetic attempt that had been made to form a laager. It was clearly less effective than that drawn up on the other bank the previous evening. A handful of wagons and carts had been pushed together in a rough semicircle, extending from the riverbank. Many gaps remained, however, and as a bugle sounded, Fonthill saw men doubling up to fill them in two ranks, the front kneeling, those behind standing.

'Stand back, we're coming through,' he screamed and led the trio towards the nearest gap. It looked at first as though the line of troopers would not break, but they did so at the last minute, as though in reluctance, and the three galloped through, closely followed by the horse whose rider had been speared. He, alas, had long since fallen from the saddle.

Half tumbling from his mount, Fonthill ran to Mzingeli. 'Not much,' said the tracker. 'Scratch.' Then, with satisfaction: 'I kill him.'

Alice, medical bag in hand, had materialised. Her face was white in the dawn light. 'Are you all right, Simon?' she called, as she knelt down to examine Mzingeli's wound.

'Yes, fine. Look after Mzingeli. Are you all right, 352?'

The Welshman was reloading his Martini-Henry. 'Right as rain, bach sir. But my God, them black fellers frightened the life out of me, comin' out of the trees like that without a sound. Not a nice way to fight, look you. I almost 'ad a spear in me belly before I saw 'em. Like ghosts, they was.'

Fonthill was conscious that men in various stages of undress, all carrying rifles, were doubling up towards the ring of wagons and the line of defenders.

'Here they come.' The shout came from Forbes, revolver in hand, who was standing on a cart to the left of the line. His voice boomed out. 'No one is to fire until I give the order. We will fire in volleys. Front rank first.' A single shot rang out. 'Blast your eyes, that man. I said hold your fire until I give the order. Wait.'

Fonthill and Jenkins ran to join the major. The sun was now beginning to peep over the top of the line of trees some two hundred yards away and the first of its rays shone directly into the eyes of the defenders. 'To hell with that sun,' swore Forbes. Then he shouted, 'Pull your hat

413

brims down. Select your target. Still wait...'

Simon shaded his eyes and saw that the line of the bush, some two hundred yards away, had suddenly erupted with a mass of Matabele, who now raised a triumphant yell and began running towards the defenders, their dappled shields seeming to form a phalanx that moved towards them at great speed. He gulped, thrust a cartridge into the breech of his rifle and looked behind him for Alice. She was kneeling just below him, carefully winding a bandage around Mzingeli's thigh. He caught Jenkins's eye; the Welshman winked before nestling his cheek into the stock of his rifle. This was Jenkins doing what he was born to do, with coolness and delight. No fuss. No fright. Lucky devil!

Then: 'Front rank, FIRE!' Simon heard the voice of Wilson, on the right of the half-circle, repeating the order, like an echo, and then he and Jenkins fired together. As the smoke cleared, he saw that the first line of Matabele seemed to have melted away and shields and black bodies were strewn across the earth. But the attack hardly paused in its stride.

'Brave buggers,' muttered Jenkins.

'Front rank, reload.' The voice of Forbes was stentorian and steady, echoed from the right by the higher note of Wilson's. 'Second rank, FIRE! Second rank, reload, Front rank, FIRE!'

Suddenly, a sound that Fonthill had never heard before on any battlefield joined in the awful cacophony. First one Maxim machine gun and then a second began their staccato chattering, causing spurts of dust to rise at the feet of the advancing warriors and then, as the barrels were raised, bringing them down in a great swathe.

'About bloody time,' grunted Forbes. 'They were almost on us. What the hell were those gunners doing?'

But the attack was not finished. From the ranks of the front spearmen appeared a line of riflemen, who knelt and discharged their weapons at the defenders. Fonthill realised with a start of guilt that these were the brand new Martini-Henry rifles that he had struggled to bring up from Kimberley. Then he saw, through the blue smoke, that the sight of each gun was raised to its maximum height and that the bullets were singing past, high over the heads of the defenders.

Forbes turned and grinned. 'They think that the higher they raise the sights, the faster the bullets will go,' he said.

Some spearmen, however, braved the bullets of the defenders – and those of their compatriots behind them – and were able to run close enough to the line of the laager to hurl their assegais. Two troopers kneeling in the front rank in the central gap toppled backwards, trying to pluck the spears from their chests. But this was the high-water mark of the surge forward, and the Matabele turned and ran back out of range.

'Will they come back again, do you think?' The question came from Alice, who, rifle in hand, had joined them.

Fonthill pulled her to him for a quick moment, as much in relief that she was safe as in affection, then said, 'I just don't know. There are so many of them. If they get near enough they could overwhelm us. Stay close, my love.'

It took only some fifteen minutes before the Matabele came again. This time they were led by the riflemen, who ran forward, fired, fumbled to open the breech, inserted another round, fired again then repeated the exercise. This time not all of the bullets sang over the heads of the defenders in the line, but the firing was ragged and on the whole ineffectual, and soon the riflemen were replaced by the more familiar surging mass of spearmen, who swept across the open space, their assegais held aloft and their cowhide shields forward as though to deflect the volleys that crashed out against them again.

The bravery of the warriors was no match for the modern weapons of the defenders, of course, and faced with the terrible fire of the Maxims and rifles at such close range, the Matabele eventually turned and ran back to the cover of the bush. There, some of them stayed to hurl defiance before melting back into the shelter of the trees. They left behind them at least two hundred warriors strewn across the open ground, virtually all of them dead.

Forbes turned to Fonthill. 'Where is my picket?' he growled.

Simon shook his head. 'I doubt if any of them escaped. The Matabele came at us suddenly at very close range out of the bush.' He sighed. 'We only just escaped, and I think we did so because we were riding slowly, carefully and quietly. I am afraid that your lads were making a bit of a noise and rather inviting the attack.'

The major nodded slowly. 'Humph. Just shows

what might have happened if they had come at us in that damned forest. Well, you warned us, Fonthill, and I'm damned grateful. Just gave us time to man the ramparts, as it were. Now, let's see what the damage is.'

Jameson and Wilson joined them with the news that in addition to the picket, only two men had been killed and six wounded, including Mzingeli, whose wound did indeed prove to be superficial. To Fonthill's great relief, six of the picket trickled in out of the bush during the course of the morning. They had, it seemed, found that the Matabele had closed in behind them before attacking, and so had simply spurred their horses on and doubled back later.

They did report, however, that they had seen the mass of the Matabele retreating back across more open ground in the direction of Bulawayo.

'Good,' said Jameson. 'That means that we can push on. I am told, Forbes, that there is far less bush that way.' He pointed to the west. 'I suggest that we break up the laager and move on. I doubt whether we shall be attacked again until we near Bulawayo – even if then, that is.'

'I quite agree,' echoed Wilson.

'Very well,' said Forbes. 'But I feel they will attack again. We have given them a bloody nose, but they still have about eighteen thousand warriors to throw at us. They are brave and they won't give up yet.'

'I say,' called Wilson. He pointed out across the scene of battle to where a solitary figure was walking slowly among the dead. 'Who's that?'

'Alice!' snapped Fonthill. 'She could get herself

killed.' He leapt over a thorn bush and ran towards her. 'Alice! What are you doing? Come back. There could still be Matabele in the bush.'

She turned, notebook and pencil in hand. 'Oh, I don't think so. They've all gone by the look of it, except these here.' She gestured around her. 'I've counted more than one hundred and fifty dead so far.' She fixed Simon with cold eyes. 'Not much of a battle, was it? I mean – spears against machine guns. More of a massacre, I'd say.'

Fonthill sighed. 'It didn't seem like a massacre when Jenkins, Mzingeli and I were caught out in the bush.'

Alice's expression softened and she put out a hand. 'Yes, sorry, my love. Do you think that this will be the end of it?'

'Forbes doesn't think so and nor do I. I am sure they will make a stand, probably just outside Bulawayo, to stop us from entering the king's kraal. After all, this hasn't exactly been a battle. Lobengula didn't commit many warriors. His army remains intact. It could be a very different story next time.'

Alice ran a desperate hand through her hair. 'Oh God! How long does this nonsense have to continue?'

Simon seized her hand. 'It will continue, Alice, until we have unseated Lobengula and he has been captured. You must resign yourself to that. Come on back now. You remain vulnerable out here.'

Hand in hand, they stepped over the bodies of the dead warriors, already attracting an army of flies, and made their way back to the laager. The wagons and carts were already being harnessed to their horses (no oxen – they would have slowed the advance), tents were being struck and mounts saddled.

'What about these bodies, Doctor?' Alice asked Jameson.

The little man frowned. 'Have to leave them to the jackals, I fear. No time to give them a Christian burial, you see. Not that they would have appreciated that, being heathens.' He gave a mirthless laugh. 'No. Sorry, ma'am. We must press on. I suggest you mount up.'

Within minutes the outriders had cantered out, and shortly afterwards, the two columns re-formed and began to snake towards Bulawayo and the kraal of the King of the Matabele.

Chapter 18

It took them seven more days to approach the capital, during which time, although there were various alarms and scares, there was no sign of Lobengula's retreating impis. Eventually they reached Thabas Induna, the little flat hill that rose some twenty miles north of Bulawayo. Nearby was the source of the Imbembesi river, and Jameson decided that the columns should laager here and water the horses before the last push on to the king's kraal.

The laager was established in comparatively open land, but the passage to the embryonic river

419

was dotted with shrub and trees. Although patrols had reported no evidence of Matabele presence in the vicinity, Forbes decided to send a light escort to supplement the black wranglers taking the horses down to the river, and Fonthill and Jenkins, anxious to attend to their horses, as well as those of Alice and Mzingeli, accompanied them.

The straggling herd had hardly had time to reach the river when the Matabele emerged from the bush. From the moment they burst out from the trees, running fast, shouting and brandishing their assegais and rifles, it was clear that their targets were the horses.

'They are trying to stampede them,' shouted Fonthill. A small group of Matabele had broken away from the main band and were heading for the horses, waving their arms and screaming. The beasts were now pricking their ears and prancing, their handlers desperately trying to soothe them. Behind the advancing warriors, a screen of natives had emerged and were beginning to direct rifle fire at the escort and the horse wranglers.

Fonthill thrust his foot into his stirrup and struggled to remount. He shouted to the escort, who, milling about and unsure whether to return the Matabele fire or gallop back to the laager, seemed leaderless: 'You men, follow me.' He pointed towards the sprinting Matabele. 'We've got to run them down before they stampede the horses. Come on, quickly.'

Impeded by the need to lead Alice and Mzingeli's horses, neither Fonthill nor Jenkins had a hand free to draw and fire the rifles in their saddle buckets. Instead, they cantered towards the escort, twenty of whom gathered around them.

'Right,' shouted Fonthill. He pointed towards the spearhead of Matabele diagonally to their right. 'Give them a volley and follow me at the gallop. Ready, FIRE!' The noise of the shots made their mounts prance, but a dozen of the running warriors spun and fell. 'Now, hard at them and use your rifles as lances. Stay together. Follow me, GALLOP!'

'Hold tight, bach,' shouted Jenkins, and they were off, heads down, rifles held low like medieval lances, a small but solid mass of cavalry bearing down on the running warriors. It was too much for the Matabele, and they scattered in all directions as the horsemen crashed through them, flying hooves sending tribesmen to the floor and rifles thumping into cowhide shields and sending them spinning away. The fact that he was leading Alice's horse in the charge had unbalanced Fonthill, never the best of horsemen, and he knew that if he hit one of the warriors he would be unseated. As it was, as they thundered towards the group he realised that he was slipping sideways and about to slide off the saddle. A strong Welsh hand from his right pushed him back again and he regained his balance, to ride through the milling tribesmen unscathed. One horseman was unseated but Jenkins reined in hard, swung round and threw the bridle of Mzingeli's mount to him, and the trooper was able to scramble away to safety.

At the end of their charge, the horsemen reined in, turned and waited for Jenkins and the fallen trooper to rejoin them. Fonthill, perspiration pouring down his face, nodded towards the Welshman. 'Thanks, 352,'he gasped. 'I thought I was gone then.'

Jenkins grinned. 'With respect, bach sir, you really shouldn't lead mad charges when you can't sit on your arse properly on an 'orse.'

Fonthill returned the grin, although there was more relief in his face than amusement. He wiped his face with his hand. 'Yes, well, not exactly the Charge of the Light Brigade, I do agree, but more effective, I would say. Well done, lads. Anyone hurt?'

The question was made more relevant by the singing of bullets winging their way over their heads. The Matabele riflemen had trotted forward and were now kneeling and firing directly at Fonthill's troop. It seemed, however, that the sights on their rifles were still set too high for the firing to be effective. More of a threat were the scores of black spearmen who were now spilling out of the trees and breaking into a run towards them. The group of warriors deputed to stampede the horses seemed to have disappeared, and down by the river, the horse handlers and the rest of the escort were cracking whips, screaming, nudging the lead horses and beginning to turn the mounts away from the water and the Matabele and back towards the laager.

Fonthill gestured towards the running warriors. 'Reload. We'll advance towards those spearmen and put one volley into them. Then let's get out of here quickly and go and help our people gallop the horses back. We will form a screen to protect the rear. Trot forward, now.'

The volley brought down a handful of the attacking warriors but did little to stop the advance of the others, who came on, spears swinging low, pumping strength into their legs, and shields pushed forward. Still they came, appearing out of the trees without break to form a black mass moving very fast across the open ground. Fonthill realised that this was no marauding party, sent out to steal horses and snipe at the edges of the advancing British columns. Lobengula had committed his main impis – probably including his much-famed seven-hundred-strong bodyguard – to overwhelm the white men. As if to underline this, he could hear heavy firing coming from the direction of the laager. He bit his lip. Would there be a laager to return to?

They rode back hard and caught up with the last of the horses, now galloping equally fast. As they broke cover, Simon realised thankfully that the laager was not surrounded and that the escorts were leading the mounts back towards a protected compound, where an opening was being kept for them. Looking behind him, however, he realised that the first of the charging spearmen were breaking out from the bush to complete the ring enclosing the laager.

'Halt,' he shouted. 'Two more volleys before we ride in.'

With impeccable – and surprising – discipline, the little troop turned round, lined up, fired their volleys and then galloped back into the enclosure.

'Come on,' shouted Fonthill, handing his two horses over to a Kaffir wrangler. 'We must find

Alice and then help in the line. I have a feeling that this is the big one.'

Alice was perched between two troopers behind the side board of a wagon, Mzingeli and her rifle by her side but her head down, scribbling furiously in her notebook. 'Make way, lads,' cried Fonthill, and they shouldered themselves in beside her.

'Thank God you're back,' cried Alice, regarding them both, her eyes wide. 'What happened?'

'The captain 'ere decided to charge the 'ole Mattabelly army,' said Jenkins, slipping a round into his rifle. 'So 'e nearly fell off.'

Alice gave a half-smile, but there was little humour in it, more concern. 'Can't be true,' she said. 'My husband is a magnificent rider, and anyway,' she gestured to the front, 'the whole Matabele army is out there, coming our way. Look!'

They followed her gaze. The spacious clearing in which they had camped was black with warriors. This time the attack was not pell-mell but coming seemingly in stages, with riflemen thrusting forward to fire, reload and fire again before the spearmen rushed towards the laager. Once again, however, the firing was wild and the riflemen could be seen fumbling with the Martini-Henry's loading mechanism, some of them dropping their cartridges on the ground and trying to scoop them up again.

This time the laager had been erected more carefully and the Maxims and the two seven-pounder guns mounted strategically, so that the former could sweep the warriors in the lead and the latter send their shells to explode in the rear.

To Fonthill's amazement, he saw that the Matabele riflemen were firing into the smoke and dust on the ground caused by the explosion of the shells. He reached across to tug at Mzingeli's sleeve. 'Why on earth are they doing that?' he asked.

A look of derision stole across the tracker's face. 'They fools,' he said. 'They think that when shell explodes it send out spirits of white men. So they shoot to kill them. Stupid!'

The concentrated firepower of the British was taking a terrible toll. There was no protection in the clearing, nowhere to hide from the volley firing, the sweep of the machine guns, nor the boom of the two cannon. The warriors seemed to be engaged in a dance of death, as they ran forward, jumped high as they were hit and then fell backwards, scattering their rifles, spears and shields before lying still, occasionally moving a limb, like injured beetles.

'Oh, this is brutal,' sighed Alice. 'Why don't they stop and run away?'

But still they came running forward, black waves beating against a hostile shoreline. Some of the spearmen somehow managed to evade the bullets and the shells and reach within a hundred and fifty yards of the laager wall, to throw their assegais in a defiant and futile gesture, only to crumple and join the ranks of the dead behind them.

After letting off two rounds, Fonthill could not bring himself to fire again and merely sat, his arm around Alice, as they watched the slaughter. Jenkins, however, at their side, continued to fire.

Then, as he reloaded and lifted his rifle again, he stiffened.

'Hey, bach sir,' he cried, pointing to the edge of the trees. 'It's 'im, ain't it? Look, just there. In the golden suit.'

Fonthill and Alice followed the pointing finger and caught a flash, nothing more, of a yellow jacket before it disappeared back into the bush.

'De Sousa?' asked Alice, her eyes wide.

'Could be,' answered Simon. 'I couldn't really see.'

'It was 'im all right,' said Jenkins. 'I'm sure of it. Dammit, I was too late in firin'. Now I've missed 'im again, blast 'is eyes.'

Fonthill stared long and hard at the rim of the bush as the Matabele continued to pour out and run across the open ground, but there was no repeat sighting of the yellow uniform. 'Well, it seems that Gouela is now definitely hunting with Lobengula,' he murmured. 'Perhaps we shall yet have a chance of settling scores with him.'

'No,' muttered Alice. 'Please keep away from that awful man.'

At last the waves began to recede and the attacks finally stuttered and died. Simon consulted his watch. He estimated that the battle, if battle it was, had lasted only forty-five minutes. A cheer went up from the defenders in the laager as silence descended on the clearing.

'There must be at least three thousand dead men out there – probably more,' whispered Alice. She turned to her husband. 'What for, darling? Why?'

Fonthill could think of nothing more to say and

merely shook his head. Then he raised it and walked to meet Jameson.

'A complete and utter victory, old boy,' said the doctor, his face beaming under the perspiration. 'And I have just heard what you did out there down by the river. If the Matabele had run off our horses we would be at their mercy, for all our firepower. We are all in your debt, Fonthill. Thank you very much.'

Simon shrugged. 'Well, Doctor, you have had your battle. Do you and Forbes and Wilson think it was decisive?' He jerked his head over his shoulder. 'There are enough dead out there, God knows.'

Jameson looked at him sharply. 'Well, my dear fellow, *they* attacked us, if you remember. It had to be done. Brutal, I agree, but necessary surgery.' His voice dropped. 'I hope that your wife was not too shocked by it all. Not good for a lady to be involved in this sort of thing, of course.'

'Oh, she has witnessed much of this in her career. She saw what happened at Rorke's Drift; she was at Ulundi, Kandahar, Sekukuni, El Kebir and Abu Klea, so she has seen more battles than most generals.'

Jameson's jaw dropped. 'Good lord!'

'What do you propose to do now?' Simon asked.

'We will march on Bulawayo, of course. My aim is to put Lobengula into custody. We have given him a hard knock here and I don't think he will attack us again, but we can't have him at liberty. He still has thousands of men under arms and I must get him to make some formal acknowledgement of surrender. We don't want this thing to go on indefinitely.'

'Where is Rhodes?'

'He is riding up from the east. We shall meet him in Bulawayo.'

Jameson took off his hat and fanned his face, then he looked around the laager, where the men were lying in various postures of exhausted relaxation, their weapons at their side. Their jaunty, arrogant air had long since deserted them, together with the smartness of their uniforms. Their hats were stained with black rings of sweat and their brown jackets were bleached by the sun. Leggings were scratched and torn by the thorn bushes and their faces showed relief, not triumph. The acrid smell of cordite lay heavily on the air and flies were beginning to mobilise on the Matabele dead. The edge of the bush offered no threat now, for the cream of Lobengula's impis lay strewn in the dust under the sun and the rest were making their weary way back to the king's kraal.

Jameson swung his head around slowly to take it all in. 'By Jove, Fonthill,' he said, his voice little above a whisper. 'You know, I was never certain we could do it. After all,' he gestured with a dismissive hand, 'this lot were not soldiers. Just farmers really. All volunteers. Oh, they could shoot and defend themselves, but they knew little about military discipline, standing firm under attack and all that sort of thing, and they all remembered Isandlwana, don't forget. Bringing 'em this far in the face of an enemy outnumbering them by twenty-five to one and winning two engagements I have to say is an achievement. Yes,

I know it's not over yet, but I feel it is bar a bit of shouting. Eh?' He looked up at Fonthill, rather like a puppy demanding praise.

Fonthill nodded slowly. 'I agree.' He regarded the little doctor with a mixture of admiration and curiosity. He was reluctant to give him the praise he so clearly desired, but he could not help but wonder at how a general practitioner from Edinburgh with no military training and little experience of the African bush, low or high veldt, could turn himself into such a determined leader and logistician. How was Rhodes, slippery, ambitious, driving Rhodes, able to recruit and motivate such men? He sighed. 'Yes, Doctor, I do think it's all over now. But tell me: did you have any strategic reserves you could call on if the columns from the east and the south had been overwhelmed on the march, as could so easily have happened?'

The doctor grinned. 'Not a sausage.' Fonthill thought of the women and children left unprotected back on their farms in Mashonaland. Then he recalled that Jameson had the reputation of being a compulsive but skilful poker player, a born gambler.

'I see,' he said. Jameson and Rhodes, he reflected, were a well-matched pair.

The column – now a single homogenous unit – laboriously dismantled the laager, inspanned and resumed its advance south towards Bulawayo. Alice continued to scribble intensely, occasionally swearing when she forgot to write in cablese to save the *Morning Post* precious pennies. Mzingeli slipped inscrutably back into his role as tracker, riding with Fonthill and Jenkins to provide meat for the column; the Welshman made no secret of the fact that he was now solely motivated by the thought of reacquainting himself with Fairbairn's liquor stock; while Simon relapsed into contemplation of the future – would Alice agree to keep their holding in Mashonaland, and could their differences over the war and Cecil John Rhodes be reconciled?

For all his defence of the man to Alice, Fonthill still could not make up his own mind about Rhodes. Was he a visionary patriot and a hero of Empire, in the mould of Clive, Cabot and Wellesley, or a selfish brigand, crushing all opposition in his pursuit of land and glory on the African continent? Back in Fort Salisbury, before setting out, he had heard rumours that the same ambivalence was prevailing back home in political circles. On the whole it was said that the liberals distrusted Rhodes and saw him as a piratical figure, while right-wing politicians applauded the fact that he was accumulating imperial real estate at no cost to the exchequer. In that context, Simon wondered how General Lamb would have regarded the invasion and the subsequent war. At least, he pondered, the original road-building incursion had been bloodless. So perhaps he would be credited with helping to keep Rhodes from invading with all guns blazing. In fact, of course, he had had little opportunity to influence Rhodes. Rhodes was the supreme puppet master, pulling strings from Cape Town that influenced events far, far away. Why, the bloody man had started and conducted a war without even visiting the battlefield!

When they were some seven miles away from Bulawayo, the marching column was startled when they heard a rumble like a roll of thunder and saw a dense cloud of smoke rising to the south. Lobengula had set fire to his kraal, put a match to his store of powder and cartridges and abandoned his capital. There was to be no last-ditch stand against the invading white men.

For the victorious entry into the smoking capital, Jameson, ever the Scot, found from somewhere a pipe major of the Royal Scots Regiment, who led the Mashonaland settlers into the heart of the ruins, where the company's flag was hoisted on the site of the king's inner kraal.

Alice, riding at the head of the column with Fonthill, Jenkins and Mzingeli, just behind the pipe major, Jameson and the two majors, let out a cry of delight when she saw the incongruous figure of Fairbairn sitting on the roof of his store. She dismounted and ran towards him.

'Mr Fairbairn, oh, I am so glad that you have survived,' she cried.

The Scotsman removed his pipe from his mouth. 'So am I, lassie,' he called down. 'So am I. I thought it would be touch and go, but the king, bless him, was a perfect gentleman to me to the end. When he was blowin' up the place, he issued instructions that I was not to be harmed. And nobody touched me.' He grinned, and then sadness descended on his face. 'I don't know what's goin' to happen here now, but one thing's for sure: I shall miss the old devil.'

Alice smiled. 'Do you know, so will I. But where has he gone?'

Fairbairn gestured with his pipe. 'Took his sons, some of his wives and a few thousand of his warriors and trekked up north. Maybe he's tryin' to cross the Zambezi; maybe he just wants to hole up in the bush. It's anybody's guess.'

'One more important question, Mr Fairbairn. Those kind people who helped me to escape, you remember, the man who lost his hand?'

'Oh aye, I remember.'

'What happened to them?'

The Scotsman paused before replying. Then: 'I'm afraid de Sousa's men caught up with them. They were found with their throats cut. Even the mule was killed.' He shook his head. 'I'm sorry, Mrs Fonthill. This is a cruel country, so it is.'

Alice felt tears start into her eyes. She turned to Simon, who had joined her. 'Those two gave their lives so that Mzingeli and I could escape, yet I hardly knew them. I feel so ... guilty.'

'I'm sorry, Alice.' Simon called up to the Scotsman. 'Mr Fairbairn, I shall ever be in your debt for what you did for my wife. I can't thank you enough.'

Fairbairn waved his pipe. 'Difficult times, Mr Fonthill. Difficult times. We must stand by each other.'

The question of the whereabouts of the king immediately became a burning issue. Alice sent off a trusted young settler back to Salisbury with her cable for the *Morning Post*, which ended with: 'But where is the king? Peace cannot be made until he is found.'

A couple of weeks later, the column from the south arrived. It had seen little serious fighting

432

but had been delayed by the desertion of King Khama's men, who had formed a not insignificant part of the unit. Shortly afterwards, the tall, rather dishevelled figure of Cecil John Rhodes galloped into the home of his old adversary and immediately locked himself into conclave with Jameson.

The explosion that had so singularly marked Lobengula's retreat had torn apart the centre of his kraal, destroying his own house and the huts of his *inDunas* and wives, although, strangely, it had left standing and virtually unsinged the great indaba tree under which he had sat to dispense judgement. It had also left undamaged the other beehive dwellings that stretched out on to the plain and formed the suburbs of the city. These had now become inhabited again as the people of Bulawayo hesitantly returned and realised that the white invaders were not intent on harming them.

Fonthill, Alice, Jenkins and Mzingeli lived in their bivouac tents that had sheltered them on the march. Presuming that the war was now over, Fonthill was anxious to return to Fort Salisbury to see how his farm was faring under the care of Joshua and Ntini, who had been left to tend it, but he found his wife strangely reluctant to leave Bulawayo.

'I am beginning to realise,' she told him, 'that this chapter cannot be closed until the king is found. There has to be a formal peace treaty, with Lobengula signing it, but he has gone off with the remainder of his army up north, it seems. While he is out there with his men he will be perceived

433

to be a threat and I must report what happens to him.' Her grey eyes took on a steely glint. 'I want to be sure that the old boy is not disadvantaged by Rhodes and Jameson any more than is inevitable. I shall be watching them like a hawk.'

Fonthill sighed. A handful of journalists had arrived with the Tuli column, all of them dismayed by the lack of action they had been able to report on the journey north and resentful but resigned that, once again, Alice Griffith of the *Morning Post* had scooped them all. The current attitude amongst them – and, indeed, throughout Fleet Street it seemed – was jingoistic. The King of Matabeleland had to be found and punished for allowing his impis to wash their spears. Simon knew that Alice would be hypersensitive to their reportage and anxious to effect a balance. It was a difficult time for everyone among the smoking debris of Lobengula's 'Place of Man Who Was Killed'.

The day after Rhodes's arrival, Fonthill received a note from the great man asking if he could spare him a minute. He walked to the tent that Jameson had set aside for the Cape premier and found the two men sitting and talking at a single trestle table. Apart from the table and three camp chairs, the tent was completely unfurnished.

'Ah, Fonthill.' Simon smiled at the well-remembered high squeak of a voice and took the hand that was offered to him. The big man was wearing his customary old cricket flannels and, despite the heat, a tweed jacket that had certainly seen better days. Underneath a large black tie that was only loosely knotted, his shirt was open at the throat and his waistcoat gaped to reveal his paunch. The air of an eccentric, bohemian country squire was emphasised by the lock of reddish-grey hair that curled boyishly over his forehead.

'Do sit down,' said Rhodes. 'Jameson has been telling me how very helpful you have been, both on the journey north with the settlers' column and with the fights you've had on the way here. Helpful. Yes, most helpful. Damned helpful.'

Simon shrugged. 'Oh, I did little enough. The doctor here did a most amazing job in getting these columns together, and Forbes and Wilson did good soldierly work.' He grinned wryly. 'Mind you, that turned out to be not so difficult, given that we had Maxims and the cannon. The Matabele were completely outgunned.'

'Mmm.' Rhodes's protuberant eyes seemed to bore into Fonthill. 'Got your land all right? Started your farm up there? Eh?'

'Yes thank you. We didn't suffer as much as many others in the storm and the rains and we have more or less established it. I want to get back there now, because I haven't seen the place for weeks and I fear I can't stay out in these parts too long. My wife is anxious to get home to Norfolk.'

Rhodes nodded and gave a half-smile. 'Yes, of course. Miss Griffith. I have a feeling, from what I've heard and read in the *Morning Post*, that your good lady is not exactly in tune with what I have been trying to do here in Matabeleland.'

Simon returned the smile. 'I think, indeed, that

would be fair to say, sir. I know that, in her role as the *Post*'s correspondent here, she would be grateful to have a word.'

'Of course, of course. I've no complaints. Rough with the smooth, you know. That's what those of us in politics have to do. Take the rough with the smooth.'

'Quite so. How are things progressing with establishing a formal peace?'

Jameson spoke for the first time. 'Ah, that is what we wished to talk to you about, Fonthill. We can't exactly say that things are going well.'

'Indeed not.' Rhodes opened a small humidor on the table and pushed it towards Fonthill. 'Cigar?'

'No thank you, sir.'

'It's the damned Imperials, you see,' said Rhodes, selecting a cigar, snipping off the end and then lighting it with some ceremony. 'Would you believe it, Fonthill, I have been told by the Colonial Office in London that all the negotiations with the king to settle the peace have to be conducted with the high commissioner that the Colonial Office has set up in Salisbury. I mean to say, my dear fellow, I have paid for this damned war myself, and what I haven't paid for my company has. For Whitehall to jump in now and insist that it wants to settle the way this country is to be run in future is not only unfair but a damned cheek.'

He blew out a stream of blue smoke. 'What's laughable about it all is that before we can seal a peace with Lobengula, we have to find him. The High Commissioner and the Colonial Office

436

haven't any idea where he is or how to go about trying to find him. Who has to do that? Why me, of course.' Rhodes leaned across the table. 'Well, I have no intention of letting the bally Imperials mess things up at this late stage. *We* will find the king and *we* will settle things with him in an honourable and satisfactory way for all concerned. Jameson here is already working on it.'

Dr Jameson leaned forward, the light reflected in his rimless, circular spectacles. 'Yes. I wrote a letter to the king and sent it off with one of his *inDunas* who stayed behind here and who had a rough idea of where the old rascal has gone. I told him that if he would come back to Bulawayo he would be safe and would receive friendly treatment. Well, I received a reply this very morning.'

He held up a wrinkled piece of paper. 'Most of Lobengula's letters used to be written by Fairbairn, one of the traders here, but this one – according to Fairbairn, who knows the man's hand – seems to have been written by that Portuguese feller that was always causing trouble.'

Fonthill stiffened. 'De Sousa, the man known as Gouela?'

'Yes, that's the chap. He must be with Lobengula. The king says he will come in but he is concerned about what happened to the two *inDunas* who were killed at Tuli. He is also worried about where he could live in Bulawayo, his houses having been burned down.' Jameson sniffed. 'I think he is just playing for time, so I am mounting a patrol to go and bring him in. We are calling it the Shangani Patrol, for we believe

437

Lobengula has gone up that way with the remnants of his army. Nothing too heavy: we shall ask for volunteers and I shall want no more than about three hundred men.'

Fonthill whistled. 'How many are supposed to be with the king?'

Rhodes intervened. 'We don't know accurately,' he said. 'Could be as many as three thousand, but after the hidings these impis have received in recent weeks, we don't expect any real resistance. Three hundred good chaps will do the job well.'

And cheaply, Simon thought to himself. But Jameson was continuing.

'I am putting Forbes in command, of course, with Wilson along as his deputy, but given that the rains are due to break any day now and the bush up there can be pretty thick, Rhodes and I would be most grateful if you, your Welshman and your tracker could go along to lend a hand. Particularly in scouting,' he waved a hand airily, 'and that sort of thing.' He leaned forward again, almost conspiratorially.

'To be frank, I am just a touch concerned about the friction between Forbes and Wilson, and the younger chap can be perhaps a little headstrong. Your experience and knowledge – not to mention the fact that you know the king personally – would be invaluable.'

'I do hope you will say yes, Fonthill,' added Rhodes from behind a curtain of smoke.

Fonthill's mind flashed to two puff adders, a searing pain in his chest, a pockmarked face close to his and the smell of cheap pomade. A chance to settle the score?

438

'Of course,' he said.

'Splendid,' Rhodes and Jameson responded in chorus. And as though to seal the agreement, a sudden crash of thunder broke over the roof of the tent, and immediately a downpour sounded on the canvas overhead and filled the interior with a noise like a hundred war drums beating. The rains had begun.

Chapter 19

Fonthill's jaw dropped in incredulity. 'Rations for only three days!' he repeated. His horse drooped its head in the sheeting rain and Simon pulled down his hat brim to protect his face. 'That means we will be out of food by tomorrow. Whose stupid planning was that?'

'Can't be helped.' Forbes's face was set in stoical gloom. 'There was little to spare back in Bulawayo and we had no time to go hunting before we set off. Jameson said we could live off the countryside.'

'Not in this weather we can't. Even if we're lucky enough to get one buck, that's not going to feed three hundred men. You know that, Forbes.'

'Yes, well ... Wilson was in charge of provisioning. We shall just have to go on short commons until this damned rain lifts. I've sent a message back to Bulawayo pleading for more rations.'

The two men, hunched on their mounts, were plodding at the head of the column as they headed northwards. Fonthill stole a glance behind him at the men straggling out behind. Three hundred volunteers had not exactly sprung forward from the ranks when Jameson had sent out his call. The men had been away from their homes for several months already, the lure of loot had receded, for Lobengula had taken his most prized cattle with him, and the prospect of tracking the king into the treacherous bush had little appeal. Every man knew what the rainy season meant: flooded trails, rivers in spate and general misery for travellers. Eventually a force of sorts had been gathered from the three columns, including that from the south, but these were not disciplined troops, and murmurs of discontent were already to be heard as the Shangani Patrol had passed through Inyati, which had been a station of the London Missionary Society. They found that the station had been wrecked and looted and it was clear that Lobengula had a large force with him. No-one knew exactly how far ahead he was, but he was out there somewhere, with a last impi covering his retreat. The uncertainty added to the mud and the unceasing downpour to unsettle the amateur soldiers pursuing him.

'I've had enough of this,' exclaimed Forbes. He held up his hand to halt the column. The wagons are slowing us down terribly in this mud and we shall never catch the old devil at this rate. In any case, I am not at all sure that many of these chaps have got the stomach for a fight. Even if we catch Lobengula, I doubt if we have the spirit to bring him in.'

'What do you intend?'

Forbes stiffened his back so that he sat erect in the saddle, despite the rain lashing directly now into his face. 'I shall send the wagons back to Inyati to form a laager there with about half the men,' he said. 'They will be a fallback base for me and they can have the extra rations that should arrive from Bulawayo. Wilson and I will take the rest of the men – the best of 'em on the freshest horses – ahead in a flying column up to the Shangani to make contact with the Matabele. We will take whatever rations can be spared and it should be easier to hunt with this smaller number. Are you comin' with us, Fonthill?'

'Of course.'

The orders were transmitted, an overnight laager laboriously constructed, and early the next morning the column was split, with the wagons turning round heading south and one hundred and sixty mounted men riding north – heading straight into the steady rain.

Jenkins wiped the water from his moustache. 'I 'ope you don't mind me askin', bach sir, but 'ow are we goin' to bed down at night?'

'No, 352, I don't mind you asking.'

The Welshman let the subsequent silence hang for a moment, as the two rode on with the advance picket. 'Yes,' he said, eventually, 'well now that we've established that you don't mind me askin', like, can you tell me 'ow we're goin' to bed down for the night.'

'On the ground,' Fonthill growled, 'in the wet, in a square, in front of the horses to protect them.'

'Ah, I see. There's cosy then, isn't it? Snugglin' up to the 'orses in the rain. Glad I joined, I am.'

And so the patrol continued heading north, towards the Shangani river. Occasionally, spears were flung anonymously from the bush at the outriders, but no attack was made. The men were particularly vulnerable crossing the river beds, formerly just dried-up dongas but now bubbling with water as brown as cocoa, but Forbes banked on the Matabele sticking to their established tactics of only attacking from the bush. He was also unsure that he was near enough to the king's party to provoke an attack.

'Are we close to 'em yet, Fonthill, do yer think?' he asked one evening, after Simon, Jenkins and Mzingeli had spent the day ranging ahead.

Fonthill shook his head. 'No. I doubt it very much. Mzingeli here is following a faint spoor – faint because of course the damned rain is washing the tracks away. If we were near, the signs would be much clearer. And such a large body of men would leave a swathe of marks in the bush. We will know if we are near the king's rearguard.'

'Humph.'

Once again the men ate cold meat and fruit that night, for no fires could be lit under the continual downpour. Then, after posting guards, they all pulled their horses down, tied their groundsheets up to their own necks and lay down on the soaking ground on the outside of their mounts, facing the bush from which an attack would come, if it came. And once more it did not.

Next morning, however, was marked by a disturbance. Just after the patrol had begun its weary march forward, four men came galloping up from the rear. Fonthill was riding in the van again with Forbes and Wilson, and he saw that the little group was being led by a young officer, and that the man in the rear was covering the two in the middle with his revolver.

'What the hell's this?' growled Forbes.

'Look at this, sir,' said the officer. He handed the major a damp hessian bag, the contents of which were clearly heavy, for the sack hung nearly to the ground. Forbes put his hand in and produced a gold sovereign, then another, and another.

'What on earth...'

The officer nodded to the two men, whose heads were bent under their sodden hats. 'These two are at the rear looking after the baggage ponies, sir. I went back to check on the rations for the day and found them with this sack. I reckon there could be as much as a thousand gold sovereigns in there. They were dividing them.'

'Sovereigns?' cried Wilson. 'Out here – in a damned sack? Were they just lying about, or what?'

'These two said, of course, exactly that. That they found them lying there. But I caught a glimpse of two Matabele slipping away back into the bush, and by the look of them, they were *inDunas*. More to the point, however, I found this note, scrunched up into a ball and obviously thrown away by these two troopers. I think it had been left by the *inDunas*, with the gold.'

Frowning, Forbes smoothed out the paper and read aloud: '"White men, I am conquered. Take

443

this and go back." He looked up. 'It's signed with a cross and a seal.'

'May I see?' Fonthill stretched out a hand. 'Yes, that's Lobengula's seal. I recognise it.' He shook his head slowly. 'He is trying to buy us off. The poor devil is obviously at his wits' end.'

Wilson face was a study in puzzlement. 'But how would he have such a large amount of gold with him, out here in the bush?'

'It must be part of the gold that Rhodes paid him,' said Fonthill. 'I brought it up to Bulawayo myself, many months ago.' He gave a sad smile. 'He never really had a use for it, you know. This must have been his last throw of the dice.'

Forbes turned to the two men. 'Well, what have you got to say for yourselves, eh?'

The larger of the two men looked up. 'Sure, it's all a misunderstandin', sir,' he said in a strong Irish brogue. 'We was just countin' the money, your honour, to bring it forward to you, so we was.'

'Here, wait a moment.' Fonthill urged his horse forward. 'Don't we know each other?' He reached forward and tilted back the hat brim of both men. 'Well, well, well. Would you believe it.'

'Do you know these two?' demanded Forbes.

'Oh indeed I do. As fine a pair of rogues as you will find in the whole of southern Africa, Major. Their names are Murphy and Laxer, and this is the second time they have tried to steal these sovereigns.'

'Ah, your honour,' Murphy adopted an in-gratiating smile, 'it's good to see you again. No, sir, we was not stealin' this time, I promise you.

444

On me holy mother's death bed I promise.'

'They are thieves,' repeated Fonthill. He related the story of the treachery of Murphy and Laxer on his journey to Bulawayo. 'I suppose they joined up in the south in the hope of quick loot. Of all the men in this column, it is ironic that the *inDunas* should have picked out these two to give the money to. I suppose the messengers were frightened to come to the front of the column in case we shot them out of hand.'

'Thank you, Baxter,' said Forbes to the young officer. 'Tie the hands of these two villains, then take two reliable men and ride with them – and the sovereigns – back to Inyati to await trial. You will be responsible for the money and the prisoners. Good work, man. Off you go.'

He turned back to Fonthill. 'It's infuriating that we didn't capture the *inDunas*. They could have told us how near we were to the king and how many men he's got with him. D'yer think it's worth going after 'em now?'

Simon wrinkled his nose. 'I doubt it. This rain is washing everything away, and looking for two men in the bush will be like trying to pick up eels in a riverbed. But we must be reasonably hot on Lobengula's heels, otherwise he wouldn't have thrown his money at us. My advice is to keep pressing on.'

That day proved unusually depressing. The rain had become no worse, but its unvarying intensity was eroding the spirit of the pursuers. None of the horsemen could find a way of sealing their bodies from the water that penetrated every nook and cranny of their oilskins, and moving in the

445

saddle produced a chafing that grew worse with every mile. Many of the horses were now becoming blown, and Forbes was growing increasingly irritable at the pace of the advance. Even worse was his fear that he might be riding into an ambush. Had Lobengula crossed the Shangani, now only a few miles ahead, or was he waiting to attack as the crossing was attempted?

He called Fonthill to him. 'Will you scout on ahead to the river and see if the Matabele have crossed? Rotten job, I know, but I would rather you did it with your two chaps, who can slip through the bush easily, than have a troop go on and blunder and splash about. Come back as soon as you can and report on the state of the river, too.'

It took the three men less than an hour to ride up to the swollen river. Despite the rain, it was clear that a large group of men had made the crossing not so very long before. 'How long, would you say, Mzingeli?' asked Fonthill.

The tracker dismounted. Here the banks of the river were not high, and though they were wooded, the bush was not too thick. Broken branches showed where a wide crossing of the river had been made by many people, and wagon tracks could still be discerned in the mud. Mzingeli shrugged. 'Only yesterday, I think. Many cross. Now on other side.'

'Mount up,' called Fonthill. 'We may have to leave quickly.'

'Blimey,' said Jenkins, squeezing the moisture from his moustache, 'you're not thinkin' of goin' across now, are you, bach sir? It looks a bit deep

446

to me. Probably full of crocodiles an' all.'

'No. There won't be any crocs in that fast-flowing water, but I don't want the three of us to ride into an impi on the other side. Let's get back while there's plenty of daylight.'

They met the column only two miles or so from the river. Forbes immediately called a halt and held a council of war as Fonthill reported. 'We are pretty certain that Lobengula has crossed, and only yesterday,' he said. 'If you want to go after him, you had better do it soon, because the river is rising all the time. It's about two hundred yards wide. You can make the crossing all right now, but you may have only about twenty-four hours in which to do it.'

Forbes nodded, his face expressionless. 'Any sign of Matabele on the other side?'

'No. But they could be in the bush, of course.'

'Umph. If we cross today and I find we've got about three thousand warriors facing us, I would have my retreat cut off.'

A silence fell on the little gathering, broken by Wilson, who leaned forward eagerly. 'Let me go now with a small patrol,' he said. 'I should be able to make contact with the Matabele and have some idea of their strength and position. I can move quickly if I take the best horses.'

Fonthill looked at the faces of the two men. It was clear that Wilson, younger, less experienced but ambitious, was anxious to have the honour of finding Lobengula. Forbes, himself not without ambition, was obviously also anxious to claim the distinction of catching the king, but he knew that one false move now could jeopardise his whole

447

command. Caution overcame ambition.

'Very well, Wilson. It seems clear that the king's camp is near, just across the Shangani. Take twenty men and establish exactly where it is. But be back by nightfall. Understood?'

'Understood.'

'We will come with you,' said Fonthill.

'No.' Forbes's face was set in granite. 'I may well need you here. We are vulnerable. Off you go, Wilson.'

The young major rode off with his party, which included several officers, and Forbes set about building a laager of thorn bushes to provide some protection for his main force. The rain at last had slackened and Fonthill, Jenkins and Mzingeli settled down around a spluttering fire that the tracker had managed to light and ate their biltong.

'I ain't no general, like,' observed Jenkins, 'but I can't 'elp feelin' that things ain't exactly as we would like 'em. What d'you think, bach sir?'

Fonthill nodded gloomily. 'You are right, General Jenkins. Major Forbes has a real problem on his hands. He can't really advance his main force – pathetically small as it is – across the river until he has established where the enemy is and how large it is, but if he leaves it much longer he won't be able to cross and the king will get away again. And if he is caught on the other side without a chance to laager, he will be stuck with the river at his back and no way to retreat or manoeuvre. 'What do you think, General Mzingeli?'

The tracker munched his biltong. 'Not good, any way.'

The three sat in silence under two clouds: the

448

first, grey and swollen with rain; the second, one of foreboding and almost as real.

Like the rest of the camp they turned in early that night, despondent not only because of the cold and wet but also because Wilson and his men had not returned. Taking this as an indication that the little patrol had been wiped out and that he was about to be attacked, Forbes set extra guards.

But the camp was aroused well before midnight when two men from the advance party rode in, to be followed an hour later by three more. They reported that Wilson had indeed reached Lobengula's camp but was in danger of being cut off by the Matabele guarding the king and had taken up a position in the bush, where he would wait until the main body joined him.

Fonthill and Jenkins arrived just as Forbes had finished questioning the arrivals, with the help of his next most senior officer, Captain Borrow. 'Dammit it all, Fonthill,' exploded the major, 'I told the man to return here before dark. Now he has set himself up right on the enemy's doorstep and as good as ordered me to come and rescue him! Bloody fool.'

'What do you intend to do?'

Forbes looked at each of them in turn, his eyes wide. Simon could not help but sympathise with the man. Soldiering in the colonies, far from home and with no major outbreak of hostilities to offer the chance of distinction, was a dull and slow business, with little real chance of advancement. Forbes had not put a foot wrong so far in this strange campaign. Now he had been offered the seemingly easy but high-profile task of bringing in the recalcitrant rebel king, to put the final touches to his little war under the eyes of the generals back in Whitehall. Yet this small matter of 'clearing up' was proving to be a nightmare, thanks to a thrusting junior officer.

'Well...' The major gnawed at his moustache. 'I can't risk crossing the Shangani with my whole force in the dark. We would end up all over the place. I've got few enough men anyway, and we could be under attack here ourselves at any minute.' His voice dropped. He was thinking aloud now. 'But I will have to send what reinforcements I can to Wilson to help the damned fool get back.' The silence descended again. Then: 'Yes ... right.' His mind was made up.

'Borrow,' he barked, 'take seventeen troopers right away, cross the Shangani and join Wilson. Tell him I will come to him when I can.' He turned to Fonthill. 'I'd be grateful if you and your two scouts would go with them. If it comes to a scrap, you will be of great help to Wilson, I know. And if you do get near the king, your knowledge of him will come in very handy.'

Simon gulped. It was more an invitation than an order, given Fonthill's civilian status, but it was one that could hardly be refused. Sending just twenty-one men across the Shangani to reinforce the patrol seemed madness. It would mean that Wilson would have too many men to help him patrol, but not enough to reinforce him in fighting a major action. It was neither one thing nor the other. He opened his mouth to protest but thought better of it.

'Very good. We will come with you, Borrow.' He doubled away to bring the glad news to Jenkins and Mzingeli.

''Ow many?' Jenkins's face registered indignation. 'What's 'e doin', makin' up a few 'ands of whist or somethin'?'

The Shangani when they reached it looked menacing by the light of a moon half hiding behind the clouds. Swirling and surging, it was now a dull yellow, and driftwood was being tossed along in the turbulence. The river hissed as it bounced over the wide and comparatively shallow drift. Captain Borrow regarded it with concern.

'May I suggest, Borrow, that we link the horses together?' suggested Fonthill. 'That way the strongest swimmer will help the weakest. Do we have rope?'

Borrow nodded. 'Sergeant,' he called, 'fix a leading rope to my horse. Men, hold your rifles high. Keep the water out of your magazines. Grab the rope and follow me. First six men across, dismount quickly and form a semicircle, rifles at the ready, until we are all across.'

Jenkins, the bravest of the brave in facing an enemy, now showed a face the colour of the moonlight itself. 'I don't like this at all, not at all, bach sir,' he gasped. 'You know I can't swim. An' then there's the crocs. P'raps, look you, I could be a sort of rearguard on this side an' protect you all as you cross...'

Fonthill sighed. 'There are no crocs in this racing water,' he said, 'and you are not going to drown, I will see to that. I will be right behind you. Just hold on to the rope. The horse will do

451

the swimming. Give him a kick to keep him going. Here we go. Come on.'

Led by Borrow, a slim man but a good horseman, the little party entered the water. The lead horse, its eyes showing as much yellow as the river itself, tossed its head and baulked, but Borrow skilfully urged it into the water and set the beast swimming. In single file, the patrol followed him, and immediately the weaker horses were swept downstream, but were held by the rope and kept roughly in line – although it was a line that bowed and sagged. It was some two hundred yards further downriver before Borrow was able to reach the far side of the Shangani, but all of his men were able to climb up the bank and reassemble, including a trembling Jenkins.

'Nothin' to it really,' he confided to Mzingeli. 'You see, the 'orses do the swimmin', like. You just sit. It's easy, see.'

One of the messengers from Wilson had volunteered to make the return journey, and he led the party as it picked its way between the trees and bushes in the semi-darkness, for the moon had now disappeared behind the clouds. Every member rode with his heart in his mouth, expecting a shower of assegais to rain in from the darkness on either side, but all was tranquil as the horses trod quietly through the bush. In fact, it was only twenty minutes after leaving the riverbank that a cry of 'Who goes there?' told them they had reached the patrol.

The men were lying behind their prostrate horses in a rough circle in a clearing. Wilson rose and shook hands warmly with Borrow and

Fonthill. 'How many have you brought?' he asked.

Barrow smiled. 'Only twenty, I'm afraid.'

For a brief moment Wilson looked dismayed. Then he grinned. 'Oh well. More than enough, I expect.' He gestured over his shoulder. 'We've found the king's camp. It's about half a mile up there. Couldn't attack in the dusk, so we will move in tomorrow at first light.'

Fonthill frowned. 'You won't wait until Forbes arrives with the main party?'

'Good lord, no. We can do the job.'

'How many warriors has the king, then?'

'Oh,' Wilson looked nonchalant, 'not all that many, I think. Couple of hundred perhaps. Maybe more. Fellow we captured thought something like that, but we're not sure, to be honest.'

'And you plan to attack the camp with thirty-odd men?' Fonthill tried to keep the incredulity out of his voice.

'Of course. Get at 'em first thing and take them by surprise. The fact that you got through shows that they have not surrounded us, so they are not anxious for a fight, in my estimation. I know natives, Fonthill. Punch 'em hard and they will fold. Believe me.'

Borrow coughed. 'Fonthill was at Isandlwana *and* Rorke's Drift, sir,' he murmured. 'He may know natives too.'

'Ah yes. Sorry, Fonthill, no condescension intended, old boy. But the Matabele are not the Zulus, you know.'

'Hmm.' Fonthill regarded the great moustache, which somehow looked lugubrious on such a narrow, young face. 'Yet the Matabele showed great courage, don't you think, in attacking us twice on our way to Bulawayo. And this time, we will not be safely laagered.'

Wilson waved a hand. 'Doesn't matter. We've got the firepower. We will move in early, grab the old boy and take him back across the river. They won't have the guts to follow us.'

'Well, it's your decision.' Fonthill tried to sound uncritical. 'I think, however, that Forbes was rather expecting you back last night.'

'Yes, well, I felt that once I had made contact with the enemy, it was my duty not to let go.' He took Fonthill by the elbow and walked him away from Borrow. 'To tell you the truth, Fonthill, Forbes can be a little ... what shall I say? Cautious, I think is the word. Natural, I suppose, given his age and all that Sandhurst stuff he imbibed when he was young. But I know Africa, y'see, and how to behave here. These Kaffirs don't follow the rules laid down at training college. We have to fight 'em the same way.'

Fonthill looked at him hard. Wilson was confident, almost to the point of cockiness. There was nothing wrong with that in warfare. Better assuredness than hesitation in a commander. But was he being impetuous to the point of foolishness? He had no real idea how many men the king had with him, so better surely to retreat to the river and form a bridgehead on the bank, allowing Forbes and his troopers to cross in the morning and make the attack with a larger force.

As though reading his thoughts, Wilson patted him on the shoulder, in what seemed a ridiculously avuncular gesture from a younger man. 'We shall have the advantage of surprise tomorrow and should have some fun,' he said. 'Now why don't you try and get some sleep? We shall move just before sun-up.'

'Very well. Ah – just one last point, Wilson. When you approached the king's camp, did you see or pick up any evidence that a Portuguese was with the king? A man they call Gouela?'

Wilson lifted his eyebrows. 'Didn't see the chap because we didn't get that close. But the native we picked up and questioned did say that there was a white man with Lobengula. A feller in some sort of uniform. I didn't pay too much attention, I'm afraid. Obviously not one of us.'

Fonthill smiled. 'Thank you. Good night, Wilson. Good luck tomorrow.'

So de Sousa was still with the king! Perhaps tomorrow would provide the chance for a final reckoning with his enemy. It was a sort of comfort as he faced the prospect of the dawn attack.

In fact, hardly anyone in that small company slept that night. Fonthill's momentary flash of euphoria at the thought of facing de Sousa again was soon replaced by a sense of foreboding. He had two main worries: Alice and Mzingeli. The tracker was a brave man and quite imperturbable in the face of danger, but he was not really a fighter. In addition, of course, this was not his war. Simon had offered him the chance of crossing back across the Shangani before it became virtually impassable, but he had rejected it. 'I stay with you,' he had said. And, knowing his man, that would be that. He must insist that

Mzingeli stayed close to him and Jenkins when the attack started.

Alice ... ah! He stirred uncomfortably on the hard ground. If the battle in this dank semi-forest should prove to be his last, then he wished – oh how he wished! – that his farewell to his wife had been warmer. Her attitude towards Rhodes and Jameson had hardened since the battle at the Imbembesi river and what she called the massacre of the Matabele. She now regarded all of Rhodes's dealings with Lobengula as exercises in dissimulation and deceit, a preface to the inevitable invasion by an army of mercenaries. Fonthill's decision to join the Shangani Patrol to capture the king had been met by her with some ambivalence. She wished him to play no further part in the violence that surrounded the creation of Rhodesia, but his presence on the patrol she hoped would be a kind of guarantee that no harm would come to Lobengula. They had kissed good bye, of course, but her eyes had been cold. It seemed as though she had not forgiven him for his part in Rhodes's negotiations with the king. He sighed and wished he had more confidence in the outcome of tomorrow's assault on the king's camp.

No bugles roused the troopers in the morning. Dawn promised another, wet, miserable day and the men rose from their damp couches without a word. The rain prevented fires from being lit, so everyone chewed cold biltong, drank water, shook the rain from his coat and silently fell into line within minutes of waking.

'Nice day for it, then,' observed Jenkins,

slipping a bayonet down next to the Martini-Henry in the rifle bucket hanging by his saddle. As cavalrymen carrying the shorter carbine, the troopers of the patrol had not been issued with bayonets. Somehow, however, Jenkins had procured in Bulawayo two of the long triangular blades issued to the infantry that, fitted to the end of their rifles, made a stabbing weapon just under six feet long. It had proved deadly in the Anglo-Zulu war ten years before, and indeed, the Zulus, so famed for their prowess in hand-to-hand fighting, had come to fear it. Mzingeli had declined to take a bayonet, claiming that it made the Martini-Henry too heavy to use.

'Look.' Fonthill drew Jenkins to one side. 'This is going to be a very tough fight, so we must stick together. In particular we must both keep an eye on Mzingeli. He's a bit old for this sort of thing.'

'Don't feel so sprightly myself, bach sir. But I see what you mean.'

The only man among the thirty-four who lined up that morning who did not seemed possessed by the prevailing air of melancholy was Major Wilson. Even his moustache appeared to bristle with happy expectation as he addressed his troop.

'Now, men,' he said, 'this is our chance to write a glorious footnote to the creation of Rhodesia. It is we who will capture King Lobengula and bring this war formally to an end. We shall be out-numbered, of course, but we have the advantage of firepower, as has been proven over the last few months. So fire quickly and accurately on order and we shall find that the Kaffirs will run, as they always do.'

He paused, as though expecting assent or even a faint cheer, but no sound came from the ranks. 'Right,' he went on. 'Ride until the order comes to dismount. Horses will be taken to the rear. Then we will advance on foot in open order. When we come upon the camp, we will move forward and fire volleys. Myself with Captain Borrow and the sergeant here,' he nodded, 'will run forward and capture the king. There will be no pursuit of the fleeing natives. Any questions? No. Good. Mount.'

'Ah,' muttered Jenkins, 'just like that, eh? No interference from the black fellers, look you. 'Ow very kind of 'em.'

'Come on,' said Fonthill. 'Stay close.'

Somewhere from behind the grey, overcast sky, the sun gave some backlight to the clouds and the patrol set off in the half-light, walking their horses slowly and deliberately through the bush. Jenkins, Mzingeli and Fonthill rode three abreast, with Mzingeli sandwiched in the middle. After approximately half an hour, as the little group approached a giant anthill, Wilson raised his hand and dismounted. A handful of men took the reins of the horses and tethered them at the rear of the hill, as the troopers doubled forward and joined Wilson to form a thin line some fifty yards across. Then, slowly, the line advanced.

Wilson turned. 'I can see the wagons,' he called. 'At the double. Charge!'

Fonthill remembered thinking that a charge without bayonets was somehow toothless when from the bush immediately ahead emerged a row of Matabele riflemen, sweeping out from behind the trees and then being supplemented by others emerging from the side to outflank the charging troopers. The soldiers and the warriors fired at almost the same time, with, it seemed, almost the same results. Captain Borrow and a trooper fell, and three Matabele. The natives were obviously still firing on sights set too high, and the troopers, shooting on the run, could not take steady aim. Nevertheless, the spectacle of a solid line of warriors being reinforced every second as more and more Matabele emerged from the bush was too much for the attackers. The charge petered out, with Major Wilson firing his revolver some twenty yards in front of his men.

The major turned and doubled back. 'Fire in volleys,' he cried. 'Front rank...' His voice died away. There were no front and second ranks; only one wavering line, in danger of being outflanked and gunned down from the side.

Fonthill sensed disaster. 'Quickly, 352,' he said. 'Run along the line and tap the shoulder of every other man.' Then he raised his voice and shouted: 'Every man touched on the shoulder will double back twenty paces and face the enemy. The remainder will fire a volley and then run back through the rear rank and cover it as it retreats.'

Wilson was looking at him in consternation. Jenkins had completed his running and touching task. Fonthill screamed: 'Men touched, run back NOW! Front rank, reload, aim, FIRE! NOW RUN BACK. Rear rank, hold your fire. Now, rear rank, aim, FIRE!'

And so, walking back, Fonthill directed an orderly retreat, with the men running back in turns, covered by the line through which they ran.

Simon had time to shout an apology to Wilson. 'Sorry,' he said. 'Infantry drill for an orderly retreat. Sandhurst stuff, you know. You wouldn't have it in the cavalry. Needed here, though.'

The major neither accepted nor rejected the apology but kept his eyes on the Matabele, who were now pouring out from the king's camp and circling wide through the bush. 'There must be a whole bloody impi here,' he cried. 'They're going to surround us if we're not careful. We need to get to the horses...'

'Jenkins,' Fonthill shouted to the Welshman, who was now directing the volley fire. 'Double back with Mzingeli and get the men holding the horses to bring them up. Quickly now.' He turned to Wilson. 'If we can mount up, we may be able to break through them and get to the river.'

'I'm not crossing that damned river.' Wilson's face was white under his tan but his eyes were determined. 'We'll get back to a clearing and make a stand there until Forbes comes across. We can still take the king's camp.'

'Don't be stup–' Fonthill bit back the words and took Jenkins's place in directing the retreat. This time he set the wing men at the end of each line to firing at the warriors who were slipping through the trees on either side. 'Stop them from getting behind us,' he ordered.

One more man had fallen from the Matabele fire, which was still, mercifully, ill-directed. Now, however, Fonthill realised that the main danger was about to come from the spearmen who were trotting out from the bush immediately ahead and threatening to mount a frontal attack. His eyes scanned them desperately. There must be at least a thousand warriors who had debouched from the camp and were intent on engulfing the little band of troopers facing them. So much for a couple of hundred! Yet, respecting the firepower of the white men, the spearmen held back, seemingly relying on their own riflemen to reduce the number of guns facing them.

At that moment, there was a muffled thud of hooves and the mounts arrived, led by Jenkins and Mzingeli on the lead horses. Fonthill looked to Wilson. Would he resume command?

He did. 'A Troop, give covering fire,' he shouted. 'B Troop, mount.' There was a howl from the Matabele as they saw their prey slipping away, and at last the spearmen ran forward, gaining ground rapidly on the troopers, whose horses were prancing and proving difficult to mount. 'A Troop, mount,' screamed Wilson. But it was too late for two troopers, who were speared as, one foot each in their stirrups, they tried to control their skittish mounts.

Fonthill, Jenkins and Mzingeli, riding flat to their horses' necks, were the last to leave the little clearing, thrown spears falling behind them as the derisive cries of the Matabele died away.

'What's 'appenin?' cried Jenkins as they weaved between the trees.

'He's going to make a stand in a clearing near the river. He ought to try and cross it while we have the chance.'

A look of anguish returned to the Welshman's

461

face. 'Oh, I don't know,' he shouted. 'I don't fancy bein' drowned with a spear in me back, look you.'

They caught up with the rest of the patrol in a wide clearing, studded with a few isolated trees and with boulders and large stones scattered about.

Wilson had already dismounted. 'This is our best chance of finding cover,' he said, his breath coming in short gasps. 'I marked it on the way up.' He looked at Fonthill anxiously, as though seeking approval for showing some form of military expertise at last. 'We should be able to hold out here until Forbes crosses over.'

Fonthill looked around. There was little cover for the horses and not much more for the men. If Major Forbes was able to cross the Shangani, all might still not be lost, although he saw no possibility of mounting a realistic attack on Lobengula's camp, given the number of warriors who had obviously accompanied the king on his desperate trek north and who were clearly determined to defend him to the end. A momentary vision of the corpulent old monarch, bouncing on his wagon, desperately trying to avoid his pursuers, flashed across his mind. He felt a pang of sympathy for this Lear-like figure. Was the old boy still riven with gout and wearing his carpet slipper?

Then the first shot hissed across the clearing. 'Put the horses down,' yelled Wilson, 'and get them behind as much cover as you can. Sergeant, give me an ammunition report.' He turned to Fonthill. 'God, they've come up fast.'

'Yes.' Simon gave him a unforgiving smile. 'Just

like Zulus.'

It soon became clear that the patrol was surrounded, for bullets were now singing into the clearing from all sides of the bush and men were forced to shelter behind their horses, which became the first casualties. Cries rose as, inevitably, bullets found their mark in human flesh. The troopers, however, were returning fire and their accuracy remained sufficient of a deterrent to prevent that overwhelming charge by spearmen that could spell the end of the defence.

An hour went by without any of the tribesmen in the bush breaking cover, but opposite where Fonthill and his two comrades were sheltering, it became clear that some sort of attack was being prepared. Many plumes could be seen nodding over the thorn bushes, and black figures were flitting between the trees.

'It looks as though they are going to try something,' said Simon. 'Fix bayonets, I think. Mzingeli, fire and then keep low.' He shouted to the troopers on either side: 'I think we are about to be charged. When they come, it will be rapid fire as they advance across the open ground, then, if they still press, use your rifles as clubs—'

He had no time to finish for, with a howl, the Matabele burst from the bush and ran towards them, shields held forward in the traditional offensive mode. It looked as though someone was testing the firepower of the troopers, for only about one hundred of the warriors were deployed in the charge, but they came very fast, their legs pumping and their plumes nodding.

'Brave bastards,' muttered Jenkins, as the

defensive line crackled with rifle fire. The troopers fired as fast as they could work the cartridge ejection handles and thumb fresh rounds into the breeches of their rifles, and the .45-calibre slugs tore into the massed ranks of the charging warriors, sending them down in swathes. Yet with the courage that had been displayed in the other battles of the campaign, those behind pressed on, hurling defiance. Given the time taken to reload the single-shot Martini-Henrys, it was inevitable that some of the attackers would somehow escape the fusillade and reach the line of defenders, three of them materialising where Fonthill and Jenkins were kneeling, desperately feeling in their bandoliers for fresh cartridges.

'Bayonets, now!' screamed Fonthill.

He stood, conscious of Jenkins at his side, and parried the thrust from the assegai of the man opposite, the steel of the clashing spearhead and bayonet clanging out over the din of the firing. The warrior pushed forward his shield, seeking to find a way of thrusting around it, and Fonthill caught a glimpse of intense black eyes gleaming at him from a perspiring ebony face. Remembering a technique painfully learned at Isandlwana and Rorke's Drift, he dropped the butt of his rifle and caught it behind the spear pole that stood out at the bottom of the shield, twisting it so that the long shield was pulled round, exposing the warrior's side. With a swift downward movement of the rifle head, he plunged his bayonet between the man's ribs, and twisting it to withdraw it, he heard again the *ikiwa*, the sucking noise. The Matabele sank to his knees and then to the ground, blood pouring from his side.

Fonthill had time to look around. Predictably, Jenkins's man was sprawled by the side of his comrade and the Welshman was wiping blood from his bayonet. 'What about the other one?' asked Simon. Jenkins nodded to the left. There, Mzingeli was calmly reloading his rifle, a tall and very dead warrior sprawled across the rock in front of him.

The tracker nodded. 'Don't like Matabele,' he said. 'They make us slaves.'

'Good man.' The clearing was studded with Matabele bodies. Fonthill stopped counting at thirty. 'I don't think they'll try that again for a while,' he said.

'But they'll come again?' Jenkins's sweat-stained face was set.

'I suppose so, but they will try and reduce our numbers with rifle fire first. That was just to test us. It's going to be a long day.'

As the morning wore on, Wilson wriggled his way towards Fonthill. 'Sorry to get you into all this,' he said. 'I'm afraid it's too late now to think of breaking out en masse and trying to cross the river. We've lost horses and we have too many wounded and I am not going to leave them to be disembowelled.' He gave a weak smile. 'God knows where Forbes is, but perhaps he has no idea of the sort of pickle we are in and is taking his time. Fonthill, your horses are still sound. Do you think you and your two chaps could make a break for it, get across the Shangani and tell Forbes to come on up as quickly as he can? You are scouts and you know the bush better than any of us. Can't order you, of course, and you could well be cut down. But I think you have a fair chance. We will set up a bit of a barrage to make 'em keep their heads down while you mount and set off. What do you say, old chap?'

Fonthill looked at the pinpricks of fire that marked the fact that the Matabele were now well established in the bush all around the clearing. He started as, for a brief second, he thought he saw the flash of a yellow garment. All thoughts of de Sousa had long since dissolved and he deliberately put the Portuguese from his mind now. It was just a question of survival. He looked into Wilson's diffident face. 'Of course,' he said. 'I will put it to the others, but I don't see them refusing.'

Nor did they. 'I go where you go,' said Jenkins, 'but 'ang on to me in that water, please.'

'I come,' said Mzingeli.

The three exchanged their rifles for revolvers – much easier to handle on horseback – spoke a few reassuring words into the ears of their patient mounts, who were lying well protected by stone outbreaks, and tightened their saddle girths. Fonthill crawled across to Wilson. 'How long do you think you can hold out?'

'Depends on the ammunition.' The major forced a smile. 'If it goes on at this rate, I should say that we will all be looking like porcupines with spears in our bellies by nightfall. Unless Forbes can get here, that is. It depends on you, old chap.'

'Right. Good luck.' The two shook hands and Fonthill crawled back to his horse, now scratching restively in the soil with its hooves. Simon took a deep breath, exchanged glances with his two comrades and gave a nod to Wilson, and as the troopers blazed away into the surrounding bush, the three men mounted, kicked in their heels and, heads down, made for the most southerly of the gaps in the trees, to the cheers of the remaining members of the Shangani Patrol.

How they survived the breakout, Fonthill would never know. He was dimly conscious of black figures scattering as they thundered through between the trees. He heard Jenkins's revolver crack to his left and he himself brought down a warrior who attempted to launch his spear at him at close quarters. A spear sped over his right shoulder and thudded into a tree trunk a little ahead of him, and a bullet tore through the sleeve of his jacket. Death, for those few seconds, was all around them. Then they broke through the bush into another clearing and sped across it into the dubious safety of the trees beyond.

Fonthill turned his head. Jenkins was riding well at his side, but Mzingeli was a little way behind, and he saw that blood was trickling down the tracker's arm. He reined in hard and caught the black man's bridle. 'Are you...' He tailed off as Mzingeli slumped on to his shoulder.

''Ere.' Jenkins was alongside. He leaned across and lifted the tracker as though he were a feather pillow and deposited him across his own saddle in front of him. 'Take his reins, bach, and follow on,' he yelled, digging in his heels and riding away, one arm holding Mzingeli upright as the tracker's head lolled in time to the beat of the horse's hooves.

They rode this way until they reached the riverbank, where they dismounted and found Mzingeli completely unconscious. A bullet had gone clean through his left shoulder and another had grazed his head.

Jenkins gave an anxious glance at the yellow water. 'It's much 'igher than yesterday,' he said, 'an' I don't think you'll be able to get us both across, bach sir. Best thing to do, I think,' he beamed confidently, 'is for you to take the horses across and go and find Major Forbes. Me an' old Jelly 'ere will creep into the bush and 'ide until you can come back for us with the rest. Makes sense, isn't it?'

'No it bloody well isn't. The Matabele are probably hot on our heels now and they will find you in a second. I shall get you both across ... somehow.' He looked around desperately. 'Mzingeli is the problem. Is it the shoulder wound, do you think?'

'No. That bullet that grazed 'is 'ead is what's knocked 'im out, I think. 'Ere, 'elp lift 'im down.'

Carefully Jenkins handed the tracker down to Fonthill, who stretched him on the ground and chafed his hands, but the man remained unconscious.

'We can't wait here until he comes round,' said Fonthill. 'The Matabele will be here any minute now. I shall just have to carry him across on my horse and hope that the two of us are not too heavy to prevent it swimming. Can you find something to lash him to me? Ah, unsaddle a horse and tear up the saddle blanket, that should do. I will stuff my shirt into this shoulder wound to try and staunch the bleeding. Quickly now, or they will be on us.'

The two men went to work in feverish haste, but Jenkins had only just thrown off the saddle when a cry made them turn their heads. Two Matabele warriors, their faces fearsomely daubed in ochre and white, throwing spears in their hands, burst out of the bush. Behind them could be heard the distant thud of hoofbeats. For a brief moment the four men regarded each other in a tableau that seemed to be fixed in time. Then, in a blur of action, the first warrior threw a spear at Simon, who was kneeling on the ground. He had just time to roll away so that the shaft buried itself into the soil, but at the same moment Jenkins's revolver barked and the thrower jerked backwards and slumped to the ground. The second man flung his spear at Jenkins, who ducked and fired in the same movement, the bullet penetrating the warrior's shield and hitting him in the chest. The shaft, however, took Jenkins's horse in the throat, so that the beast reared and slipped in the mud, bringing the Welshman down, pinning him under its weight and sending his revolver spinning away. At the same time, Fonthill's horse, eyes wide, stampeded away.

'Bloody 'ell,' shouted the Welshman, 'I can't move. Can you pull me out from under this bloody 'orse?'

'No, he can't.'

The voice came from the edge of the bush, and de Sousa walked his horse forward, his revolver covering both men.

'How convenient,' he said. 'One unconscious,

the other pinned under his horse and you, Font-hill, without a weapon.' Perspiration was streaming down de Sousa's face from his gallop through the bush, and his uniform had lost its pristine smartness: stains marked his tunic, his boots were scuffed and he had not shaved for days. The dress sword that used to hang so decoratively by his thigh had now been thrust carelessly through his belt. Life in retreat with Lobengula had clearly not suited him, but his eyes were now gleaming with anticipation and he showed his tongue between his small white teeth.

He dismounted, his revolver carefully covering Fonthill, who remained crouching beside Mzingeli. He made to get up, but de Sousa waved him down. Then the Portuguese slowly transferred the pistol from his right to his left hand and drew the sword from his belt.

'I shall kill the three of you,' he said, 'and I shall take my time about it, I promise you that.' He gestured behind him with his head. 'My men will be here soon and they like a bit of entertainment, so I shall wait until they arrive. In the meantime...' He walked towards Mzingeli.

'Even you wouldn't harm a wounded man,' cried Fonthill. He shot a quick glance at Jenkins, but the Welshman, the veins standing out on his neck, was trying without success to push away the dead weight of the horse that lay across his legs.

Simon thought quickly. 'Look,' he said, 'your quarrel is not with these two. There's half of the gold sovereigns that Lobengula left in that bag behind my saddle. Take it and let them go – then you can do what you like with me.'

De Sousa sneered. 'Oh, I'll do what I like with you anyway. And if there *are* sovereigns there, which I doubt, I shall take them. Oh, I am so glad that I saw you ride away, Fonthill, because I could not be sure that you were with this pathetic little party. Now, I will let you watch a little blood-letting before my happy warriors arrive. This sword is not just for decoration, you know. I think we'll begin by finishing off this Kaffir of yours...'

Fonthill sprang at him from his crouching position, but his clawing fingers landed in the mud well short of the Portuguese's boots. Instantly de Sousa skipped around and plunged his sword into Simon's calf as he lay spreadeagled. The pain was hot and sharp and Fonthill cried out in agony, clutching his shin to his breast.

'Bastard,' cried Jenkins, panting from his exertions but still firmly wedged under the dead horse.

'Your turn will come in a minute.' De Sousa spoke calmly, then turned back to Fonthill. 'That will stop you running away while I carve you up a little. You could call it unfinished business, I suppose. Yes, I don't think I will wait, after all.' He drew back the sword and Simon closed his eyes.

As a result, he did not see a sweating Jenkins, just able to reach up to the far side of the horse that imprisoned him, fumble in his rifle bucket hanging by the saddle, withdraw his bayonet and hurl it with all his strength at de Sousa's back. The weapon rotated through the air in a silver cartwheel. There was an equal chance of it hitting the Portuguese base or point first. If the former, then it would merely thump into him, causing him to start a pace or two forward, doing no real damage. If the latter... As it was, the point of the lunger hit de Sousa firmly in the middle of the back, penetrating tunic, shirt and flesh, not deeply enough to kill, but inflicting a painful wound.

The Portuguese, his eyes staring wildly, staggered towards Fonthill. Instinctively, Simon reached up and pulled the man's tunic so that the two fell back together, de Sousa crashing on to him and expelling the air from his body.

Fonthill heard Jenkins's despairing cry: 'The bayonet, bach. The bayonet, in 'is back.' As the Portuguese put a hand to the ground to push himself away, Simon reached behind his back and his fingers locked on to the blade, now loose from de Sousa's exertions and threatening to fall away. The heavy man's other hand had now reached Fonthill's throat and was beginning to tighten, so that stars floated before Simon's eyes. 'Damn you, English,' croaked the Portuguese. Fonthill made one last effort and slid his left hand around his assailant's back in a desperate embrace, pulling him closer and finding the blade. His two hands now joined together and jerked the bayonet down savagely. He felt the point go cleanly through de Sousa's body and lightly prick his own chest before blackness closed in on him.

He came round to hear Jenkins shouting and feel Mzingeli's hand slapping his face. The tracker had crawled to his side and had somehow pushed the dead de Sousa away.

'Ah, Nkosi,' he gasped. 'Good. You hurt but not

dead. Get up. We must move horse off 352 bach and get across river. Matabele coming. I think I hear them.'

'Oh hell, Jelly.' Jenkins's voice was hoarse. 'See to the captain. I'll be all right. Get across while you can.'

'No.' Simon was struggling on to one knee. 'If you can move, Mzingeli, help me up and get me a spear to lean on, can you? Good. Now hand me that sword. Right. Let's insert these under the belly of the horse. That's it. While we try and lift it a little, 352, can you try and struggle out from underneath?'

'Blimey, if you two cripples can do that, I can get out. Right. Try now.'

The two men may have been injured, but the hard life they had led on the veldt had toughened their bodies and given them reserves of strength. Slowly, as they heaved, the dead weight of the horse began to rise. The shaft of the spear snapped, sending the beast crashing down again, but not before Jenkins had extricated both his legs.

'Thank God,' he said. 'Now, where's that pea-shooter? I can 'ear the Mattabellies comin'. Bach sir, can the two of you get on that 'orse and into the river, while I 'old the devils off?'

'Only if you get on that other–'

His words were cut short as three panting Matabele broke out of the bush. They stood immobile for a second, partly to regain their breath and partly to take in the scene before them. Then they ran forward, stabbing spears held low. Their hesitation gave Jenkins just enough time to pick

473

up his revolver, kneel and fire, bring back the hammer and fire again. The two leading warriors staggered and fell and the third paused, hurled his assegai, then turned and ran back to seek the cover of the bush. Jenkins's third bullet took him squarely in the back.

'Bugger, no more bullets,' cried the Welshman. 'An' no more 'orses.' De Sousa's horse had bolted at the gunfire. Jenkins leapt forward and picked up the Portuguese's revolver. Then he turned and saw a staggering Fonthill pushing Mzingeli up on to the saddle of his horse. 'Get up behind him, bach,' he called. 'I'll cover you.'

'No.' Simon's voice was a croak. 'You're pathetic, 352, being afraid of a bit of water. You get up behind him; you're the only one that has the strength to hold him on. I will hang on to the horse's tail and get across that way. Go on. Get on. That's an order. Look, they're coming through now. Get on, damn you, or it will be too late.'

Jenkins gave a despairing look at the swirling water, then he turned, emptied de Sousa's revolver at the Matabele who were appearing now through the trees and vaulted on to the rump of Mzingeli's horse, clutching the swaying tracker to him to prevent him falling. Then he urged the mount into the water as a hopping Fonthill clutched at the beast's tail.

As the current swept them away, a despairing cry of 'Oh bloody 'ell' merged with the shouts of the Matabele as they rushed to the water's edge, abortively throwing their spears after the disappearing trio.

474

Chapter 20

Two weeks later, Fonthill sat on the edge of a camp chair in their tent in a Bulawayo that was no longer smoking but still smelled of charred timber, while Alice replaced the dressing on his calf. The crossing of the turbulent Shangani had been perilous and had taken all of half an hour, but had been completed successfully in the end. The yellow water, however, had bequeathed an infection to the open wound in his leg that had delayed their departure from the king's old capital and which was only now responding to treatment.

'Will you please keep still,' commanded Alice.

'I am as still as I can be when you're pulling that damned bandage so tight.'

'It has to be tight to keep the dressing on.' She pulled a face. 'Is it still painful?'

'Only when I laugh.'

'Don't laugh, then.'

'I can't help it. The sight of you on your knees before me is very, very funny. It should happen more often.'

'Oh do be–'

A ridiculously loud cough outside the flap of the tent announced the arrival of Jenkins. 'Come in,' shouted Fonthill. 'Don't knock.'

The Welshman put his head through the opening. 'I did knock, see, but you don't 'ear nothin' on canvas, now do you? Good morning, Miss Alice.'

'Good morning, 352. You would be better at this than me. Do you want to take over?'

'No thank you, miss. I 'ad enough of treatin' the captain up in the north, look you. He ain't a good patient, is 'e?'

'No he is not. What can we do for you?'

Jenkins's eyes lit up. 'I've brought some news. Just come in, it 'as. The old king 'as died – up in the bush there somewhere, miles from anywhere, near that river up north, the Lumpini ... Lapono...'

Fonthill sat upright. 'The Limpopo.'

'That's what I said. It seems that no-one knows 'ow he died. Could 'ave been poison, or sickness. 'E wasn't a well man at the end, they say. Oh, an' Mr Rhodes is back in town, I 'ear.'

'Who told you all this, 352?'

'One of the blokes in Dr Jameson's office. One of the Mattabellies 'as come in from north of that river where we 'ad our little swim, like, and says that the king bolted, o' course, when the fightin' started.' His voice dropped as he continued. 'This man was at the fightin' and 'as told 'ow everyone in Captain Wilson's party died. Very tragic it was.'

Fonthill frowned. 'Do you know the details?'

'Nothin' more than that, bach sir.'

Alice and Simon exchanged glances. When Fonthill, Jenkins and Mzingeli had staggered ashore, almost half a mile downriver from where they had first plunged into the water, they had lain exhausted for a while. They could hear gun-fire coming from across the river and, full of anxiety for the fate of Wilson and his men, had

476

pushed on, with Simon and Mzingeli on the horse and Jenkins leading it. Eventually, towards dusk, they had come upon Forbes and his command, entrenched behind a laager. There, they learned that Forbes had approached the river early that morning but had been attacked by a force of Matabele. Having lost several men and seven horses, he had decided that the river was too high to cross and had taken his men back.

'I can't risk losing my whole command by having another go,' he told Fonthill. 'Anyway, from what you've told me, we would never get across, and it's too late now in any case.'

Simon had been forced to see the painful logic of Forbes's argument, and eventually the three had accompanied Forbes and his men on their disconsolate march back to Bulawayo. The Shangani Patrol had ended in failure.

'Jenkins,' said Alice, finishing the dressing with a neat bow, 'would you like to make us all coffee while we digest this news.' She looked up at Simon. 'So, now the war is really over ... or is it?'

Fonthill sighed. 'Oh yes, it must be. Presumably what was left of the impis is still out there, somewhere in the bush. But without Lobengula as a figurehead they will be leaderless, and despite their victory over Wilson and his men, they will have lost so many warriors that I don't see them going to war again. They will just break up and go back to their individual kraals.'

'Will there be any reprisals by Rhodes for the Shangani disaster?'

'I doubt it, but I want to go and see Jameson and Rhodes, now that he is back in Bulawayo.'

'So do I. I will come with you. I have a story to write.'

The rest of the press corps in Bulawayo had returned to the Cape after the flight of the king and the virtual fizzling out of the war. Alice had stayed, of course, because both Simon and Mzingeli were unable to travel. The tracker, in fact, had recovered faster than Fonthill and had now jettisoned the awkward shoulder bandage and sling and was moving freely. The fact that Lobengula's death had been confirmed and that details had emerged of the end of Wilson and his men meant that she could now wrap up her coverage of 'this sordid war' and write her final report.

Sordid or not, the war had given Alice the chance of re-establishing herself as an intrepid and, as it ensued, lucky war correspondent. Her closeness to Fonthill, of course, had given her a succession of exclusive stories, the latest of which had been his account of the Shangani Patrol. Now she would be in a position to scoop her rivals once again with the details of the last battle of Wilson and his men.

They sent a message across to Jameson, asking if he and Rhodes would see them. Normally, Alice suspected, Rhodes would have declined to be interviewed by her, but he could hardly resist meeting and thanking Simon, the hero of the patrol's last days. And he could surely not refuse to see one without the other. She was not above using every trick at her disposal to complete her story.

Acceptance came by return, and as Simon

limped across to Jameson's office, established in a rebuilt hut on the site of the king's inner kraal, he could not forbear to warn Alice not to be antagonistic to Rhodes. 'Press him by all means, darling,' he said, 'but you must not thrust your own views on him.'

'Thank you, Simon, but I shall thrust on him anything I wish.'

They found the two men in sombre mood. They both rose to welcome them, however, and shook hands warmly. 'You did splendid work at the Shangani, Fonthill,' said Rhodes, 'and I am only sorry that Forbes couldn't follow up.'

'So am I. I have to say to you both that, frankly, I feel the effort should at least have been made.'

'Well,' Jameson broke in quickly, 'I understand that the river was terribly high. There's a difference between the three of you crossing and taking across more than a hundred men against a hostile far bank. But,' he shrugged, 'I'm afraid it's all too late to argue now.'

Alice opened her notebook. 'I understand, gentlemen,' she said, 'that you have news of how Wilson and his men finally died.'

'Yes, we do indeed, madam.' Rhodes was sitting bolt upright and he looked Alice challengingly in the eye. 'And it is a story that makes us all proud to be English. I hope that you will be able to report it fully.'

'I hope so too,' Alice replied coolly. 'May I have the details, please and the source of your information?'

'Certainly. Certainly. One of the Matabele who was a member of the king's party – not an *inDuna*, you understand, but a minor chieftain from what we have been able to ascertain here in Bulawayo – came in this morning with his family. He wants to return to live here. He fought at the final Shangani battle and then went off with the king, who was trying to make for the Limpopo. He tells us that Lobengula is certainly dead, for he saw his corpse, but he does not know the cause. However, he gave us a graphic account of Wilson's end.'

He coughed. 'Magnificent, if I may say so. He says that the troopers fought on throughout the day, their numbers gradually being reduced by the firing of the Matabele–'

'Ah yes,' interrupted Alice. 'And do you know, Mr Rhodes, from where the Matabele obtained their rifles and ammunition?'

Simon winced, but Rhodes did not flinch.

'I expect, dear lady, that they were part of the consignment that your husband took to Bulawayo, to cement the treaty I had agreed with the king. I regret very much that they were used against British troops, which was, of course, breaking the terms of the treaty, but one must take risks sometimes in these regions if one wishes to progress.'

'I see.' Alice, her head down, was scribbling fast. 'Pray continue. You were saying that Wilson's patrol was reduced by the firing during the day?'

'Indeed.' Rhodes smoothed his moustache. 'They fought off each attack with great bravery as the day progressed until they finally ran out of ammunition. Then...' The great man's voice broke. He took a large and none too clean handkerchief from his pocket and blew his nose noisily. Then he wiped his moist eyes. 'Yes, do excuse me. This Matabele said that Wilson – whom he identified because of his large moustaches – and his men shook hands all round, stood and sang one verse of "God Save the Queen", then ... then...' he blew his nose again, 'stood firm and waited for the inevitable as the final charge came. No one survived, of course. They were all speared and then disembowelled as a tribute to them as great warriors. Magnificent. Magnificent. Please do quote me, if you wish.'

A silence fell in the tent as Alice continued to scribble.

'A chapter of errors, I am afraid,' said Fonthill, 'which doesn't detract from the bravery of them all at the end.'

'What ... er ... yes, well, quite.'

'What do you propose to do about the remnants of the king's impi?'

Rhodes made a dismissive gesture. 'We shall send out messengers to say that they may all now return to their kraals without harassment, as long as they promise to forgo further hostile activities. There will be no pursuit of them in the bush. Jameson here will organise for a party to go up to the Shangani and bury the dead.'

'And your plans to expand to the east?'

'Ah, that reminds me. I wrote to you, Fonthill, of course, following the receipt of your treaty with Umtasa, to thank you for your work out there. But let me take this opportunity to thank you again. Jameson here has made contact with the king, but I have to confess that we have met

481

with difficulties with the Portuguese, who of course control the coast. This was to be expected, but the road to the east has necessarily had to take a lower priority to the establishment of our settlements here. This has now been done and–'

Alice looked up from her pad. 'So you are saying, Mr Rhodes, that your aim in invading Matabeleland was always to establish settlements here and in Mashonaland?'

'What?' Rhodes blinked behind his spectacles. 'But of course, madam.'

Alice produced that special sweet smile that so often presaged the killing point. 'But this was not what you told King Lobengula, was it? You only requested mining concessions, surely?'

Rhodes seemed quite unfazed. 'Certainly, and quite genuinely. Unfortunately, the land has proved to be comparatively unproductive so far. But I always also wished to establish good settlers here to spread the values of the English race in a territory that knew only barbarism and cruelty. If the land here seems not to have fulfilled its promise in terms of mineral deposits – and this still remains to be proven – then it is certainly, in the high veldt, good farming territory. It could never have reached its true potential under Lobengula, a feudal despot of the old order.'

Alice put down her pencil. 'I understand, Mr Rhodes, that there are many people in political and other circles back home who do not share your views.'

For the first time Rhodes began to show signs of exasperation. It was clear that a background of buying off his competitors in commerce and a

remarkably unchallenged rise to the top in South
African politics had not prepared him for debate
with a proponent of radical views – and a woman
at that.

He leaned forward. 'Then, my dear lady, those
people "back home",' he laid heavy emphasis on
the words, 'should have done something about
what you have called my "invasion".' He took a
strong pull of his cigar and waved away the
smoke. 'On the contrary, I had approval – un-
official, it is true, but approval all the same – of
my actions from government circles and I was
allowed to execute my policies at my own
expense. In other words, these people back home
that you referred to were, on the whole, quite prepared to let me carry on a programme of extension of the British Empire as long as it did not
cost the British Government a single penny. It is
others, madam, who are guilty of hypocrisy, not I.'

Jameson entered the debate for the first time. 'In
dealing with savages, Mrs Fonthill,' he said, 'one
cannot be perhaps quite as punctilious as, say, in
Europe. One cannot say, "I wish to settle your
land," because the king would have said, "No,
keep out." That is obvious. So we had to use other
means. But let me point out that Mr Rhodes has
not been motivated by personal gain. It could well
be that there are no minerals to be mined here or
in Mashonaland, and as a result, the company of
which he is chairman will gain no return on its
investment. In addition, he has deployed a
considerable portion of his personal fortune in
financing this campaign and is unlikely to gain a
return on that. His motives have been altruistic:

the extension of the British Empire and the spreading of the British way of life.'

Alice opened her mouth to speak, but Jameson held up his hand. 'One more matter. Lobengula's father took this land at spearpoint less than sixty years ago. He introduced slavery and execution on a whim. The king, then, has no more right to it than the good white farmers who are now beginning to work the land following Christian principles.'

Alice wrote something on her pad, underlined it with a flourish and stood. 'Thank you, gentlemen,' she said, her face a little flushed. 'I think I understand your position and I am grateful to you for explaining it to me. I should point out, however, that nothing you have said justifies to my mind the invasion of a land ruled by a man who has a constitutional right to it – you recognised this in your original treaty with Lobengula – and the massacre of his people by machine guns, cannon and modern rifles when they have the audacity to resist your incursion. I fear that this view must be expressed in my final report on this miserable campaign. Good morning.'

She swept out of the hut, leaving behind her a silence as heavy as the blue smoke that hung in the air. Fonthill found himself grinning as he regarded the shocked faces of the others.

'Well, my word.' Rhodes's voice had risen to a squeak. 'You don't share your wife's views, surely, Fonthill?'

'Well, do you know, sir, I rather fear that I do now.' He shifted in his chair and thrust himself upright, wincing at the momentary shaft of pain the movement caused. 'I am certain of one thing, and that is this: many brave men gave their lives for this land. I hope for your sakes that it will be worth it. Good day to you both.'

He hobbled back to their tent to find that Jenkins and Mzingeli had gone hunting and Alice was, predictably, scribbling furiously on a cable pad. She hardly looked up as he entered.

'Now, don't chastise me,' she said. 'I have work to do. I know you don't agree with me, but I had to say all that. I am only supposed to report news for the *Post* and my own opinions, as always, will only be implied. But,' she looked up at him with a triumphant smile, 'I got Rhodes to admit that he invaded to build empire, not to prospect. That damns him from his own mouth and it's a good story. Now, go away, you Imperialist, and let me write my piece.'

Fonthill bent and kissed her. 'As a matter of fact, I agree with you.'

Alice looked up, her mouth open. 'You do? Good lord!'

'Yes, and I told them so.'

A slow smiled began to spread across Alice's face. 'Simon, you continue to amaze me. I think I am beginning to love you all over again.'

'I should think so. My leg aches. I need attention.'

Then the smile was replaced by a frown. 'But you own land in Mashonaland. You have taken Rhodes's shilling.'

'I know. Listen.' He pulled up the other camp stool. 'I still love the land up there, and I agree with Rhodes and Jameson to the extent that it should be developed and farmed creatively. The Mashonas – or the Matabele, for that matter – will never do that. They are not farmers and never will be. However, I have a proposal for you.'

'Propose away.'

'I would like to give the farm to Mzingeli. He has no roots in the Transvaal, nor a proper home, working for that Boer down there. He would like, I am sure, to be near his father.'

'But is he a farmer? Could he work the land?'

'Actually, he was beginning to do very well, until we took him away to be a soldier, with the result that he got a bullet through his shoulder. No, he will cope, with a bit of help. We will give him a sum of money, which we will invest in the farm, and if he agrees, and I think he will, I will promise to keep an eye on the property for him, visiting him from time to time to help him develop it. Jenkins and I will like the game hunting anyway, and as you know, I love the country. It seems the ideal solution. The land will return to one of its native sons, in a way, and Ntini and Joshua can both work for him. What do you think?'

Alice sat for a moment, deep in thought. 'What do *we* do?' she asked.

'We go back to your beloved Norfolk and give the land there the attention it deserves after our long time away, and still retain a sort of foothold here. But...'

'Ah. I knew there would be a but.'

Fonthill frowned. 'Yes. Well, we might as well be completely honest with each other. I can farm happily in Norfolk for a time, but the place runs itself pretty well, and I know that I will get bored after a time – and so will you, not to mention Jenkins.'

Alice sucked her pencil. 'So...?'

'I think – no, I am sure – that there will be trouble soon in the Transvaal. The Boers there are still cocky after beating us so completely on Majuba Hill, and the peace agreement afterwards was a cobbled-together mess. To be frank, I sense that Rhodes has got his eye on the province and wouldn't be above stirring up trouble there with the many Britishers who have gone in to work the goldfields on the Rand to justify an invasion.' He smiled sheepishly. 'Jenkins and I know the territory better than most Englishmen – certainly better than most soldiers. With General Lamb as army commander in the Cape, there could be a job for us and a bit of excitement to relieve the ... er ... forgive me, my love, but I think the word is *tedium* of life in Norfolk, if and when the call comes.' Then the smile faded and he looked at her anxiously. 'But would you let us go?'

She stood and looked him levelly in the eye. 'Of course, if I could come too.'

Fonthill sighed. 'I knew you would say that. You would want to report it all for the *Post?*'

'Of course.'

'Well, they say all is fair in love and war, and I don't suppose we have run out of either yet.'

Alice stepped forward and put her arms around his neck. Somewhere a dog barked and harness creaked as a wagon drove past. 'No, I am sure we haven't,' she whispered into his ear.

They kissed and stood together for a moment,

her head on his shoulder, and then she said: 'And I love your idea of giving the farm to Mzingeli. It seems the perfect solution. Put it to them both – for Jenkins must be party to this, as he is to everything – when they return. Now,' She pushed him away and sat down again. 'Go away and let me write.'

'Very well. But go easy on Rhodes and Jameson.'

'Of course I will. Oh...' She looked up. 'How do you spell despicable?'

Author's Note

The Matabele War was a virtual sideshow in the great pageant of Victorian colonial wars, attracting comparatively little attention from historians and writers of biographies and autobiographies, probably because it was, on the whole, a piece of private enterprise by Cecil John Rhodes. Nevertheless, it did result in the establishment of a new nation in southern Africa, Rhodesia, and the controversy that surrounded its birth has continued to cling to it, through its split into northern and southern Rhodesia, its unification, its secession from the British Commonwealth and its present reincarnation as Zimbabwe under President Mugabe.

It was also significant in that it represented the high-water mark in the territorial gains that made the British Empire the largest the world had seen. (I discount the bits and pieces of real estate that Britain picked up as a result of the First World War.) For a novelist, however, the war's main attraction must be the clash between its two main protagonists, Rhodes and the Matabele chief King Lobengula. They never met, like those more famous adversaries Wellington and Bonaparte, and Hitler and Churchill, but their vices and virtues stamped themselves on the encounters between Lobengula's impis and Rhodes's army of settlers just as surely as if the two had crossed assegai blade and bayonet personally.

In setting the adventures of Simon Fonthill against the background of the war, I have attempted to relate accurately its twists and turns and also to paint the background to what became a classic conflict between the expansionist march of a great colonial power and the struggle of a barbaric and warlike people to remain independent. The Shangani episode was a tragedy, of course, and among the last of its kind.

As always in the Fonthill novels, I must establish what was fact and what fiction. Simon, Alice, Jenkins and Mzingeli, of course, are fictional characters, as are General Lamb and those two rogues Murphy and Laxer. All of the other main characters, however, very much existed: Beit, King Khama, Fairbairn, Dr Jameson, Chief Umtasa, Captain Borrow and Majors Wilson and Forbes. I did not create Manuel de Sousa, 'Gouela', although I confess to painting him rather more darkly than perhaps even he deserved. De Sousa, a Portuguese agent with a reputation as a rapist and a slaver, was a regular attender at the court of King Lobengula, and he did try to persuade the king to eschew all dealings with Rhodes.

Lobengula did indeed send a bag of golden sovereigns in a pathetic attempt to divert his pursuers, and the two troopers who accepted them from the *inDunas* did try to keep them and were court-martialled. Three men, all scouts, were sent back by Major Wilson to cross the Shangani in an attempt to get Major Forbes to bring aid, and for those who may think that Simon's crossing of the river by holding on to the horse's tail is a little fanciful, then I must refer them to Lieutenant Horace Smith-Dorrien, who escaped the Zulus after Isandlwana by crossing the Buffalo river in the same way.

Alice's treatment of Lobengula's gout is based on fact, in that Dr Jameson did earn the king's friendship by so treating his ailment in Bulawayo – as well as, it is said, because he could make the king laugh. Rhodes's pursuit of Simon to recruit him to take the gold and arms to the king and to prospect to the east is quite logical, in that he did, in fact, employ many young British adventurers for such tasks – particularly in exploring towards the Portuguese borders to establish contact with the tribes there and to persuade them to sign treaties with his company.

Wherever possible, I have based important conversations on the writings of the participants or those who were present at the time. Rhodes's eulogy to the strengths of British character and his vision of the map of Africa to the north 'covered in red', expressed so forcefully to Font-hill in Cape Town, are taken from his writings: Similarly, Lobengula's colourful analogy of the chameleon (England) and the fly (Matabeleland) was remembered by those who were in his kraal at the time.

Cecil John Rhodes, of course, was a highly complex and controversial character. As I have tried to reflect in the novel, the British Government, the press, the bankers of London, the public of the day – none of them could ever quite make up their mind about him. Was he a capitalistic charlatan or a great man of empire? Amazingly, well over a hundred years later, the jury is still out.

Rhodes attracted opprobrium when – as Fonthill feared – he plotted to send a party of armed men into Kruger's Transvaal under the command of the faithful Dr Jameson to stimulate a rising against the Boer government. This abortive mini-invasion became known as the Jameson Raid, and the good doctor went to jail for leading it. Somehow Rhodes wriggled out of accepting the blame, although he sturdily supported the doctor throughout, and Jameson later became reinstated in society and died an honoured man and servant of empire. He was interred in Rhodesia's Matopo Hills, near to the body of Cecil John Rhodes, the man he had served so well.

The cause of Lobengula's death was never established – he could well have been poisoned, the fate of many African despots. His people wrapped his body in the hides of two newly flayed oxen and buried it in a cave. Rhodes took charge of three of Lobengula's sons, and of their sons, and took them to his home in Cape Town, to be educated and brought up there. One of the boys survived to become one of Rhodes's chief mourners when the great man died in 1902.

The fate of the Shangani Patrol became a cause célèbre back in England. As with Rorke's Drift after the British defeat by the Zulus at Isandlwana, the heroism of the little band – their singing of the national anthem, the formal shaking of hands before they faced the last charge of the Matabele warriors – distracted the public's attention from all that had gone before: the slaughter of the natives by machine guns, modern rifles and cannon. It thrilled the readers of the Victorian newspapers and was what they expected of their heroes. The only things lacking were white pith helmets and red coats.

A memorial to Wilson and his men was erected where they fell, and the remains of their bodies were removed to consecrated ground, to be reinterred later near their memorial in the Matopo Hills, where Rhodes and Jameson were to lie. If the Anglo-Matabele war is little remembered now, the Shangani Patrol lives on in the minds of those lovers of history who respect extreme bravery – particularly when its last moments are acted out with a sense of drama and pathos that even Hollywood would consider too unbelievable to put on the screen.

J.W.
Chilmark
August 2009

The publishers hope that this book has given you enjoyable reading. Large Print Books are especially designed to be as easy to see and hold as possible. If you wish a complete list of our books please ask at your local library or write directly to:

Magna Large Print Books
Magna House, Long Preston,
Skipton, North Yorkshire.
BD23 4ND

This Large Print Book for the partially sighted, who cannot read normal print, is published under the auspices of

THE ULVERSCROFT FOUNDATION